"I want to work for you."

Effie brushed a hand in dismissal. "I need no new blood."

"Then that is a shame," Cecily said. "The name of Effie will be forgotten far sooner than it should, and the name of Lyle and Company will grow and be remembered."

She thought she had struck a response with the mention of Lyle & Co.

"We share a common enemy, Madame Duvall," Cecily said. "William Lyle tried to destroy you. The present owners of the firm have tried the same with me."

Effie seemed to lose interest until Cecily said, "I believe you have known hate the way I know hate. We would have revenge."

Costly Pleasures

Costly Pleasures

Mary Ruth Myers

BALLANTINE BOOKS • NEW YORK

Library of Congress Catalog Card Number: 84-91022

ISBN 0-345-31759-9

Printed in Canada

First Edition: March 1985

This book is for my daughter, Jessica,
who is more precious to me
than all the rubies, diamonds, and sapphires of the world.
Love,

Mom

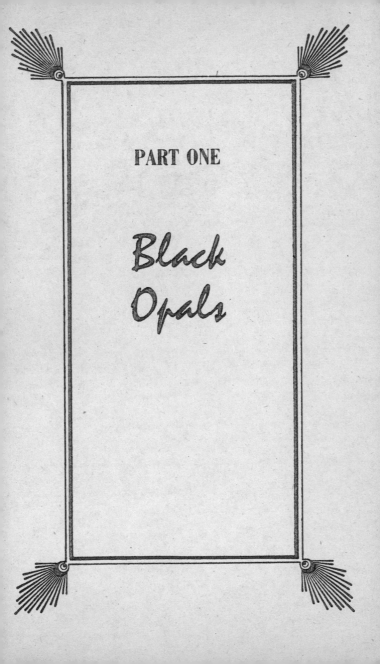

PART ONE

Black Opals

ONE

"LISTEN TO ME, CECILY! I'VE SMUGGLED DIAMONDS FOR YOU. I'VE swung by my ankles for you, but I am *not* going to get myself booked for assault because of you! Not when I have a hair appointment at Salon Margrit first thing tomorrow!"

Trailing French perfume, the woman with scrambled blond curls and a five-carat diamond winking on her well-tended fingers caught at Cecily's arm. Cecily, faster than her taller friend, slipped free, still brandishing the high-heeled lizard sandal she'd snatched off in the doorway of her condominium.

"I'm damned if I'll let some reporter lie his way into my apartment," she said fiercely. "Not after the day I've had! Not so he can write more innuendos about a decent man who happens to have been a friend of mine!"

Her silken brown hair, cut almost boyishly short, stirred with her anger. She moved toward the living room, annoyed by the thought that without her shoe she probably looked younger than twenty-seven and shorter than five feet three.

"Cecily, the last thing you need right now is bad publi—"

She ignored April's voice at her heels. They had reached their destination. Cecily's eyes swept stretches of cool white carpet, white walls, low tables, and fixed on a man rising from the L-shaped seating unit. She pointed her sandal.

"Out!"

She was almost too weary to move at the end of this long, hot, treacherous Miami day, but nearly twenty years of surviving on her own had taught Cecily a show of strength was needed most when she least felt up to it.

"Oh, now, Miss Catlow—" the reporter began.

"I don't have time to wait for the security people to get rid of you. I'm going to do it myself if you don't start moving!"

Today she had wrested more than half a million dollars in emeralds from competitors who had meant to keep them from her. She had managed to keep—for a few months, at least—control of one of the world's most elite jewelry companies. Surely she could rid herself of this intruder.

By his indulgent look she knew he was seeing what men

3

always saw in her: the contours of her face, incredibly delicate in spite of its definite squareness; the large and vulnerable brown eyes in their thickets of lashes; the soft mouth above her small, firm chin with its annoying dimple.

But I'm tougher than I look, she thought, then hurled the shoe to drive away the unsettling fear that maybe she wasn't, that maybe she was more fragile and open to hurt than she'd always pretended. Why else would the absence of one man at that meeting today produce such pain inside her? Why else, after all this time, was the spot where her heart had been still a raw, open wound?

"Hey!" the reporter howled, ducking. "If you don't talk to me, you'd better believe I'll put it in print that you attacked me!"

Cecily stripped off her other sandal. He began to retreat, his tape recorder held before him like a shield.

"I'll tell you this much," she said, advancing. "Teddy Landis never did a dishonest thing in his life! Shall I pound it into you?"

He disappeared into the foyer. A second later the front door slammed.

Cecily and April looked at one another. April's wide blue eyes relaxed above a grin and they both dissolved in laughter. Dropping her sandal, Cecily fell back onto the couch. April collapsed on a section facing her and crossed long legs.

"Jeezus!" she said. "You are the craziest person I've ever met, you know that, Cecily? And that's sure saying plenty, considering we met in a mental hospital."

Cecily laughed again, but this time the act was sobering. She looked at April in her swingy Chanel cardigan suit, then at her own expensive wine-red dress, and thought how far the two of them had come since that first meeting.

"Hey, Hester, how's about some bubbly?" April continued cheerfully as Cecily's maid, now that danger was past, sidled into the room with shoulders sloping.

"Yes, and run a bath for me, will you?" Cecily said. "I'll just have a sandwich while I soak. Some of that ham. You can leave when it's ready."

April plucked at the tight blond curls cascading down to her collar and covering her eyebrows. "Look at you!" she scolded. "Too tired to come out for dinner with me—and for what? If that cousin of yours didn't squeeze you out of business today, he'll try again, won't he?"

"Probably." Cecily pretended a calm she didn't feel as Hester returned with the champagne. She had gotten the emeralds for the Countess di Crichi's necklace. She'd managed to keep Duvall intact for a while, at least. Her back might be against the wall, but she was surviving.

"Well Jesus, Cecily, why let yourself in for it? Just look at what he and the others have done to Vanessa. Look at what they've tried to do to you! It gives me the willies thinking about it! Sell out. It's not like you need a job, for God's sake. And there's no one to protect you anymore, not Effie, not—"

"I do pretty well by myself." Cecily spoke more sharply than she'd intended, then immediately felt guilty for lashing out at her friend.

April began to work rhythmically at the gum in her mouth, a habit she no longer allowed herself in polite society. Her lashes were so heavily spiked with dark mascara that her eyes resembled a rag doll's. They studied Cecily with a native shrewdness learned in the back of a circus wagon.

"You ever miss him?" she asked bluntly.

"No." Cecily drank so quickly from the glass of champagne sitting beside her that cool, golden drops spilled in rivulets onto her wrist. Her eyes had closed instinctively. April knew her too well to be allowed to see what she was feeling.

She drained her glass and smiled across it, the smile a lie.

"He was like a—an infection. I'm cured now. Over him."

"Miss Catlow . . ." Hester appeared, her nasal voice as unobliging as the rest of her. She stood wiping her hands. "Your bath's ready."

Cecily stood up, relieved the subject was ended.

"All right, then. Just don't end up dead," said April. "I don't know what it is, but I've always looked awful in black."

After quick good-byes Cecily made her way to the skylit bathroom. Dozens of plants in hanging baskets cast swaying shadows on yards of white ceramic tile, creating of the room a luxurious refuge. Next to a sunken whirlpool tub carved from a single slab of gleaming black marble, a silver tray held a sandwich, a peach, and a bottle of Taittinger. Cecily discarded dress and lingerie. Hester had asked for the evening off but would pick them up later. With a sigh she eased herself into a world of soothing, pulsating water.

I'll think about the emeralds, she told herself silently. It would keep her from having to face that damned question of April's that was still there at the edge of her mind, clawing at her, demanding an answer.

Miss him? No, she didn't miss him. But something pressed at her eyes, something gnawed at her insides. Old bitterness. Old anger. A pain that never left.

Don't look back.

She thought of the emeralds. Five perfectly matched stones, as lightly flawed as fine emeralds could be; three-quarters of a million dollars' worth of glittering greenness. They'd made her safe. Surely Jordan Lyle and her own board would see she was as strong as they were now—that they couldn't break her.

A business is the only thing worth loving—the only thing that doesn't betray love.

She heard Effie's words.

But Effie was gone. So was . . . She shook her head, refusing to say his name even to herself. A loneliness that burned her very bones spread through her.

Cecily reached for the sandwich beside her, saw it was roast beef instead of ham, and put it aside with disgust. She poured a glass of the costly sparkling wine and sipped it pensively, wondering if Effie had been right.

The day had been so long. Her eyes fell closed. Perhaps she would sleep well tonight. Half smiling, she lay for an interval soaking in the welcome feeling of doing absolutely nothing. When hunger pangs disturbed her she reached for the champagne again.

"That how you keep going these days? Wesley thinks maybe it is."

Cecily gasped at the sound of the low, grating voice. Cold Taittinger splashed her breast as her hand jerked. She swore.

For an instant she felt her arm rising, trying to hide her nakedness from the man who stood just inside the doorway. Then she let it fall. It would give Ben too much pleasure to see her discomfited. And God knows those smoldering black eyes of his had traveled every inch of her body often enough.

A pulse hammered in her throat, a pulse at odds with the outwardly poised and competent woman she had become.

"How did you get in here?" The words squeezed out of her.

Rage flooded her that he should come strolling back into her life. The first time had been bad enough. And last year in Bangkok—she would never forgive him that, nor forgive herself.

His low laugh sent invisible fingers stroking along her nerves, drawing them into a knot which he controlled.

"What's the matter, Cecily? Don't you think I'm a thoughtful ex-husband, looking you up the minute I hit town?"

He'd adopted his favorite stance, legs spread, encased to the knee in the shiny black boots that meant he'd been flying that damned plane of his, and probably drinking. When he stood like that, with head thrown back, he called to mind some darkly glittering opera hero with his wind-tossed black hair, his look of driven anger, the sensuously narrow strip of beard highlighting the edges of his squared, unyielding face.

Only his mouth, now mocking her, could betray any gentleness in his nature. Cecily closed her eyes, remembering against her will the pleasure that mouth could bring.

He started toward her, boot heels clicking on the spotless tile. Despite her resolve Cecily hunched her shoulders together, shielding herself, feeling weakened and helpless. Then, righting her wineglass, she sipped defiantly.

"Get out, Ben. I've had a hard day and we've nothing to say to each other."

He hitched up a bench and sat down. His eyes, hard and lazy, hadn't left her face.

She was immune to him.

She'd said that to April just a while ago.

Only now his presence was filling the room, making it hard to breathe.

"Mustard," he said in disgust, lifting the top from her sandwich and licking the finger he skimmed across it. "Christ, you've had that woman almost two years and she hasn't even figured out you hate mustard." He tossed the top of the sandwich aside.

"I've come about business. I know you'll stomach anything for that—even seeing me."

There was sarcasm in his words. Cecily looked at him angrily. Had he forgotten he was the one that had walked out on her? Love had meant as little to him as living or dying did when he was flying that hellish little jet of his.

"If you cared about business, you could have shown up three hours ago to vote your shares."

For an instant their eyes met and Cecily's heart faltered. She had never seen a gaze so dark and bottomless, and the question that flickered in it had nothing to do with business.

He grinned slowly and crossed his legs, his gaze licking slowly down along her whiteness.

"You can get out and put some clothes on before we talk if I make you uncomfortable."

She'd been wrong about the question. Anyway, it didn't matter.

"You don't affect me at all, Ben. I know all your tricks too well. But since you've had the bad taste to come in here . . . yes, I will get out."

She rose gracefully and rubbed herself with a towel, her back toward him. Why must her fingers feel clumsy? Why, even in anger, was she assaulted by this sense of something yet to be resolved between the two of them?

"Well, what is it?" she asked, whisking on the white satin robe Hester had left out for her and tying the wide sash with unnecessary vigor.

Ben had risen, too, and was holding the bottle of Taittinger.

"I want a glass of this first," he said, moving toward the living room. "You'd better have one, too. Though come to think of it, judging by those glasses on the coffee table you don't really need it. Peter Kemp some kind of nut that he leaves while you take a bath? I always suspected he had the taste of an amoeba. I wouldn't have thought you'd ever get so desperate you'd take a man like that into your bed."

Cecily brushed past, provoked by the low rumble of his voice. *Watch yourself, Cecily. You know he wants to get your goat.*

"Peter makes me feel like a woman," she said coldly. Let him go on supposing April's glass had belonged to Peter.

"*Makes* you?" His tone taunted her. "You felt that way yourself, without any help, when I came along."

"Get to the point, Ben. What brought you barging in here—" She broke off, not sure what it was she wanted to say.

Ben was looking at her neck. Before she could stop herself, her hand had moved in a vain attempt to cover the beautiful gold rope interspersed with fiery opals nestling against her throat. She wore it more often than she liked to admit. The man standing in the room with her had designed it for her, made it with his own hands.

He drank steadily from the glass he'd picked up from beside the tub, then put it aside. His expression had tightened.

"It's your sister," he said.

A wave of fear hit Cecily. "Vanessa! What's happened?"

He took a step toward her. His fingers flexed but did not touch her elbow.

"She miscarried this morning. She lost the baby. Damn it, you know I like Van, and I've worried for a long time that she'd be used as a pawn again, so I've been paying someone in their household to keep an eye on her. She called me as soon as she could."

Cecily had stepped back and with two curled fists was supporting herself as she bent over the marble pedestal that held a statue of a Thai temple dancer.

"This—this will destroy her. She'll end up back in some damned asylum!"

"I'd say the chances are good. And considering the legal battle it took to free her last time, I wouldn't put money on getting her out. Meanwhile that bastard she married controls her stock and votes to carve up Duvall. They could turn around and call another meeting of the board tomorrow."

Cecily stared at him, not comprehending, not even caring. She shivered, briefly transformed again into the terrified nine-year-old whose only safety, whose only security in the world, had been her adored older sister Vanessa.

"I'm not going to let them lock her up again!" She could hear the fear in her voice. "Maybe with the miscarriage they've taken her to a regular hospital first—"

"They have."

"I'm going to her!"

She turned, reaching blindly for the telephone. Ben's hand reached it first.

"There's not a flight out of here tonight that has a seat free. You'd have to go to New York, and you'd waste hours. That's why I came."

Gradually Cecily thought she understood. Forcing herself erect, she looked at him in shaky contempt.

"Oh, yes." Her lips were stiff. "I think I'm beginning to see. You make the gallant gesture and then expect your payment, just like in Bangkok. Is that it, Ben?"

The pupils of his eyes dilated. She saw his anger.

"You didn't object so much in Bangkok, I recall."

The sound that escaped her was partly oath and partly sob. "Damn you, Ben! I don't have time to play games with you. Just—get me to her!"

She spun away, but a splintering pain in her skull, a dizziness filled her. She stopped and swayed, clutching her forehead.

"That still happening?" Ben was behind her. "Relax that stubborn jaw of yours. Come on, now. Relax it."

His hands came around to cover the sides of her face, gently massaging the bone, coaxing, as he had so many times, the mandible joint to loosen and end her vertigo.

Her back was against him. Cecily could feel his hardness. She could not remember a time in his arms when he had not been hard. The passing minutes seemed to stop, suspending the two of them like creatures trapped in amber. A confusion of thoughts assailed Cecily's consciousness: fear for Vanessa; the remembered shelter of Ben's body; the bitter disbelief that swept her even now at knowing he had felt no love for her, only casual passion.

He stepped away, releasing her. Without looking back she walked toward the bedroom they had shared.

His voice stopped her at the door.

"They're having a cold spell in London. You got a fur around?"

She nodded, closed the door between them, locked it.

There had been a time when she and Van had laughed on the beach and thought nothing evil could ever touch them again.

There had been a night in Heredia when a thousand orchids had been in bloom and she and Ben had made love beneath them and she'd thought her happiness would never end.

Opening a small closet with an individual climate control that would keep one fur safe in even the hottest weather, Cecily took out a short lynx jacket. She stared at it, then let its shaggy whiteness fall to her feet.

Her hand gripped the door frame. Her eyes squeezed shut. There, away from Ben's sight, she wept, tears falling for so many things that were past.

TWO

"YOU KNOW WHAT YOU TWO ARE? YOU'RE BASTARDS!"

Cecily tried to escape the hold her sister Vanessa had on her, wanting to fling herself on their fourteen-year-old cousin Lucy, who ran laughing ahead of them.

They'd lived at Lucy's house for three months now, ever since Van had found Mama dead. And for almost all that time Cecily had been hoping something awful would happen to Lucy. Like maybe a poisonous snake would bite her toe. Or a tarantula.

Only Van said she was dumb to be nine years old and not know there weren't either one of those at Marblehead. Cecily glared at Lucy's balloon of black hair and hoped Lucy slipped on one of the rocks on the high, narrow finger of land above the ocean.

"You're bastards!" Lucy repeated gleefully, dancing backward in her white shirt and shorts. "You're poor and your mother was crazy and your father wasn't married to her!"

Squirming, Cecily could just see the fringes of Van's pretty chin and golden hair. Van was thirteen and beautiful.

"That's not true!" Van shouted back. "They were married! Mama had pictures."

In her anger Vanessa forgot her hold on Cecily, who hurled herself forward.

"Ouch! You little brat!" shrilled Lucy as Cecily, with great satisfaction, drove her fist farther into Lucy's stomach than she'd ever thought it was possible to punch a fist. She struck again, payment to Lucy for deliberately ripping her teddy bear. For flushing Van's earrings down the toilet. For making Van cry.

Lucy's quick slap stung her cheek and made her head spin.

"Jordan, get her off of me! She's biting!"

Cecily felt two sets of hands start to pull at her.

"Cecily, stop it!" That was Van's voice.

One set of hands was covered with curly blond hair like his head and belonged to her cousin Jordan, who was oldest of them all and fifteen. The other belonged to Vanessa.

Michael, Jordan's friend, had come with them but was just standing by. He was big and Cecily didn't like him because he was always snickering with Jordan about Van's breasts, which had grown early.

Van had taken care of her as long as Cecily could remember, Mama had been in and out of hospitals so much. Now, crying in her rage and angry with herself because she knew she was too old to cry, she subsided and pressed against Van.

"It's okay," Van said, squeezing her. "Lucy's lying."

Lucy was examining her arm, her gray eyes furious. "I'm not! Your mother was a lunatic. You're living here on charity because there's no place else for you. But as soon as your stupid old uncle dies, my mother will throw you out. You wait and see!"

Cecily sobbed in spite of herself. She wouldn't mind never seeing Lucy again, but she was scared at the thought of having no place to go—of maybe being separated from Van.

She knew why Lucy was being mean to them. Lucy was jealous. Their Great-Uncle William, who had married Lucy and

Jordan's mother, had called them up to his bedside that morning. He had patted them with his frail old hand and given Van a locket with one of his rare emeralds from Colombia. Lucy had several pretty necklaces, but she didn't have an emerald. She'd pouted till lunchtime. Then she'd turned nice and suggested this walk.

"We're going back," Van said, wiping Cecily's tears with the side of her hand. Van sounded like a grownup when she made decisions.

"Oh, no, you're not," said Lucy with a sudden singsong voice. "Not until we teach you your place."

She sprang suddenly, blocking the way back and seizing Van's necklace.

"Such a pretty necklace, Van! Such a nice, thick chain on it. Why, we could hang you by it just like your mama hung herself! Tell me, Van, did her tongue get puffy and stick out like in the movies?"

"Stop it! Please stop it!"

Vanessa's voice was sharp with fear. Cecily had never heard that sound before. She tried to lash out at Lucy, to push her away, but someone had caught her from behind. Jordan.

Cecily kicked furiously backward, aiming for his shins, but he was tall, with long arms, and wrestled her out of position. Lucy had twisted the chain tight around Van's neck, laughing as she jerked it up behind Van like a noose. Van's face was white. Her hands were clawing at the noose, but not very well.

"Hit her, Van! Hit her!" she yelled. Why hadn't Van thought of that? Why didn't she do it now?

"Don't you think that's a nice idea?" Lucy sang. "You can be like your mama. We'll hang you just like they did the witches up in Salem. Won't that be a nice use for your locket, Van?"

She began to pull Van backward, making her stumble, moving farther out on the rocky finger of land that was hidden from Great-Uncle William's house by a single large tree.

"Let me go! *Let me go!*"

Van's voice gave way to a terrified scream that made Cecily's stomach lurch.

She knew it was just a game. It had to be!

"They won't really hurt you, Van! They're just being mean!" she cried hoarsely. She tried to bite Jordan, but he cuffed her along the side of her head and she saw stars.

When her vision cleared she saw Van had either stumbled or been pushed and was on the ground. The back of the necklace had been hooked up over the thick branch of a bush, imprisoning her.

"Van! You can get out now! Just slip your head out!" she shouted.

Van might have to wiggle a little. Her necklace was twisted and pulling her up. But she wasn't being choked anymore. She could free herself.

But Van didn't try. She didn't even seem to hear.

Cecily felt herself being shoved along toward Van now. Jordan caught her hands and after a minute managed to tie them with something he took from his pocket. He pushed her to the ground and he and Michael started forward. They were grinning the way they did when they watched Van in the swimming pool.

"We'll save you, Van." Jordan's voice had a sneering sound.

He glanced at Lucy and she was smiling, nodding to go ahead, as though this were something planned. She moved back for the two boys. Jordan spoke again.

"We'll save you if you let us have free feels."

Jordan dropped to his knee. His hand closed over Van's breast as though he were crumpling paper.

"No! Let me alone!"

Van's voice was shrill and terrified. She struck with her fists at Jordan.

He laughed and caught her wrists and Michael, who was squatting over her, began to unbutton her blouse.

Now Cecily understood. They were going to rape her sister! She rolled to her feet and ran, head lowered to butt like a goat. Lucy's foot flashed out. Hard granite crashed against Cecily's chin as she fell with hands tied behind her.

Sharp, prickling shocks ran up the bones in front of her ears. Lucy was holding her down.

"One for you and one for me," she heard Jordan saying to Michael.

They had Van's blouse open all the way now, and each boy had a hand stuffed into Van's bra, moving all over her. Van was screaming and crying. Not words anymore, just sound.

Maybe it was all just a bad dream. Cecily saw Jordan's tongue lick down over his lip.

"There, we've saved you from hanging, Van. Now you've got to worship us!"

Jordan nudged Michael and the two boys unzipped their zippers together. Their penises came out, longer than the pictures

Cecily had seen in one of Van's health books and horrible-looking. They pushed them against Van's face.

"Yeah, worship us!" Michael repeated. "Kiss us. Worship your masters."

"If you're good, we'll put burnt offerings in your mouth, huh, Michael?"

"Burnt offerings! Yeah. Hot, anyway."

Their laughter had a nasty sound.

Van's hands were free now, but she didn't strike at them. Instead she tried to cover her face, cringing and sobbing. They pushed at her, shoving their skin against her mouth, her eyes.

"Mama!" The shriek, in a voice unlike Van's, burst from her. She began to repeat the cry endlessly. "Mama! Help me, Mama!"

A cold feeling welled up inside Cecily's throat. Their mama was dead! What was Van thinking?

She wasn't sure what was really happening now. She saw things and then they blurred. Michael yanked Jordan back.

"Hey, stop it, Jordan! She's wigging out or something."

Jordan shoved him away. "Lay off."

"You said we'd just have a few laughs," Michael argued. "It's gone far enough!"

Jordan had crouched over Van again and was trying to get his hand down her pants as he shoved himself at her face. Michael caught him by the shoulder and jerked him back. Jordan swore. He swung at Michael and suddenly the two boys were shoving and hitting each other.

Lucy started to rise. Cecily rolled, scrambling to her feet. Lucy didn't stop her.

Lucy was stamping her foot and looking angry.

"Jordan, stop it!" she ordered. "There's not enough room up here. You'll get hurt!"

Cecily didn't care about Jordan and Michael. Half running, half stumbling, she reached Van and shouted in her ear.

"Just put your hand up, Van. You can slip the necklace off right over your head!"

Van's eyes looked funny. They didn't seem to be looking at Cecily.

"Your *hand*, Van!"

Slowly, like a windup toy, Van obeyed. She stood, swayed, looked down at Cecily with that funny expression.

A sob caught in Cecily's throat. Van wasn't hugging her.

"Oh . . . ." Van gave a sleepy smile, held out a hand.

Cecily was on her feet. They ought to run. She started to tell

Van, but Jordan and Michael crashed across in front of them, still hitting each other.

"You stupid shit! Don't try to tell *me* what to do," Jordan said between grunts.

His face looked furious and scary. He knocked Michael backward, then knocked him again.

Cecily saw Michael's hands make swimming shapes in the air. Then he dropped out of sight. He only cried once.

No one moved for a minute. Then Lucy and Jordan and Van—as though she were just sort of following but not understanding—started toward the edge of the high, rocky finger. Cecily crept to Van's side. She saw Michael sprawled amid gray rocks. His head was twisted like no one normal could twist his head, and she knew without being told that he was dead.

Beside her Van bent double. She was scratching her face and screams pealed out of her, one after another.

No one else spoke. Jordan's throat was making swallowing motions. Lucy looked at him, then at Van and Cecily. Suddenly she turned and began to run back toward the house.

"Help us! Somebody help us!" she screamed. "Somebody help us! Vanessa's killed Michael!"

"I'm telling you, Orlena, the child will talk. She'll say what she did to the gardener when he first reached them."

Orlena Lyle looked contemptuously at the man who was pacing before her in the study. Pinstripe suit with vest, gold watch, and jelly to the core. She had taken him for a lover because he was useful and because he was mildly handsome. The handsomeness wouldn't have counted for much if he hadn't been her husband's lawyer. Of course, this disaster with the children had put him through a miserable afternoon, she thought, but she'd been through it, too.

"The child won't talk," she said, her voice a light thread of steel. "I'll see to it. Anyway, the gardener's hard of hearing. You're not suggesting there's any truth to Cecily's ravings, are you?"

She looked at him through eyes as unfeeling and green as the priceless cabochon emeralds hanging around her neck, stones her sick old husband had given her from his private collection, stones taken from the Muzo mine in the sixteenth century and irreplaceable now because the first emeralds from a mine were always the best.

Harlan Nimmo ran a hand through thinning brown hair.

"No. No, of course I'm not."

Orlena nodded. "Well, there you are, then."

She smiled to reward him for good behavior and handed him a whiskey and soda, turning so a ray of light through the draperies fell on the loosely bound wealth of her honey-blond hair. She knew she was not a classically beautiful woman, but she was striking with her aristocratic nose and widow's peak. Moreover, she radiated an air of untouchable sexuality, a half-hidden arrogance, that was maddening to men. When she had nothing more pressing on her mind, the knowledge amused her. Men had always been, in her experience, such fools.

Now, as Harlan sipped his drink, she wondered privately how much of what her children had told her about what had happened out on the point a few hours ago had been the truth. Lucy, her youngest, had the capacity of lying without batting an eye. And Jordan . . . She grimaced with distaste. Jordan would be a viper, if he weren't so inept.

Not that the answer to any of her musings mattered to her. She had planned very carefully and worked very hard for the comfortable life she now led. Once a department store model, left on her own with two small toddlers, she had managed to become a clerk for Lyle & Co., then to model its jewelry, then to marry its owner. She certainly wasn't about to jeopardize all she'd earned because one of her children had had the misfortune—or bad taste—to kill a playmate. Not when Lucy, and Vanessa's very observable break with sanity, provided such a tidy story.

"Cecily was hysterical," she said, thinking aloud. "And goodness knows she's hardly a reliable witness, considering that it's her sister involved, not to mention the mental instability the family seems to have in general."

"Of course," said Harlan. He sighed and set down his glass. "All the same, I wish this day were ended."

He looked sadly at Orlena and slowly she perceived what was really bothering him.

"Why, you unfeeling bastard." She laughed with disgust. "You don't really mind that someone's dead. You haven't really minded all the messy legal details. All you're thinking about is that we were about to go to bed when it all came up!"

She arched her narrow eyebrows, lips curling, flashing her trim body in its brocade caftan out of range as he reached for her in apology.

"When William dies, I do hope you'll wait till the funeral's over before you try to mount me."

He looked stricken, as he always did when she made fun of

him. "Please, Orlena. You're not being fair! You know how beautiful you are, and I thought of you all the way up here—"

She waved a hand. "And you're going to have a longer drive ahead of you in a couple of minutes," she said, resuming a businesslike tone. "So let's get this over."

He looked slightly rebellious. He was, perhaps, more clever than the rich, indulgent old man who had married her and adopted her children. Orlena forced her lips into an appeasing smile that was vaguely triangular.

"I'll feel better when this is over. You know that, don't you, Harlan? You could take tomorrow off and come back for the night; poor William's such a valued client."

She brushed against him, knowing the tidbits she threw out were enough to keep him as content as a lapdog.

"If William thinks the girls have run off, he's old-fashioned enough not to add that codicil to his will that he's been planning. I *want* him to think that, Harlan. I don't want my children to lose any part of what we both know should be theirs." She paused, assuring herself this all was having the effect she wanted. Her voice became a purr. "What pleasure would he get in knowing Vanessa's been committed as criminally insane? You saw to it she'd be listed as having no living relatives. You can do the same for the younger one when you enter her in the children's home. Now. Let's get it over."

"Where's Van?"

Cecily held tight to the side of the chair she'd been put in and faced her Aunt Orlena. A long time had passed since people had come running to them out there on the rocks.

They'd all been brought back to the house, except for Michael, who was dead. She'd been left in one room with someone to watch her and told not to leave. Van, to her dismay, had been taken somewhere else.

"Where's Van? I want to be with Van," she said again.

She'd never been in Orlena's study before. She knew once upon a time it had been Great-Uncle William's study, but it scared her anyway with its heavy curtains and big, dark leather-topped desk. Mostly she was scared of Orlena, sitting behind it. Orlena was young to be Great-Uncle William's wife, and she wore her coppery hair swept softly up and on top of her head like a storybook princess. Her eyes were green and very pretty, but the first time she'd met Orlena, Cecily had seen in those eyes that Orlena didn't like her.

Orlena wore emeralds from Great-Uncle William's company day and night, big fat ones. They weren't the glittery kind, but were smooth like jellybeans. Her aunt had bracelets and several necklaces. The one she wore today had diamonds mixed in with the green stones. Emeralds hung in a double row from her neck and two huge ones covered her earlobes. They glowed like her eyes as Orlena leaned forward.

"Vanessa killed someone today. You know that's a terrible crime, don't you, Cecily?"

Her voice was like cool water. It made Cecily shiver. It continued now.

"Vanessa's insane, just as your mother was. She had to be sent to a hospital so she doesn't harm anyone else. They've already taken her."

"No!"

Cecily pushed forward on her chair. She was frightened—more frightened than she'd ever been in her life. Her tongue felt wobbly.

"It's a lie! Van didn't kill Michael. Jordan pushed him."

She could hear Orlena catch her breath. The green eyes behind the desk wavered slightly, toward a man standing in the shadows.

"I'm sure that's what you would like to remember, Cecily, but that's not how it was. We all know it wasn't."

Cecily stared at her. Could Orlena be right? Her voice still sounded so cool and calm and Cecily couldn't exactly remember all that had happened since they'd come back to the house. It was like one minute she'd be thinking of something and the next minute somebody was coming into the room and a lot of time had passed. . . .

"No!" She *knew* what had happened. She'd been there. "It was Jordan! Lucy had been choking Van and the boys held her down and opened her blouse and did nasty things—"

"Quiet!"

Orlena sat back. Her eyes were hard. The only thing about Orlena that was short were her fingers, with their small, pointed nails. They drummed on the desk now. One of them wore an emerald as big as a quarter.

"Lies won't help you, Cecily. In fact, you'll find things go easier for you if you don't make trouble."

Her voice had grown sharper.

"After what happened this afternoon, after this—this scandal that's been brought on your great-uncle after all he's done for you, he wants no more association with you and your sister.

You're being made wards of the state. Do you understand what that means?"

Cecily swallowed. Orlena was a grownup and she was only nine years old and she knew there was nothing she could do to stop what was happening to her.

"Van's innocent," she said in a whisper.

Orlena rose like an angry statue, jerking a piece of paper between her fingers and making it snap as she creased it.

"I will not tolerate lies about my children. If ever, *ever* you tell this preposterous tale about Jordan again, I'll see you're locked up just like your sister, do you understand?"

She tossed the paper onto her desk. "Go and pack a suitcase. Mr. Nimmo will take you to the children's home. Be down in ten minutes."

Cecily wanted to hit her as she had hit Lucy earlier, but she knew it would do no good. Orlena was bigger, and stronger, and Cecily knew her only safety now lay in obeying—or pretending to.

"I—couldn't I just see Van to say good-bye or something?"

She knew by Orlena's eyes her request was hopeless. She fought against tears. Van was gone and she didn't even know where and she didn't know where she was going, either. What could she do?

By the time she reached her bedroom on the second floor she still hadn't thought of an answer. A male nurse was standing outside Great-Uncle William's door, so she couldn't get in there. All Uncle William's servants—the nice cook and the bossy maid and the gardener, who was usually outside anyway—had disappeared. There was no one to help her.

Bitterly she kicked her empty bed, again and again, ignoring the ache that came to her leg.

"I'll find you, Van, and I'll get even with them. I will!" She couldn't see for the tears in her eyes, but still she kept kicking. "I'll get even with all of them, even if it takes a million years!"

THREE

IT WAS COLD OUTSIDE. WIND RATTLED THE WINDOWS OF THE OPEN, modern workroom of Landis and Oxenburg, Estate Jewelers. Six stories down, the crowds passing on Fifth Avenue were being pelted by a steady drizzle.

To Cecily, bent over a microscope, the phone call she'd just received had made it a beautiful day, its skies as blue and clear as the ten-carat sapphire she was examining.

"Well? What do you think?" asked the anxious young man with curly red hair standing next to her.

"There's no question," she said with a final squint at the small inclusion they'd been studying. "The edge isn't ragged at all. This stone came from Ceylon, not Burma."

Teddy Landis, nephew of the senior partner in Landis and Oxenburg, groaned and rubbed his abdomen. He was twenty-seven, only two years older than Cecily, but already he had the temperamental digestion of a much older man.

"Why," he mourned, "*why* must your hunches always be right?"

Cecily laughed, still floating over her phone call. She smoothed the cuffs of her silky dark green dress with the surplice waist, the first new dress she'd indulged in for more than a year. She'd known when she saw it in a shop window that it would make her eyes look larger and darker than ever, and even though there was no one to appreciate it but Teddy and the other men she worked with, she had succumbed. Sometimes she thought she'd spent her entire life resisting beautiful clothes, longing for them, standing motionless outside shop windows while she told herself her earnings were needed for something more important than her own pleasure. Van was more important to her than a thousand dresses, and Van had no one to depend on except her. Sometimes Cecily resented the need for her self-imposed discipline but not today.

"Cheer up," she said to Teddy. "The company won't have to lay out as much for the ring as they would have with a Burmese stone—not that it isn't beautiful in its own right; the color could pass for Burmese. But you know they won't. So we've just earned our keep for the week by saving them a buck or two."

Teddy sat down in the single chair in the small glass enclosure that was his office.

"*You* have," he said. "Thousands. Two lousy years you've been with this firm and you've been better than I am from the day you walked in. Oh, well. You've saved my ass another time." He grinned. "You look like the cat that fell into the cream today. What's happening? You in love?"

Cecily laughed again. Falling in love, like buying more clothes than she absolutely needed, was a luxury she had not permitted herself. Not until she got Van out of the hospital where she'd finally located her, she thought, and today she seemed close to that goal.

"You remember I told you about my sister," she said cautiously, for she rarely talked about Van, had only done so with Teddy, who was her friend, in fact. "Well, I've finally found a lawyer who thinks we can get her out. The one I talked to just after I started work here was so discouraging—said I'd have to have a bigger apartment and be able to give proof I could be the sole support of Van. And I couldn't then. But now . . ." She knew the contours of her cheeks were deepening as she smiled. "Now I've had two raises and I've got a nest egg. This new lawyer called just a while ago and said he'll meet me Thursday. He sounds absolutely positive it'll just be routine."

Teddy looked at her and she saw the sympathy in his eyes.

"I never knew the finances were a problem. Jeez, that's why you never eat lunch, huh? Here you said that's how you keep your weight down and I was dumb enough to fall for it.

"Well, that's great, C. C.! I'm happy for you. And look, if you ever need a loan or anything like that . . ." He grinned. "I couldn't do a damned thing for you, considering how little I manage to save, but I expect I could twist the old man's arm so he would."

"Thanks."

Teddy nodded and carefully removed the ring from beneath the microscope. He started out the door.

"Guess I better break the news about this to the front office. To think the dame that wanted to sell us this has been a customer for almost twenty years! I wonder if she was trying to put one over on us."

Humming under her breath, Cecily left Teddy's office and stepped into an identical glass-enclosed cubicle that was her domain. It was not quite an hour before quitting time. All the gems she'd received that morning had been checked in again, receipt signed. She had only paperwork.

As she sometimes saw it, the business of Landis and Oxenburg was really nothing more than a glorified version of the humble garage sale. Heirloom jewelry of the highest quality was purchased from estates and auctions and resold to wealthy clients around the world. Nonetheless, she reveled in being a part of it. The company was one of the most respected in the trade, and occasionally she and Teddy, the junior appraisers, wrested some satisfying discovery from the routine of their work as they had this afternoon. It paled next to the excitement of assessing large

lots of valuable jewelry at auction and setting the company's bid
as the senior appraisers did, but the atmosphere itself certainly
had its share of glamour. Who could ask to work in a more elite
setting, so near to Harry Winston and up from Tiffany's?

As she finished the papers before her, because she was thinking ahead to Van's release, Cecily also thought backward through
the steps that had led her to this pleasant job with Landis and
Oxenburg: two years with a wholesale dealer in colored stones,
first as an appraiser, then as an assistant buyer of amethysts and
star sapphires; before that a year as gemologist-salesclerk in a
small but exclusive jewelry store in Newport; before that the year
of intensive training at the Gemological Institute—once she'd
worked as waitress, office help, and part-time clerk to earn
tuition money; before that, of course, the foster homes.

She shivered at the memory, rising quickly and rubbing her
arms. The horror, the aching loneliness of those first weeks
separate from Van, would follow her all her life. She did not
even know where her sister was. She had no one—no one in the
world—to care about her. Nights were the worst. There was no
one to pull the covers to her chin. No one to hug her. No one
who was just always *there*, a sustaining warmth.

When she was twelve, with the help of new and caring foster
parents, she had found Van. She'd been permitted to see Van at
the mental hospital. They'd met rather awkwardly in a room
filled with people, and Van had held out some gum.

"It was all I could get. I wanted to give you a present," her
sister had said.

Van had looked so tired. Not at all like Cecily remembered.

Then suddenly Van had hugged her, stroking her hair. It had
been so long since anyone had hugged her . . . so long since
anyone had told her, by either words or touch, that she was
important and loved. The mute reassurance had broken through
the rigidity with which Cecily tried to protect herself and she'd
cried and cried in Van's arms. Van had always known what she
needed. Now they could write letters. Now they would never be
separated again.

But the next time she'd gone to see Van, Van had gone.
Eleven years later she'd found Van in another hospital, under a
false name, the work of the Lyles, no doubt.

A sob startled Cecily back to the present. Surely the sharp,
grieving sound hadn't come from her, a grown woman. She
wiped her eyes.

To compose herself, Cecily looked around her cubicle. What

irony, she thought, as she had many times before, that she should end up in the same trade as her Great-Uncle William. As Orlena.

Her fingers tightened convulsively on the sleeves of her prized new dress. She no longer dreamed and planned revenge against Orlena as she had as a child, yet the least flashing thought of the woman or Lucy or Jordan even now filled her mouth with the hot taste of hate.

Orlena had inherited Lyle & Co., the fine old jewelry house owned by Great-Uncle William and two generations of Lyles before him. She, Cecily Catlow, had inherited only those ancestors' passion for dealing in precious stones. Funny, she'd always thought it was myth that the taste for a particular occupation ran in a family's blood. And maybe it was. Maybe it was only circumstance, or subconscious, youthful romanticizing of the family lost so early that had somehow led her to her chosen field.

The phone on her desk rang, summoning her back to the present.

"Miss Catlow, Mr. Landis wants to see you," a crisp voice announced.

Cecily held her breath. "Mr. Landis" meant Jacob, the head of the firm, not Teddy.

She frowned. Except for her interview prior to being hired, she had never been asked into Mr. Landis's presence. Now she felt uneasy. Did this have something to do with their discovery about that ring?

Heels tapping, she made her way through the single large room shared by appraisers, repair department, and the armed guard who from this side controlled the electronic security door through which all entries and exits were made. Let it be a compliment, she prayed silently. Let me not have made a mistake. I need this job. I need it for me and for Van.

Jacob Landis's office was a shockingly stark room, with walls painted white, beige carpet and furnishings, and the vast windows on two adjacent walls open to daylight. It was an amazing contrast to the rich reds and walnut paneling of the company's reception room, and Cecily knew why. A gemstone would show its truest colors amid these neutral surroundings. And the most elite of Landis and Oxenburg's customers, the crème de la crème, were received here by Jacob Landis himself to inspect prospective purchases.

A short man, almost completely bald, and rounding in front, Jacob looked up from behind his desk.

"What made you think that sapphire might be Ceylonese?" he barked.

Cecily swallowed. "The facets. They were so irregular when you looked at them from one angle."

Had she made a mistake?

Jacob Landis shoved a small leather box toward her and flipped it open.

"Here. Grade these emeralds."

Strangling silently, Cecily stared at him. Her eyes moved to the contents of the box. He was testing her. She must have been wrong about that sapphire and it had damaged her credibility and if she didn't perform well now, he'd let her go.

"I—need a reference set."

It would be foolhardy to try and judge emeralds or any other colored stones without a standardized set against which to measure their color gradations. Even customers, if they were well versed, knew that.

"Try without one," said Jacob Landis, eyes narrowed.

The inside of her mouth was dry. Her heart was pounding. It was almost dark out, and the artificial lights in the room would distort her perception of color. So might the reflection of her own green dress. Picking up tweezers, she began to transfer the glittering stones before her to the natural settings formed on the back of her left hand by her outstretched fingers.

As the work drew her in, she forgot to be frightened. She concentrated for several minutes, sorting the eight loose stones before her into three rows at first, then, with intent deliberation, reversing the position of two here, two others there.

"Here," she said at last, looking up at him. "I'd grade them this way, top to bottom. And these two, I'd say, are virtually identical."

The man across from her gave a grunt. He beat together fleshy thumbs.

"There's an auction tomorrow, small but worth being represented at, I think. The deceased was known to be a mistress of one of the Hunts. I've just had a call from Waters saying the lots he's most interested in at that auction in California won't be coming up for bids until tomorrow. Arlo's out with the flu."

Cecily's blood started thundering, making up for the fear that had gripped her earlier. Jacob Landis scowled.

"I think you can hold your own—with a reference set." A smile pushed through beneath the scowl. "Your eye is very good. Not one mistake. But no one who takes chances lasts in this business. Sight's in the morning, bidding's in the afternoon.''

She could hardly believe her ears. She would have to be a fool not to know what a break this was for her, and coming years earlier than she'd expected. If she went to this auction, she would be matching wits with men at least twice her age, and in a business that still nourished a prejudice against women.

''Why aren't you going yourself?'' she asked, forgetting she'd never even spoken privately with her employer before and had no right to cross the lines that separated them.

He thumped his chest. ''Heart. My doctor won't let me.''

He scribbled out a note and handed it to her. ''Take this back to the vault and they'll have that reference set waiting for you first thing in the morning.'' He walked with her toward the door. ''Oh, and Miss Catlow. There'll be firms at that auction that don't ordinarily deal in estate items—maybe some of our neighbors from down the street, probably Lyle and Company. Only way a company can get the color their better clients are looking for these days, the quality of new emeralds being what it currently is. Don't let the number of firms involved in the bidding rattle you.''

Cecily felt her heart thud high in her chest.

Lyle & Co.!

For an instant she felt all the old anger, all the desire for revenge. She shook it away. ''I won't,'' she promised.

Emotion could only be an enemy in the workplace. She'd stay level-headed. Van was going to be free soon. She herself had just been given a kick up the ladder at Landis and Oxenburg. She didn't give a damn about the Lyles.

Yet when she returned to her office and buttoned her raincoat she found her brain running feverishly. Did Orlena and her offspring involve themselves in the actual business of Lyle & Co. or simply live off its profits? Would she recognize them if any of them were there? Would they recognize her?

Van . . . she thought with a sudden wistfulness. Van had protected her and made her feel safe all those years ago. Would she ever know the warmth of depending on the strength of someone other than herself again?

Silly thought. She was angry for letting it slip in. She could take care of herself. And yet . . . She sighed.

The intercom in the workroom stirred to life.

''Miss Catlow? Are you still in the office?''

''Yes.''

It was Thelma in the front office speaking. By the time Cecily had made her way out the electronic door, Thelma, with her own coat on, was hurrying down the hall to meet her.

"Can you help someone about a refund?" asked Thelma. "I know you helped out in sales when Marge was out with the flu and know how it's done."

"Where's everyone else?"

"Marge still feels sort of peaked, so Mr. Landis sent her home about three. He just left himself. And Mr. Tucker had a dental appointment. He left on the dot. It's ten past quitting time, you know," Thelma said virtuously. "I was just closing up."

Nodding, Cecily took off her coat. "Sure, I'll take care of it."

Whoever it was would have to come back tomorrow. Cecily wasn't authorized to make a refund, and in any case the vault was probably already locked.

"She slipped in before I could tell her we were closed," Thelma said, heading for a rear exit. "I wouldn't ask, but I remember her. She's bought things here. And she said she really had to see someone tonight. Thanks, dear."

Opening the door to the front office, Cecily saw a woman waiting on one of the love seats before a small glass display counter. She wore a fine fur but the rest of her was ravaged. Her blond hair was tucked back untidily beneath a silk scarf. Makeup had been applied too thickly in an attempt to brighten a puffy white face. She was clutching a red velvet box in one hand.

"I'm Mrs. Maxwell Kemp," she said with a smile that seemed more like a twitch as Cecily came around to meet her. "I want to return this."

She snapped open the red box, revealing a narrow chain of one-carat diamonds holding a ruby. Easily eighteen carats of diamonds there, Cecily thought.

"I'm afraid you'll have to come back tomorrow," Cecily said as politely as she could. "Our vault closed about ten minutes ago."

"Look, I have the sales slip." Mrs. Kemp's voice grew thinner and tighter. "You guarantee to repurchase an item within six months and it's only been three!"

"I'm sorry."

The woman sprang to her feet. *"I want my money back and I want it now, do you understand?"* Her veneer of well-bred graciousness had vanished. "This thing's brought me nothing but bad luck. I hate it!"

Cecily rose, too. Teddy had still been in his office when she got her coat. She'd better let him handle this.

"If you'd like to sit down—" she began.

But the main door to Landis and Oxenburg burst open and a tallish man in his early thirties strode in, out of breath. Mrs. Kemp whirled.

"You!" she shrieked and snatched the necklace to her.

"Put it down, Myra! It's not yours to sell." He lunged, grabbing it from her.

Cecily moved toward the counter, toward the button hidden beneath the carpet on the other side that would summon guards, but Mrs. Kemp spun back toward her.

"Damn you! This is your fault!"

With clawlike hands the woman snatched a heavy mirror standing on the counter and brought it in an arc toward Cecily's head.

Dodging, Cecily shut her eyes against the inevitable blow. Glass shattered. But not against her. Someone had caught her and turned her . . . the man who had burst in just seconds earlier. He had taken the blow from the mirror. He staggered with her in his arms.

She had just time enough to see a chair hurtling toward the plate-glass display counter before he spun her away. His leg struck one of the love seats and they fell on top of it, still tangled together.

"Hey! What's going on?"

That was Teddy's voice.

Cecily became aware of a guard in the room, of Mrs. Kemp's swearing. Shaken, she looked at the man whose shoulders still hunched protectively above her.

"Are you all right?" he asked.

He had hazel eyes and a thick mustache that gave an almost boyish look to his handsome features. His jaw was smoothly curved. There were two small cuts on his check from fragments of the mirror.

"Yes . . . thank you," she said.

She could feel the beat of his heart against hers. Still he didn't release her. He scanned her face with concern and some other emotion she couldn't quite recognize.

"You're sure. You're not cut anywhere?" He brought his fingers up and brushed them lightly across her face, pushing back her hair.

Cecily felt an odd sensation stealing through her body as her eyes looked into his. She nodded.

"Cecily, what the hell . . ."

Teddy was coming toward them now. The stranger who was holding her reached into his vest and held out a card.

"That woman there is no longer married to Maxwell Kemp. She was trying to sell property that didn't belong to her. My father's housekeeper called to say she'd burst in and opened the safe and was headed here. If you want to call the number on this card, Mr. Kemp will confirm it."

"You son of a bitch! You're no better than he is." The woman now being restrained by a guard was shouting. "That two-timing bastard threw me out without even a cent to live on and you know it!"

The man on top of Cecily looked embarrassed. He rose, helping her to her feet, and reached for his wallet.

"Here, Myra. Take this for your drugs or gin or whatever it is you need and get out of here."

He passed her a bill. Cecily saw it was five hundred dollars.

"I'm sorry about this," he apologized, smoothing his hair and turning to Teddy. "I'm Peter Kemp. If you'll call my father when you get an estimate for damages, he'll take care of it."

Teddy nodded.

"Some scene," he said a moment later when everyone else had left. "You sure you're okay, C. C.? Want me to drive you home?"

"No need." She picked up the coat she'd discarded and rolled her eyes. "After this the subway's going to seem positively relaxing."

A few minutes later she stepped outside the building in a constant stream of people, then stopped short. Peter Kemp was standing there in the rain with his collar turned up and his arm on the top of a silver-gray limousine. He stepped toward her.

"I feel very guilty about what happened up there," he said. "Please let me take you to dinner to try and make up for it."

On a breath that was sharply indrawn, Cecily laughed. "It's not necessary. Really."

"I'd like to. Really."

She shook her head. Though she went out with men on a casual basis, Cecily had never allowed herself to become involved with one she found truly attractive. She had an obligation to Van first, and she wouldn't risk any interest that might draw even part of her thoughts and energy away from that.

"If you don't say yes, we're likely to get soaked standing here and arguing about it," said Peter Kemp. He took her arm and urged her toward the limousine. "Where would you like to go?"

* * *

"Oh, please don't punish him! He didn't mean to do anything wrong!"

The words slipped out before Vanessa could catch herself. She bit her lip as the elderly man who had wandered to the front of the line in the harshly lit gray dining room was caught by the arm and hustled toward the exit by attendants.

Miss Mundey, the blimplike attendant with rouged cheeks who had seized him first, whirled and glared at Vanessa.

"Always giving free advice, aren't you? You know the rules, little bleeding heart. No getting out of line even if it is to ask the maître d' for a table for two."

A few patients snickered. Vanessa colored with outrage for poor befuddled old Mr. Niederlehner, who was crying now in the distance.

He just didn't know where he was, she wanted to say. *The poor man's crazy.*

But then she supposed that was obvious, or he wouldn't be here.

"You better be careful, Van," the brown-haired girl behind her whispered as Miss Mundey turned away.

"I know," Vanessa murmured.

She shoved her hands into the pockets of the gray-blue dress that was the uniform for every female patient. She hated Miss Mundey. The woman was a bully, like someone else Vanessa couldn't quite remember. Talking back to Miss Mundey was something she shouldn't do at any time, especially not now, when Cecily thought she might be released soon. Vanessa knew that staff would have to agree a patient was ready to leave, and Miss Mundey was staff.

Vanessa looked with distaste at the starchy casserole that was Friday supper. There were ten at her table on the women's side of the dining room. Things were more intimate here, less institutional than in the larger dining hall serving wards where everyone was really wacko. She guessed she should be grateful. She ate methodically, thinking that once she was free she might write the governor or someone about Miss Mundey. Jell-O, casserole, gray-green peas. There. She was done.

She placed her utensils carefully across her tray, ignoring the lumpy-looking glob of yellow that was dessert. A majority of the women on any ward she could remember were overweight, and she thought she knew why. There was nothing but meals to break the monotony of the days, and most meals were starchy.

So she almost never ate dessert. Sometimes she gave it to someone, which made her a lot of friends.

"Lost your appetite, Vanessa?"

Vanessa shrank. Miss Mundey was hulking over her. Vanessa could feel her broad and threatening shadow.

"They don't like patients to wither away here, missy. I think you'd better clean your plate."

"Yes, Miss Mundey."

Vanessa picked up a spoon, hoping that would be enough to make the woman budge. It wasn't, and Vanessa had been in the wards of various hospitals sixteen years, long enough to know when something was being demanded of her.

Slowly she began to swallow down sticky-sweet pudding. When I get out of here, I'll work and buy pretty jewelry like Cecily sells, and nobody will tell me anything I have to do, she thought.

It was raining outside. She could tell by the bucket catching drips near a door to the kitchen and by a certain oppressing heaviness of the air.

She hated rain.

But she was powerless to do anything about it, just as she was powerless to do anything about Miss Mundey's bullying or the food she ate or anything else in her life. Vanessa kept her eyes fixed on the tray in front of her so no one saw her angry tears.

FOUR

"*F*INISHED WITH YOUR SALAD, MISS?"

"Yes, thank you."

The rain seemed far away as Cecily relaxed in her lushly upholstered seat and drank in, once again, the scene stretching all around her in this magic world of mirrors and brass at the top of the World Trade Center.

"We'll just go somewhere casual," Peter Kemp had promised as his last argument before she'd agreed to have dinner with him.

He'd brought her here, to Windows on the World. By most people's standards it was hardly casual, unless you defined "casual" as meaning that the women were wearing pearls and heavy gold chokers instead of diamonds, or unless you compared it perhaps to some celebrity spot like Lutèce. The waiters gliding about wore smart white jackets with gold epaulets. Murmurs of conversation were discreet. Glad she had chosen today to break in her new dress, Cecily finished the wine in the goblet beside her, enjoying the view again.

First there was the restaurant itself to gaze at from their table in one of the many quiet, elevated niches where thick carpeting seemed to flow continuously up into modern banquettes. The tables were finely draped, the silver gleamed, the waiters and water boys murmured orders and answers in so many foreign languages that Cecily wondered how they possibly understood each other.

Then there was the view out of the windows that gave the restaurant its name, virtual walls of glass one hundred seven stories in the air. Rain had obscured the view of the city down below when they came in, but now it was clearing slightly. The lights of bridges appeared as brilliant smudges against a wet-vinyl background.

She wished Van could see this view. Van had always liked pretty things. She wondered what her sister was doing tonight.

"I do apologize for the uproar with Myra," Peter said for the third time. "The other ex-wives are reasonable, but she . . ." He shook his head.

Cecily smiled. "How many ex-wives does your father have?"

"Myra's the fourth. The first, my mother, died actually, so I guess Myra's only the third *ex*-wife."

He smiled engagingly. His vested gray suit had the fit that came only with custom tailoring. With his mustache, and the shock of brown hair that kept tumbling onto his forehead, he looked paradoxically sophisticated and rather lost.

Cecily quickly glanced down. Each meeting with those hazel eyes was making her feel warm in a way that was foreign to her.

"Does your veal look all right?" he asked as it was set before her.

"Yes, wonderful."

It *was* wonderful, and the fresh mushrooms in puff pastry that had come before had been exquisite, and Peter Kemp had insisted on buying her dinner out of simple, charming politeness. She must remember that.

"With so many stepmothers how did you ever keep all the names straight?" she asked.

They moved to other topics over dinner. When asked about his occupation, Peter said vaguely that he worked in real estate. As conversation progressed, Cecily realized he meant owning real estate—condominiums, shopping centers, hotels.

"My father would have stayed with shopping centers and nothing else," he said. "Hotels were my idea. So far they've done very well."

Cecily sipped coffee and hoped he wouldn't notice she hadn't finished her lemon tart. Its paper-thin slices of fresh lemon made it rather bitter for her taste.

"When I asked you a while ago you wiggled out of answering me," he said. "How did you end up in the jewelry business?"

Cecily shrugged. How could a man like Peter Kemp understand a childhood spent in foster homes—no sense of belonging, no color, let alone glitter.

Worst of all, though, there had been no one to talk to, no one who cared or listened to her victories and uncertainties, no one who shared with her and laughed and teased.

Never, she realized now, had there been any hope of her becoming a permanent member of the families with whom she had stayed. After all, her mother had committed suicide; her sister had been a murderess; she herself hit when angry. Cecily grimaced to herself at the memory of that childhood flaw.

"I started out as a designer working in precious metals, really. That's what my mother had done, and I wanted to be like her. I didn't know very much else about her. She—" Cecily turned dark eyes toward the wall of windows. "She died when I was young.

"Unfortunately I had no talent for working with gold. An instructor was kind enough to tell me early on and suggest gemology." She spread one hand in an expressive gesture. "That was that."

Peter crossed his arms on the table and hunched across them to speak, looking at her with a puzzled smile.

"I've never known a girl who worked for a living before. Can you believe that?"

"Yes."

Cecily let her laughter out softly. He laughed, too, still very close to her.

Their eyes met and held. Reaching across the table he touched her hand.

"You're incredibly lovely, do you realize that? Your face is so—so pure and soft."

Cecily didn't know how to answer. Neither of them moved. That lost-little-boy look was there on his face again. And he'd been listening to her, talking to her, making her feel as though she'd known him for years. His fingers slid over hers, covering them completely as his thumb rubbed gently against the curve of her hand.

"Let's go somewhere and listen to music," he said in a near whisper. "Just for a while."

Cecily felt herself waver. The hand covering hers was warm and urgent. She felt herself responding to it—to him—to this man who just hours ago had thrown himself between her and a madwoman to protect her.

"I mustn't," she said, removing her hand and avoiding his gaze. "I have some fairly important work cut out for me tomorrow."

He looked disappointed. But then, with a smile of resignation he stood up and held her chair.

"All right."

He insisted on seeing her to the door of her apartment, and Cecily, as they climbed the stairs, wondered what she would say if he asked her out again. She could think of reasons enough to decline. Peter Kemp was moneyed and would very likely tire of her as quickly as he'd shown interest.

"Thank you for a wonderful evening," he said as they stopped at her door.

Taking her hand between his own, he kissed it. The gentle act made her feel suddenly defenseless and unsure of herself. An attempt to kiss her lips she could have handled, but this . . .

Then he *was* kissing her lips, his arms sliding softly up to enfold her. The faint scent of his aftershave surrounded her. The feel of his mustache was like silk as it brushed her skin.

Cecily's fingers had wound themselves in the lapels of his raincoat. The wine they'd drunk at dinner seemed to be running in her veins, making all her senses light. His kiss, the slow-moving pressure of his mouth on hers, made her crave more intimacy than she'd ever known with a man.

"Please—may I stay the night?" he asked, releasing her just enough for them to see each other.

Cecily shook her head. Her heart was pounding.

"No."

"May I see you tomorrow, then?"

His hazel eyes were sweeping her face. She felt herself melting under their touch.

"I—don't know."

She couldn't afford to be thinking about him, not with the

auction tomorrow and the chance it brought for advancement at
Landis and Oxenburg. There was Van to consider, too.

Peter's arms tightened around her. Their mouths feasted on
each other again until she grew weak with the feeling of nearness.
She could feel the taut pressure of his thigh against hers, was
aware of his maleness. Suddenly all thoughts of Van and auctions seemed part of some other universe. Reluctantly she drew
herself from his embrace, unlocked her door with trembling
fingers, and closed it between them.

"Congratulations, Miz Catlow."

"Thank you."

Cecily glowed as she and Teddy touched plastic cups above
the small split of champagne opened on her desk. He'd brought
it in just minutes ago, after her return. With shoes kicked off,
nerves jangling in relief, she sipped it happily.

"My God," she said, overwhelmed by reality now that the
auction was past. "I actually *survived* it!"

Teddy laughed, his wiry red hair disarrayed as usual at the end
of the day.

"Not only survived but returned in triumph, I hear."

Cecily laughed, too. She wondered whether or not to share the
delicious news that Jacob Landis had told her. She would be sent
to another, larger auction next week. No, she decided, it would
sound too immodest.

Teddy straightened gravely and bowed above his wineglass.
"Madam, will you be my chief appraiser when I run this show?"

"You bet," said Cecily, gesturing airily with her champagne.
"If you pay me an arm and a leg."

Regretfully she looked at her wrist. The narrow bracelet set
with small emeralds that Jacob Landis had apparently put together years ago as his ingenious reference set winked back at
her.

"Guess I'd better turn this in to the vault before it closes. I
just about died when they handed it to me this morning."

"Looks good on you. I'll bet old Waters looks like a fag when
he has to wear it," Teddy said, grinning.

"Waters is built like a fullback. He could wear dangly earrings
and dare anyone to smirk." Shooting a parting glance of good
humor across her shoulder, Cecily headed for the vault.

By the time she reached her cubicle again, her phone was
ringing.

"Cecily?" said the voice on the other end. "This is Peter.

Will you join me for supper and a play tonight? Please say yes."

Cecily closed her eyes. She should be sensible. She should stay home tonight and write to Van. She should remember attention from someone like Peter Kemp wasn't likely to last.

But this day had been very special to her. She couldn't bear to see it end so quickly.

"Yes," she said. "I'd like to very much."

"Do you mean to tell me you're completely empty-handed? I sent you to that auction and you didn't come back with a single lot?"

Orlena Lyle wrapped a sheet around her and sat up on the massage table. She was naked except for her collar of emeralds and a matching two-inch bracelet.

"That's impossible, Jordan! Even for you."

Her green eyes blazed. The masseur who came each day to attend her in the private massage room adjoining her office was already scuttling toward the door, aware of her coming fury. He had more sense than her son did, she thought darkly. A better sense of timing, anyway.

"Are you *aware* how badly we need some good emeralds?" she demanded, tucking one end of the sheet in at her breasts and stalking dangerously across the room. "Are you *aware* we have a chance to do business with one of France's greatest champagne barons if we can meet his quality standards?"

"If you want his business that badly, why not give him some of those from around your neck?" asked Jordan insolently.

Orlena stopped, head turning like a swan's. She looked at him from her full height until, although he towered over her at six feet four, she had the satisfaction of seeing him fidget. "You are a fool," she said, each word ice.

He had been standing like a lump, fists on the hips of the silk suit he'd had tailored in Italy. He was fine window dressing, she thought through her anger, but not much more.

But now, to her surprise, he broke the pose to wave his arms and take a step toward her.

"What the hell right do you think you have to call me that? What the hell right do you think you have to chew me out?

"I could have had several of those lots—all of them—if I'd had the power to set our top bid myself. But no, you're so power-hungry you can't stand to admit my judgment might be right on anything. You gave our bidder his orders on what the top line was to be on any one lot and he wouldn't cross it. What a goddamn farce—I'm vice-president of Lyle and Company and I can't even have the final say on the prices we pay. I have to stay within your guidelines.

"Well, you just take the blame for this one yourself, Orlena! I tried to tell you the price of good emeralds is going up more than you realize. You know how many of those lots we could have taken? Four of them!"

He waved his spread fingers in her face. Orlena struck them away, incensed at this rebellion. Still he kept spewing like some minor volcano.

"There were six lots and I could have dumped four of them in your lap if I'd had the power to offer just five hundred lousy bucks over your limit, Orlena!"

"Shut up, Jordan." It annoyed her that both her children called her by her first name. She had borne them, endured them, provided for them, and should be accorded respect as their mother. "Be glad I made you vice-president. I didn't have to!"

His face was red. It looked ridiculous with his curly blond hair.

"You need me for a front—just like you needed Harlan Nimmo until he dropped with a heart attack! No one would have taken you seriously running this business. A woman, an ex-model . . ."

"Don't be a fool, Jordan." She smiled because she knew it made him furious to be dismissed like that—and to hide the fact there was the tiniest grain of truth in what he was saying. "Every man who works for me knows quite well I run Lyle and Company. Our competition does, too. *I* made this company triple in sixteen years. *I've* brought it to the edge of international recognition!

"Be glad you have a title that can impress the girls—or is it boys you're after these days?"

She smoothed her hair and peered archly over her shoulder at him. It always gave her satisfaction twitting Jordan. He had such a nasty temper. He wasn't at all like Lucy, who was eternally sulking, mostly because she knew her looks were no match for her mother's beauty, Orlena thought smugly.

Jordan crossed his arms. "I want a share in the company or I'll walk out."

"Oh, you greedy young idiot. You don't have the spine." She pointed a stubby finger, impatient now with this impotent bid for power. "Sit down and stop whimpering. I pay you a very generous salary—more than you're worth. You're as tiresome as your sister. *She's* always whining because I won't give her part of my emeralds. Well, I've earned my emeralds. I've earned my power. I have a right to them. If you pay attention and do what I tell you, you might learn something by the time you're my age."

Orlena preened as she tossed her sheet aside and slipped into a low-wrapped wool dress the same shade as her ivory skin. She looked younger at forty-eight than she had at thirty-two, thanks to her visit to a certain hospital in Sweden.

A knock sounded on the door.

"Mrs. Lyle, Mr. Zumwald is here," announced her secretary.

Orlena swept past Jordan and out into her office with hands outstretched.

"Milton, how good of you to come," she said in her most charming voice.

Jordan slunk behind her. He, too, could be charming when he chose—he had apparently inherited that much from her. Annoyingly, he didn't seem to choose so now. Perhaps he was rather like his sister after all.

"Orlena, it's a pleasure to see you," the short, rather hooknosed man in front of her was saying almost bashfully.

He was putty in her hands.

"I've thought about you so often since that night we were introduced," she said, positioning her hand lightly on his sleeve and steering him toward a jade silk settee. "Do you know my son Jordan?"

The men grunted pleasantries while she contemplated her annexation of this man whose own business holdings would complement her own. His store in Palm Beach would give her the outlet there she craved. With it she could reach the wintering European royalty, the international clientele that had so far eluded her.

"Oh, dear. It's so hard to know where to begin," she said with a small, apologetic laugh as Milton Zumwald looked back at her. "So hard being a woman in this business. . . ."

She made her eyes sad and coaxing, then let them fall modestly to her lap. "I miss William so. He sheltered me, you know." Orlena thought she let her eyes flutter up again with just the proper hesitancy. "The fact is, Lyle and Company has grown so rapidly these last few years I'm not comfortable with the decision making. I don't feel up to it. I need someone with experience as our senior vice-president."

Jordan's indrawn breath was audible. She had not told him she had this in mind. What was the point when Lyle & Co. was entirely hers?

She ran an innocent finger along the neck of her dress and watched Milton Zumwald's gaze bob down in spite of himself.

"I—well, I thought I'd try you first because it would be even nicer if I could have an attractive man around as part of the deal." She laughed demurely. "I'm sure that must sound absurd from someone my age."

"Oh, no, Orlena. You're not even in your prime. But I have my own company, as you well know. I've never even dreamed of selling—"

"I know," she interrupted quickly. "We'd have to pay you a great deal, and of course trade you stock in Lyle and Company if you joined us."

Jordan had risen. She broke off to look at him. "We'll talk later about those stones I want, Jordan. Who did you say the high bidders were this afternoon?"

Jordan glowered at her. Really, what did he want? To have her job as president?

"Herbert Shrier took one lot and Vince Vincinte took another," he said. "The other four went to some girl from Landis and Oxenburg."

FIVE

IT WAS TEA TIME, AND AMID THE GREENERY AND AIRY OPENNESS OF The Palm Court a violinist, accompanied by a grand piano, was playing a sedately lilting medley from the musical *Showboat*. Lulled by the sounds, Wesley Bell stared at the photograph just handed him and faced a crisis of conscience.

He wondered if he should confess to Cecily Catlow that he'd invited her here so she wouldn't see his small office and guess, correctly, that he was the least esteemed attorney in the gargantuan firm of Fitch, Fitch & Cromwell.

He wondered if he should admit he was such a klutz at conversation that, in spite of his rather nice-looking build and sandy hair, women rarely went out with him more than once and Fitch, Fitch & Cromwell confined him to research rather than meeting clients.

He knew he ought to because Cecily Catlow was different, somehow, from other women he'd met, and very nice.

But he wasn't going to.

Guilt struggled with tenacity in his breast as he faced the reason. He'd just fallen in love with a photograph—with a delicate-looking blond woman who'd spent most of her life in a mental hospital.

Though Vanessa Catlow must never learn that secret, Wesley knew, as he sat unable to pry his eyes from this image of her face, that he was prepared to die rather than see her locked up like that.

"You really don't think there'll be any problem, then?" asked her sister.

Drawn out of his shyness by her concern, Wesley readjusted the thick frames of his glasses, which had an annoying habit of slipping sideways on his finely chiseled nose, and smiled at her.

"I can't see a one. She'll have to go through some sort of evaluation there, of course—go before a board. But as long as she's . . . uh . . ."

The enormous brown eyes looking back at him took on a warning look.

"Vanessa's perfectly sane."

He nodded, aware he'd blundered. In her green dress the pretty young woman across from him looked like she'd been made to match this room with its mossy green carpet bordered by pink roses. Her lips were as velvety as the bud in the silver vase on their pink marble table. Yet attractive as she was, it was another face, the lost, sweet face in the photograph, that tugged at his heart as no other ever had in his thirty-nine years.

Wesley felt half-absent from this present conversation. Anger, an almost unknown emotion, had been rolling through him in ever-increasing waves since Cecily had described the incident that had caused her sister's madness. Two young girls scared and mistreated with no one to help them, he thought. Compared to that, the haggling over wills and alimony that Fitch, Fitch & Cromwell dealt in was clearly the inconsequential tripe he'd always half thought it.

"Damn it!" he said, surprising himself with his vehemence. Reluctantly he passed the photograph back and reached for a tea sandwich from the plate between them. Another reason he brought his few clients from FF&C's overflow here for tea was that it spared him fixing something to eat when he returned to his bachelor apartment. Now he bit savagely into the morsel between his fingers without even tasting.

"Damn it, she's so beautiful!"

Cecily looked startled. Then she smiled, but he saw tears starting in her eyes.

"Yes, and she's good and she's gentle and . . ." Her fork hung motionless above the marbled chocolate cheesecake she'd been eating. "Please. Just help me get her out. It took so long for me to find her because of the phony last name, and I can't even get up to see her during the week, the trip takes so long."

Wesley did something he'd never done before in his life. He reached across the table and touched a woman's hand.

He wasn't a bad lawyer. In fact, he'd had the high score in the state on his bar exam, he recalled with a growing stubbornness. It was just that the law had never especially interested him, though at eighteen it had seemed vastly more appealing than entering his father's savage arena as a Wall Street stockbroker. It also had been respectable enough to pass muster with his family, unlike his real desire to be an historian.

There would be no complications, he decided. He would have Vanessa Catlow out in a few weeks. Wesley bit vigorously into the last sandwich.

"I'll go up and begin the procedure for her release tomorrow," he promised.

One of the senior partners had assigned him to spend tomorrow drawing up a will for one of the firm's biggest clients, who wanted to leave her millions to her Pekingese and an animal psychotherapist. Wesley contemplated telling the lady and the senior partner they could fornicate with her dog.

He wouldn't, of course. He'd spent his whole life being practical.

"I may or may not get to meet with Vanessa herself," he said, being practical now and thinking ahead to the technicalities that were always present. "But I will be there."

Cecily was glancing discreetly at her watch. "Good," she said. "Oh, that's wonderful!"

Wesley nodded. He'd grown up in a family that didn't express emotion, but he could recognize it in other people. Cecily Catlow's face was fairly glowing now with love for her sister.

"Am I keeping you from something?" he asked, remembering that glance at her watch.

With a smile and faint blush she held her hand out to shake his.

"Not if there's anything more we ought to discuss. But if not, I do have plans to meet someone."

She could hardly believe she had known Peter only four days. Eyes closed, Cecily relaxed in his arms, floating with him in dreamlike circles across the dance floor on the mezzanine of a private, moneyed hideaway known as Le Club. Above them a soaring skylight was draped in sheer fabric. Around them, on intimate tables, candles glowed beneath fringed silver shades. The music was piped in, but a famous actress many years her senior and the Count and Countess Somebody were among the dancers around them. Her body and Peter's moved as though they were one.

"Want to try somewhere else?" he asked, his breath stirring her hair.

Reluctantly Cecily left her reverie and shook her head. "I can't. I'm a working girl."

She didn't feel like it tonight. She had done the unthinkable—bought a special dress to come here. Even though it was secondhand, discarded by some socialite at a resale house off Seventy-ninth Street, the tube of shimmering white silk with its single wide strap made her feel like someone from a fairy tale. Tonight she'd sipped champagne from tall crystal glasses unlike any she'd ever seen. Tonight she'd eaten caviar from plates edged in gold. Tonight had been glorious, but now it was two in the morning.

"I don't want you to be a working girl," said Peter soberly, looking into her eyes. "I want to take care of you."

She melted into his arms, the words singing in her ears. When his arms were around her like this, she did feel taken care of.

"I—Peter . . ."

She didn't know what else to say. He smiled at her.

"I ought to go home."

His moment of resistance was surprisingly brief. "All right," he said.

The minute they were in his car he drew her against him and kissed her. Only slightly aware of Peter's chauffeur in the front seat, Cecily met the kiss with an intensity that matched his own. Then, when she could bear its building frenzy not another instant, she drew slightly away. This was flirting with danger. There had been too much of champagne and romance tonight, and she sensed she and Peter both were walking a tightrope with control of their own emotions.

Moonlight slanted through the rear window of the limousine.

"I love you," Peter said, voice low.

Cecily felt his fingers tightening over hers. She fought for breath, hypnotized by the shadows playing over his face.

"I . . . love you," she whispered.

The moment was magic.

Peter looked at her thoughtfully and then, abruptly, gave a crooked smile.

"Almost there."

They walked from his car to her building in silence. Four nights she had known him and four nights they had made this walk together. Crazy. You didn't just meet a man and start spending every free minute with him. It didn't give you time to sort things out. But she knew what she'd said just a minute ago was true. She was in love with Peter.

It made her feel fragile and unprotected. What if he didn't love back?

But he'd said he did—he'd said it first. If she felt exposed, she also felt more security in his arms than she'd ever known.

They had reached her apartment. Peter opened the door. Inside he placed light hands on her shoulders and she yielded up her face to him. Their bodies swayed together.

His mouth moved hungrily on hers, more demanding than in nights past. Cecily tried to restrain the response of her own lips and couldn't. She threw back her head, riding waves of pleasure as Peter kissed her throat. His hands moved on her bare flesh, revealed by her evening dress, and she gasped at the feel of it. She wanted their hard, stroking surfaces to touch every inch of her.

"Cecily. I want to make love to you. I *have* to make love to you," Peter said hoarsely.

The words brought her partway to reality. She writhed away from him and shook her head.

"No. I want that, too, but I can't. I have . . . responsibilities."

"*What* responsibilities?"

She had not escaped his arms, only put her back toward him. He kissed her neck.

"Please, Peter. I don't want to explain it now." This was hardly the time to discuss Vanessa.

A shudder of desire coursed through her as he kissed her neck again. Cecily fought it.

"I'll share whatever burdens you've got. I'll take care of you, Cecily. That's all I've wanted from the moment I met you. It's all I want on this earth!"

His hands, planted on the front of her waist, moved as he spoke. One swept up to caress her breasts. One dropped ever downward in slow, burning arcs. His lips began to explore the bare skin of her shoulders, his tongue swirling pleasure where it touched her. The widening circles of his hands pulled her into a floodtide of spinning sensations. Then Peter was on his knees in front of her, lowering her loosened dress and kissing her belly. Cecily knew it was too late to stop for either of them.

Holding him tightly, she knelt, her dress pooled around her. They finished undressing each other with feverish fingers.

This was right. Peter loved her and she loved him. She was being lifted on the crest of wonderful, hitherto unknown feelings.

"You're beautiful," Peter whispered. "You're beautiful and you're mine—forever!"

Locked in each other's arms, they rolled on the carpet and Cecily, for the first time in years, knew the sweetness of not being alone.

The woman with the blond curls fascinated Van. She watched surreptitiously, aware of Miss Mundey's hawklike eyes.

Yes, that was someone related to poor old Mr. Niederlehner. The woman was smoothing his white hair and pecking him on the cheek in greeting, her tight blond curls tumbling over her eyebrows. Vanessa busied herself with the piece of needlepoint that bored her silly but seemed to please everyone who saw her work on it. The blond woman had linked her arm through Mr. Niederlehner's. They were heading out to the sun porch, which was separated from the visitors' room by a wall with large glass windows.

Now was the time. Van pawed frantically in her sewing box, then gaped up at Miss Mundey with a face as idiotlike as she supposed Miss Mundey thought it ought to be.

"I don't have my scissors," she said. "They must still be in the sun porch. May I go and hunt them?"

Miss Mundey looked daggers at Van.

For days now she's had it in for me, Van thought, ever since I argued with her in the cafeteria. Well, she can't do too much to me today. It's Saturday—visiting day. She likes to put on a good face for the people who come here.

Van swallowed, remembering for a fleeting moment a wall of years when she hadn't known what day of the week it was.

"Come right back as soon as you find them," Miss Mundey snapped. "There are people out there trying to have private conversations."

Van went as swiftly as she dared, the round-pointed scissors she was supposedly looking for stuffed in her shoe. It worried her a little that Cecily wasn't here yet. Cecily was almost never late.

The sun porch was nearly deserted—just three people besides Mr. Niederlehner, who was small and dapper, and the blond woman with him, who was chewing gum. Even though it was warm on the porch, people seemed to stay inside when they visited.

From the corner of her eye Van looked and saw Miss Mundey watching her from the distant nurse's station. Dropping her head, she pretended to hunt her scissors. She stooped as though to investigate under a chair. Miss Mundey couldn't see her now.

"They're not very nice to Mr. Niederlehner," she said in a soft voice to the blond lady. "He gets out of line at meals and they send him all the way to the back. He cries."

The blonde stopped chewing her gum. Her lashes were very dark with mascara. She was thin, and pretty, Van guessed, though her earrings and bracelets all seemed a little too dangly and her skirt was short.

"That right, sweetie?" the blonde demanded of Mr. Niederlehner, stroking his cheek.

Vanessa smiled. Mr. Niederlehner never said a word, except in the cafeteria when he tottered toward the front of the line waving jaunty fingers and saying, "Table for two."

Van freed the scissors from her shoe and held them up. "I'm supposed to be hunting these."

The blond woman nodded. "Who are you?" she asked, her gum chewing starting up slowly.

"Vanessa Catlow." Van shrugged. "I'm a patient."

The woman looking at her had sharp eyes, not cruel like Nurse Mundey's, but quick and thoughtful.

"I'm April," she said, sticking down a hand which Van shook awkwardly. "His wife. How often does he get sent back? Thanks for telling me."

Van felt faintly embarrassed now. The woman named April was talking to her as though Van were a friend, and a normal person.

"It's—well, it's happening more often, almost every night this week, I guess. He just doesn't know where he is. He gets out of line and asks for a table for two, but that's against the rules, you know."

A movement of April's eyes alerted Van, who made a pretense of reaching under a couch as Miss Mundey opened the door.

"Oh, here they are," she said. "I'm awfully sorry if I bothered you."

She started to scurry away, but to her dismay April gave the attendant a look that nailed her in place and spoke in sharp tones.

"Say, look here. I understand you've been sending my husband back to the end of the line at meals and I don't like that."

Van caught back a gasp.

"You telling her tales?" Miss Mundey demanded, her eyes making a target of Van's forehead.

Van trembled.

"Who, her?" asked April in a brassy and threatening voice. "Why should she? Jeezus, does everyone in this place know what's happening to Herbie but me? She's just some girl who came out here hunting her scissors!"

Miss Mundey looked unsure now, but hostile nonetheless.

"Who did tell you?" she asked, changing to a falsely sweet voice. "We try to remind patients they mustn't gossip about other patients—part of the training they need before they get back outside, you know."

April considered Miss Mundey, who was three times her size, and chomped on her gum.

"Herbie told me." Her hands were on her hips.

Miss Mundey eyed her coldly. "Mr. Niederlehner never talks. Everybody here knows it."

April gave a devilish grin. "Ever hear of sex therapy? I gave Herbie some good times in bed. He talks to *me* just fine!"

Miss Mundey, known to the patients for never letting anyone crack a joke, turned redder than her rouge. Van bit back a laugh and hurried into the visitors room, and there, walking toward her with springy step, came Cecily.

"I got you a pass," said Cecily, waving it. "Want to go out for lunch?"

"Oh, yes!" Van sighed, sure she would be safe from Miss Mundey for a while now. On days they had visitors they were allowed to wear real clothes, and today when she'd put on the pretty skirt and sweater Cecily had bought her, she'd hoped they'd have an outing.

"You're late," she said. "I was getting worried."

A funny expression touched Cecily's face. "I . . . I had a late night last night. I'm sorry."

Van frowned. Had Cecily's answer been a little abrupt, or was she just imagining it because that was one of the problems you had when you'd been crazy?

They sat on a couch in a corner of the visitors room. Van decided she'd better change the subject.

"The lawyer came."

"I know."

Cecily smiled now. She was pretty, Van thought, but better than pretty. The snap of her eyes and the way she carried her chin still hinted of that stubborn, tomboyish streak she'd had when they were children. Now, though, it made you sure she could do anything she set her mind on.

"What did you talk about? Did you like him?" Cecily asked.

"Well . . ."

Van laughed merrily as her attempt to conjure up Wesley Bell brought back the image of how he'd blinked behind his glasses and stammered every time she'd looked at him.

Then, hearing herself, she smothered the sound. Maybe laughing when no one else did was a sign she still wasn't like normal people.

"He's—he's awfully nice," she said uncertainly. "He told me I'd have to go before the board, but I already knew that."

"And he told you the board won't meet again for a month?"

Van nodded.

Miss Mundey stalked by on the way to her coffee break. April and Mr. Niederlehner came in and sat down not far from Cecily. Van thought of telling her sister about Mr. Niederlehner and the cafeteria and the funny thing April had said about sex to Miss Mundey. But maybe Cecily wouldn't be interested, and anyway April was sitting close enough that she might overhear and be embarrassed.

"I've been thinking about what I ought to do when I get out of here," she said, moving on to a subject she'd enjoyed of late when bored, and that she thought might amuse Cecily. "I thought maybe with my background I should try brain surgery."

There was silence.

Cecily looked at her blankly.

"It—it was a joke." Van felt suddenly like crying. She'd made a fool of herself. She'd proved she didn't belong out with normal people.

"Brain surgery! Jeezus, that's rich!" said a voice. Someone started to laugh.

Looking up from her tightly pressed hands Vanessa saw April trying to hide her mirth as nearby visitors looked.

"You sure must have all your buttons to be able to make cracks like that after being in this place," April said. "What are you doing here?"

Cecily was looking worried now. Van knew she shouldn't have drawn this attention to herself.

"I say the wrong things." Her hands curled into fists. She looked at Cecily. "Maybe I'm not ready to get out."

"Van, that's not true!" Cecily squeezed her hand. She smiled quickly. "I'm sorry I missed your joke. I—I was thinking of something."

"Look, honey, if you're not ready to leave this place, nobody's ever going to be," encouraged April, joining their conversation without invitation. "Poor Herbie now, he'll never get sprung. And that stinking rich family of his won't put him in a private place where they might have to claim him."

Vanessa tried to think of an appropriate answer.

"But you come to see him every Saturday. I know that cheers him up," she faltered.

Beaming, April fluffed at her curls. She had six bracelets on her arm, and all of them jangled.

"I owe him. He was good to me. Still would be if he'd been the one to control his money, but his family got lawyers to just dole it out to him like an allowance, see?" She shrugged. "I didn't know he was a loony tune when I married him—just figured he was a sweet old geezer with money to burn and an eye for the girls. Hey, that was pretty clever, that bit with the scissors so you could tell me about what had been happening to him."

Van knew she'd better explain to Cecily about Mr. Niederlehner. Then she introduced the two women. Introductions were something she did very well, she thought. The Niederlehners ended up going to lunch with them at a little restaurant just down the road from the hospital grounds.

"I like April," she said when they separated late in the afternoon. April had left her a book and asked if she'd read it to Herbie because the ones in the library here looked pretty dull. The lady on the cover of the book was mostly naked.

"She certainly isn't boring," said Cecily.

They looked at each other and laughed.

Cecily threw her arms around her. "Oh, Van. I can't wait till you're home with me. And I've met the most wonderful man! I want you to meet him."

Vanessa felt suddenly cold inside. She had that feeling sometimes when she thought about men and dating and things.

Cecily consulted her watch. "Oh, damn. I've got to go or I'll miss my train."

Vanessa swallowed. She always felt a little scared when Cecily left her. And Cecily had never mentioned a man before. Van had always assumed it would be just the two of them when she got out. Of course that was silly.

She tried to smile. She didn't want Cecily to worry about her.

"Oh, I'm so glad they're letting you go to another auction," she said. "Be sure and do a really good job."

SIX

"YOU ARE SHOPPING FOR SOMETHING IN PARTICULAR, MISS CATLOW? Rubies? Diamonds?"

Startled, Cecily glanced at the bearded, heavyset man who had come up beside her. It was hot in the small auction house, and the seats they were about to take were not so comfortable as the padded ones at Sotheby's, where this event would be taking place if it were more important.

"No, nothing in particular," she answered cautiously.

She knew the man with the pipe who had spoken was head appraiser for another small but respectable jewelery house just off Fifth Avenue. Louie, her bidder, had pointed him out to her when they'd arrived. He was European, and his eyes settled into comfortable slits as he heard her answer.

"Do you know Martin Cohen?" he asked, indicating a man behind him. "He's from Cohen Brothers."

Cecily nodded acknowledgment. In only a few minutes it would be time to take seats for the auction. She wished she dared glance at Louie to see if he had any sense what this was about.

It wasn't necessary.

"There are six major items among all the others here," Cohen said, keeping his voice low. "Our firms are the only three who could afford to bid for them. Everyone else here will settle for lesser offerings."

Cecily considered but did not answer. She had come to the same conclusion herself but didn't want to tip her hand.

"The reserve prices seem dear on those pieces, don't you agree?" continued Cohen.

After the briefest of hesitations Cecily nodded. If the bidding grew heated at all, there would not be much profit to be made on the pieces in question. She already had faced the fact she was not going to emerge from this auction with anything near the triumph she had the first.

The man who initially had approached her took out an unlit pipe. He chewed it thoughtfully.

"You understand a knockout?" he asked.

Cecily felt her stomach muscles tightening.

She knew the term. It meant several dealers agreeing not to bid against one another. The maneuver kept down the selling price on a particular stone or piece of jewelry. Afterward the conspirators got together privately and worked out who really got the item and what was paid for it. But whether it was completely ethical . . . whether it was worth the risk . . .

"I'm interested in the two sapphire pieces," said the man with the pipe. "Like you, Cohen isn't particular but would like a better price than seems likely if we all compete. If you're willing to let me have the sapphires, we can try a multiple knockout. You choose any one of these four remaining." He tapped lightly at four entries in the auction catalog. "Cohen will have the other three. What do you say?"

Cecily twisted the finger-wide gold bracelet Peter had given her. It seemed like a pledge, a promise of their life together. He'd been waiting on Saturday when she'd gotten back from seeing Van. He'd given it to her then, the night after they'd become lovers. They'd spent every night together since, and he'd filled her small apartment with flowers and jars of caviar and most of all his presence.

She brought her mind sharply back to the question it had been evading. Should she risk this scheme? Could she trust these men? She wanted desperately to look at Louie, whose job, apart from bidding as she instructed, was to close sales, write checks, and arrange for safe delivery of purchased goods.

As though he had read her mind, the man with the pipe looked over the filling auction room and spoke from the side of his mouth.

"Don't worry, we wouldn't trick you, young one. Ask Louie. He's here as a witness."

She did look at the veteran bidder from Landis and Oxenburg and he shrugged.

"Waters joined a knockout about two months ago. He didn't get the bracelet, but he thought the gamble was worth it."

A gamble. It all boiled down to that. Cecily bit her lip.

"What about these emeralds?" She pointed to a number in the catalog, an early-nineteenth-century parure consisting of necklace, brooch, earrings, bracelet, and small tiara. The stones were of good size, but the color was on the light side. She'd guess them to be Russian or Brazilian. Moreover, the color was patchy within many of the individual stones. It had taken her three extended periods of studying the stones to reach that conclusion, the filigree settings were so dazzling. The set would make a nice acquisition for her firm, but only at a very low price and for its antique charm, not the value of the emeralds themselves, she thought.

Cohen shrugged. "If the price is right, I might try to get them. But Lyle and Company wants emeralds badly, I understand. They may drive the bids up."

Cecily felt her heart give a hard, angry beat. She'd seen Jordan at that first auction, last week. She'd recognized him immediately, though he was on the other side of the room. Today he wasn't in evidence. Maybe someone else was here.

"Ah, speak of the devil," said Cohen as the door opened and Jordan's tall form, stylishly attired, came in. "Late as usual. I see he's acting as his own bidder today."

The man with the pipe grunted. "Not the best judge of stones, in my opinion. He may well want emeralds badly enough to make the bidding too rich for my blood."

"The emeralds aren't covered in our arrangement," Cohen said bluntly.

Both men eyed Cecily. She knew they wanted her decision.

"Okay," she agreed.

Jordan had taken a seat across the room from her. He turned now, glancing in her direction, and her blood froze, but his gaze moved on. He either hadn't seen or hadn't recognized her.

Cohen and Jordan had taken their seats, well separated. Cecily found hers. The auction began almost immediately, and for the next forty minutes she was too busy to think.

"A black opal? You're not serious!" Louie exclaimed as his finger slid down the printed auction list after placing Cecily's successful bid for two minor purchases. He scowled at her next checkmark. "They bring bad luck."

She smiled at his superstition. "Come on, Louie. You know no one believes that anymore!"

Of course, none of the items being sold were on display. They were locked in a vault and would be presented when all this was over and payment was made, but she could still visualize the black opal ring. The dark central stone was as large as her thumb, its flashes of brooding red fire as rich as the rubies encircling it.

"Anyway, I suppose it would be my bad luck, not Landis and Oxenburg's," she whispered mischievously.

Louie sighed and they got the ring.

The knockout worked as planned. She and the man with the pipe offered token competition against Cohen, then dropped out early. When she bid for the item she'd chosen, a choker necklace of canary diamonds, Cohen offered one bid against it, then backed off when she topped his bid. He shook his head as though to indicate to one and all she didn't know what she was doing. Cecily hid a smile. She rather liked his style.

"Item forty-two," the auction executive droned from his podium. "A parure of emeralds."

Cecily felt her breathing grow more shallow. Jordan Lyle hadn't bid on any other item. Unable to stop herself now, she turned and looked at him. Narrow, arrogant nose, tightly waved blond hair—he was merely a grown-up version of the sneering cousin who had tied her hands and assaulted Van at Marblehead.

For a minute a physical sickness filled her. She closed her eyes.

"You okay?" Louie whispered.

"May I have an opening bid of seventy-five thousand?" intoned the man at the podium.

Cohen opened. Jordan followed. There were other bids, all of them moving up by cautious increments of five thousand dollars. Louie's arm raised to register hers. Except for the auctioneer's voice, seeking ever higher bids, an auction was a silent thing. Silent enough to let the past flood in.

Cecily sat reliving the horror of seeing Van for the first time after almost thirteen years and trying so hard to find her. Van's eyes had been frightened and nearly lifeless. Her once silken hair had hung in limp strands. She'd resembled some pale, discarded mop, not the sister whose image Cecily had clung to for her only support through the years.

"Raise." That was her voice, speaking to Louie.

Jordan bid higher.

Cohen looked briefly back at her, cautioning her, his recent ally and new at this game, that she should perhaps call it quits. Cecily liked him for that.

An impulse gnawed at her, pleading for release. "Raise," she said automatically.

Cohen had told her Lyle & Co. wanted emeralds badly. That would explain why Jordan had fought for them so hard at the last auction. The price here was already at the borderline. Much higher and the purchaser would take a bath.

Jordan topped her again, the movement of his arm less desultory than it had been last time.

Not a great judge of stones, the man with the pipe had described him. Was that true? He'd been greedy for power as a child, and the way he held himself now suggested he still was.

"Raise," she said.

Louie hesitated. "Are you sure?"

She nodded. "That's beautiful filigree. I'd hoped nobody else would notice. I guess they have."

God, if you're really there, be with me on this, she asked silently.

The desire for this one small revenge was so strong she could taste it. She was putting her reputation, her chance for further advancement, on the line, and maybe risking trouble for Louie as well. But seeing this man who had spent his whole life free while Van was locked up had triggered something inside her. This chance to repay, in some infinitesimal way, what had been done to her and Van had fallen into her lap.

"Do I have one twenty-five?" the auctioneer was repeating.

Louie bid.

Jordan turned to look directly at her, his eyes scorching through her, and Cecily knew, at last, there was no recognition in them. She also knew he was falling victim to an absolute rage.

"Do I have one hundred thirty thousand?"

With a final glare, defiantly, Jordan raised his hand.

Cecily's own hands felt cold to the bone. She thought uneasily about the black opal ring she'd just purchased and the old superstition that such stones brought bad luck.

"Once more," she said to Louie as she fumbled in her purse. "Then we drop out."

Louie shook his head in disbelief. "That's—"

"Do it, Louie."

"One hundred thirty-five?"

The voice from the podium sounded distant now. A ripple broke the quiet of the room.

Jordan turned to look at her again. Cecily flicked open the compact in her hand. Tilting her head as though to examine her reflection, she glossed on lipstick as Louie's hand, reluctantly, went into the air for a final time.

Somewhere in the rows of chairs behind her someone gasped.
"One hundred forty?"

Nothing happened.

Jordan was glaring at her, fist curled, clearly agitated, while she knew her performance with the compact was making her look calm.

"One hundred forty?" came the question for the final time.

Slowly Jordan's hand rose. Cecily slumped back, free to breathe again.

Jordan Lyle had just spent one hundred forty thousand dollars for emeralds that were probably worth only half that amount.

"You, Jordan, are an idiot!"

Orlena slammed down the phone and glared at her children. They were in her office, Lucy sitting on one of the jade silk settees on the other side of Orlena's desk and Jordan lounging behind it. Orlena fingered the double choker of emeralds around her neck, knowing what must be done even as she spoke.

"That 'girl' from Landis and Oxenburg who proved to half the jewelry world this afternoon that you haven't a brain in your head just happens to be your little cousin Cecily!"

"What?" Lucy had a vaguely squeaky voice that grated on Orlena's nerves.

Jordan's mouth popped open and closed like a guppy's.

Orlena adopted a quiet, threatening tone as she walked toward them. The silk of her white suit rustled.

"I've always known you two didn't tell me the truth about what happened the day that boy was killed out on the point. Apparently your cousin means to settle scores. My God, she had such a distinctive face! Were you sleeping, Jordan, that you didn't recognize her?"

He squirmed and Orlena tried to avoid distaste. How had she managed to produce a son with so little spine?

"Maybe it was an accident," he said sullenly. "Maybe she didn't even recognize me—"

"Of course she did!"

Was he really stupid? It was bad enough that pigheadedness had just cost the company fifty thousand dollars—had cost the entire price of those emeralds he'd bought, in fact, since Lyle & Co. didn't deal in antiques and the stones were decidedly inferior for resetting. Was he also blind, that he couldn't recognize revenge?

"Well, you wanted emeralds, and I thought Landis and

Oxenburg must want them, too,'' he began. ''When a market gets tight, prices do shoot up some times—''

''Sit,'' she said, cutting him off.

She faulted herself for never realizing this might happen. Cecily Catlow had been an uncommonly stubborn child, as she remembered.

A rare ripple of uneasiness passed through Orlena. It wouldn't do to have an old death made into scandal, if that was Cecily's next move. It wouldn't do to have people question why William's great-niece was working for another company, either. Most of all, it wouldn't do to have someone threatening Jordan's image of competence, which Orlena had so carefully crafted for him. God knows what this one episode had already done. They couldn't risk a repeat. Though she didn't admit it to Jordan, there were certain men who responded better when they thought they were dealing with another man, even though she pulled the strings. She needed him. Besides, he was her son.

''I'll make her pay through the teeth,'' he said sullenly, breaking the silence.

''Cecily always was a brat,'' Lucy chimed, pushing back the black hair that puffed out unstylishly behind her ears. ''She bit. What are we going to do?''

Lucy always had been the more practical of her children, Orlena thought with satisfaction. Lucy knew Jordan's threats were pipe dreams, and Lucy was ruthless enough to see immediate action was needed. The girl had not, Orlena suspected, done as well as she had as public relations director for Lyle & Co. by being a pussycat.

''I haven't decided yet,'' Orlena said slowly, fingering her necklace again.

''In that case,'' said Lucy, riveting her gaze on her mother's action, ''there are things to discuss before I leave for Palm Beach.''

The new direction startled Orlena. Lucy had done well to see their jewelry would be part of the style show at an exclusive charity luncheon scheduled for next week. There were so many international people filtering into Florida with their titles these days. If Orlena succeeded in her plan to open a branch office there, this exposure would be invaluable.

''What have we left to discuss? We've gone over what pieces we'll supply. They'll go out by bonded messenger at the first of the week.''

''And *I'll* look like the hired help sitting down with those women you want for clients! How do you think that looks for the image of this company?"

Orlena sat down, feeling put upon that the wretched child was going to start whining about something trivial at a time like this. Her eyes misted over. Her children didn't like her. She had tried to give them everything and they always wanted *more*. They never seemed to *care* about the worries she faced or the struggle it had been for her to hold and build this company while fearing daily it might slip through her fingers because she had not been born into this business and did not, even now, have all the skills and shrewdness her competitors did.

"Oh, yes. We're back to this lust of yours for my emeralds, aren't we?" she sighed. They never seemed to understand that everything she did was for the two of them, that when she corrected them or denied them something it was only to make them stronger. "You have perfectly splendid necklaces that half the women in this country would die for! Twenty carats of rubies in that last one as I recall."

"Twenty *one-carat* rubies," Lucy pointed out nastily.

"Well, if that's not enough, you have an extravagant salary and a company discount."

"*You* didn't buy your emeralds."

Orlena arched an eyebrow. "Indeed I didn't. And you're more than free to come by yours the same way I did mine.

"Which brings us to another point about why I have no intention of sharing. You haven't the eyes to go with them."

She looked pointedly at Lucy's nondescript gray eyes and mincing features. There was silence. Lucy resembled a thundercloud.

"Now then," Orlena continued. "If you're both over your tantrums, I suggest we start dealing with this matter of your cousin Cecily. If we handle this well . . ." She slipped out of a diamond bracelet and let it swing on one finger as she thought. "If we handle this well, there'll be no more problems. We'll absorb Milton Zumwald and have our Palm Beach branch and your salaries will go up."

She paused, smiling at them and shifting an aristocratic chin.

"If we don't, Lucy won't have money for her pretty baubles and Jordan won't have a job. Is that clear?"

Sometimes she wondered if the two of them would ever act like adults. Sometimes she wondered if they both expected her to live forever. Neither of them was satisfactory, really. She'd hoped for a son as smart as she was and a daughter as pretty.

Nonetheless, her blood ran in their veins. Perhaps they'd learn something yet.

"Who's our poorest customer?" she demanded of Jordan. "I mean, who would give their soul to afford more than the meagerest purchase?"

Jordan looked at her blankly. Orlena sighed.

"Nola Levesque." Lucy's answer was prompt and definite. "She owns that little dance theater, would like to be thought of as impoverished French gentry."

Orlena favored her with a genuine smile. There was hope for Lucy.

"Wonderful," she said. "Send her to me."

SEVEN

CECILY NESTLED IN PETER'S ARMS, DRIFTING IN THE ISLANDLIKE seclusion of his king-sized bed. Her ear, pressed to his bare chest, heard the beating heart beneath it slow to normal after their recent lovemaking. Turning her face, she kissed the smoothness of his skin. Never, she thought, have I been so happy.

Even in darkness she could feel the glimmer of the pear-shaped diamond circling her finger. Peter had placed it on her, in this bed, just two nights ago.

She could scarcely believe what that ring promised: Peter would love her forever. They would spend their lives together. She would be his wife.

"What would you like for your birthday?" he asked now. "A fur coat? Pearls?"

She laughed, brought back from her happy reverie. "Oh, Peter, don't be silly. My birthday's still months away!"

With one fingertip he traced the line of her jaw and chin. "But I like to buy you things, darling. Couldn't I get you something early? Or what about a gift for absolutely no occasion—that's it. What shall I get you to wear to that party tomorrow night?"

Just for a second Cecily felt a hesitancy she'd felt before. What if she looked discernibly out of place when, for the first time, she met his friends and business associates?

Maybe Peter had been thinking of it, too. Maybe he was worried about it. Maybe that explained this offer.

"Peter . . . I'm not sure I want to go. I won't be comfortable—"

His lips smothered hers to end the protest. "Of course you're going to go! I want everyone to meet you." He rolled over on top of her, pinning her arms with his. "Say you will now," he teased like a spoiled child. "I'll keep you here until you do." He began kissing playfully at her neck.

Cecily laughed. How could she ever have imagined he was less than totally content with her the way she was?

"All right."

Releasing her, Peter sat up fully and turned on the light. She loved the sight of him all tall and pale, his innocent nakedness accented, somehow, by his mustache.

"It's not even midnight," he said. "Let's go somewhere and dance for a while." He started out of bed until she caught him back.

"Peter, I can't. I'd be dead on my feet tomorrow—"

"Call in and take the day off. Give them your notice while you're at it. Darling, I'm going to *marry* you! I've never had anyone to care for. I've never had anyone to care for me. Why should you work when you don't have to?"

It flattered her, in a way, to have him want her to be his so exclusively. Yet it made her uncomfortable, too, for some reason she could not name.

Sighing, she ran a hand across his chest. "I have to go in tomorrow. There's a brooch to be appraised first thing, and I'm the one who has to do it. I. Me. No one else can."

She smiled with amusement, remembering Teddy's head popping around her door that afternoon as he said breezily, "Hey, C. C., need your help with a nutty customer." For a second she'd feared he meant a real nut, like Peter's violent ex-stepmother.

As it turned out, however, this customer had simply seemed to be of the feminist persuasion. After making sure there was a female in sales, she had looked at necklaces and had purchased a very fine rope of pearls with amethysts. Then she'd produced a ruby brooch she wanted appraised by the following day, but only on the provision that she could deal with a female appraiser. That was when Teddy had come hunting Cecily.

She yawned, wondering whether having lots of money made people a little loose upstairs, like they were at Van's hospital. The thought of Van triggered guilt. Cecily hadn't written to her this week. Things had been so hectic. But in little more than a week Van was going to be free, and then Cecily would have so little time with Peter.

"You're sure you don't want to go anyplace?" he persisted, settling down beside her and smoothing her hair.

"I'm sure."

He gathered her to him. His kisses were long and sweet, an incredibly wonderful nectar they could drink only from each other.

"Then let's make love again," he whispered.

The next day was a Friday, always festive at Landis and Oxenburg. The people who worked there liked their occupations, but they also liked weekends. It was half-past ten when Cecily finished another job and started the appraisal of the ruby brooch.

She looked at it and frowned. She put it under the microscope, then carried it to one end of the workroom and placed it under an ultraviolet light.

"Teddy, come look at this," she called as it turned a fire-engine red.

Teddy, who had been in the hall between their offices, sauntered down and looked.

"Synthetic," he said with a *tsk*ing sound. His forehead wrinkled. "Poor woman's been had somewhere along the line. It's always a shame to tell them that."

"Fortunately I don't have to," she said. She took the stone to Jacob Landis.

There were other chores to round out the morning. She'd just reached in her drawer for the apple that was to be her lunch when commotion erupted at the entrance to the workroom and came noisily toward her. Looking up, she saw Jacob Landis, a security guard, an unknown man, and a woman Cecily recognized as the owner of the ruby brooch.

"I want her searched! I want every inch of her office searched!" the woman screeched, pointing. "You've seen the earlier appraisals on that ruby! I brought you a real stone and I want it back or I'll sue!"

In shock, Cecily realized the woman was pointing at her, accusing her of theft.

Jacob Landis looked uneasy.

"Please, Miss Levesque. I'm sure we can get to the bottom of this," he soothed. He glanced at Cecily. "I'm afraid we're going to have to search your office, Miss Catlow."

Still stunned, Cecily nodded. The threat of a lawsuit was not taken lightly by a company like this one, whose business would be only as good as its reputation. It was insulting, of course, being accused by this woman, but she was innocent! And she was sure Jacob Landis knew that despite these motions. She sat down and tried to fight off a trembling in her limbs as the drawers of her desk were methodically removed and searched.

"There's nothing here," said the security man.

Foot tapping, Miss Levesque gestured with the cigarette glowing in a holder between her fingers. "Search her! Search her wraps!" she demanded. "Or are you all in on this?" She looked haughtily at Jacob Landis and at Teddy, who had come in and was looking as stupefied as Cecily felt.

The security guard, with obvious embarrassment, looked to Jacob Landis for instructions. Landis nodded. His face was set. His grimness spread fear in Cecily. She thought, involuntarily, about the black opal she'd bought and Louie's superstition. In a few minutes, surely, this awful nightmare would end.

She stood up, offering herself for the search.

"I'll do the wraps first," mumbled the guard.

He examined the umbrella she hadn't carried for a week, her green wool muffler, her coat. As his hands passed over the hem of it, he stopped.

"There's—there's something in the lining, Mr. Landis."

Her employer straightened. His eyes swung to Cecily. Her heart sank under his look. But this was ridiculous! There was nothing in her coat.

"Look," Landis barked.

She wasn't sure what the guard used, knife or fingers. All she knew was that his hand came up holding something red.

"See! She looked at the stone when it came in yesterday—made sketches or something!" shrieked her accuser. "She had a copy made and brought it in! She was trying to steal my ruby!"

Tons of gravity seemed to push against her. There *couldn't* have been a ruby in her coat! This was some kind of dream.

No one spoke.

Jacob Landis looked at her with outraged contempt. "I advise you not to move," he said. "The police will be here shortly."

Orlena spun in her desk chair to face her daughter. The scarf of her peacock-green dress fanned behind her as she rose and crossed the room, completely satisfied by the call just received.

"Well?" asked Lucy.

Sometimes Lucy's impatience annoyed her. Both her children forgot too easily the power she held and that their very existences were owed to her.

Today, though, she was pleased with Lucy's near edginess. Lucy perceived the importance of the little arrangement they'd made with Nola Levesque and had checked in several times, anticipating this phone call. It was far more than could be said for Jordan.

"Everything went splendidly." Orlena poured herself a glass of sherry. Normally she avoided the calories, but today she had earned them.

"You could stand to take off a few pounds," she observed to Lucy. "Call your brother and tell him I want to see him."

Lucy obeyed, but when she had finished her lower lip protruded slightly. The wretched girl never had been able to take constructive criticism, Orlena thought. Still, she was in a good mood now, so she wouldn't scold.

"Nola called from the Waldorf. They found the ruby and were predictably relieved when Nola said she wouldn't press charges. Jacob Landis was calling the police when she left.

"That was really very clever of you, Lucy, finding someone who could spot the brand of raincoat Cecily wore—someone from Alexander's did you say? Are you sure she won't talk?"

"She *used* to be a buyer at Alexander's. She's married very well. And no, she won't talk. She believed me when I said it was a market study. The girl's an absolute idiot except when it comes to clothes."

Orlena smiled. "Come and have some sherry, dear."

Lucy looked at her warily. The girl was so sullen.

"Matching her coat was easy compared with switching them." Lucy said. "That man she goes out with takes her to very nice places."

Lucy had proved quite resourceful, staking out Cecily's place of business, following her on the subway, watching her every move, thought Orlena. Thank God she was more persistent than Jordan. It had taken more than a week of watching before Cecily had stopped at a public place without a cloakroom, a beauty school that fixed hair at cut-rate prices. Then it had been easy for Lucy, wearing a blond wig and glasses, to go in, shed the coat with the ruby, hang it by Cecily's, and a few minutes later walk out in the innocent coat.

"I believe I'll let you have that little opal with diamonds around it that you've been coveting," Orlena said.

Lucy showed promise.

Now she sneezed—not quite as delicately as Orlena might

have hoped—and dabbed at her nose. "I want more than a ring. I want to be made a vice-president, like Jordan is."

Orlena paused with her glass to her lips. The greed of her progeny was simply disgusting.

"You'll be satisfied with what I give you," she said coldly.

The door opened.

"Ah, Jordan," she purred.

There was one more thing to do for safety's sake. Her children didn't recognize it.

Advancing to her desk, she checked the notes she'd made earlier in the day on the address and visiting hours of the asylum.

"Tell me, Jordan, how would you like to renew acquaintance with pretty little Cousin Vanessa?"

Cecily sat in total shock, gripping the sides of her chair and unable to move. She knew time had passed. She knew she ought to act . . . do something . . . call Wesley Bell, perhaps, and tell him she needed a lawyer. They were going to arrest her. But she hadn't stolen that ruby.

She looked at the coat in the corner. *Her* coat. Her gloves in the pocket. How had this happened? She was innocent, but how was she ever going to prove it?

A sound broke through to her consciousness. Her door was opening. Teddy looked toward her, but not at her.

"You can get your things and go," he said.

"I . . ." She tried to understand and couldn't. Her brain felt numb. "The police . . ."

"They're not coming. He changed his mind."

Teddy's eyes avoided hers. Cecily realized that somehow, miraculously, Teddy had set things straight. She sprang to her feet.

"Oh, Teddy! Thank you—"

She stopped. He still wasn't looking at her. His expression was odd.

"Teddy . . . you don't believe I'm really guilty, do you?" The sound of her own anguish echoed in her ears.

Teddy's hand swept his red hair. There was pain on his face as he stared at the floor.

"I know you need money—because of your sister. I don't know what to believe."

This second shock was harder than the first. Teddy, her friend, had saved her from total disgrace, yet he thought her guilty.

The sting of her hurting pride brought the world back into focus. Cecily straightened.

"You're right. I do need money," she said tightly. "I have two weeks' pay due me. I don't suppose I'll be likely to get a recommendation so I can get another job, so I'd appreciate it if a check for that amount were sent to me."

Teddy nodded. A moment later she was alone. With shaking fingers she did something she'd never done before, dialed Peter's number at work. Her world was collapsing, but if she could just reach Peter, he'd take care of her.

"Good God, I'd better call and make some excuse why we can't attend that dinner tonight!"

They'd been riding for miles in the back of Peter's gray limousine. All Cecily's pain and anger continued to spill out in sobs, though she'd finished her story.

In the silence of the cavernous car she raised her head and stared at him. She'd taken his silence while she'd talked as reassurance, the warm presence of his arm as commiseration. The detachment expressed in his words hurt.

"*Damn* the dinner!" she said with force. "How can you even be thinking about a dinner? I've just been fired and accused of being a thief!"

Her voice rose with increasing anger. Peter frowned at her as though she were being unreasonable.

"It happens to be a rather important dinner. I was hoping to settle a deal about a new hotel with some people there, in fact. Now we can't possibly go!"

He checked himself and tried to smile, the effort pale. "Look, Cecily, I realize this is awful for you. But it's awful for both of us, surely you understand that. My company—my father's company—deals with some very stuffy people. If we go tonight and word of this has leaked out and someone recognizes your name . . ."

It was the third shock of the day, and it was the worst. Cecily drew back as he reached for her hand. Peter looked apologetic. Engaging. Charming.

She'd believed almost blindly that he would share her anger, that they would weather this together. Peter loved her! Instead, he was upset about how this would affect his business—not about her.

Fighting new tears, she stripped off the diamond engagement ring and held it out to him. "Do you want this back?"

"Darling, don't be ridiculous!"

"Then damn it, instead of worrying about someone recognizing my name, help me clear it! I want my job back. I don't know how that ruby got in my coat, but I know I was framed and I want to know how and why! I have a lawyer, but I don't have the kind of money it would take to fight this. Will you lend it to me?"

He bit his mustache. His uneasiness was apparent. "Cecily, I'm not sure this is the sort of thing you ought to fight. You'll only end up with a lot of notoriety."

Her heart cracked. The man who had begged so fervently to take care of her had vanished.

"Stop the car."

"Cecily—"

"Stop it, I said. I want out!"

With seeming reluctance Peter leaned forward and tapped on the window, signaling his driver to the curb.

"Please, Cecily. Let's talk this through. I still care for you very much, but we have to be practical. If it's known my wife was involved in a scandal, it's not going to help my business. I think you ought to go away for a while—just until this is all forgotten. Let me set you up in a little place somewhere, maybe in Westchester."

Cecily's eyes took in the familiar contours of Peter's face. Her bones seemed to break inside her with the weight of his betrayal. Wordlessly, as the limousine stopped, she dropped the diamond from her finger into Peter's lap.

She opened the door.

"No, Cecily. Please." He caught her arm. She saw him swallow awkwardly. "I—I want you to keep it."

As she moved away without listening, out toward the curb, his hand thrust into her pocket. Too numb with her own grief to fight anymore, Cecily shoved at the door behind her. She stood staring into a shop window. She did not even know where she was. When she finally turned, the big gray car was gone.

Aware of tears streaming down her cheeks, aware of being alone, she reached into her pocket. Her fingers curled around the hardness of the glittering ring. There was a storm sewer just a few steps away. She would throw it in. It would be carried miles away, to the river, to the Atlantic, out of her life.

She had been a fool. She wanted no reminders. Her arm drew back.

And then she thought of Van.

Van was due for freedom next week, only Cecily no longer

had any way of supporting her. The diamond in her hand was a top-grade white stone with a weight well over three carats. She knew men in the small, teeming stalls of the Diamond Exchange who would buy it from her, though not at full value. She hailed a cab.

"Madison and forty-seventh," she said.

Her tears were drying. A bitter resolve was replacing her heartache. No matter what she had to do from this moment on, she and Van were going to survive.

EIGHT

"Is NOLA LEVESQUE THERE, PLEASE? SHE'S FORGOTTEN HER DENTAL appointment and we're trying to locate her."

"Miss Levesque? I don't believe so. Let me check with Mrs. Lyle."

Cecily broke the phone connection quietly, jaw set. She had learned what she'd wanted.

She had lain awake all night in the narrow bed of her silent apartment trying to make sense of yesterday's nightmare. She had tried and tried to find some explanation, some hand responsible for what had happened. It was almost noon on Saturday morning, and, trembly with coffee, half-sick with the tears she'd shed and tormenting questions, she'd seized only minutes ago on a random thought so incredible that she'd feared her mind was confusing itself with childhood demons: Maybe Orlena or one of her children lay behind that business with the ruby.

It was crazy to think it. They had no reason to hate her, did they?

Wretchedly she'd remembered baiting Jordan at that auction. Though she'd expected it to lead to ruthless rivalry the next time they met, she'd never imagined . . .

She'd made the phone call.

Now, closing eyes too parched for tears, she sat down on the simple tweed couch beside her telephone.

"Shit," she said.

She still had no idea how that ruby had come to be in her coat. The fact the receptionist at Lyle & Co. had recognized the Levesque woman's name proved a connection with her relatives, though, and that was enough.

Less than twenty-four hours ago she had lost both her job and
Peter. Today, when she so desperately needed to see Van, to
touch the only human link she had in the whole world, someone
had called to say Van had the flu and couldn't have visitors.
Now Cecily's discovery that her own impulsive behavior was
partly to blame for the shattering of her world felt like the last
straw. She buried her head in her hands. She had to believe
things would somehow get better. It was all that stood between
her and total despair.

I have to eat, she told herself, the very act of thinking painful.
If I don't eat, I'll get sick and I'll be defeated.

Forcing herself to move, she went to the kitchen. She swallowed down cheese and bread. It made a lump in her stomach.

There was certainly nothing more the Lyles could do to her
now, she reflected bitterly. And she had money in the bank,
thanks to the sale of the cold little diamond she'd once trusted to
bring her so much happiness.

Well, she'd been a fool to trust. Her age of innocence was
over now. She'd never again fall for a man the way she'd fallen
for Peter, nor believe in friendship as she had with Teddy. She'd
believe in nothing but herself. And Vanessa, of course. Van
would be with her in another week. Wesley Bell was arranging
not only for her release, but for a court hearing to make Cecily her
legal guardian. They'd go somewhere with her nest egg and Cecily
would take care of both of them. She started toward the shower,
determined to batter her brain, if not her spirits, back to life.

She was toweling her hair, an old red sweat shirt giving her
comfort, when the doorbell rang. Her heart leaped painfully.

No. Even if it was Peter, she would tell him to go away.

Throwing the door open on its chain, she saw a woman with
Raggedy Ann eyes and tight blond curls. Oh, yes. They'd met at
the hospital. Maybe she'd brought some word from Van.

"Hello," said Cecily, freeing the chain.

The woman stepped in. She was chewing gum rapidly. Cecily
remembered now her name was April.

"Have they called yet?" her visitor asked anxiously.

"Who—" began Cecily. Then premonition chilled her. She
gripped the blond woman's arm. "Van! Something's happened
to Van!"

The bright little eyes looking back at her from their nest of
mascara held sympathy. April didn't cringe. Instead she put a
reassuring hand on the fingers digging into her. The telephone
began to ring.

Dazed, Cecily tore to answer it. The door was still standing open. April closed it.

"Miss Catlow?" a voice at the other end was saying. "This is Dr. Lenox. I'm afraid your sister's had a setback. We've had to move her to a confinement ward. It's going to be some weeks before it's advisable for you to resume your visits. . . ."

The rest of what he was saying twisted, unheard, past her ear. Something about possibly having a better understanding of Van's problem in a day or so. Cecily let the receiver fall back into its cradle.

April was shaking her head. "You got a bottle around?" she asked.

"I . . , yes. In the kitchen."

Cecily sat down heavily. She'd never kept liquor, but Peter had bought a supply of the Scotch he liked. April disappeared. There were sounds of opening cabinets and a few moments later Cecily felt a glass shoved into her hands.

"Drink it down."

Cecily obeyed. She felt no effect, only the awful numbness that had started when she'd answered the telephone.

"Jeezus, kid! You must have needed that," April said, and was gone again. She returned with Cecily's glass refilled and one for herself. "They tell you about the guy who visited your sister before she . . . ." April made a vague, embarrassed gesture with her hand to indicate the mental snap.

Cecily, fighting to keep what was happening around her in focus, looked at her without comprehending.

"Didn't figure they would," April continued. "They may not have known. She was out under one of the trees when they found her—alone, I mean. But I thought maybe you'd want to know, and I figured how hard this would be for you anyway . . . I mean, Van told me last Saturday about you two being all alone in the world. So I thought I'd come." She sipped swiftly, deftly, at her drink. "He was tall and good-looking with hair kinda like this." She pointed to her own. "Said he'd wait for Van in the garden."

Outraged understanding began to make its way through to Cecily. Her hands tightened on the glass.

"You mean Van had a visitor? They told me she was sick!"

April looked surprised. "She was waiting for you, said maybe the four of us could go out for lunch again. She's such a sweet kid—"

"*Van had a visitor? And—and then she went crazy again?*"

April shifted uncomfortably as Cecily set her glass aside with a clatter and rose.

"Well, I'm pretty sure. . . . I mean, he spoke to that awful Miss Mundey and he almost whispered, but I'd swear he said Vanessa Catlow. She'd gone back to her room to get a book she'd finished with—"

Cecily's hand swept sideways, sending her half-filled glass to the floor. The action could not relieve the anguish inside her. She struck again, flinging a lamp off, watching it shatter.

"Damn them!" she sobbed. "Damn them, why did they have to hurt *her*?"

April, her slim legs crossed, had frozen.

"Hey, look." Her voice took on a light, placating tone. "If you want to throw booze on the floor, you ought to buy something cheaper than Chivas Regal."

Although shakily, Cecily realized April probably feared this flare of destructiveness was a sign she, too, was loosing her grip on reality. The woman had just come from visiting a hospital filled with mental patients. Agitation was often the first sign of psychiatric problems.

"I'm sorry," Cecily said carefully, resuming her seat and shading her eyes. "It's just she was so close to getting out. And I know who must've done this to her."

"Jesus God! You mean it was deliberate?"

Cecily nodded.

Silently April slipped into the kitchen, returning with a fresh glass which she handed to Cecily.

Cecily drank doggedly until half its contents were gone. It made her feel calmer. She'd never had a woman friend before and now, just when she'd vowed to live completely within herself, this rather flashy-looking little blonde she hardly knew was showing her kindness.

"Thank you." She struggled to smile. For the first time she noticed that April wore dangly earrings again today, and a bracelet with clanking gold coins—hardly like the customers who had patronized Landis and Oxenburg.

April's blue eyes were wide. "Yeah, sure. You going to be okay?"

"Oh, splendid." Cecily couldn't keep the bitterness from her voice. "Yesterday I lost my job, and now . . ." There were tears left in her. They blurred her vision. "She's all I have!"

"Life's shit, isn't it?" April trailed into the kitchen and came back with the bottle from which she'd been pouring. "You know, I was born in a circus wagon, and all I ever wanted was to get away from the stink and the noise and live like regular people.

"But you know what? I saw a girl killed by a lion once, and the look on her face, it wasn't near as horrible as Herbie's was after they gave him shock treatments."

She dabbed carefully at an eye. "I know I'll never get him out, but you, sister—Jeezus! I just figured today was an accident, some dumb-ass boyfriend showing up and upsetting her, but I thought you'd want to know. If that guy who came upset her deliberately, he ought to lose his balls!"

"I intend to see he does," said Cecily.

Harm to herself she had almost accepted. Harm to Van she would never forgive.

Jordan licked his lips and leaned back in his darkened apartment to watch his latest videotape. It had been a stroke of genius taking Trace MacDonald along with him to film when he'd visited Cousin Vanessa. MacDonald was an ad man and was hot to get his hands on Lyle's account. Jordan had always known how to manipulate people. Look how he'd kept Lucy and Orlena against each other all these years—having accidents as a child so Orlena would fuss over him, then, later, pretending to be on Lucy's side and feeding her jealousy when she whimpered Orlena never paid attention to her.

It was his favorite game.

His second favorite game, he amended, licking his lips again as images began to flicker on the screen before him. Vanessa's shining gold hair. Her startled look as he stepped up to her and covered her mouth. His slamming her against a tree and hurting her. The terror in her eyes.

He was in control. It scared women when they knew that. He liked to see women scared. Orlena and Lucy were always nagging at him, thinking they were better than him. They were cunts. All women were cunts.

But he got even. He showed them they weren't men's equals after all. Because underneath they were always so easy to scare.

He watched himself shoving Van's skirt up. He watched himself sawing away between her legs. She'd fought at first. He could hear the sound of her muffled screams. She'd bitten his hand.

He was starting to get an erection. Jordan rose and switched the tape off. He'd save it for later.

Going to see his cousin had been a pleasure, Jordan thought, prowling restlessly into the kitchen and making a sandwich. He bit off hunks of white bread and rare roast beef and ground them vigorously between his teeth. He hated Cecily Catlow. She'd spoiled a good time for him that time in Marblehead and she'd made a fool of him at that auction. He owed her plenty. He'd enjoyed the chance to get back at her through her sister, but it was only a start.

The videotape was going to bring him lots of satisfaction. He'd enjoy it first, and then he'd hit her with it—call and tell her he had it. She'd be hysterical. She'd be sorry she'd ever crossed him. She was like all women—like Orlena and Lucy. Hovering, just waiting for you to make a mistake so they could snicker at you and act superior. She'd see.

He thought of her at that auction, putting on lipstick to mock him. He'd like to see her scared and underneath him.

Suddenly Jordan had a memory of her struggling when he'd held her back that day in Marblehead. How she'd bitten and kicked.

All at once, angrily, he felt himself ejaculating on brand new slacks.

That was another thing to hold against Cousin Cecily.

"Without any proof there's no legal action we can take. Not with any hope of winning, anyway."

Wesley Bell watched Cecily's face. He had a feeling she'd known he was going to tell her that, but it didn't keep him from feeling miserable. He had every confidence what she'd told him about the ruby in the raincoat and the loss of her job was true, but gut feelings didn't help much in court.

"I understand," she said tonelessly.

Wesley stirred his coffee so he wouldn't have to notice how her face had changed since he'd first met her. Dark, dark circles rimmed her eyes. They almost made her prettier. But she looked so much thinner, and a pain she didn't express that looked like it never left her burned in her eyes and made him wince.

Didn't she have anyone to rely on? the lawyer wondered. He straightened his glasses. He'd never heard her mention a boyfriend, but surely she had one.

"Are you sure you don't want something to eat?" he said.

She shook her head.

They were meeting this time in a small coffee shop on Forty-seventh Street. Wesley had sensed they both wanted the kind of privacy they could find here. She had called him on Monday about being fired and about Vanessa. His stomach knotted.

"I'm sorry," he said, and wished he were more articulate.

"Thanks." She managed a smile.

"I made some enquiries about Miss Levesque and Lyle and Company. The thing is, Cecily, from what I've learned, and heard from you, about your Aunt Orlena, she'd be too clever to show any out-and-out payment to Nola Levesque on her books. So Levesque was a customer of Lyle and Company and for some reason came to Landis and Oxenburg. So what? After a bad experience there, it would look completely natural that the woman went back to trading at Lyle and Company."

"And of course there's no way of proving it was Jordan who visited Van. There's probably no law against harassing mental patients, anyway."

With an angry movement Cecily shoved away her half-finished coffee. Wesley looked at his hands. He hurt for her.

And Vanessa. She had been more beautiful than her photograph, and sane and sweet. He would have walked through fire for her. Now someone had gone and hurt her. Maybe destroyed her.

"How—how is she?" he asked.

Cecily swallowed hard. "They won't let me see her. I called her doctor—told him what April said happened—but he said at this stage of treatment—" Her voice broke. "I know what they do to her there is all that can be done, but it's so awful!"

He was silent a minute.

"Do you mind if I go up to check on her from time to time?" he asked.

She was biting her lip, hunting desperately for something to fix her eyes on so she wouldn't cry.

Every day of this last week had been like reliving the time when she was nine years old and torn away from Van the first time, Cecily thought, a nightmare with no end and no margins, where anything could happen because she'd seen firsthand how puny her own strength was. Sleep wouldn't come to her because she was afraid to close her eyes. By day she faced the constant fact of her own powerlessness, unable to right the wrong against her, unable to help the one person she'd been given on earth to love, unable to protect herself or her sister. Worst of all, perhaps, unable even to sustain herself economically.

And Peter's faithlessness burned like a great, festering gash across the surface of her isolation. Three days after he abandoned her, he had sent flowers, a check enclosed with the card that bore his name. She had ripped both up. She was not for sale. She had moved to the Y on 47th street that night and left no forwarding address.

With a breath Cecily fought back the anger and despair that were rising inside her. Thank God Wesley Bell wasn't one of those pompous types who tried to impress you by talking on and on, she thought. He was sitting quietly, letting her have time to compose herself.

"There's no chance of getting Van out for months now," she said answering his question. "Years, maybe."

"I know. I just want to keep checking. If they know we're monitoring, they're less likely to keep her on any ward longer than necessary." He paused. "I'm fairly certain Vanessa was ready to leave the hospital last year—maybe long before. But she was useful to the ward attendants, did their work for them. I talked to a psychiatrist who interned in a state institution and he told me that isn't uncommon. One afternoon when I showed up unexpectedly to see her, I'm pretty sure she was measuring out medications."

Cecily felt a little gasp catch in her throat. The man across from her looked stricken, as though he thought he'd erred in some way.

"I—" he began uncomfortably.

She put a hand out, pressing his.

"Thank you. Thank you for telling me. And yes, please monitor. Just send me a bill."

"No bill. I want to do it."

She looked at him in puzzlement now. He shrugged, changing the subject.

"Any hope of a job yet?"

A week had passed. If she had any chance of finding employment in the city, she'd know it by now.

She set her jaw. "It's fairly clear the word's been passed that I'm a security risk. After twenty-two firms I started to realize I was wasting my time. No one in Manhattan wants to trust their jewels to an appraiser who might be a thief. The only thing I'm likely to find is clerking in some little store—if I'm lucky."

Wesley frowned. "What then?"

Cecily drew a breath. "I have plans."

She'd learned a valuable lesson out of the nightmare of this past week—the most important thing in life was survival. Not love, not putting down roots, not hanging onto a job—just survival.

She'd spent days amid microfilm, gone through stories, read

every line ever printed about Lyle & Co. Finally she'd found what she wanted: A name. An enemy. Someone who might have reason to hate Lyle & Co. almost as much as she did.

F. E. Duvall, known as Effie.

The woman was ancient. Shrouded in mystery. From the little Cecily had been able to learn about her, she was universally feared and hated, probably corrupt.

And powerful.

Cecily gathered up her purse. "I'm going to Miami," she said, forcing lightness.

She was not going to rest until the Lyles's business, their peace of mind, everything they owned had been destroyed.

She was going to bind herself—as apprentice or even slave, if necessary—to Effie Duvall.

PART TWO

Emeralds

NINE

"YOU HAVE AN APPOINTMENT AT THIS PLACE?"

The boat-taxi pilot jerked his head toward the island that was still just a dot of grass in the blue Atlantic and Cecily nodded. What business was it of his that for more than a week she'd tried futilely to reach Effie Duvall? The woman wouldn't answer her letters, wouldn't take her phone calls, was not interested in discussing business because she no longer did business, an officious secretary had told Cecily.

Cecily knew better. To this island halfway between Miami and Palm Beach came Arabian princes, Bavarian duchesses, Brazilian planters, and the mistresses of Texas computer kings. There, on that dot of land, they could purchase gems finer than any supplied by Cartier or Bulgari. And no one seemed to know how Effie came by them.

"Good thing," said the boatman. "Guards all over the place, and the ones I've seen carry machine guns. Show up without an appointment and they'd just as soon shoot as ask questions."

Cecily tried not to swallow. She wondered if she'd done the wrong thing coming here. Maybe Effie *was* crazy as well as reclusive. She'd heard that rumor from more than one source. Maybe the woman had been dead for years. She'd heard that story, too.

Her gray linen suit and high-heeled sandals seemed out of place in the small motorboat. Ignoring uneasiness, she watched the contours of the land ahead of her take shape. Tall lines that looked like matchsticks soon took on the forms of coconut palms. Behind them were flashes of white and a red tile roof. She looked in the direction they had come. Miami had vanished, the buildings of its shoreline becoming a tiny strand of pearls floating on the horizon.

"Best get ready to shout out your name," the boatman advised.

Turning, Cecily saw a small boat landing rushing toward them. Striding down it came a lean, mustached man with an open white shirt and gold cuff links. His hands were on his hips and he looked wary, but he was unarmed.

75

"No docking here. This is private property," he called as the boat cut its motor.

Cecily motioned the boatman toward the landing. "I've got business with Effie."

Two men stepped from the palm trees and moved toward the dock. They carried not machine guns, but high-powered rifles.

"Madame Duvall is expecting no one," snapped the man in white. "Turn back."

Cecily was close enough now to lunge and seize a rung of the dock ladder. "All right. Go back," she said to the boatman as she swung onto it.

The boatman was clearly nervous. She'd lied to him. She'd paid his fee when they left Miami, too, so he had no reason at all for heroics.

"Okay, lady," he said with a shrug. "I warned you.'

"Hey, you! Come back here!" the man on the dock ordered sharply as the motorboat opened its throttle. His attention divided between the two of them, he took a menacing step toward Cecily, who was scaling the ladder.

What could he do to her? Kick her into the water? Order her shot? She clung motionless to the rough wood of the top rung, regretting her impulsiveness yet determined not to back down. If she seemed indecisive, she'd stand no chance at all in this situation.

Setting her teeth, half expecting a blow, she heaved herself onto the dock. The maneuver was clumsy in her insubstantial shoes, but at least she was still alive.

The man standing over her put out a warning hand as she straightened.

"Stay where you are. You'll go right back in one of these boats—whoever you are."

"No, I won't," she said, flinging her head up and starting past him. "I'm Cecily Catlow. I'm here to see Miss Duvall. You can tell her I intend to stay right here until I do."

The man who was barring her way spoke in Spanish to the other two men, a rapid command that Cecily couldn't understand.

"I will go to the house for a boat key," he said to her. "I warn you, if you attempt to leave the dock, they will shoot."

Cecily sat down on a coil of rope and tried to think. She was on a dock being watched by two men with rifles. The distance between her and Effie Duvall seemed almost as great as it had in Miami. She'd shown her nerve and it had gotten her exactly nowhere. Damn. Locking fingers around her knees, she thought furiously, hunting some way around those men.

The one in charge reappeared in what seemed a surprisingly short time. He spoke again to the guards, this time nodding toward the house.

"Go," he said succinctly, and turned to speak into a small box in his hand, a radio of some type.

At first she thought he meant onto a boat. Then she understood. Apparently her gamble had paid. Effie Duvall was going to see her.

The land rose slightly up as they moved through the outer ring of palm trees, the swell of the island giving its occupants a view of miles of ocean. How many occupants were there? Cecily wondered. From the little she'd been able to learn, the place was Effie's home as well as her atelier. Ahead of her she saw two white towers with a building connecting them and smaller, lower, additions extending from each side. She stepped beneath Moorish arches, past plantings of Natal plum bushes, fan palms, and neon-pink Bougainvillaea. She stood now in a great hall floored in tile.

The guard in the lead motioned toward the right, and an elevator. Cecily's sense of direction told her it must lead to one of the towers. There were only two stories. Did Effie's health require an elevator, or was that one of the standard items in homes along Florida's gold coast? The elevator stopped, opening onto a hallway with carpet as blue as the ocean outside.

The carpeting led through an open door. The guards fell back and a thin, curved man with a hooked nose looked up from his desk, unhinging his jaw to speak and nodding toward another door.

"Go in," he said.

Though she'd thought herself unaffected by such things, Cecily found her senses overwhelmed by exotic stimuli: the private island; the fortresslike mansion, so much more beautiful than she'd expected; the brilliant colors. Boldly she stepped to the great carved door. After all she'd encountered so far, meeting Effie herself could hardly hold any surprises. She pushed the door open, then gasped at the scene that met her.

Midway through the room, the carpeting underfoot flowed up onto a raised dais. At its center stood a vast carved and lacquered Chinese table, flanked by a golden Buddha on one side and a multiarmed Hindu deity on the other. Both were life-sized. There were low lacquered benches instead of chairs, and the walls were covered in thin gold paper enlivened by tiny, cloisonné droplets of red and blue. The whole room shimmered darkly. But Cecily could hardly take in its details or even the occupant of the desk, for there, blocking her way, growling low in its throat and swinging its tail, stood a sleek, gleaming, yellow-eyed black panther.

"Don't worry," rasped a voice. "He is quite tame."

With effort Cecily raised her eyes to meet the hooded gaze of a figure behind the desk, a figure so gnarled and androgynous she could not look away. As though from a throne, a pair of black eyes watched her. Maybe this wasn't Effie, she thought, taking in the rounded shoulders and mannish black suit. Surely a form so solid could not have conceived the ethereal necklaces that seemed to capture dewdrops in flight, sunbeams against spiderwebs, the dancing magic of stars on water.

"Sit," said the figure, pointing.

A ruby the size and shape of a large olive flashed on a bent finger, its fire drawing Cecily's attention from everything else. It was perfect pigeon-blood red, a stone like none she'd ever seen and would never have thought to see outside crown jewels. Its exceptional size alone would have made men kill for it.

The panther sauntered slowly away, behind the desk, where a hand stroked his head.

"You are quite persistent," remarked the rasping voice.

And now, in spite of the short-cropped white hair, in spite of the fact the stocky figure encased in an Oscar de la Renta tuxedo could have been either male or female, Cecily knew beyond a doubt she had met Effie.

"So are you," she said quietly, walking forward. "You were very persistent in refusing my phone calls."

The woman behind the desk grunted. The dais and the tall carved chair she occupied fostered that initial impression of a throne room. But a modern, powerful throne room, thought Cecily, noting a white console telephone with computerized call buttons on one corner of the desk.

"I do business in my own way. Why should I be interested in talking to someone who has nothing to do with me?" asked Effie bluntly. "Why, especially, should I be interested in talking to a crook?"

Ice shot along Cecily's spine. Even in Miami her name had been slandered.

As swiftly as anger and fear, shrewdness came to her.

Effie knew what she'd been accused of in New York not

because the story had spread, but because Effie had taken pains to discover it after those phone calls. She'd thought to intimidate Cecily by confronting her with the knowledge—and she'd almost succeeded. Increasingly, Cecily found herself wary of and fascinated by this ancient woman. Embittered rivals accused Effie of blackmail, smuggling, piracy, even murder. All might be true.

Ignoring the bench that had been indicated, Cecily stepped up on the dais.

"If you believed I was a crook, you would never have permitted me to leave the dock."

Or unless you are likewise and think I might serve some purpose of yours, she added silently.

The hooded eyes were quick behind their wrinkled flesh. They had followed Cecily's movement but betrayed nothing, not displeasure at bounds overstepped, not approval.

Cecily plunged onward, guided by instinct. "I want to work for you."

Effie brushed a hand in dismissal. "My work is set. My client list is small. I need no new blood."

"Then that is a shame. The name of Effie will be forgotten far sooner than it should have been, and the name of Lyle and Company will grow and be remembered."

She thought she had struck a response with the mention of Lyle & Co. There was the barest tightening of a crease of skin on Effie's cheek.

A nerve-rubbing sound spilled into the silence. The panther was making some sound of contentment that was not a purr. The bizarre noise made it hard to concentrate. Was the beast but another of his owner's psychological weapons? Cecily wondered.

"We share a common enemy, Madame Duvall." Effie had been half French, had married a Frenchman. The title came easily. Heart beating with the need to reach her, Cecily took a step forward, searching desperately for some yielding in a rock-hard face. "William Lyle tried to destroy you. The present owners of the firm have tried the same with me."

Effie seemed to lose interest, turning back to her desk to sign a paper lying there and push it aside.

"William Lyle is dead and I'm alive. The names of his clients . . ." She sniffed. "They are nothing to mine."

A pang of pity touched Cecily. Effie's great fame had come in an era when the only advertising regarded by the super-rich was word of mouth—when inspired designs and gems of superior quality required no publicity. Now things were different. Ads mattered. Publicity mattered. And Effie, though continuing to serve established clients, had not shown a collection in more than ten years.

"Lyle and Company plans to expand," said Cecily carefully. "Rumors are that they're eyeing a branch in London, and they've made firm plans to open a store in Palm Beach. They'll soon be poaching on your territory. Their list of clients may not be half as prestigious as yours, but it's four times as long. We could stop them, even destroy them, madame. You and I!"

Effie pushed back from her desk. For the first time Cecily realized her ornately carved chair was also a wheelchair.

"I have told you, William Lyle is dead!" she said sharply. "What do I care what happens to his company? What satisfaction would I get from waging war against it?"

"You'd show the world it was the brilliance of Effie that brought Lyle and Company customers when they were desperately needed—that it was *your* designs that won those awards, even though he denied it publicly and fired you, hoping to silence you."

Poring over microfilm, reading news accounts more than sixty years old, Cecily had pieced together what she was sure was the truth behind them. Effie had been young then, scarcely twenty, an assistant to Great-Uncle William.

"I believe you have known hate the way I know hate," said Cecily. "We would have revenge."

Effie turned abruptly and wheeled toward a window to look out at the distant ocean. There was a flair to her—a stylishness—even now. The unorthodox attire and the calmly worn ruby were not the province of an ordinary woman.

"Hate," she spat. "You know nothing of hate!"

Her fingers snapped. The panther sprang to her side. Together the two of them moved back, circling Cecily, subtly threatening her.

"You thirst for revenge," said Effie sharply. "Why? What is Lyle and Company to you?"

Unnerved by the prowling cat and the hard black eyes boring into her, Cecily stepped back. Aware her knees were trembling, she took a seat on the carpeted step of the dais. She had never encountered a force of will like Effie's. Her fists pushed into the blue plush.

"William Lyle was my great-uncle. His widow and her children blamed my sister for a murder she didn't commit. They drove her crazy! They put her in a state asylum where she went through hell, and now, when I almost had her out, they've caused her to stay there.'' Anger exploded in her and she could no longer keep her voice even. "Do you know how hideous those places are? The cold tubs—the straps they tie them down with? I want the Lyles destroyed for what they've done to her! And to me."

Effie made an impatient gesture. "You *want*. And what have you to offer me? Why should I help you?"

Cecily swallowed. She looked boldly at Effie, determined to win in spite of the nervousness filling her.

"I'm mobile, madame, and you are not. If you let me work for you, I could double your business within two years—"

"I'm not interested in increasing my business," Effie interrupted. "I've outlived my need for revenge. There's one thing and one thing only that could interest me."

Cecily waited. Effie was watching her shrewdly. The old woman touched a button beneath her desk and a wall of draperies opened, flooding the room with light.

"Stand over there," said Effie, pointing. "Take off your clothes."

TEN

NIGHT HAD CLOSED IN AROUND THE ISLAND. WONDERING WHETHER she was guest or prisoner, Cecily walked the open, rather tropical living room where she had been shown and waited nervously. Almost as nervously as when she'd discarded her clothes in front of Effie that afternoon, she thought.

She had sensed the challenge behind that sharp, unexpected command in Effie's office, and in some fraction of a second Cecily had determined to match it. Even now she wasn't sure what the test had been. An attempt to see how easily she scared? An assessment of her resolve? Effie had run unwavering eyes along the lines of her body, then grunted.

"Dress and go down to the living room," she'd said. "You are keeping me from my work."

Hearing footsteps, Cecily looked up, remembering belatedly that footsteps wouldn't be Effie.

She was only half-right. Effie, in a high-backed chair of gold damask, was gliding into the room. Behind her came the slightly curved man who appeared to be her secretary. Last in the procession was a linen-clad butler, the tray in his hand bearing three identical drinks.

Effie stopped, took a glass from the tray, and tasted its contents with gusto.

"My guests drink whatever I drink," she announced, and smacked her lips. Cecily had the feeling all of them in the room had been holding their breath, awaiting some hint of the snow-haired autocrat's mood.

Effie raised a finger and the rest of them were served. Though aware of the woman flaunting her power, Cecily found the drink she sipped surprisingly pleasant. She was glad of it, starved and put on edge by this waiting.

That's what Effie intends, she warned herself. *Learn from her.*

Effie still wore her black dinner jacket and satin striped pants, but she had added a diamond bracelet and art deco brooch. She nodded approval above her now empty glass.

"I hope you like veal."

The unexpected comment caught Cecily off guard. She could not resist a smile. "Madame, any meal with you would be an experience."

To her relief, a rasping chuckle escaped the woman in the wheelchair.

"You are a bold little thing." She wheeled closer to the couch where Cecily had seated herself. "Jenkins, let Bibi in."

Cecily looked up in time to see a glass door slide open and the panther glide toward them. Her eyes were drawn irresistibly to the animal's paws and the claws just visible there.

Effie, watching her, gave a sly smile. "Don't worry. He is a vegetarian."

A joke? Effie's black eyes were shimmering.

"So," she said suddenly, the lulling charm vanished. "You say you want to work for me. How do I know you're not a thief as you're reported to be?"

Cecily's fingers tightened on the glass she held. "How do I know you come by the stones you sell by any means but thievery?"

The first hint of anger seemed to touch the face looking back at her. Then Effie's white head fell back and she laughed. "I like you. You are not afraid of me."

"Perhaps I hide it. I'd be a fool not to."

Somewhere in the room a phone rang sharply. Jenkins, as though he'd been expecting it, shot forward.

Effie's eyes, narrowed in assessment of Cecily and her words, barely stirred until the secretary spoke.

"Madame, his boat's at the marina. Let Raoul send two men up to—"

"No." She cut him off with a lift of the hand that wore the huge ruby. "Let him come."

Anxious lines had pressed themselves across Jenkins's forehead. Cecily could feel a stir of tension. At this hour, on an island ruled by one old woman, the conversation she was overhearing seemed stranger and more threatening than it would have in other surroundings.

"Tell Raoul I wish to be accessible to my family," Effie said, and then without a breath turned her attention back to Cecily.

"The customer who accused you at Landis and Oxenburg does not have the means herself to afford the necklace she bought. She has shopped for some years—when she could—at Lyle and Company. You see, I have garnered many little details this afternoon. I know you are not a thief.

"Since you favor me with wondering about me in return, I will show you how I come by my stones. Jenkins—hand me the phone."

She punched a single button as her secretary, with a slight, wary glance toward the sliding doors, held the console. This phone, too, was computerized.

Effie's next words were in French and fraught with simple power: *"Ici Madame."*

There was a pause, long enough for Cecily to speculate this was an international call. Then Effie spoke.

"I need five well-matched stones for a necklace, baguette or pear-shaped. The central one must be significant, twenty carats or more . . . no, no smaller ones. I am mixing with sapphire.

"He will leave at once with them? Good."

She hung up and looked steadily at Cecily. "I do not do business with De Beers. It is too inconvenient."

Cecily tried not to look impressed. The call could have been staged. Yet gut instinct told her Effie would not bother with such stratagems.

" 'Inconvenient' is a modest choice of words," she said. "If you had done nothing except buck the cartel, you'd be a legend."

Effie looked pleased. How anyone could obtain fine-quality free-world diamonds outside De Beers's enormous and carefully guarded cartel was one of the world's great mysteries.

"You see, I am quite mobile," Effie said.

Cecily looked quietly down, then smiled at her. "Yes. I see that. But you have hidden yourself, Madame. There even are rumors you are dead."

Effie's face showed nothing. Her secretary, Jenkins, watched in silence, his eyes traveling to first one of them and then the other. Cecily wondered why he didn't enter the conversation. Wasn't he allowed?

Turning her chair with one hand, Effie made her way to a lavish bar, where she began preparing herself another drink. Was her failure to ask of her guests' thirst deliberate or did she assume they could fend for themselves? Was she mean-spirited or merely brusque? Cecily couldn't decide.

Neither could she decide if she liked the woman or mistrusted her. Both, maybe.

"It is the second wife who intends to expand Lyle and Company," Effie said, her back toward them. "A former model, I am told. Very young and beautiful, as his first wife was."

She glided back toward them, toward the place where her great black cat lay waiting. It struck Cecily that despite being a prisoner in that chair, Effie was constantly in motion, constantly restless.

"Two wives and no children," she continued. "I produced four."

The information was somehow surprising. Cecily had read nothing about Effie's children, had seen no photographs in evidence, could hardly imagine her as a mother.

"Does she wear emeralds?" Effie asked abruptly.

"Orlena? Why, yes," said Cecily, surprised. "She used to, at least."

For an instant the hoods raised on Effie's eyes and she seemed to look backward in time.

"Those emeralds . . ."

The gullies of her face grew harder. She raised her glass and drank methodically.

"Show her the ruby we'll see set tomorrow, Jenkins. Don't you think it's a nice little stone?"

Jenkins had produced a chamois pouch and was offering its contents to Cecily.

"It's quite light, Madame," she said slowly, frowning at something amiss in the looks of it that she couldn't explain except as her own instinct. "From Ceylon?"

Effie chuckled lustily. "So anyone would say—but you are holding a fine red diamond. Never believe what you are told.

Always question.'' She snapped her fingers for Bibi. ''Come, let's go to dinner.''

They ate by candlelight and once again Cecily felt herself overwhelmed by the rich beauty of her surroundings. Effie sat at the head of a long table so highly polished that its dark surface gave back perfect reflections of an extravagant bowl of roses and pale orchids. The china placed on it was white and delicate and banded in gold. The flatware was rare antique vermeil. Effie's sense of balance and loveliness took Cecily's breath away. There was nothing in excess here, nothing used simply to show its owner's wealth, and everything was in such contrast to Effie's own plainness of dress. Jenkins asked several murmured questions about one of the gem-setters. Cecily wondered if the secretary lived here, or if he had been held here for this dinner.

''There is one thing you don't understand about my business,'' said Effie, cutting into a tender spear of asparagus on the plate before her. ''When you do, if you still are interested, then we'll talk.

''Do you agree, Jenkins?''

He blotted his mouth and nodded. ''Yes, Madame.''

Cecily felt her heart begin to hammer. She put down her fork.

''My business is a success because it's a family business,'' Effie said. ''It is the only way to maintain loyalty. So you see, the only way anyone comes to me is by marriage.''

A chilling uncertainty traveled down Cecily's arms. But no. Surely Effie was making this up. This was another test.

''If you want to work for me, you will marry my grandson Ben.''

''Madame, surely—''

''You will not find him unappealing, I assure you. Show her the photograph.''

Jenkins extended a small framed photograph over the table, but Cecily saw only eyes—black eyes crackling like Effie's, but angry and scornful, eyes that scorched her and drained all the strength from her body.

Not at all like Peter's eyes, she thought, and tried to close her mind. Her fingers shook. She thrust the photograph back at Jenkins. It was as though the man in the photograph had reached out and touched her, burned her flesh.

''Madame, even if I were willing, I could hardly promise to make a man marry me!''

Effie ate placidly. ''Of course you can. You have a fine body. What do you suppose it was meant for? A woman with any ambition must learn to use every weapon. Men don't turn their backs on using every advantage. This is why, by and large, they rule the world. Unless you would be ruled, too, you must use both this and this." Her hand flicked toward her head, then swept dramatically down her own stooped length. "Are you willing to be ruled?"

Cecily's thoughts were a jumble. The old woman's eyes were so keen it was impossible to doubt her wisdom.

"No. Of course not."

Effie put down her fork and leaned forward, gaze piercing. "Bring me Ben and I will give you your chance to annihilate Lyle and Company. I will give you a show, power as my assistant, whatever you require." She leaned back and her teeth showed in a cunning smile. "I suspect you might find my grandson very pleasing in bed. A good bargain all around."

Lucid now, Cecily reacted. "I don't give a damn what he's like in bed! Nor am I going to spout any drivel about love in marriage, if that's what you think."

"Good, then. It's settled."

"No it's not! You're asking too much and you know it."

"Too much? I paid the identical price three times to get what I wanted!"

Effie's voice had grown harsh. Cecily stared.

"You do not know what it is to want revenge," Effie said with contempt.

Anger fought with some fluttering feeling inside Cecily's breast. Was she not as strong as Effie, then? Was what Effie said true?

She did want the destruction of the Lyles—recompense for all the hurt inside her, salve for her loneliness. Certainly she was no longer dreamer enough to believe there was something called love, she thought bitterly. Marriage meant nothing. Engaging in sex meant nothing.

"I'm willing to use my mind *and* body in any way that will please you, Madame," she said carefully. "But I will not marry. Why should I, when I'm asking no share in your business—as your family must have? I'm not even asking a salary. Only expenses."

Effie tapped a knife impatiently on the edge of her plate. She started to speak, but before she could, a sliding door in the wall to the left slammed open. The panther sprang to his haunches, ready to launch himself.

"Down, Bibi!"

He was stayed by Effie's command, and Cecily, chilled by

fear, looked at the scene of which she slowly realized she was a part. A slender young man with raven hair stood framed by the open door. There was a pistol in his hand. He was breathing hard, but the pistol didn't waver as he fixed it on Effie.

Though she watched him, Effie stuck her fork tines into a bit of meat and transferred it to her mouth. "So," she said, chewing. "You've come. Raoul has kept me posted on your movements."

"Hah! You lie. They would never have let me reach you."

The man with the gun took a step toward them. He had the look of a dandy from his arrogant nose to his emerald cuff links. He waved the gun slightly.

"You gave my father a check on a bank account you had closed! Did you think he would accept that? Did you think he would let you steal a third of a million dollars' worth of emeralds?"

Effie had put her fork aside. Her hand rested in her lap. "Did your father think I would shrug at the murder of one of my best couriers?" she rasped, leaning forward. "Did he suppose I am senile, unable to guess who betrayed my source of diamonds to the syndicate? I have known for a long time that he was a traitor."

The gun in the young man's hand had dropped slightly. Now, as it started to lift, there was a loud, sharp crack and he pitched backward. Blood spread in a great, opening blossom through his white shirt as he fell. There were sounds of running footsteps, indoors and out. The guards who had confronted Cecily at the dock that morning arrived with others like them. They all carried rifles.

"Take him back to his yacht and leave him there," said Effie.

The panther was standing stiff-legged, growling softly. He watched as four men picked up the fallen intruder and carried him from the room.

Effie placed her own gray-barreled pistol on the table and picked up her fork. She ate a few bites in silence. Her heavy gaze moved from Jenkins, who was sitting white-faced with lips pinched closed, to Cecily, who still felt frozen.

A small red stain glistened on the carpet. Cecily wondered whether the man who had fallen there was dead or alive.

"If Bibi finds a wet spot on the rug, he is likely to forget his manners," Effie said. "Perhaps we should take our dessert in the living room." She tossed her napkin aside and rang a small bell.

Cecily watched. Rose. Speechless. Wondering if the woman who now turned her chair toward the living room was madder than Van.

"Without Ben, what you want for this company is not possible," Effie resumed as though there'd been no interruption. "My own genius is long gone. Ben, the young fool, refuses to acknowledge his. He was on the verge of great recognition. Bring him back to me and we will have a triumph. I will give you a show. I will help you destroy Lyle and Company—whether or not you marry him."

Cecily tried to speak and couldn't. Was Effie so cold that she could witness the scene just finished—could even shoot a man—and continue not only with her own plans but with her dessert?

"You will find toiletries and nightware have been provided you in a guest room," she was saying. "Tomorrow you will go to Palm Beach, to Worth Avenue, and buy a wardrobe suitable for your role as my assistant. Also a watch, a Patek Philippe."

She must be heartless. Or she had nerves of steel.

"Have all the immunization necessary to go anywhere on this globe," she said. "My grandson can be difficult to locate. Try Costa Rica first. He seems to like the airfield there. My board meets the first of next month. I'll want you both there."

"Madame, I—"

Cecily found her voice, but not the words.

"Bring me Ben and I will free your sister."

Effie took a small glass of Cointreau from a waiting tray and raised it in salute. There was a sly look in her eye. The gleaming panther leaned against her knees.

"Shall we agree?"

ELEVEN

BEN DUVALL PLUNGED HIS DARK HEAD INTO THE BASIN OF WATER before him and felt his brain throb. He had not felt so hung over in more than five years.

"Damnation!" he growled, leaning on the tile that edged the sink of his uncluttered bathroom and letting one lean thigh slant outward. "What the devil did you say the woman's name is, Rudolfo?"

"Catlow, señor. Cecily Catlow."

Squinting, Ben tried to remember a Cecily from the night before. The casinos closed early in San José so he'd gone to an after-hours place. It had turned into quite a party. There'd been plenty of good-looking girls. Women, really. The sort of restless, international mix San José attracted. He couldn't recall a Cecily.

He ran his mind back through the last months, wondering, at the same time, whether at thirty-six he was getting too old for unbridled drinking.

"Christ," he said to his servant. "What time is it, anyway?"

"Ten o'clock."

Ben wanted to make some comment about this Cecily Catlow picking a hell of an hour to come calling but knew he couldn't. He slipped into the white shirt Rudolfo was holding patiently, rolled the sleeves to the elbow, stuffed the tail in, and yanked up the zipper on tight tan slacks.

"You tell Luis if he ever lets anyone in to see me before I'm up again, I'll skin him."

"Yes, señor."

Ben shoved at the high crest of his black hair, aware the fine-looking beard that edged his jaw probably needed trimming and perversely pleased by the knowledge. When women chased after him he liked to set the record straight on what he thought of it, which wasn't much. He did the chasing—when it suited him. Heels clicking on polished tile, he stalked down the hall.

Sunlight flooded the long, informal living room at the back of the house. That was one of the things Ben liked about Costa Rica, the plentiful sunshine mixed with a moderate temperature. That and the fact the place was so small and sleepy no one ever breached his privacy. Not until now, anyway. Head still throbbing, he scowled at the girl who began to turn from her contemplation of his garden as she heard him enter.

Three pairs of French doors stood open to midmorning sun bouncing back from the warm, polished, cinnamon tiles of a narrow terrace. The girl who had turned to meet him looked as fresh as the world beyond, her skin as white and fragile as the delicate gardenias growing at the foot of the terrace. Her eyes were enormous and soft, set in an unforgettable face. She had square little shoulders that made it hard not to glance at the breasts hiding under her silky rust-colored dress.

"I've never met you," he said, draping his arms on the back of a chair and regarding her irritably. He would have remembered. "You make it a habit to push your way into houses of people you've never met and demand to see them, do you?"

His headache had vanished. His fingers yearned to touch her

petallike skin. He wondered if she was a virgin and why he should even be thinking about it at ten in the morning.

She crossed the room. Her lips stirred and Ben found himself more aware of them than he wanted to be.

"Effie sent me."

His skull caved in as though hit by a wrecking ball. *"Mierda!"* he said.

His swearing was like enough to the French for Cecily to understand. Antagonism that was not of her making crackled between them as they faced each other, his arms hanging insolently across the back of that chair.

Maybe part of the hostile current was of her making, she amended. She hadn't wanted to come here. For the past three weeks, as she'd carried out Effie's orders, she'd resented being sent on this mission. She'd nursed a faint hope Ben Duvall would prove reasonable, a man driven from his grandmother because he was the very antithesis of her obstinate temper. Now, looking into eyes as angry and black as newly formed obsidian, she had a strong hunch she'd been wrong.

"You might as well clear out now," he said, his voice an unnervingly deep bass. "I'm disappointed to hear the old lady's still alive."

His deliberate harshness sparked Cecily's anger. Effie must have known he would be like this and had set her an impossible task.

"Really? In view of the time you spent with her when you were younger, I'd think you might show a modicum of concern for her."

He shifted, straightening lazily and hooking one thumb in his belt.

"I've also spent plenty of time in the company of ladies whose services I paid for. You think I should inquire after them?"

Cecily glared at him.

"Go back and tell Effie I want nothing to do with her," he said, and turned on his heel.

Realizing he meant to walk out on her, Cecily caught sharply at his arm.

"Look here! I've been in this city almost twenty-four hours, and I've spent most of them tracking you down. I'm damned if I'm going to leave without even talking to you!"

The sinews beneath her fingers felt like steel cables, tempered and hard. His simmering eyes narrowed.

"Lady, I don't happen to care if you camped on my doorstep all night! You woke me up. I haven't even had my coffee. And the last thing in the goddamn world that interests me is talking to you or anyone else remotely connected with Effie!"

He shook her hand off as though it were lint. By the hotness of her face Cecily knew it must look as angry as his.

"Oh, really? That's surprising, since you own a good interest in her business. Or didn't you know the whole thing's about to go down the drain?"

Something stirred in the set of his square jaw. She'd surprised him with her knowledge, she thought. Or struck a nerve. He made a scoffing sound and strode from the room.

After a second's hesitation, Cecily followed. She found herself in a small corner room with windows on two sides showing a patch of lawn brightened by clumps of orange lilies and spikey-topped Joshua trees.

Ben Duvall had flung himself into a chair at a round table and was drinking coffee.

"You don't object if I have breakfast in my own house, do you?" he asked with sarcasm. His hands, with long, restless fingers, reached out to cut a slice from a fat length of hard sausage which was sitting before him surrounded by blocks of cheese, papaya wedges, and glistening limes. With knife and meat suspended, he paused. The eyes she remembered from Effie's photograph—eyes unlike Peter's gentle ones—took her in at a glance. "You working with Effie?" His question, though disinterested, held the barest edge of disbelief.

Cecily was conscious of her dress from Martha's, of the choker of fine, rare amber that Effie had given her to wear with it. She knew she was, at that moment, very much Effie's woman.

"I am if I bring you back for the board meeting," she said cautiously.

He shot her a look. "Fix some coffee and milk if you want it. Effie's built her empire. If she can't run it alone, it's too damn bad."

"I don't use milk," said Cecily as he nudged a pitcher toward her. He was trying to patronize—to cast her as the little lady.

That was probably Ben Duvall's style. He was the sort of man women fell over themselves to attract and please, she guessed as she sat down opposite him. Good-looking? Not especially. But male to a fare-thee-well. It would be impossible to sit in a room with him and not be aware of his body. She tried not to notice the deliberately unconventional cut of his beard, or the way he sat easily with legs well apart.

She took a sip of coffee and swallowed in shock. The liquid slipping into her had the strength and bitterness of slightly thinned tar. The narrow mouth of the man watching her quirked with satisfaction.

"Amazing you like it straight," he drawled. "When I'm down here I use everything I can to soften the taste myself."

Nettled but not willing to show it, Cecily set her cup aside and splashed in milk. "I'm surprised you're not interested in what happens to Effie's business," she said calmly. "Especially since you'd welcome the money to build a prototype of the computer-radar system you and your partner have put together."

He stopped with his own cup halfway to his lips. "How the hell—"

"I talked to a pilot friend of yours. Some people at Aerotech. Quite a lot of people who know you, actually, and know about your experiments."

A maid in a white blouse and blue skirt appeared with a newspaper. Ben unfolded it with a crack. He meant to ignore her, Cecily saw.

"An old rival of Effie's is expanding into Palm Beach."

Silence.

"She's willing to fight them. She's willing to mount a show and try for a bigger share of the market—which means bigger profits for you as well as her. But she'll only do it if you provide the designs. She seems to think your work's brilliant. I can't say I especially agree, but those are her terms."

He stopped chewing but did not look at her. She'd gotten his goat with that.

"I'm not interested in design. I haven't been for years—if ever. There's no more to discuss."

Cecily's determination wavered. She wondered what else she should try. That she'd learned he'd been married? That with simple logic she'd seen that the end of his work for Effie coincided with his wife's tragic death?

Or maybe what he'd said just now was true. Her eyes moved desperately around the room as she tried to decide what to do next. They were caught by a stack of magazines on the bottom shelf of a corner cabinet holding mail and out-of-date issues of *Newsweek*.

Wordlessly she crossed the room and picked up one of the

magazines. "You read *Eighteen Karati* for the centerfolds, do you, Mr. Duvall?"

She riffled the pages of the elite Italian magazine given to jewelry design. He looked so caught out that she smiled.

"Damnation!" he said, and she could feel the breath behind his exclamation warm her face as he stood up. He seemed poised above her, half a head taller, and some force emanated from him that she could feel.

Their eyes locked. Cecily was conscious of their two wills clashing as they stood there, neither backing down.

"What the devil's Effie promised you for coming here?" growled Ben Duvall. "No, wait. I'm in no mood to hear. I'm going back to bed. No scheme of Effie's could pay me enough to go back to her, but if you're still here when I wake up, we can talk after dinner."

Someone had come to see her. Van struggled with drowsy eyelids and tried to remember. She'd been at the end of a long tunnel, but she was coming back now. Sometimes she saw faces. They popped up suddenly because of the tunnel. The sides of the tunnel curved and hid things until they were right in front of her.

"Do you know where you are, Vanessa?"

She'd been in the tunnel before. It made voices sound funny.

"Vanessa . . . do you remember where you are?"

This voice was gentle. Vanessa blinked and saw a face and tried to remember. It wasn't Cecily. It was a woman.

She looked around. She was in a room with a small desk. The door was open. It wasn't where you sat in the cold tubs and then got tied up in sheets. She hated that place.

"It's an office," she said. "Are you my social worker?"

"I'm a doctor, Vanessa. I'm Dr. Baumgardner."

"I've never had a woman doctor before."

"I know." The new woman doctor frowned and her mouth looked angry as she pushed around some papers on her desk. "And you've been afraid of your other doctors because they were men, haven't you, Vanessa? That's why you always did well on the ward but were marked as very nervous when a male psychiatrist saw you. . . ."

But it was getting too hard to make out the words of that voice droning on and on. It sounded so watery. Van gave up the effort. She hunted for that memory about who had come to see her.

Someone nice. A nice man. Had she seen a doctor somewhere who told her she was afraid of men? She wasn't afraid of this

one. He was a friend of Cecily's. He'd sat a long way from her
and been very quiet and then he'd said something that had made
her feel almost safe.

It felt like someone was holding her arms. She liked that
feeling, she felt so cold sometimes. There were voices whispering around in her tunnel. She wished they'd go away and let her
sleep.

Oh . . . where was she? She'd been with a lady doctor. She'd
been with a doctor and thought about other things and that
wouldn't do at all.

"I want a blanket," she said. "When is Cecily coming?"

She thought she said it. Sometimes she wasn't quite sure.

The man who had made her feel almost safe, his glasses had
slipped a lot.

"She's shivering," he'd said.

But nothing had happened.

He'd handed her his jacket.

She couldn't remember the rest . . . something about Cecily
. . . something about being moved. She hadn't asked where. She
hoped it was someplace warm.

TWELVE

CECILY CATLOW'S FACE HAD HAUNTED HIM SO THAT HIS REST HAD
been fitful. Now, in the small garden outside the breakfast room,
Ben Duvall sat with a foot cocked on the table next to him, a
scrawny kitten in his lap, and watched her sleep.

He'd bet she'd never been in a hammock before, he thought,
studying her high-heeled sandals and the way one hand clung
unconsciously to the netting under her. He'd bet she'd never
intended to nap there, either. She'd probably thought the whole
house had been deserted when it had closed down for siesta;
maybe even had started to wonder if he'd flown the coop.

Ben grinned at the thought. Never hurt to engage in a little
psychological warfare. So long as she'd been brought some
lunch—and he knew she had—he felt no guilt at all over leaving
her to cool her heels. He watched the stirring leaves of the lemon
trees where the hammock was anchored cast shadows on the soft
velvet of her lips. This garden background suited her. He'd like

to see her in jeans, though, with her hair ruffled up—odd, but he could almost picture her as a tomboy. He'd like to see her in bed with those brown eyes of hers staring up from the pillows, too.

Shaking his head, Ben brusquely dismissed such thoughts. If the girl was working for Effie, she must be as hard and ambitious as Effie herself.

His hand tightened on the icy rum drink in his hand at the thought of Effie. It was through her ruthlessness his pretty, laughing mother had died when he was only ten. It was through her unfeeling hunger for power he'd lost his wife and their unborn child.

Ben drained his glass. Perhaps the rum would make him numb. It was easier that way. Not to feel. Never to feel.

Living or dying didn't matter a damn to him. That was why he could get such speed from his single-engine jet, which in another, still experimental version, had been named the Peregrine. It was why he didn't shrink from testing equipment too new for other pilots to touch.

Damnation. He wished the girl in the hammock hadn't thrown out that about making money enough to install the CDTI system if he came back to Effie. He and his partner Pepe wanted the backing for that project so badly their mouths filled with saliva just thinking about it. Yet nothing could bring him back to Effie. The stubborn old woman ought to know it. She'd be eighty-five in December and was talking about a show. Incredible. Of course, there was always the likelihood Aurelio or Harry would succeed in cutting her throat first so they could rid themselves of obligations to her and Duvall.

Effie got about the same affection from her family she deserved. Still, for a fleeting second, he felt almost sorry for her.

No. No sympathy, no concern at all for Effie. He was merely curious because this girl had shown up; this girl, who must not be married to anyone in the family. He'd have heard if she was; he wouldn't turn his back on that pack of wolves without keeping tabs. He'd let Cecily Catlow speak her piece, then send her on her way.

She couldn't be as fresh and uncorrupted and capable of being hurt as that face of hers made him think. He wondered if she knew working for Effie meant she might have to lie, to smuggle, to kill and risk being killed.

A goddamned waste, he thought bitterly. He looked at the curve of her throat. Annoyed that she still hadn't stirred, he set his glass down loudly.

*   *   *

When her senses awakened, it was to the fragrance of cooling earth and the unfamiliar sounds of crockery clattering in a less than modern kitchen. Aware she'd slept when she'd only meant to rest a minute, Cecily forced her eyelids to part. Immediately her blood surged with resentment. Ben Duvall lounged in one of the nearby chairs, observing her. His foot was on a rung of the table beside him and his forearm rested lazily on his knee. A minuscule kitten that had joined her earlier now napped comfortably on his groin.

"Hope I didn't wake you," he said.

She could scarcely draw breath knowing she'd been watched as she slept. The discovery made her feel incredibly violated.

Nonplussed, she made a quick motion to sit up, forgetting the care with which she'd been forced to approach the hammock. The mobile net spun. Her feet hit the ground before she was in full possession of them. She'd have fallen except for the strong arm that came out to steady her.

"Doesn't do to move too quickly," her host said in a needling tone.

His eyes were fascinating—dark, brilliant. His hand still steadied her and his arm lay against her waist. For an instant Cecily feared he might pull her down against him, his manner was so filled with dry amusement at her predicament.

Heat flooded her face. She'd needed to keep the upper hand with this man, and she'd just made a fool of herself. Aware, as she had been at their first meeting, of the cablelike muscles twining beneath his flesh, she freed herself.

"It strikes me as pretty poor form to watch someone sleep."

"May be." His lips parted in a narrowly defiant grin. "I enjoy myself."

All at once she didn't know which one she found more taxing, him or Effie. Clearly she was being used as a pawn in some war between them, and she resented it.

"You know, you could at least be civil!" she snapped. "I don't consider being here one of the high points of my life. Effie's first demand was that I marry you if I wanted to work for her. I could have gone along with that. I could have barged in without knowing about your wife. Thank God I took time to find out a few things about you—Effie sure didn't bother to tell me! Is that why you quit working for her? Do you blame her for your wife's death?"

He'd risen, amusement gone, and his eyes were shooting fire. "No," he said in a harsh tone. "I blame her for her murder."

The words shocked Cecily. "That's—absurd!"

Although his height exceeded hers by only a few inches, he seemed to tower over her. Anger burned in his face.

"You don't know her very well, do you? What do you think, she's just some entertaining, strong-willed old lady?

"She cares nothing for anyone or anything except her empire and never has. You're naive if you can't see that—or maybe you're as treacherous as she is. I've had your bags sent over from your hotel. Dinner's at eight."

Before she could speak, his back was disappearing into the house. The depth of his rage echoed in his departing steps.

Cecily felt shaken by the explosion without knowing why. Her hand gripped her arm. It throbbed where he had held her. More uncertain than she'd felt in years, she moved toward the house.

The man she'd come to see hated Effie, was embittered beyond all reason. Surely what he'd said about Effie causing his wife's death hadn't been true! Still, she remembered that first chilling dinner at Effie's table. She wondered what the wife he'd loved had been like. She couldn't help thinking Ben Duvall's brand of love might be like a roaring flame, consuming its object in a wind of colors and heat.

The window in her room looked out on a wild hill hugged by hundreds of coffee trees. Cecily pressed her forehead against it. A woman must use her body as well as her mind, Effie had said. But Cecily knew she'd made the right choice in refusing to consider such a ruse with Ben Duvall.

Wondering why she felt so restless, she washed her face and looked out the window again. Almost two hours had slipped away from her by the time she glanced at her watch.

When she ventured out into the long hall, a houseman directed her to the living room where she'd waited that morning. The man she was to bring to Effie stood on the veranda beyond the open French doors, a drink in his hand. It was totally dark. Scattered candles, flickering in translucent white capiz shells, illuminated the shape of things just enough for her to see the set of his head and know he'd been watching her.

"How'd Effie find you?" he asked before they were even close enough for conversation. He came toward her.

Cecily tipped her head back to face him directly. It was, she suspected, the only way to hold her own with him.

"She didn't. I found her."

Indoors and out seemed to mingle in this room, filling it with the whisper of leaves, the sweet scent of flowers. Though only half an hour from San José, this spot seemed cut off from all other civilization.

"And what's she promising you if you succeed in wooing me back to her?" his deep voice asked.

"It's—personal."

He had asked the only thing that could make her stumble. Cecily dropped her eyes, aware of the closeness of his gaze. Music with a soft but insistent beat filtered into the room from a stereo. The houseman was placing silver on a small table draped in white that had been set up near the open doors.

"Drink?" Ben asked.

She nodded.

He moved toward one of the heavy, intricately carved cabinets that formed an entire wall. Taking out a glass, he filled it and freshened his own. By the looseness of his movements and words, Cecily wondered if he'd been drinking steadily since she last saw him. She sat down on one of two facing couches and felt the silken smoothness of well-worked leather.

"I wouldn't give you five minutes to hear what Effie wants if I didn't need money for my plane," he said shortly, handing her a glass and sitting across from her.

She couldn't suppress a smile. "I wouldn't be here if I didn't want to work for Effie," she countered.

"Because of what she can do for you?"

"Because of what she can do for someone very dear to me."

"A lover?"

Cecily drank quickly, thinking of Peter, avoiding the probing sharpness of Ben Duvall's eyes.

"No," she said. Only now she wondered if he'd interpreted her actions for exactly what they were. "For my sister," she said briefly, drinking again. The glass held rum mixed with fruit juices. The taste was unfamiliar, potent, another factor in the sense she was starting to have of moving and breathing in a world cut off completely from the one she'd left.

Ben stretched his legs out comfortably. It was a disturbing trait of his, the ease with which he displayed his maleness.

He was breathtaking with his black hair and the curl of his mouth daring anyone to get near him. But she was only thinking that because . . . because something about the climate here and the scent of flowers was affecting her. Because her brief time with Peter had awakened things in her blood.

"Haven't met the rest of the family, have you." His voice grated out in statement, not question. "Too bad. I hear Aurelio's divorced just now. Effie could have made good headway offering you to him."

Cecily ignored the insult. "It's you she wants."

He drained his glass. "She's using you as bait."

"She's using me as legs."

He stood up, refilled their glasses, and held hers down without releasing it. Their hands lay side by side. In the flickering candlelight of the room, his eyes themselves were flames.

"Effie tell you she introduced me to my wife? It suited her to gain access to the family, but of course I didn't know that then. Marguerite was just a kid—seventeen. Three years later she was dead because of Effie. She was pregnant at the time."

Cecily heard the bitterness in his voice, understood it at last. "I'm sorry," she said softly.

"Yeah. Well." He let go her glass and took a deep drink from his. "Since I no longer have dealings with Effie or her business, it doesn't much matter."

The houseman appeared with a steaming platter. "Ready, señor."

Ben stepped back, but not, she discovered as she arose, enough for comfort. For a moment they stood so close their legs brushed. His black gaze challenged hers. Almost inaudible the music played, its base line filling the moment, thump . . . thump . . . thump.

There was wine on the table, but Ben ignored it, bringing his glass with him. They ate in silence.

"It's beautiful here," Cecily said at last, looking out at the shapes of shrubbery and Joshua trees.

Ben paused, his glass in front of him. "Yes," he said briefly.

She tried to ignore the fact that his eyes, when they stirred, covered every inch of her.

There was the barest whisper of movement, then a squeak. The very young kitten she'd seen earlier launched itself into Ben's lap. The man took meat from his plate and fed small bits to it, half glancing at her with the first trace of anything she could recognize as embarrassment.

Cecily felt her chin giving way to its dimple.

"That's a big improvement over Effie's panther," she ventured.

"The panther's a psychological weapon." Ben pushed back his plate. "Effie uses a lot of them. Tell me why you think she's going to have competition and what she wants to do about it."

Cecily did.

"Why are you so set on working for Effie?" he asked when she'd finished.

They'd been served coffee and Ben was stroking the kitten. Cecily sensed something happening in the fluttering circle of candlelight at their table. Their eyes had met and now kept catching, sliding away and coming back to catch again. The low bass note of the music continued to throb, a drum, a pulse.

"She's smart. She's strong." Cecily tossed back her hair, her mouth hard. "I was caught in a scandal where I was working before. What else is there?"

"What else is there?" he repeated under his breath. "Christ Almighty, don't you have a mirror? Lots of men would kill to give you what you wanted!"

He stood up abruptly and walked toward the bar. After a moment Cecily rose, too, moving to the open French doors. She acknowledged a sudden tension but didn't know how to diffuse it. She felt as though she'd run a race with him and was fighting for breath.

"Here."

She turned as he handed her a fresh drink, his dark eyes slanting down at her. Her breasts felt hot and overfull. They drank in silence. She fixed her attention on the distant shapes of the garden. Never, she thought, would she forget this mellow taste of rum.

Ben's thumb was hooked in his belt. "Are you a virgin?" he asked.

Cecily's head swung back indignantly. She stared at him. "That's a hell of a question!" A small panic beat in her. She sipped again, quickly, eyes downcast. "No. I'm not."

"What happened?"

She faced him as steadily as she could. The night breeze stirred the front of his white shirt. His eyes had caught the shadows of the moon.

"I told you, there was a scandal. He was afraid I'd ruin his reputation."

They were silent, observing one another.

This has nothing to do with Effie, Cecily thought. It has nothing to do with anything.

Ben took her glass and set it aside. "You can go on to your room and not be disturbed, if that's what you want."

Her breath came hard. The entire evening seemed a prelude to this, a prelude she didn't understand.

"That's—not what I want."

He caught her and his kiss was hard. Not just urgent, as Peter's had been, but hard and certain.

Their mouths parted hungrily. Rivers of fire rushed through her. It was as she'd imagined with this man, the wind, the leaping colors, the consuming flames. In it she was totally lost, totally freed from physical boundaries to be carried skyward in a glorious column of sheer sensations.

They revolved slowly once . . . again . . . again, trying to draw closer to one another than clothes and bodies permitted. His hands devoured the curve of her throat, the softness of her cheeks. Then they were in another room, their clothes tumbling to the floor. Ben's kisses covered her throat, her breasts, the vulnerable flesh behind her ear, until she could not have given her own name for the whirling passion inside her.

"I don't give a damn if you are some trick of Effie's! I'm going to make love to you!" he said savagely.

And it was lovemaking. He was giving her pleasure as well as taking it. She could feel it before Ben laid her on his bed and his exploring hands, then his lips, began to shoot small sparks along the inside of her thighs.

Her fingers wound in his dark hair, hungering for its thickness. For one flashing, conscious second, she was shocked that this was happening. She had never experienced a touch like this, an ecstasy like this.

Her eyes had long since fallen closed. Through the meeting of their bodies she knew the strength of his arms, the flatness of his backside, and the wonderful feeling of fullness as at last he eased into her.

Within and without he possessed her. His strokes were even. His mouth caressed the pulse point on her throat until her head rocked side to side in frenzy. A wild, rushing feeling began to build inside her. She dug her nails into his flesh and clung to him, crying her frightened bewilderment. Her body, in his hands, was turning into molten gold, melted by his touch and set into motion, freed by fire to run toward its destiny.

THIRTEEN

ORLENA HAD MADE IT A POINT TO SHOP IN BRIGETTE'S, WHERE BLOUSES ran five hundred dollars; had hidden her amusement when, on her third visit, her name and position with Lyle & Co. were known there. The deference was satisfying, of course, but far more bankable was her certainty that she had established a useful connection—as she had at three other shops in Palm Beach that were called upon frequently to put together the endless style shows women with money to burn attended in the name of charity.

Now, balancing the Spode cup and saucer Brigette Chasen-Palme had served in her private office, she prepared to make the first use of those connections.

"We're so pleased you like our merchandise," Brigette was saying. "And we're delighted you've added your store to Worth Avenue. Such an incredible change from when Zumwald's was there!"

"A change for the better, I hope," Orlena said mildly. She thought Brigette's shoulder-length platinum hair had probably been bleached by the hands of a skilled technician instead of the sun that had left her skin golden.

"But definitely." The woman settling a wide gold band more snugly around a bare upper arm and propping thin elbows on her desk was a good deal more composed than Orlena would have expected. "Now then, what was it you wanted to see me about?"

Orlena set her cup aside. She had worn a white silk suit this morning, and a single large emerald set simply in gold hung around her neck. When she was seeking advantage, she was careful never to give cause for envy by wearing her best emeralds.

"I understand you're presenting the style show for the Friendship benefit luncheon. My company would be quite interested in coordinating jewelry for you. My daughter Lucy provided our services to the Overseas League a few months back, and I believe they were quite pleased. Naturally, the exposure would be good for us. In exchange, I think the prospect of seeing something by one of the newer shops might be counted on to move a few more tickets, don't you?"

She paused, vexed by uneasiness as Brigette Chasen-Palme's composed little mouth began to curve with something near to gleefulness. The shop owner shook her head.

"I'm flattered by the offer. Perhaps another time, Mrs. Lyle. But the Countess di Crichi is honorary cochairman of the event and she's volunteered something that will guarantee a sellout. She's a longtime client of Effie Duvall—I'm sure you're familiar with that name! She's persuaded Effie to furnish us half a dozen pieces from her private collection. It will be the first time in years anything of hers has been shown in public." Brigette Chasen-Palme was scanning an appointment calendar. "I'm scheduled to meet with her assistant, Miss Catlow, next week."

"Catlow!"

Orlena let the name escape like a hiss of steam. She saw the startled look of the woman across from her and calmed herself. "Ah, well. I'm pleased for you. And yes, perhaps we can work together another time."

She rose, shook hands, and made her exit sedately. Ten minutes later, with snapping steps, she threw open the door to the private offices above her long-sought new store on one of the world's most affluent streets.

"Come in at once!" She did not even slacken her pace as she sailed past Lucy's open door.

Her daughter looked up from the ad boards that she was consulting with a young man who was handsomely and prematurely gray and hurried after her.

"Orlena, what is it? I'm with Trace MacDonald. He has to get back to New York as soon as we approve the final details on those ads."

Orlena flung her handbag toward a fawn suede chair. She was well aware her daughter was gaga about their splendidly clever account executive from J. Walter Thompson, and Trace MacDonald was being more than attentive—though whether because of Lucy or because he recognized the profitability of their account she wasn't quite sure.

She made a quick decision.

"Perhaps he should be in on this. I think we can trust him. I think he's close to being part of our inner circle, don't you?"

Lucy preened, as Orlena had known she would. Orlena had been sure for some time that the ad man and her daughter were sleeping together when business gave them the chance. MacDonald was a purchasable item, unless she missed her guess, and far smarter than Jordan, who was running things in New York now,

she thought wryly. Amazing that the two men had become well
enough acquainted—even though it was through playing raquet-
ball—to spawn this working relationship. Perhaps she should
encourage MacDonald's interest in Lyle & Co. She could hardly
go astray providing Jordan with an extra prop.

"Well, we don't have a style show," she said when Lucy and
Trace MacDonald were seated in front of her. "In fact, we have
a very nasty stumbling block."

She raised an eyebrow at Lucy. "It seems your cousin Cecily
has found a job with Effie Duvall. I doubt you've heard the
name, but the woman—"

"Had at least three princes among her clients and made everyone in the business hate her because of the quality stones she
could lay her hands on. I know, Orlena."

Orlena felt her mouth tightening with impatience. There had
been no need for Lucy's little display of knowledge.

"You weren't listening, Lucy." Her voice was an icy trickle.
"I said Cecily *has* a job with Effie Duvall, who is very much
alive—and who, it seems, has titillated half of Palm Beach by
promising to show *her* jewelry at that luncheon—after being
retired for years!"

There was silence, during which she watched her daughter's
small eyes widen.

"Who is this Cecily?" asked MacDonald.

Orlena gave him her silkiest smile. "A shirttail relative of my
late husband, Trace. William tried to show kindness to her and
her sister, but . . . well . . . that shoot of the family was prone
to mental illness, I'm afraid. And violence. Crime. I'd hate to
spell it all out. If she's taken it into her head to be a stumbling
block to us, it's going to be very difficult!"

Lucy's fingers, short like her mother's, drummed on the arm
of her chair. "Well, that's just fine," she said peevishly. "The
ad slot we wanted in *T and C* wasn't available, either. Someone
else had already booked it for fall-winter."

"Who? That's not the page Tiffany's uses. Or Harry Winston.
Or Graff."

MacDonald smoothed his eye-catching gray hair. "Maybe I
can find out. Would you like me to try? I can use Lucy's
Rolodex."

A few minutes later he returned, looking as unflappable as a
man in advertising—or any job of consequence—ought to look,
Orlena thought with growing interest.

"It appears we've got ourselves a little vendetta here," he

said. "The slot you wanted, in the issues you wanted as well as a few more, were reserved a couple of weeks ago by Duvall Inc."

Orlena was silent a moment, then furious. Her green gaze fell on Lucy.

"She knows about Nola Levesque."

"That's impossible!" Lucy argued.

"Jordan didn't give his name when he went to see Van. It must be that! What else can it be?"

Orlena paused a moment. She suddenly felt like weeping. *They* thought she was made of iron, no doubt, these two watching her. They didn't realize how scared she was by these latest events. She'd learned her role to perfection long ago, and no one had ever realized how uncertain she was of her own abilities, or how weary from constantly, second to second, having to bluff.

Always afraid someone would find out her deficiencies, as she herself had through the years. Always fighting not just to camouflage those deficiencies but to correct them so they wouldn't trip her. Learning to read an account sheet though she'd barely passed freshman math in high school. Learning what percent of her gross it was safe to spend in advertising, and where it would be most effective. Always, it seemed, she had been scrambling and there was no time for fun. No time to go to the ballet and off-Broadway plays. No time to plan entertaining little dinner parties. No time to go to Paris and visit all the galleries she'd dreamed of as a girl.

She had her emeralds, of course, and without them she might not have succeeded. They allowed her to bluff. They allowed her to seem both rich and confident. Amusing, really, how much a woman was judged by what she put on her back or around her neck.

If you wore a designer label and stones of first water, you were looked on as rich. If you managed to keep a less than vacant expression, you were taken for clever as well. If you had the least initiative, made plans, gave orders, you were accepted as powerful. It was as simple as that.

Unless, of course, you relaxed for a moment. Orlena sighed. She never dared relax, not even during her massage.

"If it's not Nola Levesque," she said aloud, "then your cousin's nursed a grudge all these years over whatever you and your brother pulled in Marblehead. See the trouble you and Jordan caused with that childish prank of yours?"

Lucy, for no reason at all she could see, exploded, her hands curled into fists.

"It *could* be Jordan's fault, you know! Someone could have seen him when he went to the asylum. He's careless, but you can't admit it because he's always been your favorite!" She sounded near tears. "*I* set up the plan to get Cecily out of your way in New York—and it was an elaborate plan, and it worked, and what thanks do I get? The first time—the *first time*—something goes wrong you want to blame it on me! You never even *mention* Jordan!"

There had always been such rivalry between her children. Orlena shook her head.

"Lucy, dear, you're too sensitive. I was only mentioning possibilities. Anyway, what matters is the spot we're in now. This old woman Cecily's working for must be in her dotage by now, but she could ruin every plan I've laid if she decides to compete with us."

"I'd say we need to stop her then," said Trace MacDonald.

Lucy, after a moment's stiffness, nodded.

Orlena smiled, increasingly pleased with both of them.

"I'd say so, too."

William Lyle.

The name hung like a necklace of serpents' teeth in Effie's mind as she sat in her office lost in thought, spinning the wheels of her chair idly between her fingers, rocking slowly forward and backward, forward and backward.

Her eyes rested on the statue of Shiva, creator-destroyer, with his four waving arms. She had been looking over reports from Lynette in Sri Lanka. Then her mind had skipped. She had found herself thinking of William Lyle as a young man of thirty, and it was all the fault of the girl named Cecily Catlow, who had come into her life and tempted her to expunge the single great scar, the old, unforgivable pain buried deep in her soul.

And the girl thinks my grudge against William is over the designs he stole from me.

Effie chuckled harshly.

When she looked in a mirror at her stout, wrinkled form, she no longer could picture herself as Françoise Enyart, who had been so slender and straight and filled with energy when William Lyle became her lover.

Ah, but she still felt that former self!

What a naive young fool she'd been. She'd adored the daz-

zling young man who'd reached to her across lines of social class
and proper employer-employee relationships—discreetly, of course,
for everything was done discreetly in those days. Out of her love
there had flowed a floodtide of creativity. That William had
claimed credit for her finest designs was unimportant; that was
how things were done between a master artist and his assistants.

Then she'd opened a paper one day and faced the news of his
engagement.

"I need the connections this marriage will bring me," he'd
said bluntly. "And I don't intend to jeopardize it. This means
the end of any relationship but a working one between us."

It was at that instant, with pain stabbing into her, that she had
felt the first desire to see her own mark, her own small F. E. cut
on the jewelry she'd created. If she meant nothing to him, she
must mean something to the world, in her own right.

"Then acknowledge me as the designer of these pieces for the
International Diamond Competition," she'd said boldly. "You
owe me that."

He'd been indignant. "I owe you nothing!"

He fired her on the spot out of cowardice—she recognized that
with newfound wisdom. Ah, how quickly wisdom came! So hurt
she forgot all reason, she publicly claimed her work and he
denied it. That quarrel was all people knew of any connection
between Françoise Enyart (soon to be know as Effie) and William Lyle.

Turning so abruptly that Bibi, napping by her desk, was
startled, Effie wheeled to the window that gave her a view of the
sea and the margins of the island fortress she'd created. She
looked out.

"Madame . . ."

The voice behind her was soft in quality, though not in sound.
Rearranging her chair, Effie saw the slip of a girl whose persist-
ence in seeking her out just weeks ago had struck some chord
long muted inside her. So, she thought, the girl had returned
from Costa Rica. She tried to still her curiosity, to hide her
hope.

"Jenkins buzzed you, and when there was no response he
thought perhaps your intercom might not be working," Cecily
said.

Effie kept her gaze deliberately less decipherable than usual. It
was rare she indulged in daydreaming.

"I was thinking over the past four months' transactions in
sapphires," she lied. "Did you find my grandson?"

From the drop of the girl's shoulders Effie knew she would not like the answer.

"I found him."

Mounting the dais, Cecily walked to the window Effie herself had abandoned only seconds earlier. There was a locked look to her jaw that Effie had never observed before. An agitation to her step. She held herself too rigidly.

"I talked to him, but the effort was wasted. He won't come."

Effie frowned. Something had gone wrong. Something had upset this girl. She could see it in the tension in Cecily's hands, which she clasped cleverly behind her in hopes of hiding it.

"You did not try hard enough," Effie rasped.

The girl at the window looked back sharply. Her face was as white as a pearl.

"I slept with him," she said with an odd, angry dignity.

For a rare instant Effie did not know how to respond. This girl was a proud one. If she'd chosen such a tactic, she'd surely looked upon it as just another gamble. Nothing to be ashamed of. Yet something troubled her. Those words had been an accusation.

"So you failed," said Effie with generous mildness. "A pity."

The girl shot her a look and there was loathing in it. This one could go far in the world, thought Effie. She had fire.

"If that's all, Madame, I should like to go. I want to call my sister. I'm sorry I failed you in this. I'll do anything, *anything* else, to accommodate you."

Effie waved a hand. She began to wheel energetically back toward her desk.

"You will need a new number for your sister. I've had her moved. I talked to your lawyer while you were gone. It seemed to me recovery might be hastened in a private hospital. He agreed most enthusiastically and made the arrangements."

She heard a small sound like a sob. Cecily's hands had unclenched.

"Oh, Madame! I—I—thank you. I don't know what to say. . . ."

There were tears in those grave brown eyes of hers. Haunting they were, as soft and luminescent as brown star sapphires, Effie thought.

A scarcely known emotion stirred in Effie's breast. She'd seen greed from those around her in her life, and hate, and sometimes even craven, prostrate cowardice from those who had crossed her. But it had been a long time—a generation, perhaps—since anyone had looked at her with tears of gratitude. Not since—

A chill passed over her and she blotted out thought of the child she had wronged, the child she had lost, the late, last child, to whom she'd felt a genuine attachment.

"I am a fool," she said aloud. "My brain has softened. Call your sister now and see me tomorrow. We have odds and ends to prepare for a charity luncheon. After that's tied up, we can make our plans for a full-blown show."

FOURTEEN

"S HE'S WANTED THE SAME THING, ALWAYS THE SAME THING. IT'S ALL she's ever wanted to *see* for fifteen years!"

Mortimer Kopek, bald and shorter than Cecily was herself, threw pencils and fragile instruments into a wooden box on what had been his workbench, winking furiously as he talked.

"If I have no originality left, she has no one to blame but herself. I brought her fresh designs, but she said she knew what her clients liked. Heavy. Big." He waved his arms. "So now I'm fifty years old and being fired! Where does she think I'll find a job? Where does she think she'll find anyone to work for her? I—*I* could produce for her if she'd give me an ounce of freedom!" His flat thumbs struck his chest. He was red in the face.

Cecily looked despairingly at Jenkins, who had come with her on this mission. It was altogether the worst she'd faced in the ten days since she'd returned from Costa Rica. It was teaching her the high price exacted for being Madame Duvall's assistant. By morning she was being required to observe the craftsmen of Effie's workroom—the stone-setters, two goldsmiths, the skilled gem-cutter whose father before him had been enticed from Antwerp to work for Effie. By afternoon and into the evening she was expected to meet with Effie. Now, though, she was being asked to fire a man.

In looking over photographs of the jewelry created by Duvall Inc. in the last five years, Cecily's spirits had sunk at how repetitive, how unimaginative it seemed to be. Oh, yes, the designs showed off large, fine stones to good advantage. "But shouldn't a piece of jewelry do more than that?" she'd wondered aloud.

Effie, after a long, thoughtful look, had made her pronounce-ment. "We will find a replacement for Mortimer. Go tell him at once."

Now, standing in the design room with its slant-top tables, hearing this outpouring from the man just given his notice, Cecily felt guilt. She more than half believed that Mortimer's every word was true. Effie could be hardheaded. And dogmatic. She'd learned that already.

Maybe Mortimer *hadn't* been given a real chance to prove himself.

Where *did* Effie think she would find another designer who would please her on such short notice?

Perhaps she still nursed some secret belief that Ben would come back, thought Cecily crossly. And just for a second that thought of him brought back the shock, the bewilderment, the disbelief over what had happened that night in Costa Rica. She still could find no reason for it, not the rum they had drunk, not loneliness. . . .

She jerked her thoughts back to the present moment. "Are you making excuses or saying what you could really do?" she asked.

Mortimer glowered. "I'm telling you I *could* design things that didn't look as though they'd been made thirty years ago!"

"All right. You've got a week."

Cecily glanced at Jenkins. The secretary looked stunned, dismayed, more curved than ever as he shook his head.

"Miss Catlow, I admire what you did," he said as they stepped out into the hall again. "I think you were probably fair. But Madame will have your head. She does not like her orders disobeyed."

It was more than he'd said to her in an entire day before. Jenkins was so silent, so unquestioning, that Cecily sometimes wondered how Effie stood it.

Now she wondered if he'd been made Effie's secretary for that very reason. He held his tongue. He didn't argue. His skin was so nearly transparent, his manner so mild, that he became almost invisible except when needed.

Cecily gave him a teasing smile. Surely he couldn't enjoy an existence as colorless as the one he led.

"She'll have to find me before she can have my head, and I intend to make myself scarce until she's had time to cool down. Tell me, she doesn't send the panther out to fetch people to her, does she?"

He gave a pale, uncertain smile. "Not so far," he said. "But then, she always surprises me."

Cecily laughed. He had the makings of a sense of humor, anyway. Since the two of them seemed to be destined to work together a good deal carrying out Effie's bidding, she was glad.

"Thida! What are you doing up here? I have warned you!"

As they rounded a corner Jenkins snapped out the words with an authority Cecily wouldn't have thought possible. A figure had frozen in flight ahead of them, a small, slender Asian girl with glistening hair and an exquisite mouth.

Anger now lent a red blush to Jenkins's transparent skin. The girl they had surprised shrank back, quivering. She wore a white dress considerably more laundered and frayed than the uniforms of most of the household staff.

"I—I only wanted to see the picture," she whispered.

Nearby her a tapestry with a Buddha on it filled an entire wall.

"You will lose your job if you come up to see that picture again," Jenkins scolded. "Madame lets you work here, but kitchen workers remain in the kitchen. Do you understand?"

Nodding, with her face still toward him, she edged down the stairs.

"It's a good thing Madame herself didn't see you," Jenkins muttered under his breath. He seemed to remember Cecily then and looked embarrassed. "Madame doesn't like her."

Cecily was puzzled. "Why does she keep her on, then?"

Jenkins's eyes had followed the girl named Thida. There was sympathy in them.

"Madame's grandson Ben sent the girl here. I don't know the story. He flew people out of Phnom Penh when the Communists were killing people in the streets. Foolish. Dangerous. He's been courting death ever since he left Madame. He sent a note saying he was obliged to the girl." Jenkins paused and coughed discreetly. "Madame thinks perhaps they'd been intimate."

Cecily was silent a moment, imagining, against her will, Ben Duvall with his dark crest of hair and driven look, rescuing people from a world gone mad. She and Jenkins began to walk down the hall together.

"Effie told me when I came here that everyone who worked with her was related to her. Is Mortimer? Are you?"

"Not Mortimer. Not the men in the workroom. Their loyalty is guaranteed by their pride in working for her—and by a certain leverage she holds over each of them. The servants she screens ruthlessly. Not one of them would cross her." He looked down

at the brilliant blue carpet. "I'm on the fringes, you might say.
I'm . . . the product of an indiscretion committed by her first
husband."

For the second time that morning Cecily felt the discomfort of
being a newcomer to this small, closed empire.

"Oh, Jenkins, I'm sorry. I shouldn't have asked—"

"No, no. A logical question." He gave a perfunctory smile.
"Someone would have told you. Madame has been very good to
me. She's a charitable woman in her own ways."

At the door to his office now, he stopped and sighed, looking
with obvious reluctance toward Effie's throne room, into which
he would have to step now to tell her Mortimer had not been
fired.

"Just tell her I gave him a week," said Cecily, guessing what
was on his mind. "She can't blame you. If she has a chance to
cool off, I'm hoping she'll see some merit in what I decided."

Jenkins nodded. "I'm glad you sought her out," he said.
"She's showing more vigor than she has in years—since Ben
left."

Ben, thought Cecily, escaping outside and heading toward a
wild stretch of rocks on the far side of the island. Was she going
to be cursed to eternally hear that name? She walked quickly, the
legs of her trousers and sleeves of her white gauze shirt billowing in the wind.

Confused, as she had been since her return, she sat down, out
of breath, and pillowed her head against her hands. She had not
slept well in days. Every time she closed her eyes she found
herself seeing Ben Duvall's black, angry ones. She found herself
feeling the hardness of his arms. *What had happened between
them?*

Angrily she picked up a piece of rotting palm shell and hurled
it toward the beach. She had never had an experience like the
one with Ben Duvall. With Peter there had been attraction, a
tumbling head over heels into romance, a desperate hope for
commitment. With Ben there had been an explosion. The thing
that disturbed her, the thing that annoyed her, was that she could
not put the whole of it from her mind.

She felt as though she didn't know herself because of what
had happened in that quiet, sun-washed spot known as Heredia.
She'd never just fallen into bed with a man before. And she
hadn't even liked Ben. She'd found him bitter and unpleasant.
Damn.

She threw another piece of coconut shell, wrenching her shoul-

der with the force of her frustration. The only good thing that
could be said for the ten days that had come and gone since was
that her period had come and gone with them. She'd stopped
taking pills when Peter left her. She could have been facing a
real disaster because of her foolishness.

Cecily lay back in the warm, bright sun.

*Oh, come on, Cecily! Snap out of this mood you're in. You
know you've had everything to be happy about these last ten
days. Hasn't Effie done a wonderful thing for Van—more wonderful than you'd ever dared hope for? Haven't you got a job, in
spite of the fact you didn't deliver what Effie wanted?*

The thought of Effie made her sit up, open her eyes, and
concentrate. It was lunchtime now. Effie was usually in a good
mood after meals. She must get back soon and face whatever
wrath there was to be.

"I did not think you were a coward!"

Cecily had looked up at the sound of her office door opening
and now watched Effie roll relentlessly toward her. She was, in
spite of Effie's goodness to Van, in spite of her own bravado, a
little afraid.

"I didn't give Mortimer another week here out of cowardice,
Madame. I did it, I hope, out of good business sense."

The hoods were low over Effie's eyes. "You know more
about business than I do?" she snapped. "That's not the cowardice to which I refer. I refer to the fact you have hidden from me
for almost two hours—that you missed your lunch."

An imp of daring tugged at Cecily's mouth.

"Ah, Madame! Now *that* I prefer to think of as self-preser-
vation."

The words did not soften Effie. "When I give orders I expect
to have them obeyed!" she barked. She snapped her fingers and
Bibi, the panther, came close for her to scratch his ears.
"Remember that, or you will find yourself without a job," she
said in a voice of steel.

Abandoning her desk, Cecily came around to sit on a corner of
it, leaning forward earnestly.

"Madame, I think with the prospect of losing his job hanging
over his head, Mortimer will put that week to excellent use. We
will know by the end of it whether he is, as he insists, capable of
being more creative than he's felt free to be in the past."

Effie poohed in dismissal. Cecily hurried on.

"If he can show us something fresh, it will save us a great deal of time. You already know him, his personality, as he knows how to work with you. With someone new—once you found them—it would take many weeks to reach that stage. Time is precious. That style show is nothing, but we have those ads to fill—"

"A little pressure is good. Good for everyone," Effie said, rolling energetically around the desk and stopping again. "If you do not like pressure, you do not belong here."

Cecily sighed. Effie was the most exasperating person she'd ever met, and buying seven months of advertising in *Town & Country* without even one outstanding piece made up and ready to photograph was sheer lunacy. Apparently Effie wasn't the type to go from virtual retirement to full competition in modest steps.

"Next to having a wisdom tooth pulled without anesthetic, I can't think of a thing I find more fun than a little pressure. But seven full-page ads to provide for in less than three months? A major show to have ready two months after that? Madame, be reasonable!"

"You are impertinent!"

They glared at one another.

"I am being reasonable," Effie said. "I used to present three collections a year, and single-handedly."

Seizing the opening she'd needed, Cecily nodded.

"Now *there* is an important point. That's what we need now. *You* designing—as well as Mortimer! It's the only thing that can give this project your own imprimatur. *And* it's the only thing likely to give us the number of pieces we need."

Effie sat to one side, a stubbornness in the posture.

"Impossible. I do not have the touch. I dried up long ago."

"Sit down, Bibi. You have just been out," she added to the panther, who, having just settled at her feet, stood up again and trotted restlessly toward the door.

"Picasso didn't dry up. Dali didn't," persisted Cecily.

"Ah, but those are Spaniards for you! They also lack the taste to know when to give up lust."

"How can you say Mortimer is not inventive, then? How can you judge anyone who designs for you if you no longer have the touch yourself?"

Effie snorted angrily. She began moving toward the door, the ruby ring on her finger flashing as she propelled herself. In the hallway a faint step sounded and she stopped abruptly.

Cecily's gaze moved up just in time to see the opening door. She sat welded against her desk by the dark gaze sweeping from Effie to her. Her nerves gave a single, discordant jingle like discs of a struck tambourine.

Ben Duvall had entered her office in one easy stride.

"So." Effie's voice sounded oddly hoarse as she broke the silence. "You've come to your senses."

Like a housecat, the panther rubbed against Ben's legs. They were sheathed in black leather boots that drew attention to the lean thighs above them and made him look like some soldier of fortune out of an earlier century. Reaching casually down, he scratched the panther's head.

"I need money to test a new piece of equipment. Your pigeon here said you'd be willing to pay for my services."

Though he looked at his grandmother, Cecily could feel the heat that seemed to rage inside him.

"You may have your old room and Mortimer's studio," Effie said, starting past him with no further word of greeting. "I will see you at dinner. I have no time to spare you right now. I'm working on some designs of my own for a show in the fall."

Cecily had just enough of her senses left to hear, with disbelief, Effie's turnaround. The impossible, smug old woman!

Then she could hardly think at all for knowing she'd been left alone in the room with Ben Duvall.

He sauntered toward her, the light fabric of his slacks molded to his legs. One thumb was hooked in his belt. Cecily, instinctively feeling some need to protect herself, threw up her chin.

"You've got lousy manners, not even leaving a note behind when you decide to vanish in the middle of the night," he said, stopping in front of her.

The muscles of his face were tightly drawn. She remembered the hard feel of his kiss. She could hear him breathing.

"It didn't seem to me there was much to be said." She slid from the desk, avoiding him, though she kept her gaze locked warily with his own. Moving deftly behind the desk, she gathered up papers.

"You're right about that." He circled the desk, as restless as Bibi was, and as unnerving. He made no move to touch her, but his voice dropped lower and his mouth twisted humorlessly. "I've got to hand it to Effie. She used good bait this time."

Aware of his nearness, Cecily had to wet her lips before she could speak.

"I don't know what you're talking about. If you're here . . . I hope you didn't come here with any kind of expectations."

There was mockery in his eyes. It made her breathing falter.

"Now that I'm back with Effie I expect to get whatever I want," he said. "And I will. Or hadn't you heard how Effie spoiled me? She's always seen to it I got whatever suited me."

FIFTEEN

CECILY LOOKED OUT A LONG WINDOW DRAPED IN THE COOL CELERY green of the bedroom behind her. The others would be starting dinner soon. She'd sent word to the kitchen that she'd be absent tonight.

Blood surged through her veins as restlessly as the sea surged around the margins of Effie's island. Seeing Ben Duvall again face-to-face had been a shock. Worse, though, was the knowledge the shock had been a physical one, the jolt of her body responding to his, the weakening of bone and connective tissue because his dark gaze pierced her. She shifted, trying to rid herself of those sensations. What was wrong with her that she could be affected like this?

Angrily she ran a hand through the thick crown of hair grown suddenly too hot and heavy for her head. It was illogical that she should respond to any man like this, with the scars of Peter still so fresh. Even before Peter, she'd never been aroused by a man's mere presence or the sound of his voice.

Obviously, she thought in disgust, this was what had happened to her in Heredia. A simple, lightninglike sexual magnetism.

She needed something to divert her mind. In her office there was a current inventory of items on hand she wanted to study. She would get it and bring it back here.

The way to her office led past the back hall of the house where stairs descended to the kitchen. As she passed them her peripheral vision registered a shape. She looked again. The Asian girl named Thida was sitting on the stairs, head bent above a stenographer's notepad where she was scribbling furiously.

"Thida." Cecily spoke in a muted voice she hoped was also firm. "You're not supposed to be up here."

The girl's shoulders spun. The notepad catapulted from her hands to fall at Cecily's feet.

Regretting the fear she'd caused, Cecily bent to retrieve it. A gasp escaped her as her eyes deciphered the shorthand markings on the page before her.

"This is our conversation from Madame's table last night!" she said accusingly. "Who did you record this for?"

The frail girl at her feet had locked her hands together in supplication.

"No, please! It was not like that! I was practicing for dictation, nothing more! See, look! Just now I practice from a book. I've done nothing wrong!"

She snatched up a book from the stairs and shoved it at Cecily. The words on its open page matched the scratchings on the last filled page of her notepad.

"Please don't tell Madame Duvall," she whispered. The skin beneath her eyes was tight with fright. "I know I should not be here, but it's quiet. And to be here on the stairs—it's like in my father's house when I was a little girl."

Shame and sadness rose in her face as she looked down. Cecily felt a flood of pity she could not stem. Thida might be lying. Only there was something in her downturned face—a pride in spite of her fear and her frayed white uniform. She was so young, not twenty yet, Cecily judged. She must have been very young when she came here, and if her childhood home had had stairs like these, working here must bring equal parts of help and humiliation.

"All right. I won't tell on you." She returned the notepad. "But if I see you up here again, I'll report this. And don't you ever record another word of Madame's conversation."

"I—am very grateful." Thida held her supplies against her chest and began to retreat. "I will do you any service! My little cousin—without my job here I could not put food in her mouth."

Turning, she disappeared like a shadow. Was the girl actually supporting someone besides herself? wondered Cecily. She hoped she wouldn't regret this softness of heart. Continuing to her office, she found the inventory sheets.

Back in her room she studied them for a few minutes, then, with irritation, tossed them aside. Encountering Thida had diverted her, but now her mind was back on Ben Duvall. Could he really have taken to bed the incredibly young and easily frightened Asian girl? Impatient with herself for not concentrating, she started crossly in to wash her face.

A barrage of impatient blows jarred her door, making her jump. Effie, she thought, even before she opened the door and her employer wheeled in, stern-faced.

"What is this about not coming to dinner?" Effie snapped. "You look perfectly well."

Cecily gave her a long, thoughtful look and decided against evasiveness.

"I think you can guess why I choose not to come, Madame. I told you what happened in Costa Rica. I'd rather not have to sit down with your grandson tonight."

Effie brushed her hand against the air. "Don't be tiresome! All of us do things we'd rather not." She turned her wheelchair sharply, taking in every trace of Cecily's personal habits as she moved across the room. "Someday perhaps I'll tell you what I did to get those emeralds for William Lyle."

There was a roughness to the words. A sound of self-contempt. The subject sprang forth so unexpectedly that Cecily, though angered by Effie's lack of understanding, nonetheless remembered an earlier question about her great-uncle's wives.

"Madame," she gasped, the anger giving way to sudden, groping curiosity, "were you and my great-uncle lovers?"

Effie whirled. "Look at me!" she cried. "Do you suppose any man ever loved me? I am not a lovable woman. Ah, the great fools women make of themselves for that word! I chose to love the only thing worth loving—the only thing that returns your love—a business.

"Now come along. You've made us wait too long already for our dinner."

Cecily knew it would be futile to argue. The panther was waiting outside her door, and she and the animal followed Effie to the elevator.

Now he knew where little Cousin Cecily had gone. She was here in the Palm Beach area and making trouble again. Jordan sat in his sister's office, watching Lucy yak on the phone, and gloated at his newfound knowledge.

He had a score to settle with Cousin Cecily. She'd made a fool of him over that parure of emeralds. It was her fault, too, that he was stuck in New York while his mother and sister were here in the sunshine—that he'd been left in a stinking city he'd never liked, a figurehead in a branch operation, punished like a child for a single blunder.

He should be here, at Lyle's headquarters. He should have power. They should be listening to his opinions. After all, he was going to run Lyle & Co. someday.

Jordan glanced impatiently at Lucy, still on the phone.

He was glad Cousin Cecily had made trouble for Orlena. It gave him secret satisfaction watching Orlena dither and fume. Let her see what it was like to be outsmarted by a little bitch nobody. She'd lost her choice ad spot. She'd lost that fashion show she and Lucy had been drooling for. And she didn't have the guts to wipe out the source of her trouble.

That was the trouble with women. They were weak. He'd handle Cousin Cecily, and it would be a pleasure. First, though, he had to make sure Orlena moved him here. He'd get that through his little sister.

At last she was hanging up.

"That was Trace," she simpered like a lovesick cow.

"Do tell."

He'd always been able to make Lucy do what he wanted.

"Sounds like you're having a good time here."

He rose and strolled toward her chair.

"Well of course there's lots of *work*," she said, instantly defensive, as though suspicious he was going to try and take it from her. She stood up.

"I'd like to be here, too," he said. "Beaches at the doorstep. Nice weather. It's not fair for me to be left in New York, do you think, Lucy?"

"Well, Orlena—"

He caught her from behind, by her black hair.

"I want to be here, too," he said, jerking her so she fell back into her chair.

"Ow, Jordan! You're hurting—"

"I'll hurt you more if you don't do what I want."

Without loosening his grip on her hair he swung his elbows forward to imprison her shoulders. She was trapped in the chair now, unable to do more than scratch ineffectually at the sleeves of his jacket. He yanked her hair back harder, bringing tears to her eyes.

"Say you'll make Orlena move me here. Say it, or I'll hurt you some more!"

His sister was so stupid. She always whimpered and whined as if that would make him stop before she gave in. Jordan hadn't done this to her for a long time—five or six years now. Other women were far more interesting.

"Let—me—*go*!"

He pulled her head back until her eyes stood out and she was looking straight up at him. Jordan smiled slowly.

"Don't you miss me?" he asked, making his voice coaxing now. He leaned over so his breath brushed the side of her neck. He crooned into her ear, his lips against it even though his hold on her hadn't slackened. "I miss you, Lucy. That's why I want to be here."

He twisted her neck to one side until she whimpered. His lips were just above her other ear, his voice seductive.

"I'm the only one who cares about you, Lucy. Orlena never has. I'm the one who brought you Trace, remember? You like Trace, don't you, Lucy?"

She was crying now, small gulping mewing sounds.

"We've got to stick together, Lucy. Otherwise she'll never be fair to either of us. Don't you want me on your side, Lucy?"

She was uncertain. He could feel it in her body. He could also feel something else. Where they pressed against his arms, her nipples were growing hard.

"All—right—"

Lucy's answer was a whimpering gasp.

Jordan let her go.

He knew she'd never go back on a promise to him. She was too afraid of the consequences.

"Take care of it then," he said, eyes narrowing at her in warning.

By the time they got downstairs, Effie was discoursing so agreeably on the excellence of the report she'd received on sapphire production in Sri Lanka that her whole personality seemed to have changed. Ben was in the living room, standing impatiently and downing the last of a drink as they came in.

"You drink too much," said Effie as he turned back toward the bar.

He shot her a dark look, lifting a crystal stopper from a bottle and pouring.

"That a fact? Well, if you care so damned much, maybe you should have worried about it ten years back." He let the stopper fall back with an insolent clink and raised the glass to his lips. "Your conscience let you sleep nights, Effie? I can. With this."

He drained the glass of half its contents, the hand on his hip thrusting back the jacket of the black suit he wore. Cecily noticed the small finger on his left hand was crooked. A ruby the perfect color of Effie's, but much smaller, winked in the lamplight.

Effie made an angry sound. Cecily sat down next to Jenkins, feeling the tension and wondering whether this would become an explosion. Instead Ben's gaze swung to her. She steeled herself.

"I see you dressed for dinner," he said, observing her slacks and blouse. His mouth gave an unpleasant twist.

"Enough of this!" said Effie in a warning tone. "I'm hungry."

In the dining room Cecily saw immediately that this was not to be Effie's everyday dinner. There were three different wineglasses at each place instead of one. There were poached quenelles of fish as well as soup and salad before the main course, sliced breast of duck.

"So," said Effie, taking a spoonful of soup and looking over it. "Cecily, explain to Ben what plans we have made for the next six months—what we will have need of."

Cecily gritted her teeth. Effie was deliberately seeing to it that she and Ben must talk to one another.

"That *you* have made," she corrected. Doggedly she looked across the table and began to outline for Ben Duvall, as he asked occasional terse questions, his grandmother's projects: the charity luncheon now three weeks away, which seemed well in hand, the full show in October. "And ad space has been reserved in *Town and Country* September through February," she concluded.

"Damnation!" Ben pushed away the duck he'd hardly touched and stared at Effie. "Effie, you've bitten off too damned much. Don't you agree, Jenkins?"

The hoods above Effie's eyes did not stir, but the corners of her mouth raised, Cecily noted. Was she pleased by this anger, concern, whatever it was Ben was showing?

"I like a challenge. My customers are dying off around me, just like everyone else. New ones must be attracted if the business is to profit." She paused, looking at her grandson. "You must agree. Why else would you have come?"

Their gazes locked. Effie's, though it did not precisely retreat, was the first to slide away as she reached for her bell. Its sweet, sharp tone broke the silence, summoning dessert.

"My family needs to be reminded who runs Duvall," she continued, her voice a growl now. "Some seem to anticipate either my death or my senility. Otherwise they would never have caused the murder of Joao's best courier."

Ben looked up sharply. "Rosas?"

"Yes. Pedro Rosas. And the following day number two mine

was closed with labor problems and Joao was approached with an offer to sit on the cartel's board if he'd sell.''

Ben made no comment, drinking slowly from the cup of coffee just poured for him. A silver tray was being offered now, and Cecily looked, then looked again with a start at the dessert displayed there. The sophisticated dinner just concluding was being brought to its finish with fat sugar cookies, tops glittering thickly with the sweetness that gave them their name.

Ben, too, looked startled at the sight of them. His eyes, as though involuntarily, shot to Effie.

"You make them?"

The question was brutally harsh.

Effie's eyes were heavy-lidded. "I have better things to do with my time. The cook made them." She paused, then added with brisk indifference, "From my recipe."

Ben's hand moved to the tray. Slowly, woodenly, as he watched the old woman watching him, it returned a second time.

Jenkins broke the silence, his voice thin and nervous, his subject irrelevant.

"I was thinking, Madame, that one of the motorboats ought to be replaced this year."

Cecily knew she had witnessed something symbolic in the serving of these cookies. Had they been a favorite of Ben's once upon a time? One Effie made herself?

"If I'm to produce a design, I must work at night, when my ideas are best," Effie announced when they had finished their coffee. "Come, Bibi. Come, Jenkins. I want your advice on something."

Not anticipating the abrupt departure, Cecily found herself left alone in the dining room with Ben, her coffee cup still in her hand. A china clock with a high-pitched tone struck faintly.

The maneuver of leaving them here was so pointed it felt absurd not to comment on it.

"Effie's not exactly subtle, is she?" she said under her breath.

Ben pushed his chair back. "Never."

Cecily dropped her napkin onto the table and stood up. "I wouldn't have taken her for a romantic."

He looked at her, derision in his eyes. "She's not. She's pragmatic. She gets what she wants."

There was taunting in the words, and a deepness as they left his throat that made her wet her lips and look away from him. She took a breath.

"Look, just for the record, when I slept with you it was—an

isolated incident. A one-time whim. Because I was getting over someone else. That's all.''

She saw his jaw shift.

"That a fact?"

She nodded. "So you see, you haven't been dragged here by any ruse of Effie's.''

She started around the table but he blocked her way.

"I know what Effie's like better than you do.'' He caught her arm. "And just for the record, I'm capable of taking all the sex you want to offer and not giving a damn. Remember that, if you mean to play Effie's game.''

"Let go of me. I've said all I have to say on the subject. Think what you want!''

She twisted, trying to hide the shiver their contact produced in her.

His lips curled as he observed the tremor.

"What's the matter? You fighting off one of those whims? Or is that just part of the act? Effie's trained you well.''

He had drawn her so near that she could see the fine lines fanning out from his eyes. The heat of his more powerful body seemed to be melting hers.

"You conceited bastard,'' she said between her teeth. "Take your hand off me.''

His eyes burned into hers. His mouth was set.

"Sure thing,'' he said, and freed her, his hand moving on to pick up the glass of now diluted liquor he'd abandoned on a sideboard when they'd come into the dining room.

Cecily felt herself momentarily paralyzed before his lingering gaze, and in the fraction of a second before she moved there was a commotion in the living room. The front door had opened. A welter of voices erupted, all of them angry. Effie spoke sharply from a distance, from the direction of the elevator. Ben turned and moved through the door and Cecily stepped past him.

A silver-haired man stood at the center of the room, a guard restraining each arm. The chief guard, Raoul, held the tip of a rifle to the stranger's head.

"Let him go,'' ordered Effie, wheeling toward the scene, which also included her butler, Charlie, and another servant. Jenkins, with the panther, was hurrying behind her.

"Madame, we took this from him.'' Raoul displayed an automatic pistol.

Effie grunted, bringing her chair to a stop. "Were you testing my security, Aurelio? The board doesn't meet till tomorrow.''

The man's face was enraged and garnet with fury. "My son has lost the use of an arm forever because of you!" he cried.

Effie's eyelids were heavy. "He intended that I'd lose my life, which is far more troublesome. Apparently you were fool enough to intend the same."

"Ha!"

Aurelio, freed by the guards, tugged arrogantly at his cuffs, where large emeralds flashed. His shirt was open, revealing a silver-haired chest and two heavy gold chains, one with another emerald. Cecily knew she was seeing the brother-in-law of Effie's first husband, one of two original partners in Duvall Inc. surviving besides Effie.

"I carried a gun to protect myself from you!" he said, taking a step toward Effie's chair. "You are senile! A madwoman! No longer competent to run Duvall. And if you do not agree tonight to step down, the board will force you tomorrow! Joao will not be here to help you. Our votes will equal yours. I am—all of us are—sick of dancing to your tune! I will be the new head of Duvall. That is more fitting punishment for you than killing!"

"You seem pretty sure of your votes," drawled Ben, lounging in the doorway. "You push Joao off a cliff to stack the cards in your favor, did you?"

Aurelio whirled at the sound of his voice.

"You!" There was venom as he spit the word. "What are you doing here?"

Ben sauntered forward. Did he care about any of this, or was he simply at war with everyone? Cecily wondered.

"Came for the board meeting," he said, his thumb in his belt. "Thought I'd vote my ten percent."

Cecily sensed she was seeing lines drawn for a fight tomorrow.

"Show my brother-in-law to a guest room," Effie said, beckoning the butler. "Get him dinner if he requires."

Her upper lip raised over ivory teeth. She stroked the panther's head.

"I advise you to stay in your room until called to breakfast, Aurelio. Bibi often likes to prowl at night."

SIXTEEN

SURPRISE. THAT WAS HALF THE SECRET TO SUCCESS IN BUSINESS, EFFIE thought. And by keeping Cecily chained to her desk with work and out of sight, she had seen to it that the girl would be a surprise to most of the board members now assembled.

She looked with satisfaction at the somber-eyed girl walking down the hall beside her. Cecily was intelligent. A little annoyed because she'd been forced into company with Ben last night. Good. It proved she had fire. A little wary because she sensed some purpose in keeping her out of the thick of things today. Good. It showed she had a survivor's instinct.

With such qualities, this girl who had come to her in the last years of her life could be shaped very nicely. Effie entered her boardroom with its quiet, beige linen walls, enjoying the whispers that circled the conference table as eyes turned toward Cecily.

"Ah, Aurelio. I hope you slept well," Effie said in a strong voice.

She turned her chair skillfully into the vacant spot at one end of an oval mahogany table. There were vacant spots at either side of her. Cecily took one of them.

There was no sign of Ben. He had been such an unpredictable child—like his mother before him. For an instant there lodged in her breast a loss, a sadness, an emptiness of something never known. Then she looked down the table at the rest of the dynasty she had spawned.

There was Harry, her grandson from her first marriage, forty-ish with fading good looks and from his villa in Bangkok overseer of her ruby supply—smuggled in from Burma.

Next to him sat Lynette, still blond and attractive in middle age and wearing one small, tasteful cornflower sapphire from the mines she controlled in Sri Lanka. She had come to the family through Effie's second son, now dead twenty years, as all her offspring were.

She passed over Aurelio, who sat at the end of the table opposite her, by his position directly challenging her. She would deal with him later.

On his right and next to Cecily was Kim, an obese, moon-faced, perspiring Japanese, who owned the giant pearl export firm in which she'd become a partner by marrying Kim to the daughter from her second marriage. The girl had resisted with tantrums, understandably repelled by his corpulence. She'd refused to see the advantages for Duvall—for her as an heir to Duvall; had not been appeased by Effie's suggestion that she could take a lover. Before she had even borne a child, she had killed herself.

"Joao's not coming, I understand," said Kim, glancing at the empty chair to Effie's right and then at his watch. "Troubles with his heart again, I expect. If we could begin the meeting, there's a late plane I'd like to catch."

Effie's fingers drummed the table. Perhaps her unpredictable grandson, issue of a last and unexpected daughter who had been so stubborn she'd refused to marry, was not even coming.

The door opened.

"You are late," said Effie, barely glancing up.

"Hadn't had a tetanus shot in a long time." Ben strolled toward the table. "Thought I'd better go to the mainland and get one before I sat down with this group."

There were angry sounds. A gasp somewhere.

"Did you know . . . ?" Lynette began, looking fearfully at Aurelio.

"Not until last night." Aurelio sat calmly in his chair, his silver hair and motionless pose giving him an air of competency.

So, thought Effie, observing. Aurelio had turned Lynette.

Her eyes traveled down the table again as Ben took his place.

"I understand there is some dissatisfaction with how I am running Duvall," she said without preamble. "Perhaps we should discuss that first. Then I'll tell what I require of you."

There was no response. Kim had taken a folded handkerchief from his pocket and rubbed it down over his mouth, then rubbed it again. Lynette reached uneasily for the pitcher of water that sat on the table and filled a glass, splashing. Harry, with a sideways look, was watching Aurelio, who glowered now from eyes in which hate burned.

"Ah. Perhaps I was misinformed," said Effie. "In that case we will hear reports."

From under lowered lids she watched Cecily's face and knew satisfaction as she saw the disbelief that showed there as the volume of stones and dollar worth of mining enterprises were reported around the table. They'd begun as merely the avenues to bring her the stones she needed, the beautiful, superior stones she'd craved to make her name spoken as no other jeweler's, least of all William Lyle's, had ever been. She'd chosen her first husband because he'd had some ambition, and because he was the third generation in a family of little known gem merchants who had settled in Brazil. She'd seen the possibilities: his cousin Joao already branching off to mine for diamonds, his pretty sister about to be married to a Colombian who sold emeralds to the Duvall merchants, another sister available to make another good match—and willing. Such matches had helped the business of families in the trade since time immemorial.

The difference was, she had seen the possibility to forge an empire through such family ties—an empire that would encompass not only diamonds, not only emeralds or rubies, but all, all that she needed. She would have the best stones from each mine with no competition, no fear of supply being cut off.

Her plan had worked. The lesser goods, for which she had no use, had been sold on the open market. And the companies that had sold them, controlled by her though never identified with her, had made the puppet owners she'd created very rich.

"An excellent report, Lynette," she said as the summary of sapphire production was concluded. "Your written reports have been very thoughtful lately—very forward looking."

Lynette wet her lips and looked uncomfortably at Aurelio. "I—thank you, Madame. Margaux is responsible for them. She's very interested in the business."

Effie grunted. She could never remember which of Lynette's daughters was the giggler and which was the quiet one. Apparently they had never caught her interest enough to make the effort. She would do so now.

"My own report is brief," she announced. "There will be no profits paid out from jewelry this trimester. I am putting them into advertising and a full show in October. My new assistant, Cecily Catlow, will be handling details. I expect that she will have your full cooperation."

Like a diamond turning lifelessly until it caught the light, there was silence. Then a howl of protest rose around the table.

"Quiet!"

Effie lifted her hand, but they paid no heed to her.

"Advertising! Ridiculous! A waste of money!" sputtered Kim.

"You are—commandeering our profits?" Lynette gripped the table's edge.

"You see, she is dangerous. The control of Duvall does not

belong in her hands," Aurelio said, looking with expectation at those around him.

Ben sat with his chair tipped back. "You want to put it to a vote?" he asked, speaking for the first time since he'd joined them. "The way I figure it, Effie and I have fifty percent of the votes between us and you have forty."

"You little *swine!*" Lynette stood up and shook a finger at him. "You haven't shown your face here in ten years. You don't do a damned thing to deserve your percentage! Stay out of this!"

Effie listened with a mild enjoyment. The members of her board had grown altogether too complacent.

"Perhaps Ben likes incompetence," Harry said with sarcasm. "Perhaps he doesn't realize his grandmother has grown too old and out of touch to know her new assistant was fired from her last job for being a thief!"

Effie watched with interest as Ben's eyes swung in brief amazement to Cecily, who had lost her color and now, with stung pride, lifted a small, set chin.

"Good God!" cried Kim. "I say we're fools to put up with this. I say Aurelio should take control—"

"Shut up," said Ben, his chair tipping sharply forward onto all four legs. Harry twisted to face him.

"You inform yourself well of things, Harry," Effie sneered. "How unfortunate you didn't inform yourself of loyalty."

But she'd spoken too late.

"What's in this for you?" Harry was demanding, red-faced. "You want back in the ruby trade? Or is this some other little whore Effie's picked up for you for her own convenience?"

The last word was muffled as Ben, jerking him to his feet by the front of his collar, sent him sprawling back into the table with a punch to the mouth.

"Enough!"

Effie's palm struck the table. Maneuvering one wheel of her chair, she pressed a buzzer in the floor. It had been a wise decision leaving Bibi with Jenkins so he would not misinterpret such excitement, she thought.

Now she watched as the door opened and a man strode in and everyone turned. Surprise . . . surprise was always the key.

"Perhaps some of you haven't heard Pedro Rosas was murdered, shot when he was en route with a shipment from Joao." She began to glide slowly down one side of the table. "Aurelio, whom you are so eager to place in my chair, is the one you may thank. He squealed to the cartel, told them who the principal owner of the mining company is and where the best goods go. The man who has joined us was in their employ when the contact was made. He finds it more appealing to work for me now.

"Why are you so pale, Aurelio? Are you afraid the others may lay the losses this has caused at your door?"

Even now the old fox was calm—or pretending to be.

"These are—"

She cut him off.

"Lies, Aurelio? The only lies which have been told here are about my assistant!"

The girl Cecily was looking at her with sparkling, fierce admiration.

Effie continued around the table, behind Aurelio, behind Harry. No one spoke. Returning to her place, she again pushed the bell in the carpet. This time a striking young man who moved with ease in his white suit and studied the group with the long-lashed eyes of his Spanish blood came in.

"I do not like treachery," Effie said severely. "I will not have it in my company. Aurelio, I am sure you recognize your son by a certain secretary? He has not had the advantages of your legal son, whom you sent to kill me, but I think he will prove most adequate in charge of your mines."

Aurelio slumped in his chair. His face had gone as pale as his silvery hair.

"No! No—I . . . I was mistaken about your competence to run Duvall. I see that now. And you misjudge me. I will serve you well—"

"You will not serve me at all! When you return to Bogotá you will sign the papers waiting for you. You will name Martin as chairman of your corporation and retire to the country. Otherwise you will never see another nickel from your own mines."

"No, please! I will be disgraced!"

"You should have thought of that before you crossed me. Sit down, Martin." She looked sharply around at the others. "To remind you all of this, I am cutting the vote of the Colombian mines to ten percent. The remainder will be split—half to Joao, who has always been loyal, and half to me. Do you wish to vote on that?"

No one moved. She flicked an eye to the first man she'd called in, the one now in her service.

"See Señor Solis to the mainland."

"I'll see you dead!" Aurelio screamed as his arm was seized. "I'll see you pay for this!"

"I shall tell you each now what stones I anticipate needing for the show I plan," Effie resumed, ignoring him. "When we have finished with that, we'll adjourn for dinner."

Cecily would have welcomed a chance to escape this gathering in Effie's living room. Looking at the others, captives awaiting a meal they did not want, milling restlessly and talking little, she sensed most felt the same.

Effie's family stood in small groups. The women, Lynette and her daughters Maigrette and Margaux, had changed for dinner, with sapphires glittering on arms and ears. In spite of her pencil-thick chain of gold with its central love knot, in spite of the coffee-colored silk dress she wore, she felt like an outsider.

She was not of the family.

She was not linked to Effie or any of them through blood or marriage.

No wonder they resented her, she thought darkly.

For some reason she hadn't expected that. She hadn't, until that meeting, realized she was an interloper in a closed society. Now, if she hoped for acceptance, she'd better work at it—and at selling Effie's plans.

She walked toward Maigrette and Margaux. Lynette's daughters were twenty-four and twenty-five respectively, both blond, both with eyes as blue as the sapphires coughed up by streams and riverbanks on their distant island. Their conversation stopped at sight of her. Cecily smiled.

"Hello," she said. "So one of you's been doing the reports for your mother? Effie's awfully impressed."

"I like the work," said Margaux somberly. "Mother hates it in Colombo, thinks it's boring. But as long as you've got work to do and someone to talk to, it's not bad." She shrugged. "I've got my sister."

The words pierced Cecily's heart and loneliness trickled out as she thought about Van.

"I've always thought Ceylon—Sri Lanka—must be quite lovely," she said. "I'd like to visit it."

The sisters looked at each other. Maigrette laughed self-consciously, the sound thin and grating. She seemed giddier than Margaux.

"Maybe Effie will send you to see us," she ventured.

Both girls dissolved in laughter.

Aware of some joke between them, Cecily frowned.

"Do you always come to the board meetings?" she asked, determined not to be put off by it.

Margaux recovered and looked at Cecily with a trace of apology. "Whenever we can," she said.

"Uncle Joao has a handsome son who usually comes with him," said Maigrette. "And after all, our share is only five percent. Why not consolidate?"

For a moment Cecily was unsure what to make of the statement. Was it offered in jest? Or had Effie instilled in her heirs a hunger for useful alliances? She felt a chill.

"I have a feeling we're both looked on as outsiders here," Martin said a few moments later, coming up and steering her away from them. An accent gave a lovely roundness to his words. "I am grateful to Madame Duvall and intend to serve her faithfully. Tell me, please, about this show she's planning."

Cecily began to do so with enthusiasm. She, too, was grateful to Effie and by winning support for Effie's project could start to merit the job—and the opportunity to further her own ends—that she'd won.

On the other side of the room, by the bar, Ben was watching them. The realization rattled her, made her concentration lag, made her wonder if he, too, was judging her and why he had come back. Did he care about his grandmother and her business as his intervention at the board meeting seemed to suggest, or did he care only about money for his plane?

Lynette, inclining her head so the light caught highlights in her feathery blond hair, inched in and began to edge Martin back toward her daughters.

"You'll excuse us, won't you, Miss Catlow? I want to talk to Martin a minute."

Cecily smiled stiffly, remembering Maigrette's blithe comment about consolidating her mother's five percent. The possibility that all the people around her lived and made matches from such motivation was overwhelming.

"Snatched him right away from you, huh?"

Startled by the abrasiveness of the words, she looked up to find Harry standing beside her. He held a fat glass in his hand. "Scheming broad, Lynette," he continued. "You better watch out for her."

Cecily looked through him. Even before he had smeared her in front of the board with his reference to the scandal at Landis and Oxenburg, she had known she did not like Harry. He was smug.

He stood too close and the waves in his hair were too carefully placed.

"Look, no hard feelings about calling a spade a spade this afternoon," he said with a genial lift of the eyebrow she supposed was expected to charm her. "I mean, hell, when I heard the old girl had hired an assistant I did some checking. I've got an interest in Duvall; I had a right to. Maybe what I heard was wrong."

Cecily regarded him coldly, not about to answer.

"Guess I was wrong to think Effie might be entering some kind of second childhood, too," he said, grimacing.

"Yes, I think so."

She was pleased to see his lower lip was swollen and purple. The moment when Ben had inflicted it had played through her mind more often than she wanted. It was hard to imagine Peter striking anyone. She supposed it was wrong for anyone to approve of such an act, and yet . . .

"If you're half as smart as you are pretty, maybe you'll really bring off this renaissance the old girl's planning," Harry continued.

She gritted her teeth. "I certainly hope so."

"Need anything from me, just ask. Okay?" He draped an arm over her shoulder as she tried to turn away. "Let's see if Effie won't send you out to check on me. I'll show you a good time and fill you in on all the politics of this outfit."

She shrugged off his embrace. "Why don't you tell me where you get your rubies and how they arrive here. I'm not too clear on that part of the operation yet."

Nearby, one of the Sri Lanka girls—Maigrette, was it?—laughed in her nervous, high voice.

"I'm not sure Effie would want you to know that," said Harry, leaning toward her, his tone suggesting she must treat him well to learn the answers.

"They're mined in Burma and smuggled out so he can pass them off as something from his second-rate mine," a scornful voice answered. It was Ben. "He finds peasants desperate enough to take the risk, and as insurance they won't squeal, he holds their wife or kid hostage till he gets the goods. Isn't that how you've set it up, Harry? How many got their throats cut last year? Two? Three? It doesn't matter much, since he's the only one who knows how they hide the stones."

"You bastard!" Harry snarled. The hand with the glass in it drew back as though to take aim at Ben's face.

Hate flowed between the two men. Ben's jaw tightened. Maigrette and her sister and Martin had turned to watch.

Ben tipped the glass in his hand in salute. "Better a bastard than a fool."

Cecily, feeling she had had enough of conflict in this house, this family, turned her back on them and walked quickly toward the sliding doors and out into Effie's courtyard. Smuggling, she thought. And murder! The first time she'd met Ben he'd warned her they were part of Effie's web.

Her breath came raggedly. Was it worth it, joining forces with this family? Was her own hate as bitter and evil as the deeds committed in the world of Effie Duvall?

She leaned one hip against the edge of a Moorish fountain splashing in near darkness. She felt far from the lighted arches of the house and yet too near. A footstep sounded. Looking up, she saw Ben. He had followed her, or maybe like her he had simply had his fill of the seething rivalries in the room inside. He stopped and looked at her.

Cecily felt awkward at cutting off his escape to solitude, if that was what it had been. There was a side to Ben Duvall that puzzled her, occasional flashes of something likable beneath the unpleasantness.

"I enjoyed seeing Harry's lip just now. Thanks for punching him."

It was hard to get the words out. Hard to admit the humiliation she'd felt when the ugliness of the past had been thrown at her.

"I'd been hunting an excuse. That's all." His voice was flat.

Slowly swirling the contents of his glass, he studied her. "Any truth in what Harry was accusing you of?" he asked abruptly.

"No."

There seemed no point in further denial. She hugged her crossed arms tighter against her. It was a gesture she'd learned in childhood, an instinctive self-support when she knew no other was forthcoming. He tipped his head back, killing his drink.

"Effie's right. You do drink too much," she said without knowing why.

As though caught off guard, he froze for an instant.

"What difference does it make?" He lowered the glass as his eyes picked her out in the starlight.

Cecily shrugged.

There had been an edge to his voice. There was always an edge to him. More and more she found herself wondering what had created it.

"You loved your wife."

It was a statement, not a question.

"I don't know," he said shortly. "We were both just kids."

In spite of the answer she sensed the match had differed somehow from other ones made in Effie's empire. He stirred impatiently.

"Anyway, love's just a catch phrase. A word that's thrown around. Something people believe in because they want to believe in it, like religion."

Cecily felt a sudden ache she could not explain. When she looked up he'd vanished back into the house. She stood in the moonlight and in spite of the murmur of voices spilling out, she felt alone on the planet, cut off from a warmth and a shelter for which her heart was longing.

Slipping into the house by a back entrance, she made her way to her darkened office and dialed the number of the one person whose voice could push back the loneliness.

"Hi, Van," she said a moment later. "It's me."

SEVENTEEN

"VANESSA, DO YOU KNOW WHAT SEVEN THOUSAND FOUR HUNDRED seventy divided by nine is?"

Vanessa considered the question briefly. "Eight hundred and thirty."

"What's twelve and a half percent of forty-two thousand dollars?"

The new psychiatrist, a lady with iron-gray hair, had stumbled across this game their last time together. Actually, Van thought ruefully, it was her own fault. When she'd come in that last time, the doctor had been on the phone discussing hotel rates.

"A hundred forty a night for seven nights," she'd been saying. "That's—"

Van had supplied the answer.

The doctor had stared at her, figured briefly on paper, then stared again.

Vanessa sighed now.

"Twelve and a half percent of forty-two thousand is five thousand two hundred fifty dollars."

"Very good, Vanessa! You're amazing."

The psychiatrist smiled so brightly and looked so aggressively chipper that Van felt awkward.

"That's how it works when you have a screw loose, isn't it?" she ventured. "You're twice as good at something else. At least that's what I've read."

"That's a negative way of phrasing it, Vanessa. We don't get well by being negative. . . ."

We don't have to worry about getting well, thought Vanessa. *I* do.

She was not afraid of this new doctor, but she didn't especially like her, either. The woman reminded her of her kindergarten teacher, who was always unfailingly cheerful. Funny she could remember that. . . .

"You weren't paying attention to what I've been saying, Vanessa. We need to use every minute of our time together, you know."

"I suppose so." Van tried to look however she was expected to look. "But you ought to see it my way."

"Your way?"

The doctor looked somewhat insulted. Shocked a patient would even suggest it. Van hastened to smooth things over.

"Well, it's just that I've been going through sessions like this for . . ." She couldn't remember for how long. "For a very long time. They're getting pretty repetitive."

The woman behind the desk tapped the point of a pen in angry beat. "I see."

Oh, rats. I've messed it up again, thought Van. And I really do want so much to get out of this place.

Not that the place wasn't nice. It was so much prettier than the state institution, and there weren't any bullies like Miss Mundey. At least she hadn't met any.

But she'd been thinking more about getting well of late. Once it had scared her a little. Now she *wanted* it. And she'd realized something, she'd realized that in spite of her relapses she seemed to bounce back from the darkness and awful tunnels faster than other patients. That must mean she wasn't as sick as they were, mustn't it? She'd been almost well as a teen—several times—she knew she had. Only then some boy would try to get her off in a corner of the fenced-in school ground and she'd start screaming and the screams would swallow her up into darkness.

She frowned. When you realized something, it seemed to make a lot of difference. It made you stronger somehow.

"May I have a typewriter?" she asked the pen-tapping doctor, hoping that would get her forgiven. They liked for you to ask to have things here.

She'd been thinking about a typewriter. She never thought about long division and interest rates. For heaven's sake, did this doctor suppose she sat in the corner and drooled and recited the multiplication table?

"Of course!" There was approval of her positive attitude in the answer. "Are you thinking of taking up writing?"

Van sighed. Sometimes she thought the doctors she saw were sillier than her wardmates.

"No," she said patiently. "I was thinking of brushing up on my typing so I'd have some sort of skill when I get out of here. I was thinking, actually, of typing a letter to my sister."

"What the hell's this message mean?"

Cecily looked up from her desk to see Ben in the doorway, a sheet of paper in his hand. She'd waited until he was out, then had left it in his studio to avoid face-to-face discussion. Though she detested admitting it, she felt some unwelcome cord stretching between them, ever closer to snapping, whenever they were in a room together.

"Just passing along Effie's orders," she said, standing up and stacking the tearsheets provided by several photographers whose work she'd been considering. "If we don't have two designs ready to go into production by the end of the week, we'll never be able to meet the deadlines for these magazine ads."

"Effie draw up this timetable?"

"No. I did. But Effie agrees."

"Well that's too damned bad! I can't spit up a design just because you snap your fingers. That's not how it works."

Cecily stalked toward a white file cabinet. "I'm not snapping my fingers. I'm passing along the realities of the situation—"

"Effie got herself into the situation. She can get herself out."

"Look . . ." Cecily fought for patience, slamming a file drawer and starting back toward her desk. "Effie never meant to be designing and—damn!"

She staggered, hopping awkwardly as her left foot wobbled beneath her and the heel of her shoe toppled loosely away, throwing her off-balance.

Angrily she snatched up the shoe. This whole morning had been off-balance, she thought. Brigette had called twice about the infernal style show, the end result being that she was going to have to go into Palm Beach this afternoon to calm the woman. The amount of work to be done in the next three months was appalling now that she'd put it on paper. The photographer whose work she most wanted to see was out of town, and when she'd called Van she'd been put on hold and forgotten. She hadn't needed this argument. And she hadn't needed a broken shoe. She stumped toward the desk.

"Sort of cuts you down to size, huh?" Ben drawled, coming on into the room. His eyes, with evident enjoyment, followed her progress.

Cecily kicked her other shoe off and glared at him. She could feel the distance between them shrinking. His shirt-sleeves were rolled to the elbow. He looked very much a temperamental artist. Unfortunately he was sounding like one, too.

"You should have guessed what the schedule would be when you came here," she said crisply. "Unless you didn't bother listening when I told you Effie's plans."

"Effie's already working on something. So's Mortimer, I understood. I won't be pressured—"

"Oh, *blast* Mortimer! He's fired. Hasn't anyone told you? And she's so stubborn it would take a miracle for her to admit she was wrong and take him back!"

He provoked her as no one else did. Maybe because he also aroused something in her, she acknowledged, angered by the awareness.

"What is this shouting? It sounds like a Turkish market!" growled Effie, rolling through the doorway. "Who's so stubborn?"

"Ah, Effie." Ben turned and, with a slanting look at Cecily, favored Effie with the first real smile Cecily had seen touch his mouth. It made him look both devilish and irresistible.

"What do you want?" asked Effie dryly. She continued past him with Bibi behind.

"Just a little practicality. Cecily here seems to think I can pull a design out of thin air to meet some schedule—"

"I don't think I ever made it sound like that," Cecily broke in. She was starting to think he cared about this, was not merely being stubborn. "I'm aware it's asking a lot. But facts are facts. There's a cutoff date for the photograph for that first ad. We have to get moving—"

"You know no designer worth his salt could work under that kind of pressure, Effie!" he interrupted. "I can't. I need more time. Two more weeks."

"Well, perhaps you are right," mused Effie.

Cecily caught her breath. "But Madame—"

"Come, Cecily. Surely you can stall them." Effie waved an imperious hand.

Cecily clamped her jaws together. Just a few hours ago Effie had been more than a little adamant about meeting this schedule. Now she was taking Ben's side.

"Why are you walking about in your stockings?" She scowled at Cecily. "You look undressed. I do not like undressed."

"My heel broke."

Ben, looking at her across his grandmother's head, grinned smugly and straightened his belt.

"Ah!" snapped Effie. "And have you no other shoes?"

By the time she got back from seeing Brigette, Cecily felt more frustrated and out of sorts than she had that morning. The charity style show seemed to be shaping up nicely—was sold out already—but Brigette was offended that Effie insisted on having four of her own men in charge of her jewels, as well as hotel security men at each door. They had argued about it for two hours with a careful politeness Cecily found especially draining. As she walked from the boat dock toward the twin towers of Effie's house, all she could think of was relaxing and not talking to anyone for the rest of the evening.

"Give my regrets to Madame and the others," she said to Charlie as she came in. There were voices in the living room where before-dinner drinks were being served. "Tell them I'm very tired and don't wish to keep them from dinner."

She climbed the stairs, avoiding the more visible elevator. She'd change quickly and escape to the small patch of beach she'd discovered on one end of the island. It was more private than the pool downstairs, where last night she'd seen Ben, and besides, if Effie came up to drag her to the dining room, she'd be gone.

In ten minutes' time she stood where water as blue as Effie's sapphires washed gently against white sand. Adjusting the strap of her jade-green maillot, Cecily plunged out into the waters of a peaceful cove and swam. When exercise had driven the tension from her body, she sat on the still warm beach and watched the lulling movement of the ocean. What a shame Effie couldn't enjoy it here, she thought. She wondered if Effie had ever rambled about this small piece of land, had seen its beauty or only its usefulness.

Lying back, she let sand trickle through her fingers. This island was so peaceful. Yet it seemed to have given Ben, who'd grown up here, no peace at all. What had made him so angry? What had really happened to his wife? She almost wished she hadn't had a part in bringing him back here. There was some sort of pain she did not understand between him and Effie.

It was dark by the time she returned to the house. A clock somewhere was striking nine. There was work on her desk she wanted to finish by morning, so with her towel around her neck Cecily slipped down the hall to get it. In her office she flipped on a single desk light, then paused and frowned. An anteroom connected her office with Effie's, and the door between the two was open. More important was the fact she could see a slab of cold gray steel, the door of a huge walk-in vault that the anteroom housed. The door to the vault stood open.

"Madame?" she called hesitantly.

The vault was always closed at night. Effie alone knew its combination. Receiving no answer to her call, she moved slowly to the anteroom and on into Effie's office. It was deserted.

Her heart was pounding now with her uneasiness. Cecily stepped back into the anteroom. She had not been in the vault, but she knew it housed a fortune—unset stones, finished pieces, tens of millions of dollars in inventory.

"Madame, are you there?" she called again.

She was afraid to look inside, afraid of what she might find. There must be some sort of burglar alarm around, but she didn't know where.

Swallowing, suddenly chilly in her damp bathing suit, she entered the vault. There was no one inside, but the sight that met her eyes held her motionless. Some of the drawers that lined the vault were ajar, and out of one hung a torsade of frosty white diamonds, the rope half as thick of her wrist. Emeralds cut in unconventional geometric shapes and hung on a beaten gold chain lay over the top of another. Drawers that had been removed to a shelf held unset sapphires, pearls, but before she could register their contents fully a voice spoke behind her.

"Like the view?"

She whirled. Ben must have stayed nearly as long at the pool as she had on her stretch of beach. The shirt he'd worn that morning hung open like a jacket above his trunks. He was blocking the door.

"What's this doing open?" she asked immediately.

His eyes were fixed on her. They didn't stir.

"I opened it. I was in seeing what sort of goods Effie had on hand that I might build around, but I had to use the facilities. What are you doing here?"

"Just checking. I'd come for something in my office." She felt defensive. He was authorized here; she wasn't. And his eyes still hadn't left her. They were measuring her as she'd seen Effie measure a stone of unusual color. "Don't worry, I wasn't walking off with anything," she added.

An expression she couldn't quite read enlivened his mouth.

"Pity," he said. "I'm afraid I'm going to have to do a body search anyway."

With a backward movement of the hand he closed the door. Cecily jumped, more alarmed at the thought of being trapped in the stuffy vault till morning than she was by his words, which she felt sure had been uttered only to annoy her.

"Don't worry," he said, a hint of mischief in his face as her eyes scanned the door. "Ventilation comes on in a minute and it opens from the inside anyway. What do you know about this sapphire here? Why hasn't it been set? It looks good to me."

He moved toward one of the drawers on the shelf as he spoke and took out a blue stone roughly the shape of a scalene triangle. Cautiously, thrown off-balance by his abrupt change of subject and manner, Cecily moved closer to see it.

"I don't know. Effie's grumbled a time or two about one that needed recutting to a more conventional shape."

"Figures." He dropped it back irritably, his eyes raking Cecily at close range. "You swim in the cove? That's a hell of a stupid chance to take, going alone."

She did not like this seesawing business one minute and a look that made her feel trapped here in the vault with him the next. It confused her, too, this concern for her safety. Very few people had ever worried about her.

"I heard about you reprieving Mortimer," he said before she could speak. "Here's an idea for that ad." He reached into his pocket and tossed a paper at her.

Wishing she had left, Cecily unfolded it and studied careful pencil strokes. The item sketched was clearly a necklace.

"Hammered gold and star sapphires?" she said, reading the notes on the side and translating them to a visual image. "*Brown* star sapphires?"

It was an unusual combination. She could almost envision its sheen as the glittering gold reflected back the changeable luster of smooth stones an inch in diameter. But although it would be a costly piece, it would not be as outrageously extravagant as the pieces Effie usually issued.

"It's . . . lovely," she said. "But it's not Effie's style."

"It's mine. Take it or leave it."

His voice turned cutting, almost vicious.

She folded the paper, torn from the vision that had mesmerized her. "Between you and Effie I'll have to take it, won't I?" she said shortly, and handed the paper back to him.

"You could quit." He sounded oddly satisfied with himself. She started around him.

"Don't think I haven't thought of it!"

He shifted into her path. "Why stay, then?"

Angered she must spar with him like this, and be a tool in whatever warfare there was between him and Effie, she gripped the towel around her neck. She faced him with all the lonely harshness of her existence welling up inside her. He couldn't know how it felt to have no one, no ties to anyone at all except the slender ones that bound her to Van. He couldn't know how it felt to be powerless to help the one person you had to cherish, or to spend every holiday alone.

"I have a sister in a mental hospital, if you must know. I need the job."

A despair that had been hovering over her since morning suddenly fell. It had been such a lousy day, and she was tired, and maybe she was only deluding herself thinking Van would ever get out. Maybe Van was already destroyed—lost forever.

"I want the people who put Van where she is to *pay*," she said with a sudden, convulsive vehemence she couldn't control. A wetness was starting down her cheeks at the memory of how lost Van had looked last time she saw her. "Working for Effie's going to give me the chance to make them pay—"

"Don't talk that way! You sound just like her."

The sharpness in his deep voice halted her. He caught her arm. The tips of his fingers brushed her tears back softly toward her temples even as she tried to pull away.

"That's what I want. I want to be just like her!"

His touch made her tremble.

"No, by God! Effie's tainted. She taints everything she touches!"

"I don't care—"

She tried to free herself, but his arms were unyielding, as hard as she remembered, yet quivering with some fierce emotion. Cecily knew, as his mouth captured hers with bruising force, what would happen. She struggled, then yielded to a dizzy, tumbling, too-many-somersaults feeling. Ben's thumb still moved gently against her temple, smoothing away the tears that had escaped there when she'd spoken of Van. His hands devoured the softness of her hair with a strange, inflaming tenderness.

"Don't," she whispered, but she knew the word was wasted on both of them.

Heat spread from his bare chest through the thin film of her bathing suit. Ben's mouth moved to her neck and he kissed it repeatedly, thoroughly. The exquisite movements became one endless chain of sensation. Cecily felt her mind grow thick.

"You're not going to be like Effie—I'll see to it!"

His words were a savage outrush of air as he drew back to look at her. His dark eyes were brilliant. He began to kiss her again.

Much as Cecily longed to deny it, she wanted this feel of his hand on her breast, this incredible stroking that made her body shimmer with fire like the torsade of diamonds in the drawer beyond them. She was frightened. She was yielding something to this man she did not want to yield—something more than her body.

The damp cloth of her bathing suit was being eased from her. She and Ben were on their knees. She had never known such pleasure. Ben's lips explored her belly, the tender, outer parts of her breasts, her throat again.

Their mouths joined hungrily. With tongue and tumescence he moved inside her. There was the hot, mercurial gliding of molten flesh against molten flesh.

"Oh, my God!" she whispered, eyes tightly closed against what was happening between them, cheeks wet afresh with tears.

And then she felt only the matched gyrations of their mutual seeking, until the world around them exploded in meteor showers of ruby red, sapphire blue, and blinding, diamantine light.

EIGHTEEN

"IF WE BRING THE STONES WE THINK WE MIGHT WANT IN NOW, WE'LL avoid delays," argued Cecily.

"If we bring in stones we *don't* need, we'll waste a hell of a lot of money on import fees!"

Cecily brushed a hand through the roots of her hair, so vexed she felt like pulling it. She carefully avoided looking at Ben, who stood with legs planted intractably, turning what should have been a simple morning planning session with Effie into a battle across the length of the desk on the dais.

"The import duty on brown star sapphires is not going to be excessive," said Cecily, a bite in her words.

She felt alternately hot and chilly here in this room, remembering what had happened a few steps away in that vault last night. She had moved out of hunger and instinct alone, like some wild creature.

"I realize you share Effie's view that a stone ought to be the size of a cowpile and the talk of three continents—" Ben began sarcastically.

"Enough!" Effie's hands smacked her desk. Her eyes glided back and forth between them. "All I have heard this morning is the two of you sniping. If you would go to bed together, you would do us all a favor. Perhaps then you would not both act like powderkegs. Perhaps then we could accomplish something besides this quibbling."

Ben, hands on his hips and looking impatiently roguish, bent from the waist to face her across her desk.

"We have, thank you, Effie—in your vault last night. Any other suggestions?"

An exclamation of rage caught in Cecily's throat. To add to her indignation, Effie cocked an eyebrow and chuckled. Without a word Cecily turned on her heel and strode toward the door of the anteroom.

"Now what's the matter?" Ben's voice demanded as she yanked it open.

She tried to slam it, but he was behind her, his leg brushing hers as he closed the door himself.

"I assumed you had more taste than to broadcast the facts of whatever you happen to do with a woman, that's what's the matter!"

He laughed. It was an unfamiliar sound. Seductive. Attractive.

"What the hell kind of woman are you to be ashamed of what you do? Do you suppose anyone in this house gives a damn if we're lovers?"

"*I am not your lover!*"

Cecily ground the words between her teeth. Last night they had taken their fill of each other not once, not twice, but endless times. There was nothing wrong with it, but neither did it promise anything.

"I was just as willing as you were," she said, controlling her temper. "I'll admit that. And I may sleep with you again. It's likely. You're . . . attractive." He grinned and she tried to ignore it. Some barrier had gone down between them and she wanted it back in place. "Just don't get the idea you own any part of me, Ben. I'm not going to be in your bed every night. I'm not going to be . . . something you can put a label on!"

"Why?"

There was an undercurrent in his voice that she'd not heard before. She shook her head, unable to answer. All at once a rapping sounded on the door.

"If you two are in there, come out at once!" commanded Effie. "There is work to do. If you spent last night together, whatever you're starting in there can surely wait until lunch!"

Jordan checked the clock in his new office across from Orlena's. It was smaller than he deserved, but its air smelled of power. Yes, he decided, this should be a fine time to call Cousin Cecily.

He didn't know why he was thinking about her. One hand moved absently to caress the bite marks on his arm. The woman he'd been with last night had not liked being tied up. She'd fought a lot. It had been good.

He considered a minute what he was going to say. This was only the start of course. He was going to get lots of satisfaction out of Cousin Cecily.

He punched out the number himself. The sound of a voice he knew was hers sent a strange excitement through him.

"I have some movies of your sister Vanessa you might like to see," he began without preamble. "Foaming at the mouth like a mad dog. Fucking without even knowing it, crazy as a loon."

He had the satisfaction of hearing her gasp in horror.

"If you want them," he said, "walk into a place called Three Sailors at ten past eleven tonight. I'll be waiting."

He spoke the address twice so she wouldn't forget.

Cecily sat at her desk trembling uncontrollably, a pool of coffee from her overturned cup spreading over the papers in front of her. One sleeve was in it, soaking up the still-hot brownness, but the nerves in her arm, in all her body seemed dead.

She felt like an animal running with no place to hide, Van . . . no Van was safe, surely.

Jordan Lyle. That had to be it.

He'd gone to see Van that time and had done awful things to her and made her sick again. Movies, he'd said. God. It was grotesque. It was unthinkable. She leaned forward until the edge of her desk was cutting into her and fought against nausea.

Why, *why* couldn't she and Van have had someone to help them? She breathed quickly as her mind raced trying to sort out what Jordan wanted. Maybe she and Van were not defenseless this time. Not as long as she stayed with Effie.

The door to the anteroom opened. She looked up with vision distorted as though by fever to see Ben standing there.

"What's wrong?" he asked. "I was in the vault and heard you cry out. Are you all right?"

"Yes . . ."

His eyes had found the spilled coffee on her desk. He came forward and lifted her gently up out of it. Embarrassed, she disengaged herself.

"It was nothing. Just a crank call."

His eyebrows raised.

"I can't believe you'd act that way about a crank call."

Cecily swallowed.

"About my sister," she said in a low voice. She found she could not keep it steady.

Before the phone rang she'd been wondering whether she could stand another day at Duvall Inc. Over lunch Ben had inquired about Lynette's ability to furnish alexandrite. Effie had exploded in a tirade at the mere hint he would contemplate a design using "insignificant" gems. Ben had promptly stalked out. Effie had descended on her workroom like a whirlwind, finding fault everywhere and ordering twenty small rubies, just set in a clasp, reset.

Now Cecily realized she was drawing her only sense of strength from being part of the Duvall domain. With that weight behind her, she knew she could keep Van safe.

"What about your sister?" Ben persisted.

She shook her head. This new side of him, this side that was not her foe and was almost comforting as he stood here, was too unexpected.

Her intercom sputtered, Effie demanding her presence.

"You don't have to face her, you know," said Ben, still studying her. "Not if you don't feel up to it. She wouldn't fire you. She's taken too much liking to you."

The impulse to smile was very strong. She did so in spite of herself.

"You don't have to wait around for a cobra to strike, either, so I'm told."

"But most people do?"

"Right. Something about hypnotizing the victims, I seem to remember."

He grinned. The strong lines of his face were filled with a genuine humor and his dark eyes danced unguarded.

"That's Effie all right. So damned unpredictable a body keeps coming back to watch her strike."

He tossed her a neatly pressed and folded handkerchief.

"Here. Blot your sleeve so she doesn't yell about that."

She took it, trying to understand some change in dynamics happening between them. A moment later, nearly dry and almost steady, she stood before Effie.

Enthroned behind her desk, her employer upbraided while Cecily listened.

"Look at the work you have made for me!" Effie was shaking a sheaf of yellow notes in Jenkins's neat handwriting. "Here are half a dozen people wanting interviews, at least. The phone rings constantly. All because word leaked out I had rented a ballroom for that ridiculous show I promised you. You handle them!"

She shoved the sheaf of messages toward Cecily.

"Madame, it is *you* they want to talk to. *You* are the celebrity, returning to the public eye after a very provocative absence. You interest them. Besides, how can I tell them about the show when I haven't the least idea what there'll be?"

Effie looked at her steadily. "I keep you for something, surely."

Cecily sighed.

"Do I exasperate you? Don't forget it was you who came here begging this job."

Cecily bowed her head. "I know. And I am grateful . . . ."

The door burst open.

"What is this?" Effie demanded angrily as Jenkins rushed in with Ben at his heels.

"Mortimer's sketches." Ben snatched a manila envelope from Jenkins's hands and spread them on the desk in front of her. "Look. *Look.* They're good. He's pulled your buns from the fire!"

Effie scanned them without comment. Cecily came around to stand behind her.

"About his usual," Effie said. "I have seen better—"

"Bloody Christ! I'd like to know when? Not around here you haven't! Not in years at least," Ben said passionately.

Effie's eyes shot sparks to match his own.

But Cecily was looking at the designs before her. One in particular had caught her eye. The necklace was to be an enchantment of glistening snowflakes, each tinier and more fragile than could be wrought by folded paper and scissors, each as exquisite as nature itself could make them. Every crystalline shaft was to be of fiery white opals, every sparkling tip and center was to be a shimmering diamond.

"That, *that* is good, dammit!" Ben said, pounding a finger against the sketch.

Effie looked at him blandly. "And you plan to force me to use these by producing nothing of your own, I suppose."

Her voice was cruel. Cecily felt the barest twinge of sympathy for Ben.

"Bloody Christ, Effie! I gave you a design for that ad you needed," he protested, sounding slightly harried. "I need time. I'm rusty."

"Ah. And did you do nothing at all these past ten years?"

Cecily sensed the two were really talking for the first time since their reunion.

"Yeah! I flew my plane!"

"*I* think you should both stop shouting," Cecily interrupted with a boldness she did not quite feel. "It's finally starting to look as though we might get our heads above water with all this, don't you think, Jenkins?"

He was trying to suppress a smile. She could not imagine why.

"I think the one design is very lovely," he ventured. "I think Miss Catlow was very wise to give Mortimer this chance to prove himself."

"You are not paid to think," said Effie shortly. She turned her back on them and wheeled toward the window.

"All right, all right," she said with a brush of the hand. "Tell Mortimer to unpack his things. The two of you get back to work. I have things to discuss with Cecily."

When the men had gone, Effie returned to her desk and looked reflectively at Bibi, who yawned and resumed a nap that had been interrupted.

"Take care of those interviews," she said again. "And call Joao to change this order. Call Lynette—ah, no. I will make that call myself." Something secretive flickered in Effie's eyes before the hoods settled over them. She was up to something. "Here is a name in Sydney. Arrange to have some opals shown to me. How like Mortimer to require some stone we shall have to shop for. Be done by four. I may have more chores for you."

Cecily let her breath out carefully. "I'll try," she said.

The list that Effie was laying on her for this one afternoon was staggering. And Effie's mood all day had been a strange one, smug and unusually tyrannical, as though she were testing Cecily in some way. Hoping it had nothing to do with that stupid revelation of Ben's, Cecily turned toward the door.

"Cecily."

Effie's voice halted her. It was gentler now. The old woman rolled toward her, then stopped.

"Hire a secretary if you need one. Someone you can trust."

"Someone related to me?" asked Cecily dryly.

Unruffled, Effie nodded. "That is the safest way. Someday you will see. But for now, find someone who would die for you if necessary." She made a gesture with her hand. "It will free you for more interesting things—for more interviews, since one tiny moment of weakness of mine now threatens to make me an institution."

The last words had an echo of suppressed pleasure in them.

Back in her own office Cecily wondered for the thousandth time what manner of woman Effie really was. Heartless or kind?

She called Brigette, made the intercontinental call to Joâo, wasted time over busy signals while wading through tricky negotiations over interviews.

"This is Cecily Catlow. I'm calling for Effie Duvall," she said when finally she had reached the Australian number.

She *did* need a secretary. She. Cecily Catlow, who just months ago had been at the lowest point of her life, in utter disgrace.

On the other side of the world a voice stirred to life, saying it was a pleasure to hear from her, asking in what way the huge opal dealer she had reached could help her.

What were Effie's brusque orders and harsh demands?

What was loneliness?

What was overwork?

Here, with Effie's name behind her, she had power. She could ask for fine stones of any sort and know they would be brought to her. Suddenly her whole soul was filled with the single zeal to perform for Effie.

A few moments after she hung up, her phone rang in sharp demand.

"Cecily? Someone has come to see me, and I am not in the mood. Go down and greet them. I am sending Ben, too. He will wait at the elevator."

It was ten till four. Cecily rose, thinking how quickly Effie could make one's spirits swing.

"Now what?" she asked Ben.

"I don't know." He looked out of sorts. "She dragged me away from the best idea I've had all day."

He pushed the elevator door and they started down.

The living room was filled with sunlight. A golden-haired figure stood looking out at the courtyard with its splashing fountain.

She turned at sound of them, a figure and moment encased in soft lilac cashmere.

"I'm out," said Van, a smile breaking over her face. "I'm out! I've come to stay with you!"

NINETEEN

"OH, CECILY! ARE YOU SURPRISED?"

Van's voice was delighted.

Unprepared for this moment, Cecily couldn't speak. She sagged, and Ben's hand touched her back suddenly, keeping her upright.

"Vanessa . . . oh, Van! I can't believe . . ."

Tears were flooding down her cheeks. She looked dazedly at Ben. She wondered if everyone had known of this but her.

But Ben was staring at Van. He looked sharply down at Cecily's wet face, a strained look passing through his eyes. Van was coming toward them, laughing happily. Ben turned and strode from the room.

"Oh, Cecily! Why are you crying?" Van asked, catching her hands.

They clung to one another and Cecily began to laugh through her tears.

"I'm so happy! I can't believe it! I didn't know. . . ."

Cecily felt the walls of loneliness crumbling. It seemed as though she'd been wandering for years, cold and terrified, in some great woods and now saw a lighted window. Forgetting herself, she wiped her damp nose on the back of her hand, a child again.

Van was here. *Van was here!* They were whole. They had each other to cling to. They would never be apart again.

All the riches that passed through Effie's hands had just been given her. The person she loved best in all the world was free. And to think today she'd been half-resentful of Effie, had felt used at times, and pressed. At this instant she knew anything Effie ever required of her she would do willingly. It no longer mattered what kind of person Effie was. It no longer mattered whether Effie was ruthless. She had used her power to win for Vanessa what had been denied her for so many years, a right to sanity, a right to happiness.

And I'm going to be like you, Effie, Cecily promised silently. *I'm going to grow powerful enough and hard enough that nothing will ever hurt Van or me again!*

"How did you get here?" she asked, eyes still feasting on Van. She looked so *well*—hair beautifully styled, an expensive dress that Effie's money must have supplied.

Van was bubbling as she turned, a little bit nervous but unmistakably happy, Cecily recognized as the shock of the meeting started to loosen its grip on her.

"April brought me."

Van gestured and Cecily saw for the first time that there were two other people in the room. April, with her familiar yellow curls and spiky lashes, came forward shyly.

"Jeezus, and we've had first-class treatment, too!" she said.

"Oh, yes! We came in a little plane all by ourselves with a lady pilot—did you know I've never been in a plane before? Of course you know. How could I have been? And Wesley drove us out to the airport and helped us get on. He's so nice."

"I—April . . ." Cecily put her hand out. "I'm so grateful. It was good of you. And I haven't even written to you. I should have thanked you for staying with me that afternoon when— when things were bad."

"Hey, I was glad to do it." April shifted her gum. "I mean, Herbie's gone. He died a month ago." She shrugged. "Van's about the only friend I've got. Saved me plane fare down here, too. I figured with Herbie gone I might as well go to Winter Park, see if I could hook up with a circus. Or maybe find a job as an exotic dancer. That's what I did in Manhattan.

"I'll give you a call when I'm settled, huh, Vanessa? Maybe we can get together."

Van nodded.

"Who else came with you?" Cecily frowned as she tried to identify an unknown woman waiting on a chair at the end of the room.

"Oh, Cecily . . ." Van's eyes were suddenly pleading. "She's a nurse. But I don't *need* a nurse. I'm so tired of always having someone watching me. I'm so tired of being treated like a child. Can't you send her away?"

Cecily swallowed. There was a poignancy in the words that went to her heart. Van was looking at her so expectantly.

"She's just to see I take my medication and don't get upset and go in to see the psychiatrist I have appointments with twice a week. Oh, Cecily, for heaven's sakes! I *know* when to take my medicine."

Cecily smiled at her fervor.

"I think we can manage just fine by ourselves," she said to the nurse. "If you'd write down any instructions for me, you could go back with April."

As soon as they were alone they sat on a couch together and words rushed out. There were no barriers here. They were reunited in a way they'd never been with Van in the hospital.

"I'm starting to understand some of the problems I've had," Van said earnestly. "I know I can be well. I *know* I can!"

"Vanessa, of course you can be—you already are."

They sat for a moment in silent happiness. Then Cecily laughed.

"Aren't you simply smothering in that dress? I've been dying to know."

Van laughed, too. "I'm a little bit warm. But oh, you can't imagine what a wonderful feeling that is!"

Charlie appeared from the elevator.

"Miss Cecily, I've put Miss Vanessa's luggage in her room. Shall I take you up now?"

Van had grown suddenly quiet. Was she frightened? Cecily worried.

"Yes. We'll go up," she said. "Are you tired, Van?"

"A little."

Perhaps she shouldn't have sent the nurse away, Cecily thought as the elevator stopped on the second floor and Charlie led the way down a hall and opened the door next to Cecily's, revealing a room done in fresh, soft shades of blue.

"Oh, it's wonderful! Beautiful! Look at the paintings!" Van threw out her arms and spun around like a child.

She *was* a child, she had missed so many experiences. Thoughts piled on Cecily with alarming swiftness. Was the higher pitch of Van's voice a product of mere excitement or of nervousness?

This was a new place for Van, and as large as the building Van had been in at the state hospital. There was the household staff to get used to. And Effie. And that damned panther prowling about and howling every evening—she must warn Van of that. God, yes, she'd made a mistake dismissing the nurse. Dinner, in a strange setting, with new people, was going to be an ordeal for Van after all the unknowns she'd been through already today.

"Madame thought perhaps the two of you would prefer to dine alone tonight," said the butler, backing toward the door with a kind smile that reassured her. "I'll bring a table up whenever you ring."

Ben sat in his studio drinking at intervals from the glass he refilled from a bottle that sat next to him. The room he'd known since childhood was like a dungeon to him.

It was nearly eleven, and somewhere in endless burrows of this house Effie was awake and working. He knew her habits, knew her style, knew the silent obsession with which she labored into the small hours of the morning when she was creating. She was creating now, though he doubted anyone else recognized her symptoms after so long a time of near barrenness—the distant glint that fired her eyes, the set of her mouth.

The silence of the house was making him restless, tormenting him with memories. Of his mother—beautiful, always laughing, always squeezing his hand in affection, always warming. She'd been nothing like Effie. Then there'd been the not unpleasant years with Effie and the brief ones with Marguerite.

He drank slowly from the glass in his hand. It wasn't the house making all these ghosts rise up inside of him. It was Cecily. Damn those haunting eyes of hers. They made him feel things he hadn't felt in a long time. Where did she think he'd gotten the idea for that necklace with the brown stars, all soft and shining?

He hurled the glass in his hand and watched it shatter. Why the hell had he come back here?

Ever since he'd met Cecily Catlow he'd told himself she couldn't be as innocent or as open to hurt as those eyes of hers made him want to believe. She couldn't be; she'd been spoiled by Effie.

Then this afternoon he'd seen her twice with all defenses down, once scared to death over something there in her office and not admitting it, and then with those tears sliding down her face when her sister came. He'd seen her heart on her face that time. Now he didn't know what he thought.

Anger unabated, he went to a cabinet and found a replacement glass. A moment later he drank deeply again. He dialed a number, her room, hoping she'd still be awake.

"Cecily?" He couldn't remember saying her name before. Not like this, anyway. He felt subdued and annoyed with himself. "Look, I'm taking off for Heredia for a while. Can you stop by my studio a minute?" He paused, knowing what must be on her mind because it was on his, too. "You can leave the door open."

He sat back, drank, waited, until he heard a brisk knock and she came warily in.

"You're leaving?"

She repeated it with only the barest edge of curiosity. In fact, she seemed distracted. She was watching him, though, keeping distance between them.

Ben snatched at the opportunity to fend off something gnawing at him. He used her cautiousness to feed his sarcasm.

"All alone? I never took you for that brave. I figured you'd at least wake Jenkins to come along and make sure you escaped untouched—if not Effie herself."

She ignored his baiting. "What do you mean, you're leaving?"

Ben tried not to think of that minute when she'd seen her sister, when she'd looked all small and vulnerable.

"I can't think here. Besides, I've got things to do on my plane. Thought I'd better let someone know and I figured there'd be less of a row with you than there would with Effie." He paused, then added grudgingly what he wasn't sure he'd meant to: "Don't worry. I'll deliver some more designs."

He didn't want to, but they were pressing out of him now, bottled up for years. Anyway, he'd taken Effie's money.

"But *when?*" She sounded more than a little distressed now. Business to the core. Just like Effie, he thought sourly.

"When they're ready. I don't know. A couple of weeks." He stood up, curling his fists impatiently on his hips. "Look, dammit, I *will* come back!"

Not because he detected a slowness to Effie's movements that hadn't been there before. Not because he hated that bastard

Harry and thought he might try to double-cross Effie and Cecily both.

"How's your sister?" he asked abruptly.

She looked startled, then softened through every inch of face and body.

"She's asleep. She was worn out. I think she's going to be fine. I'm—" She pressed her lips together and looked away, blinking quickly. "I owe your grandmother more than I can ever repay for doing this for me."

"Yeah. You can be sure Effie knows it, too," he said. Trust Effie to find every weak spot. She always did.

Cecily gave him a cold look, silently registering how little she cared what he'd said.

He poured into his glass again and took a drink. When the door had closed behind her, he sat down. He'd spend tonight and maybe tomorrow night in Miami, away from here. When he started out for Heredia it would be with a clear head.

He never discouraged people from thinking he drank and flew. Maybe he'd encouraged that image, knowing they'd give him a wide berth and be less likely to cross him believing he was a madman. But when he pushed the Peregrine faster and faster through boundless skies, he liked to be fully conscious of the seconds whirling past. When he pushed it past its limits and met the dark gods, he wanted to be fully aware.

TWENTY

"CECILY, DID YOU HEAR WHAT I SAID?"

Cecily blinked and looked vaguely up from the sand at the edge of the water where they were walking.

"Oh . . . I . . ."

Vanessa laughed. She loved it when Cecily let her mind wander off and then looked so guilty.

"That's what the doctors are always saying to you, you know. 'Vanessa, did you hear what I said?' 'Vanessa, were you listening?' " she mimicked in a singsong voice. "It ruins some of the nicest daydreams!"

Cecily looked embarrassed. Sometimes Van couldn't understand why Cecily seemed to take things so seriously.

"I guess I'd drifted off," she said with a smile of apology. "I'm frantic I'll have forgotten something for that style show and . . ." Her eyes clouded and she looked into the distance as she seemed to do a lot of late. "A lot of things."

"Oh, *I* don't care." Van swung her arms and sniffed the morning air. "I know I rattle. But it's just because I'm so happy. Can you believe I've been here two whole weeks? And look, shorts!" She held out the sides of white ones like Cecily wore and twirled in a circle. "Just think, I didn't wear them for so long, and now I practically live in them—except for dinner, of course, the dining room's so elegant. I feel just so free! I feel like a pirate shipwrecked on a beautiful island."

They were at the cove and a large rock they rested on during their morning walk. Van sat down first and Cecily joined her. Their shoulders rubbed.

It was all so perfect, Vanessa thought. The blue water. Cecily with her. No nurses and no needlepoint. The whole world was out there waiting. She was no one's prisoner.

And suddenly, unable to control it, she began to cry, covering her mouth with her hands so Cecily wouldn't be alarmed, but Cecily was anyway.

"Van! Van, what is it?"

An arm was around her. Van tried to choke words out, but couldn't for sobbing. She was stupid. She *was* a prisoner—of what she was and what she'd been.

"It's nothing . . . nothing. . . . I just . . . sometimes when I'm happy and feeling like I can do anything, I turn right around and think of all the things I've never done that other people have—of all the things I'll never be able to do. . . ."

"Van dearest, that's not true—"

"It is! Look at me! I'm twenty-nine years old and I've never had a date, I've never gone into town alone, I've never made a decision—"

"You decided to get well. You decided what dresses to buy when April took you shopping—"

"I'll—I'll never have a family of my own. Who'd want to take a chance on me?" Her current sob turned into a hiccup. "How am I even going to find a job?"

She felt Cecily squeeze her hand. She knew that was because Cecily couldn't think of anything to say to contradict her.

"Van, walk before you try to run! You don't have to find a job. Lots of women don't have jobs, but some of them still certainly contribute to society—volunteer work, being really good mothers, just giving a stability—''

"I need to be able to earn a living. What if—what if something happened to you? I need to learn how to stand on my own. Like you do. Like Effie. Cecily, why are you shivering? Are you chilly? It's so warm out here . . .''

"It's nothing. Look, Van, of course you can have a family. You're beautiful. A lot of men will be interested in you—if that's what you want.''

"That's another problem, too, isn't it?'' Van fished a tissue from her pocket and blew angrily. Aware the storm had abated, she gave a sad little laugh and hugged her sister. "Oh, Cecily, I'm sorry. Did I terrify you? These—these moods just happen sometimes.''

They sat in silence together. The lapping of the water seemed to wash away her worries.

The water here was wonderful, Van thought. Not like the awful cold tubs. Last weekend she had finally ventured into Effie's pool with Cecily. Now she loved it. She loved the big black panther, too. It was ridiculous that Cecily was always a little scared of him.

Suddenly she laughed.

"Do you remember when you put the Kool-Aid in Great-Uncle William's swimming pool? Three great big cans of it! The water turned purple, and so did Orlena when she caught you.''

She laughed harder remembering the sight of it. Then she became aware of Cecily's stunned silence.

Van wiped her eyes, removing the wetness of merriment now. Sometimes it felt as if they had a whole lifetime to patch back together—all kinds of things to start to know about each other. She knew she'd startled Cecily.

"I—I do think about Great-Uncle William sometimes,'' she said slowly. "I just don't think about what happened . . . that boy being killed. It was so awful!''

Cecily's continuing silence made Van defiant, though she didn't know quite why. Why couldn't Cecily understand?

"I don't *have* to think about it! I don't want to!''

She shouted the words, feeling scared, threatened, like she'd been in the hospital when some boy in her school class had tried to get her alone somewhere. But she was *here*! With Cecily. She was safe!

The water lapped. She saw Cecily swallow. She felt her own breath rushing and tried to control it.

Vanessa looked toward the ocean. Stupid topic. Silly. Whatever had made her bring it up?

"I wonder if Effie will have a Christmas tree," she said at last.

"I don't know." Cecily sounded cautious.

"I hope she does. It's such a big house. We could have an enormous one. Oh, Cecily, I'd like that so much. There's such a lot I've missed, but I'm going to make every day count from here on out."

"We'll demand a tree—say we won't eat our supper if we can't have one." Cecily made it a game.

Relief was evident in her voice. An awkward moment had passed. But how many of those moments would there be? Van wondered. They stood up in unspoken agreement and began to walk toward the house.

Effie was on the back terrace having breakfast.

"There you are," she said, a hard roll spread thickly with butter poised in one hand, a cup of coffee and milk at her side. "The water is pleasant today?"

"Yes, lovely." Van sat down, out of breath. "At Christmastime may we put up a very large tree?"

"Ah, Christmas. That comes in December, if I recall." Effie chuckled. "Yes, very large. Very large."

Cecily looked a little uncomfortable. Maybe this hadn't been the proper time to bring up Christmas, Van thought.

"I am expecting Prince Karim today," said Effie. "I will want you to call Harry and see what goods he has on hand. The prince is very fond of red. And call that Chasen-Palme woman. She is driving me crazy with need for assurances about that show tomorrow.

"The price of gold is dancing like a drunken gypsy. Get hold of Susanita and tell her she must not sell a grain unless the market is up three points by noon. Have you heard from my grandson?"

"Ben? No."

Cecily looked down at her hands and Van thought that was strange. It wasn't like Cecily to be shy.

Effie grunted angrily. "He'll produce no designs. I should not have believed he would. He's as unpredictable as his mother was before him. He'll kill himself in that plane of his as she did in hers."

Van felt left out when they talked about business. It was something she'd been considering. Everyone Effie knew was part of her business. Susanita, for example, sent Effie the gold she needed. Cecily said Susanita's husband had been a member of Effie's board once, years ago. But he'd gotten mad at Effie, shot her, and caused her to be in that wheelchair. Susanita had wrestled the gun away from him and kept him from killing Effie. The husband had lost his place on Effie's board, but when he'd died Effie had signed over all her own shares in his gold mines to Susanita to repay her friendship. That showed how wonderful Effie was.

"When will I start working?" she demanded, giving voice to the question she'd been hiding.

The other two stopped talking and looked at her.

"Vanessa," Cecily said, "you needn't—"

"In a while," interrupted Effie. Her eyes ran over Vanessa. She gave a little chuckle. "Enjoy your vacation while you can. I am laying some plans for you."

"Stop hounding me, Jordan. I moved you down here to be useful—not to tell me how to run a business I've been running for twenty years. How many times must I tell you I've taken care of your Cousin Cecily?"

Orlena was giving him an impatient look. Jordan returned it with malice. Her idea of taking care of things was to sabotage tomorrow's lousy fashion show. Did she think that was really going to stop that little bitch? She probably wouldn't even lose her job.

He'd given Cousin Cecily a good scare with that phone call about the videotapes. He knew he had. But she hadn't shown up for the meeting he'd arranged. The knowledge was a continuing irritation, like an unhealed sore.

She thought she was smarter than he was. That's why she was ignoring him. Orlena and Lucy liked to think they were smarter, too. He'd let Orlena see how ineffectual tomorrow's tactics were, and then he'd move. He was going to need money, though.

His eyes traveled over the emeralds she wore. It would serve her right to lose some of them. She'd be quick to believe Lucy was the one responsible, too. His idea grew in appeal.

"I'm sorry, Orlena. I shouldn't have brought it up," he said with sudden contrition. "You have a lot on your mind. I should be helping, not hindering. Here, let me massage your neck."

She looked surprised.

"Really, Jordan, that's not necessary—"

"I know. But it'll relax you. And I worry about you, Orlena."

He stepped behind her as he spoke. For an instant, putting his hands to her neck, he was tempted to hurt her. Except what he was about to do to her was even better.

She gasped as he began to manipulate the muscles beneath her skin.

"Let me know if I'm too rough," he said. "Has to hurt a little to do any good, you know."

She nodded.

He was pressing a nerve that caused a temporary deadness of feeling. He'd read about it and tried it on women a time or two, but never for anything like this. Orlena wore two necklaces today, one long and heavy, the other, more narrow, just above it. As his fingers moved on her skin, they also worked at the two clasps on the narrow necklace. When it parted and slid back into his hands, she didn't notice.

"There now," he said, patting her on the shoulder.

"Thank you, Jordan." She rubbed her hand across her neck and he held his breath, but Orlena looked pleased. She rose.

Jordan knew it was his dismissal, and that she was heading for a conference with the head designer. She'd been on her way when he'd entered her office and she'd sputtered about the delay.

He walked out the door ahead of her. By the time she reached her meeting, she would probably discover her necklace missing. He'd have just enough time to tell Lucy she was wanted in Orlena's office. His sister would be caught flat-footed—though of course with no emeralds. And Orlena's necklace would bring enough cash for him to bribe someone in Cecily Catlow's company.

Leaning into the fawn-colored leather of her swivel chair, Cecily tried not to let herself be chilled by those words from Effie. Surely they'd been meant as evasion, nothing more. Surely Effie would never use Van, would never consider tangling her in some marriage to consolidate her empire.

The thought was so unsettling that she spun around and sat with hands drawn into fists, staring at the wall. No. Effie wasn't so depraved as that. Yet she already had showered on Van things neither of them could ever repay. Clothes. A pretty sapphire ring that matched Van's eyes. Thank God it hadn't been a necklace. Would Van have a horror of anything around her neck? Cecily's thoughts bounced erratically before she steadied them. She would bring the subject up with Effie. Confront her. She wasn't afraid of Effie, and she wouldn't let Van be used. Not by anyone.

She looked at her list of things to do today. It was endless. After twenty minutes she still was unable to get through to Lima.

Her own phone rang.

"The Chasen-Palme woman just called again," barked Effie. "I thought I told you to contact her!"

"I'm sorry, Madame. I've been trying to reach Susanita—"

"You've been wasting your time dialing numbers? Your brain could be better used calming this woman—or finding a theme for our show next fall. I have told you to hire a secretary. When I made you my assistant I did not anticipate that it would make my life more difficult!"

Cecily gritted her teeth. Effie had become a tyrant these last few days, perhaps because of the show tomorrow, perhaps because she had once again lost Ben.

"No, Madame. I'll see to Brigette right away."

When she'd handled that call she found the lines to Peru, and Effie's niece Susanita Olivas, were still busy. In frustration she swept a hand through her hair.

Of course Effie had suggested a secretary—with the absurd admonition it should be someone willing to die for her. Not only was the advice melodramatic, it was impractical. No one thought like that in the twentieth century.

But she *did* need help. She needed someone efficient, and, remembering the pain of her expulsion from Landis and Oxenburg, she acknowledged a longing for someone loyal. What chance did she have of finding someone like that, especially with the schedule she had to keep currently, especially since Effie must insist on checking and double-checking the background of any individual she let on the island?

Very briefly she toyed with the idea of giving Van a chance. But no. The pressure would be too great.

Suddenly out in the hall there was a shout, a thump, a scream. Cecily's head jerked up. At the sound of Effie's angry voice and another scream, she ran to the door.

The scene that met her made her freeze in disbelief. On the brilliant blue carpet the Asian girl, Thida, lay whimpering with an arm flung up to ward off blows. At a word from Effie, Raoul brought the stock of his rifle crashing down against the girl's ribs.

"Where is my earring?" Effie was repeating harshly. "Raoul! Jar lose her answer!"

Jenkins, behind Effie's chair, looked positively sick at what he was witnessing. Raoul's face, too, was ashen, though his arms moved up as if by their own volition to swing the rifle.

Cecily's midsection burned. She felt not only the blows, but the horror the girl before her must feel. She remembered how it had been when she'd been dragged away from Great-Uncle William's and there'd been no one to help; how it had felt that awful afternoon at Landis and Oxenburg; when Peter had turned against her. Knowing there was no help forthcoming was worse than any illness or injury because in that moment of knowledge you lost all hope.

"Stop!" Cecily protested, thrusting herself between Raoul and the girl.

"Strip!" hissed Effie to the prostrate form. "Strip or he will hit you in the face this time! I will see where you've hidden your thieving!" She glanced at Cecily sharply. "Get out of his way. This is no concern of yours!"

Raoul tried to shove her aside, but Cecily caught hold of his rifle.

"It is my concern! Just because you own this island and everyone on it doesn't mean you can act like a maniac!"

Effie's eyes were volcanic with fury.

"Hold your tongue! I caught her up here where she has no business, and when I searched my bedroom, there was a diamond earring miss—"

"Then perhaps you misplaced it, Madame! And it happens Thida was up here because I'd sent for her."

There was no retreating now. Effie's eyes fixed on her dangerously. Though Cecily's heart was pounding, she saw that by drawing Effie's ire toward herself, she had managed to keep from Effie, and perhaps from all of them, Thida's brief expression of betraying surprise.

"I'm hiring Thida as my secretary," Cecily plunged on. "I need someone now. I can't wait while you check the background of an outsider. Thida takes dictation, types and speaks fluent French. She's wasted in the kitchen."

She hoped she was right about the typing. She also hoped she didn't end up regretting this.

If possible, Effie looked more furious than ever. She rocked her chair forward and backward, as though about to attack.

"Fah!" she said. "Fah!"

Almost convulsively she whirled her chair around, ignoring all of them. There was absolute silence as she wheeled down the hall to her office.

Jenkins, with a backward look in which there was silent

approval, hurried after her. Raoul, though seeming undecided, stepped back and lowered the rifle.

"Come with me," said Cecily to the girl she'd just made her secretary. In her office she closed the door firmly and walked to her desk, her back toward the Asian girl.

"Give me the earring, Thida."

It was a bluff. A gamble. She waited. Behind her, after a moment, there was the sound of movement. A hand appeared at the margin of her vision and a diamond earring slid onto her desk.

Thida was weeping.

"I—"

"Don't lie." Cecily held up a hand to forestall the explanation. She slipped the diamond earring in her own pocket. She'd drop it in the carpet where she was sure Effie would find it.

"I'll give you an advance on your first month's salary," she said crisply. "Take the afternoon off and buy the sort of clothes you need for working up here. And Thida—don't *ever* cross Madame Duvall again."

Thida nodded, backing toward the door.

The girl she'd just hired might not be willing to die for her, thought Cecily, but she'd be willing to bet Thida would prove loyal to her. Knees trembling at her own audacity, she went out, dropped Effie's earring in plain sight, and returned to complete her call to Lima as well as other items on her list.

When at last she paused to catch her breath, her thoughts returned immediately to Van sobbing on the beach that morning. Her sister's plaintive anger at years and experiences lost to her came back to Cecily as sharply and as painfully as if they'd been her own.

Lyle & Co.

She wrote the name in careful, dark letters, then traced over them, each stroke a promise. Someday there would be no Lyle & Co.—no Orlena, Lucy, or Jordan to worry about. They were going to taste loss as Van had tasted it. They were going to be stripped of everything. Effie might no longer be concerned with revenge, but she was. Especially after Jordan's call. The dimple in Cecily's chin deepened with a grim determination.

There had been no repeat of that call. She prayed there wouldn't be, yet she found herself increasingly tense that there hadn't been. She kept waiting for something to happen. What was Jordan Lyle scheming?

Hate and a fragmentary feeling of defenselessness warred

inside her. Only when the Lyles had been stripped of the money and status which gave them their clout would she feel she and Van were truly safe.

Her door sprang open so loudly she jumped.

"Everything going okay?" asked Ben, stepping in with a casual nod.

She couldn't speak at first. A fragile, desperate yearning that frightened her held her mute.

"Oh . . . yes. . . ." She found herself on her feet, speaking without knowing how.

He strode toward her, around her desk. He seemed to have no regard at all for the privacy meant to be conveyed by that piece of furniture. Breathing was painful for her and she was seeing the ebony crest of his hair, his eyes, the hard arms under his shirt, not his movements.

"Have some sketches for Effie." He gestured with a padded manila envelope. His eyes were on hers.

"Good. She'll be pleased. Have you seen her yet?"

"No."

He was taller than she was. She could feel the disparity of their two bodies. The words they were saying sounded far away and silly. Cecily swallowed.

They moved at the same instant and she felt the restlessness of his mouth on hers. His hard arms surrounded her, his hand against her backside pressed her against him in tight proximity. A glorious flashing heat made her liquid inside. Her fingers swam in the thick, heavy hair at the back of his head.

Her lips were swollen when he released them. She hungered instantly for the taste of him, knowing she was losing a part of herself and yet not caring.

"Why did you leave?" she asked in a whisper.

She was terrified by how often she had thought of him, confused by this impulse to hold to him tightly, knowing his return could only complicate things.

She could feel his spread fingers and, in his other hand, the envelope he still held scraping her neck.

"Why the hell do you think I left?" His eyes shimmered down at her. "To get away from you. It didn't work."

"I'm—glad."

She parted her lips to him. She heard the envelope land sharply on her desk. They explored each other, and Cecily knew through the bright haze settling over her that their movements were without the restraints of their other meetings.

"I'll see Effie later," Ben said, drawing her toward the door.

Then they were in a bedroom—his—with white walls and a tropical four-poster bed. They began to undress each other.

"Bloody Christ but I want you!" Ben said hoarsely. "I've wanted you for days—ever since I left."

She laughed, but the sound caught on a sob. There was harshness in his words, a buried anger. And she was feeling . . . Cecily shut her eyes, afraid of what she was feeling here in the arms of a man who wanted only to possess her body.

The bed was high and old-fashioned. He lifted her onto it. His arm brushed her naked breast and her senses swirled.

Cecily caught his head and urged it down. His mouth began to traverse the soft swelling of her flesh, warming it, moistening it, drawing it gently into a cavern of unbelievable pleasure. There was no need for speech.

"Ben," she whispered. Her fingers moved in trembling wonder through his hair, along the strong bones of his temples. Did he understand that she was casting pride away? That she had longed for him? She spoke his name again.

He looked up, and his eyes seemed startled for an instant. Their bitterness faded. He cupped her face between his hands. His kiss was sweet and slow.

Their bodies lay motionless, quivering with expectancy. Ben raised his head to study her face, then kissed her again. Rippling waves of completion crashed through them both as his flesh joined hers.

TWENTY-ONE

THEY HAD MADE LOVE TWICE IN RAPID SUCCESSION. NOW, SPENT AND aware of her own vulnerability, unsure of anything about the man beside her, Cecily lay studying the partial canopy of the bed above them. Her arm, flung back in a curve on the pillow beneath her, was shielding her face, she hoped, from too close scrutiny by Ben Duvall.

The bed had shifted. He was looking at her. Pale daylight filtered through curtained windows etching shadows down his bare chest, along his tightly formed muscles. She wondered what time it was.

"If you were as reluctant as you let on last time I saw you, I must have missed something." His words were low and faintly mocking. His thumb traced the curve of her throat.

Cecily pushed his hand away. On a nearby desk she could see two photograph frames, one holding the likeness of a striking woman with short hair and dark eyes like Ben's, the other empty. His mother and the emptiness where his wife's picture once had been, she guessed. They haunted her. They made it hard to resist whatever was drawing her toward him.

"I wasn't reluctant," she said in a low voice. "Obviously. You're—very good."

Unconsciously she let her gaze be snared by his.

"By damn. The *Good Housekeeping* Seal of Approval." There was sarcasm in his voice, but his smile held only humor. Cecily sensed she was glimpsing a gentler Ben, one who could charm her, yet one who might likewise vanish at any minute.

"Christ, Effie sure knew what she was doing when she threw us together," he said, sitting up and thrusting his hair back. And now the edge of anger was back in his voice again, Cecily recognized.

"The way I see it, we've both fallen into Effie's fire," he said bluntly. "We can both sizzle in it, or we can either one get away from her for good."

His eyes were piercing. Cecily looked away.

"I—can't leave her."

She thought of the Lyles and what they had done, of Van's tears on the beach that morning, and the phone call that still hung like a threat above them. But her pounding heart, as the prospect of distance from Ben Duvall was offered her, told her it was thinking of something other than the need for Effie's strength to obliterate old enemies.

Ben swung restlessly from the bed. Crossing to the window, he jerked a drapery cord, flooding the room with light, and stood looking out.

Cecily sat up, hugging her arms around her knees, and closed her eyes. She *couldn't* care for him! It would hurt too much. She didn't know what attracted him to her, but she knew it couldn't last. It had something to do with his war with Effie. It had something to do with manipulation.

"I can't leave, either," he said. "I've just sunk every cent I own into having our nav screens put on the Peregrine."

She was silent, limp with relief.

"I don't understand," she said after a moment. "How can something for your windows cost that much money?"

To her amazement he laughed, the effect spellbinding as his face went unguarded.

"You don't know the first damn thing about airplanes, do you?"

In spite of the question, she felt the distance between them narrowed suddenly to a thread. She shook her head.

Ben moved without warning, catching her by the hand and pulling her to her feet.

"Get dressed and I'll show you, then. Christ, of course it's not something for the windows! It's a whole new flight system. Computer-controlled, with ability to pick up and integrate air traffic information, radar fixes—a system that's going to prove more reliable than any human pilot if this first step works!"

"It's beautiful," Cecily said, and Ben thought she meant it.

She paused, taking in the sight of the white plane striped in red, bronze, and blue.

Ben wondered if she saw, as he did, its sleek, sharply angled nose poised for flight. Even motionless its lack of propellers and uncluttered lines spoke of speed. It was like a perfect piece of sculpture. He ran his hand along the curve of a wing and thought of caressing the soft skin of the woman beside him just a while ago.

"Going to cart her off pretty soon now, Mr. Duvall," called a man in coveralls working on a smaller plane nearby.

Ben nodded. The Peregrine would be towed into a hangar this afternoon to await installation of the system he and Pepe had designed for her. They'd drawn the plans up a year ago, watched a model tested and retested. They both felt sure beyond a doubt the system would work. It promised to be the biggest breakthrough he and Pepe had made to date. For months he'd been hungering for the moment when he'd land with all standard navigational aides sealed off from him and know another adaptation for the Peregrine had worked. The two of them would have pitted themselves against odds most men and planes didn't want to touch—and won. Yet now, standing here with Cecily, he felt the first stir in years of something approaching caution.

Forget it. If this was the time he and the Peregrine didn't make it back, there wasn't much loss.

Cecily was only marking time with him, forgetting someone else; she'd told him that the first night he'd come back to Effie's. It was okay. Maybe he was only marking time with her. And neither of them was the sort to attach any moonlight and roses sentiment to the act of sex.

He stepped up onto the wing, which was almost as high as Cecily's shoulder, and held down a hand.

"Come on in," he said.

Something warm always stirred in him at his first inner view of the Peregrine. To the left was a two-seated cockpit, to the right was what looked like an elegant cocktail lounge with four comfortable leather chairs and a drop-down table, all in rich honey tones.

"Our cabin attendants will be serving lunch shortly," he said, imitating commercial airlines. He tossed her the well-wrapped hotdogs they'd stopped for along the way. "There. You've been served."

She laughed. He'd hoped she would. He didn't know why he'd brought her here. It had surprised him. Just his own restlessness to see the plane again before it spent time in someone else's hands, he guessed.

Opening a small refrigerator, he took out a split of white burgundy and served it.

"So what do you think?"

"It's unbelievable. Unlike anything I've ever even imagined. Why do you fly?"

She'd been looking around, but now her eyes came to rest directly on his. There were shadows around them, small, delicate, brooding shadows that were always there, only darker somehow. Maybe that was what it was about her that got next to him, those shadows. Like she was always a little bit afraid but didn't dare show it. Like she was lonely.

"My mother flew. She had a little Beechcraft. I got the bug early."

"You flew people out of Phnom Penh."

"Somebody had to." He felt vaguely annoyed someone had told her about his stint with Air America. He took a deep drink of wine. "Figured I owed it, considering how many rubies Effie had gouged out of Southeast Asia."

"I've hired Thida as my secretary. She's going to start Monday."

He felt silence crackling around the narrow channel filled with their words. She was drawing him out when he hadn't meant to engage in a conversation like this. She was too damned direct.

"So?" he said. Lines were tightening between them. Ben could feel the tug.

"I've heard she might have been your mistress."

"Or my daughter?" Ben took a long drink from the glass in his hand. "You curious?"

Her steady gaze met his. "Yes. I guess I am."

Maybe it was the wine; or his long trip back. He felt things being said that weren't being said.

"Her mother died saving my ass when I took my last planeload out. I figured I owed the girl something."

Cecily made what they were talking about seem like a long time ago. A hell of a long time. He reached out slowly and drew her toward him. Her lips trembled under his. She was something he was beginning to need. Something he was beginning to want. And maybe she hadn't been spoiled by Effie.

All he had to do was figure out how to snatch her away from Effie before she was.

Wesley Bell supposed he looked foolish steering a boat while he carried roses. But after all, he'd boated off Cape Cod since he was a kid. It had just seemed simpler to rent a boat with a good motor and take himself out to Effie Duvall's island than to make conversation with some stranger going and coming. Besides, he only needed one hand for the job. He hoped Van liked flowers. He didn't think she'd been aware when he'd brought them to her in the hospital.

He supposed he should have let somebody know he was coming—gotten directions, maybe. Except then it wouldn't have looked like a casual, spur-of-the-moment thing dropping in. Anyway, they'd given good directions where he'd rented the boat, even if they had looked at him oddly when he'd told them where he wanted to go. With the thumb that held the cone of flowers, he pushed his glasses back up his nose and peered at the island ahead.

By the time he was able to see the dock he was also able to see the big boat moored there. A yacht. A good-sized one, too. That was interesting, as he'd somehow thought the elderly lady he'd spoken to on the phone a time or two wouldn't be the frivolous sort.

He could see men on the dock—three of them, four of them— with sticks across their arms. Fishing poles, he guessed. Only they looked like . . .

"Hey, you! Change course! This is private property."

Guns! Wesley stared in indignation, hardly hearing the call.

Guns! Rifles. What sort of place had Van come to? Was she some sort of prisoner?

"Turn back!" The order was barked more sharply this time.

Wesley shook the roses angrily. "I've come to see Vanessa Catlow! I'm her lawyer."

He cut the throttle. A zinging noise passed over his head. The men on the dock looked like movie bad guys, and they were shooting at him to scare him away, he thought in disbelief.

He set his jaw. "I'm here to see Miss Catlow," he yelled again.

He'd noticed a boat in the distance. Someone else was coming in this direction. The toughs with the rifles wouldn't dare use them in earnest.

"Go back. Call for an appointment!"

The yacht flew a foreign flag. Wesley was starting to worry that something was wrong.

His hand held the boat on a straight course toward the dock. The zinging sound came again. Fire burst down his arm and he gasped and fell back. Against the throttle. His glasses had slipped. The pain in his arm was making the scene around him flicker on and off. He saw disconnected images. The dock veering steeply away. The land rushing toward him. And then the crash. He held the roses above his head and hoped they wouldn't get crushed.

Ben reached the house at a steady lope. Effie might have heard those shots. Her hearing had always been keen. And if she'd called Raoul, no telling what kind of garbled account she'd get of a man being shot at her dock.

He shoved the sliding door to the terrace open. There was a cry. A blond woman standing in the hall beyond the dining room had turned in alarm. It was Cecily's sister.

Christ. He hadn't thought of her when he'd rushed up. He guessed Cecily hadn't, either. Cecily had known the fellow in the boat and been concerned, even though his wound was only a flesh wound.

"Van?" He was glad he'd remembered her name. "I'm Ben— Effie's grandson. I've been away for a while."

She looked frightened. He didn't move, though it made him impatient.

"Sorry if I startled you. There's been a minor accident down at the dock and I didn't want Effie and Prince Karim to be alarmed."

That was the second reason he'd come running up. He'd

recognized the flag on Karim's yacht and remembered the man had bodyguards. No need to get him upset thinking this was some attempt on his life. Ben edged inside. The noise of footsteps erupted from the elevator. Jenkins with Effie, Karim, and his two bodyguards. Ben turned his attention.

"It's nothing down at the dock," he said. "Just a misunderstanding. Cecily's lawyer coming to call. Apparently he didn't know he needed clearing to land here."

"Apparently no one sees fit to tell me of their comings and goings these days," Effie shot back. "Are you here to work, or did you drop in for tea?"

"Wesley's been hurt?" Van spoke for the first time. Her voice was shaky.

"His arm's a little bloody, that's all, and his glasses are cracked." Ben felt a little annoyed as he saw Effie and her entourage returning toward the elevator. Didn't anyone think about Van?

He was worried she might be going into shock or something. He tried to distract her.

"He could probably use a sandwich or something when they bring him up. So could Cecily and I. Go ask the cook to put something together, will you?"

She didn't move. "I—"

"Go on," he urged gently.

When she'd gone he shook his head in relief and went to the bar to fix a drink.

But Van was back almost immediately.

"I told them," she said stoically. "Is there anything else?" Her face was pale.

"No, that's fine," he said, surprised and a little ashamed at how she'd moved into action. He thought of what he was doing, remembered his manners. "May I fix you a drink?"

She was very nervous. "I can't. I'm on medication. I've been—"

"I know." Ben felt awkward. Might as well cut through the crap. "What's the best thing about being out?"

Van blinked. "No one ever asks me things like that," she said seriously.

Ben grinned. "Didn't figure they did."

After a missed beat she laughed uncertainly. Ben wished he could mend her. He liked her and he'd done that once with a bird with a broken wing.

Then the others were coming in from the terrace. The lawyer, supported on one side by a guard and gritting his teeth against pain, still held tenaciously to his cone of mangled roses.

TWENTY-TWO

"**I** HAVE NOT BEEN SO NOTORIOUS SINCE MY ARGUMENT WITH William Lyle," chortled Effie. "Imagine! Mention in a gossip column. Photographers waiting to take my picture."

Cecily smiled, enjoying Effie's smug delight though anxiety scoured the lining of her own stomach. It seemed they had been in the Fontainbleau for hours. Effie stopped to inspect every detail of the great hotel—the wares visible through the open door of the Cartier boutique; the grand piano around which cocktails were served; the small, twinkling lights of a dining room, which, Effie said, had been redone "considerably" since her day. How could anyone rush a woman who had not enjoyed such sights in almost twenty years?

"If you don't get a move on, you'll miss your own damned show," Ben growled.

"This is not *my* show. This is only my jewelry on a lot of twittering models parading clothes. My show is not for months yet," Effie corrected.

She stopped her chair to cock an appraising eye at a mirror. "Yes, their quality still is good," she said.

Ben grinned at Cecily across the top of Effie's head. It made him look younger, and wryly, devilishly good-humored. The privacy of their shared glance brought a lightness to Cecily's step. He reached across and brushed her fingers.

The right combination of chemicals, he'd said in bed last night. Was that all there was to their attraction? It was for Ben. She tried not to think of it, brought her mind back to Effie's dawdling progress through the infinite halls of this great hotel.

"Damn it, Effie, if you don't get a move on, I'm going to give that chair of yours a shove," Ben threatened.

"I do not recall inviting you here. Nor do I flatter myself it was the prospect of my company that lured you along."

Effie angled a look at him.

Ben bowed from the waist in that manner he had when sparring with her.

"Right. I came for the chicken salad. Unless you'll let Cecily out of her duties here long enough for me to rent a room."

171

Had there been some thawing between them, even though less than a day had passed since Ben's return? Cecily sensed a strange, cautious pleasure behind their exchange. She cast an uneasy glance in Van's direction but was satisfied that her sister, walking behind with Wesley, had been too far removed to hear Ben's comment. Sex wasn't a part of Vanessa's world, not a part of her thoughts. Even teasing about it might upset her, let alone the reality of Cecily sleeping with anyone. Van was hovering between excitement and nervousness as it was, being here today.

But Cecily couldn't afford to worry about such matters just now. Wesley was so sweet and serious. He'd take care of Van.

"I think I'd better go ahead," she said. "You look wonderful, Effie."

The name slipped out. Effie, wearing her eternal black tuxedo suit, beamed back. She did look splendid. A hairdresser had come to the island that morning and her snowy mane was fuller than usual. She wore jet-black earrings, and her white silk necktie was adorned and held in place by a rose made of diamonds and rubies. With Ben in a superbly cut black suit standing by her she looked grander and more vibrant than Cecily ever remembered.

"Go," said Effie. "Perhaps that ridiculous Countess di Crichi will satisfy herself kissing your cheeks instead of mine."

Cecily hurried along, the hem of her saffron wrap-dress fluttering with her speed.

"Looks good," said Brigette in greeting as they met in the backstage area. "Three TV stations covering it. One's setting up already."

Cecily peeked out, down the runway the models would walk. Round tables topped in pale aqua cloths held floral arrangements. A few of them were filling already. Tickets for the show had sold out the first day they'd gone on sale, which had amazed Brigette as much as it had Cecily.

"I knew her name would be a draw, but not such a big one," the thin blonde had said.

Four hundred tickets at two hundred dollars a ticket, Cecily thought now. Amazing.

She was glad Ben had come. She thought Effie was too, in spite of her snappishness.

A tremor skipped through her and she found herself remembering the way Ben had held her chin and kissed her yesterday in his plane, the strength and sureness of his fingers. Drawing breath, she disciplined her thoughts. While Brigette snapped effectively at her models. Cecily slipped out to join the others in her party. She had seen what she needed to see. Effie's guards and the hotel guards were in place. All was going according to plan.

The pieces being shown today were not spectacular—an art deco necklace and a sautoir with a black pearl, both items from Effie's heyday and with which she'd never part, plus a smattering of items from the last few years. Still, their presence—or Effie's—was enough to produce the crowd that was starting to filter in. The Countess di Crichi, a dowager with a humped nose, came over to pay her respects to Effie. Heads turned. A silver cooler of champagne arrived at Effie's side, though there was wine at the tables.

Cecily fidgeted. It seemed as though they'd been waiting forever, though of course they were early and barely half the tables in the room were filled.

She sneaked a glance at her watch and her heart thumped with the first premonition of something amiss. It *wasn't* early. The show was due to start in less than ten minutes. The ticket holders already present were buzzing and anxious. Why weren't people buzzing around those other tables, too?

"I . . . I want to check a few last things with Brigette," she murmured, rising and catching Ben's eye.

Something flickered there and he looked quickly at Effie. Did he understand? She hoped so. A cold, sick feeling was creeping into her stomach.

"Brigette!" She found the show's coordinator backstage amid the bedlam of models twitching pleats and straightening belts. Another woman, who would be the commentator for the show, was flipping through cards, preparing to go on. "What's with those empty tables?"

Tucking a stray hair into her pale chignon, Brigette shrugged.

"Late, I guess. Or no-shows. Every seat is sold, and money in."

"Why would anyone buy the tickets if they didn't . . ."

Cecily let the question die. She was peeking out through the curtain. Another camera crew was arriving. The tables that were vacant left gaps around the runway and throughout the room.

From every angle they were visible. They would look bad on camera. Bad for Brigette. Worse for Effie. Which was maybe what someone wanted, thought Cecily, letting icy fingers slip numbly down the edge of the velvet curtain. Had someone deliberately bought those tables to leave them empty?

She drew in her breath. "How long can you stall?"

"What?" Brigette looked up from conferring with the commentator. "I can't. It's time right now. And the waiters are set to bring in the lunch in forty-five minutes. They'll be on our heels as it is."

Cecily's jaw set. The fashion show and then the lunch during which the women guests could talk things over and decide to stop by Brigette's or maybe even make an appointment with Effie for some coveted item. That was the logic behind the scheduling. Only now it wasn't going to work like the clockwork intended.

"Well, you'd better hold that curtain ten more minutes or you'll have egg on your face with all those empty tables and the press here."

As she started to move she heard Brigette's voice behind her. "What—"

"Ten minutes!" Cecily spun and locked eyes with her to drive home the words.

Then she was off, moving swiftly, stopping to speak in her silkiest voice to the two women standing at the door collecting tickets.

"Sit down and enjoy yourself with your friends, please. I'll take care of the latecomers."

One of them started to argue. Cecily cut her off with a smile.

"Madame Duvall's so pleased with all your efforts. She hopes you'll accept some champagne with her compliments before the show starts."

As they turned away, Cecily caught the sleeve of a waiter.

"See where those women sit. Get a bottle of champagne to their table. And get bottles to half a dozen other tables up next to the stage. Bill it to Madame Duvall. I'm her assistant."

The activity would catch people's curiosity, give them something to watch. She wanted to run and knew she couldn't. Eight minutes left.

She approached a group of six women chatting idly in the hallway. The clientele this hotel drew would look completely suited to those vacant tables.

"Excuse me, ladies. If you haven't had lunch, there's a style show in the Gold Room. Madame Duvall, who's showing her jewelry in public for the first time in many years, would like you to be her guests."

They looked at each other in mingled surprise and enjoyment, then turned in the direction Cecily indicated.

"Oh, I heard something about this," one of them said.

She reached the dining room with the small, twinkling lights. People were arriving, waiting, being seated.

"Excuse me, Madame Duvall is inviting a few hotel guests to join her for lunch and a fashion show in the Gold Room today. . . ."

She repeated it endlessly, in a low voice, first to larger groups and then to couples.

"Say, what is this?" one man demanded suspiciously.

But others went.

It wasn't enough. She moved into the lounge, then threaded her way back, catching more newcomers. Too slow.

Her eyes caught the busy lights of a bank of elevators. She met an arriving car. Her manner was calm. Her smile that of someone who did this every day, she hoped.

Five minutes now. The press might get wind of this. But then again they might not. In any case, anything would be better than those empty tables.

With two minutes left she gave up the effort, rushing back to the room where discreetly placed spotlights were already coming on. A few empty tables remained, but not many. And the latecomers, still settling in, were attracting a little curiosity but not much.

The mood in the room was expectant.

"Where the devil have you been?" Ben hissed as she slid in beside him. "Is something wrong?"

She shook her head.

A curtain twitched. She guessed it was Brigette, searching for her. The third camera crew had arrived, and turned on its floodlights. The show was beginning.

"Unremarkable. Every piece unremarkable," Jordan sneered.

"I can't understand why those tables are filled!" lamented Lucy, watching the evening news beside him.

"I told you it was a stupid plan," said Jordan blandly. "What are a few empty tables? If you wanted the old bitch out of the way, you should have arranged an accident. Her and her piddling jewelry both in the boat coming over this morning. Nothing for the show, and she'd get fished out and die of pneumonia—innocent as you please."

"Shut up!"

Orlena rubbed her neck while her eyes, fixed on the fifty-inch TV screen, took in every detail of the diamond-and-platinum sautoir with its fine black pearl. Every set in Miami would show this tonight. *Three stations had covered it!* Her son's smug dismissal of the Duvall collection because it contained nothing dazzling only proved that he hadn't a brain in his head. It was almost as upsetting as her discovery yesterday that her daughter was a thief. Oh, of course Lucy had whined and wailed and denied it, but the fact was, Orlena's small emerald necklace was missing. The only explanation was that it had somehow slipped from her neck—perhaps she'd forgotten to fasten one of the clasps and the other had given way. And Lucy had been there in Orlena's office for no good reason, though of course she'd invented some cock-and-bull story about Jordan sending her.

Both her children were great disappointments, and the television footage, the applause of the crowd which she'd watched already on another channel, was giving her a headache.

"Left on your own you would get yourself in enormous trouble, Jordan," she said coldly. "Only an idiot would think of murder as the first solution to anything. It's clumsy. And how would eliminating Effie Duvall rid us of your cousin Cecily? God knows—"

"Turn up the volume!"

Trace MacDonald, though enduring Lucy's schoolgirlish grip on his hand as he stood behind her, had been watching the screen with an ad man's interest. It suddenly filled with Cecily Catlow answering some reporter's question.

"Why were people so excited about this show? Because Madame Duvall has come out of retirement, of course. And because of her reputation for quality. Her cachet on an item conveys a prestige no other jeweler in town can even begin to match— especially the newer ones."

A pair of doelike brown eyes looked unwaveringly into the camera.

"Did you hear that?" Jordan howled. "She's challenging us!"

Orlena caught her breath. For once her son was right. Those eyes seemed to be in the room with her, looking at her, glinting with determination as they had when William's great-niece was a child.

"Today, of course, was primarily nostalgia . . . a retrospective," the cool little voice at the microphone was saying. "We'll show a new line in the fall—by invitation."

"Turn it off!" Orlena ordered.

She was shaking. Her plan to keep those tables vacant had

fallen through. This insufferable little ghost from the past was causing more trouble than she'd thought possible in her darkest moments. Cecily could bring Jordan down. She'd ruin him if she had the chance. Orlena knew it now.

Trace MacDonald smoothed a hand along his youthful gray hair and Orlena knew he was thinking the same. She twisted her emerald ring. Her voice sounded harsh in her own ears.

"As I was asking you, Jordan, what good do you think it would do to get rid of Effie Duvall? That girl might end up running her company! *She's* the source of all our trouble. *She's* the one we have to squash. Or Duvall Inc. Or both—if we want to survive."

"Don't you think I know it?" Jordan asked nastily, as though he liked rubbing it in.

Something glittered in his eyes that she'd never seen before. It made Orlena shiver. Sometimes it worried her thinking about how rashly Jordan might behave if she weren't around to keep him in check.

"Say, is that the one that used to be in the asylum? That cute blond fox?" asked Trace.

Annoyed Lucy hadn't turned the set off, annoyed Trace had spoken, Orlena raised a chilly look to find him staring with interest at William's other great-niece, caught in the background of the scene before it faded.

A little of the panic she'd been feeling started to leave Orlena. She allowed herself a smile and stopped twisting her ring. Her narrowed eyes studied Trace MacDonald's back with speculation.

TWENTY-THREE

"IDIOT! THE MAN WHO WROTE THIS ARTICLE IS AN IDIOT! LOOK at his words—he does not even have the vocabulary to discuss either jewelry *or* fashion!"

Effie hurled a folded newspaper from her hand and rolled back to the end of the terrace where she'd been just minutes before. Her expression remained as scornfully indifferent as her words, but her eyes were crackling. Anger, thought Cecily. And under the anger she'd been wounded by that awful review in the morning's paper—though she'd never show it.

Cecily felt guilty and helpless. Yesterday had been such a triumph. Last night they'd watched Effie on every newscast, laughing and celebrating, all in high spirits. This morning's coverage made it sound as though Effie had been of interest only as a curiosity, a museum piece who had outlived her era and had not designed a worthwhile item in years.

Cecily looked up to meet Van's grave and troubled eyes.

"Have your coffee, Effie," Van said shyly. "Things always look better after coffee."

"Of course he didn't know what he was talking about," said Cecily. "It was supposed to be a retrospective, not an unveiling of new designs. Anyway, he's probably one of those men who thinks covering a style show is beneath him."

Bibi sat in a corner in sunshine, grooming himself. Effie wheeled toward them.

"I do not want coffee!" she said sharply. "Someone does not say my 'genius withered years ago' because he does not like style shows! Do you take me for a fool? You have made me look like one with these—these great plans."

She waved her hand. Cecily swallowed.

"I suppose I shall look like a greater fool with these magazine ads." Effie's mood was darker than Bibi's coat. She snapped for the animal. "Where is Ben? I want you both in my office in forty-five minutes. Vanessa, I must see you first. You finish your breakfast and then come along."

She'd been moving in restless circles. Now, before either sister could answer, she headed back into the house.

For a moment, in the bright morning air, Cecily heard nothing but the sound of a pan in the kitchen and the clear, distant cry of a seagull.

"She's hurt," said Van.

Cecily gave a nod.

There were footsteps on the flagstones. It was Ben. He looked less quarrelsome than usual, but he was frowning. He reached for the coffee.

"What the hell's wrong with Effie? She just took my head off."

"This morning's paper says—"

"I know. I saw a copy upstairs. Pretty bad, but she's had bad reviews before—a time or two—when she'd crossed someone."

"Not for a long time, Ben. Not at this age." Cecily's voice was gentle.

He considered, then nodded slowly. His eyes held hers, and

for an instant Cecily felt his desire to touch her, even though she had left his bed not half an hour ago. She wanted the same thing and was painfully conscious of Van's presence. Ben sat down, his leg deliberately brushing hers beneath the table.

"Van, have you remembered your medicine?"

Cecily knew her question was abrupt. Was she so afraid Van would see what was happening?

"Cecily, why do you keep asking me that? You know I've never forgotten." Van sounded hurt.

Cecily hated herself.

"Stop mothering," Ben said with tolerant humor. "I've got an idea Van's at least twenty-one, aren't you, Van?"

Vanessa looked startled. She was wary of Ben, as she was around all men, Cecily had noted. Now, though, Van caught his joke and laughed a little.

"Yes," she said with a blush and sudden spunk. "And if there's any mothering to do, I ought to get to do it! I'm older than Cecily."

She flounced up with her plate. Her moment of boldness was over as quickly as it had come. "I guess I'd better go and see what Effie wants. I hope it's not canasta this early in the day."

"Thanks," said Cecily when they were alone.

Ben nodded. A dark mood seemed to have settled on him now.

"There's truth in what that article says. Effie hasn't done a really original piece in years. She's relied on those goddamn big stones of hers. She's relied on sales to a bunch of dinosaurs that're dying off around her."

There was bitterness in his voice, but sadness, too.

Cecily felt a pressure inside her throat. Did he think Effie was incapable of a comeback—that even her company was? Did he perhaps harbor some concern for Effie herself?

Well, it was too late. She was in this game to stay, and Effie was too. Yet at the moment she could not quite close her ears to what Ben was saying. Her own doubts were too near the surface.

"Be that as it may, we've got to choose some designs for those ads," she said. "And a theme for them—for her show, too, for that matter, but it's the ad that's pressing us right now. A photographer's coming at ten. I've tried to talk her into consulting an ad agency, but of course she refuses even to consider that."

Ben gave a short laugh. "I understand we're due in her office soon. Let's get going. Maybe we can brainstorm for five or ten minutes before going in."

All at once they seemed to be on the same side, with Ben every bit as interested in the future of Duvall Inc. as she was. As he stood up he shoved aside a half-finished slice of papaya. There were rapid footsteps behind them. Jenkins, looking slightly less stooped than usual, burst into view.

"Madame is in a fury!" he announced from the doorway. "She wants you at once."

He disappeared immediately.

"Now what?" said Ben.

By the time they reached the living room the usually unshakable Jenkins had a decanter in one hand and was tossing back a drink with another.

"Perhaps you'd better have one, too," he said with a grimace. "Her advertising space in *Town and Country* has just been canceled. I haven't seen her this angry in twenty years."

"What?" Cecily heard her own crescendoing voice.

Jenkins moved at once to modify the shock of his announcement. "No, no, she hasn't lost her space completely—just that particular spot she wanted in successive issues. There was some sort of mix-up."

"Christ, maybe she'll cancel the damned ads, then," muttered Ben as they hurried upstairs. But he sounded as upset by that prospect as Cecily herself felt at that moment. No matter that they weren't remotely ready to run ads, the affront to Effie after that slap in the paper was too much to endure.

"Mix-up, ha!" snarled Effie as Jenkins followed them in, still trying to explain the situation. She was circling her dais, the chair beneath her suddenly become an appendage which she seemed to lash behind her as the panther lashed his tail. "I had an agreement for a fixed spot in the magazine. Now I am told some previous contract had been drawn and misplaced. What lies!"

Bright spots of color had risen to her cheeks. She thrust viciously at the wheels beneath her fingers, her great ugly ruby flashing.

"Ah, yes. My competitors must be terrified, even if some newspaper writer sniffs at me. And they are wise! My genius has withered, has it? I will show them just how plump it is." Her voice had dropped to a mutter, but now she raised it. "Vanessa!"

Cecily started. Ben put a hand on her arm. He did not appear as alarmed by Effie's half-coherent ranting as Jenkins, who was frowning in concern, or as she herself felt.

The door to the anteroom opened. Van, wearing a black velvet dress and bearing a tray whose contents were hidden by the same material, came in with a secretive look.

"Bring it here," ordered Effie.

She moved toward her desk, leaving Van to follow. Her eyes beneath their wrinkled hoods were hard yet brilliant, like gems themselves. Cold. Fiery. Glittering. They swept the assembled faces.

"I dreamed of the circus one night—of a circus I went to when I was a little girl. The ladies on horses . . . the acrobats . . . and the ringmaster. Ah, but he was handsome all in black."

Effie was starting to ramble. Cecily couldn't believe it. Horrified, she bit her lip, wondering whether it was the shock of those canceled ads that had caused this to happen, wondering if the others in the room were dying inside as she was.

"So handsome . . ." Effie chuckled, then stopped abruptly. Her eyes swept all of them again, and they seemed jarringly alert. "I have used the last of my genius now, but perhaps it will be enough to remind the world I had a genius. What do you think?"

At a movement of her finger Van flung back the pieces of black velvet covering the tray. It revealed a pad of shining white satin. And from the pad rose a choker at least four inches high, shooting black magic from a thousand glittering midnight-dark stones set side by side *en pavé*. The stones gave off such radiance that the whole creation seemed alive. Their exotic splendor stole away Cecily's breath. And joining the black stones, intended to clasp at the center of a woman's throat, was one dazzling white oblong diamond, almost two inches high.

"What do you think?" repeated Effie. "I call it my Ringmaster Necklace."

No one spoke. Ben reached out one finger and touched the collar. His hand was trembling.

"Bloody Christ, Effie. It's wonderful! The finest thing you've ever done. I've never seen anything like it. I don't know what to say!"

There was moisture in his eyes. Cecily felt the same in hers and wiped it away. Effie noted the movement and grunted satisfaction.

"It's beautiful, Effie!"

"It will be hard to sell," Effie said.

"It won't!"

The contradiction from Jekins was so vigorous Cecily laughed. Euphoria seemed to catch them all and everyone spoke.

"Are they black diamonds? Not from Joao's mines, surely!"

"Sapphires. From Lynette. Something in my gut has made me save them for decades. Now I know why."

"It solves the question of what that first ad will be."

"No! This is for my show. After it has been unveiled—in December, perhaps. Put it on, Vanessa."

Cecily felt the bottom drop out of her stomach. Van would panic.

But Van, with her golden hair arranged high on her head, clasped the necklace on with a smile. She stood before them, proud and stunning.

"You see, I have found a perfect model," said Effie.

Cecily heard with more dismay than she'd heard Effie's earlier command. Effie's web was suddenly there in the room with them, spreading out toward Van.

Her sister frowned, though.

"Oh, Effie, I'm not going to pose for some magazine, if that's what you're thinking. I'm glad enough to wear it here for them, but . . ." She nibbled her lip as though to align her thoughts. Her eyes were intensely serious. "I know you're trying to be nice to me, but I want a *real* job. I want to *do* something with my life, not just stand around and be looked at! That's what I did in the hospital."

Absurd as it was, Cecily found herself all at once encouraging what had made her uneasy just seconds before.

"Van, it's not like that." She wanted her sister to believe in herself. "You'd really be working. It's *hard* work—"

"Horse droppings! Van's telling you she wants to be more than a piece of fluff. Why don't you both listen?" Ben interrupted tersely.

Cecily looked at him in surprise, a little indignant. Van seemed startled, too.

"Yes. . . ." she said hesitantly, then with more confidence. "Yes, that is what I'm saying!" She looked at Effie with a small smile of apology. "Is it all right if I take this off now?"

Effie made a snorting sound, but waved her hand. "Now what am I to do for a model? Advertising should have a theme—an image. I've been reading about it. And that photographer will be here in"—her eyes sliced across to a clock—"ten minutes." She rubbed at her forehead.

Jenkins, at a glare from Effie, slipped away now.

"Well . . . ." said Van, chewing her lip again. "You could use Bibi. Not to wear things, of course, but to be there with them. People would remember Bibi."

Starting toward the window now, Effie turned back abruptly.

"By Christ!" said Ben beneath his breath.

Effie lost the glare she'd started with and chuckled lustily. "So you think that's the perfect image for Effie, do you, Vanessa? I shall have to pay the photographer a fortune extra, I have no doubt. But yes, but yes!"

She laughed again, then brought a hand to her forehead as though in pain.

"Madame! Are you feeling unwell?" asked Cecily in alarm.

"A touch of sinus." Effie's voice was harsh.

"A doctor could give you something for that, you know. Let me have Jenkins call—"

Effie waved a hand in negative command. "I have outlived two doctors. It's nothing. Too much champagne last night. Stop fussing."

Ben stirred. "It's your goddamned blood pressure, isn't it, Effie? Your doctor's died and you're too damn stubborn to find another one and take your medicine—"

"I do not need advice from you! I have managed without it for ten years now!"

Effie's words were a snarl. She and Ben faced one another, the truce between them gone. Cecily felt a blow to her heart as she realized how much she was coming to care for this hard, unpredictable woman and how Effie's angry look and suddenly rapid breathing was frightening her.

Effie's intercom buzzed.

"Madame? Wesley Bell is here," said Jenkins's voice.

"Wesley?" Vanessa's exclamation echoed Cecily's surprise. It seemed to end the moment's confrontation, too.

"I thought you were flying back to New York this morning," said Cecily as Wesley entered. She wondered what this was about, him here at this meeting in Effie's office.

"I caught him at the airport." Effie rolled back toward her desk, her vigor restored. "I have outlived my lawyer as well as my doctor. I can make good use of him."

"It promises to be more interesting than working for Fitch, Fitch and Cromwell," Wesley said, straightening his still cracked glasses. His eyes twinkled shyly.

"I guarantee it will be interesting," said Effie, swinging into place behind her desk. "The first thing you will do for me is find out who owns the building housing the Palm Beach outlet of Lyle and Company."

TWENTY-FOUR

"MRS. LYLE, WE'VE BEEN STUDYING THIS FOR A WEEK. THERE'S absolutely no loophole, no way out. You'll have to relocate."

Orlena's chilly green eyes bored into the bald attorney standing in front of her as he continued.

"Your lease—Mr. Zumwald's lease, which you acquired when you bought him out—was with the building's original owner. It's invalid, now that the building's been sold. If you'd like us to start investigating another location—"

"I'm more likely to start investigating another law firm. Out!"

She hugged the sleeves of her green jersey dress, eyes fixed coldly on his departing figure. She was furious. These legal advisers she paid so lavishly should have noted that obscure detail. They should have warned her about it, even though it seemed unimportant. Then she would not have found herself in this unbearable predicament, with Effie Duvall suddenly owning the roof above her head.

"I told you you shouldn't have let Trace pull strings to cancel her ads," Jordan drawled with insufferable smugness. He was getting big-headed. Just because—at Orlena's suggestion—he had wined and dined enough society cows to bring in a few new clients, he thought he was running the business.

"Shut up, Jordan!" She was more irritated than usual with him. "I'm well aware your solution to dealing with people who cross you is killing them!"

Lucy, sitting next to Trace MacDonald, stuck her lip out. "Really, Orlena! I don't think you should keep bringing up that old accident! Trace will get the wrong impression."

Orlena eyed her wearily. She did feel weary. Sometimes the effort of carrying this business on her back, all alone, threatened to flatten her.

"I don't think you need to worry too much, Orlena," Trace said calmly. Reaching into the vest of a silver-gray suit that matched his hair, he brought out a cigarette. "We have that ad space locked up. We can run the new address in every one of them. Have a party at the new location. Invite every client. It will get good press coverage."

Orlena nodded. Trace had a far better head on him than Jordan did. Still, what he was suggesting would cost them not only money, but time.

The disappointment of it pressed on her. Jordan hadn't established a name for himself—except for a whisper about that stupid move when he'd bought those emeralds back in New York. Cecily, on the other hand, was already becoming known in the Miami–Palm Beach area. Last week, at the Café L'Europe, she'd heard the girl's name fall from the tongue of one of the Princess Maria Pia's friends. The girl posed too great a threat to Jordan, was much too competent and too vindictive.

Effie Duvall could be counted on to accommodate them by dying in a few years, considering her age. It was Cecily they must derail—and before she established a following. Perhaps she must be given obstacles on a personal as well as professional level.

Orlena looked at Trace MacDonald, liking more and more the plan she'd been contemplating. The way to cripple Cecily Catlow was through her sister.

Cecily heard the battle in the workroom before she entered.

"Who gave you permission to use this?" Effie was shouting.

"You told me I could use anything I bloody damned well pleased!" That was Ben's voice.

Alarmed, Cecily moved more quickly. She had heard them argue before, but never like this.

"Anything that would look civilized!" Effie snarled. "Not something miscut! Not something to make a mockery of my name!"

Cecily saw a flash of blue in Effie's hand. It was the sapphire shaped like an uneven triangle Ben had asked her about that night in the vault. Now, surrounded by diamonds, it swung from a boldly asymmetric necklace, two chains of diamonds connecting to one side and one to the other.

"There's nothing wrong with the cut. It's exactly right for the fire of the stone."

"It's a deformity!"

"Madame . . ." Cecily tried to interrupt to say Effie had a call from a client in Switzerland, but they ignored her.

"I thought I'd stuck enough diamonds on it to keep you satisfied," Ben said bitterly.

Effie spat. "I will not have such—such *playthings* spawned in my house. A gem has precision, or it does not come from Effie! You know my standards."

She slung the necklace as though it were an offensive scrub rag. It hit the top of the worktable Ben used when not in his studio with such a crack that Cecily winced. With one hand Effie turned her wheelchair to glare at two stone-setters who were looking on in wordless uneasiness.

"Which one of you set these for him?"

One man stepped reluctantly forward.

"Go. You are finished with Duvall." Effie turned her back. She looked defiantly at her grandson. "Perhaps this will be a lesson to you. From now on clear things with me!"

The man dismissed looked as though she had shot him.

Ben's face went white.

Cecily felt her own breath blocked up inside her. She was aghast. Effie was firing a man out of simple spite, to show her own power.

"If you get rid of him, I'm leaving, too." Ben's voice was deadly.

Both stone-cutters already had fled.

Effie sneered. "You'll not leave." Her eyes flicked toward Cecily with unmistakable meaning. The look of triumph on her face was evil, manipulative, immensely satisfied. "There is too much in your blood here now for you to leave, and we made a bargain when I gave you money for your plane. You will not break a bargain."

Surely this wasn't the woman she'd come to care for, the woman whose headaches had worried her and whose goodness to those around her seemed limitless, Cecily thought. She felt cold all over.

"And what are these?" continued Effie, reaching out to sweep aside two carefully divided piles of stones Ben's table held. "Citrine. Peridot." Contempt was in her voice. "You are a Duvall, not a Bulgari! Get rid of them."

She was gone and Cecily still felt shock waves. Concern for Ben was foremost in her mind as she saw the tight set of his face. She touched his sleeve.

"It wasn't your fault, Ben."

They'd been together three months now, day and night. Still, she didn't know what to say to him. In many ways she still didn't know him at all. He didn't allow it.

"It was my fault," he said shortly. "I should have cleared it with her, but I knew she'd never approve it. She wants the goddamned thing cut more conventionally—even though she'll lose a third of it." He rubbed the heel of his hand up over his head, the defeat in the gesture tugging at Cecily's heart. "Well. At least there's enough in my bank account right now to give that man a decent payment for costing him his job."

Hesitantly she let her hand slip to his chest.

"It's a lovely necklace, Ben." She tried gallows humor to comfort him. "Maybe we could find a buyer for it before she carves it up."

He looked at her and a faint smile edged his mouth.

"Yeah. Maybe. You've bitten off one hell of a challenge getting Duvall back in the market in a big way, do you know that? She's forty years behind the times when it comes to lesser-known stones. She's pricing herself right out of the market because of it. By Christ, Tiffany uses stones like these—Van Cleef and Arpels does—everyone does."

"*And* we now have a stone-setter to replace," said Cecily, sinking into a chair and folding her hands sedately around her knees, still trying to joke about things that otherwise would be thoroughly discouraging. "Plus—are you ready for this?—I think Lynette's been doctoring her books."

He looked up from the lemon-hued citrine he'd been brooding over.

"You're kidding."

She shook her head. "Judging by her production, the incidence of large goods—and quality goods—should be higher than it is. Ten years ago it was. Two years ago it was. I've been looking at records all morning.

"I don't think the soil's playing out. Her profits from melee and second-quality stones are extremely good. If she sold some of her choice sapphires, listed them as second-rate, and pocketed the difference, she'd turn up with considerably more money in her own hands than if she shipped them to Effie. The question is, is Lynette the one who's doing it, or is Margaux? She's doing the records."

Cecily took a breath. What he'd said just a moment ago about the task ahead of her made her sure the course she'd been considering was right.

"With all there is to do in the next couple of months, I don't think we can afford the kind of squabble there'll be if I tell Effie—especially since we're getting all the stones we need. I think Lynette and the girls could be scared back into line with a warning and a second chance. They may be the only ones who could be, God knows, but I'm going to try it."

"No!" The word was sharp and Ben's forehead furrowed. "Don't mix in."

His reaction surprised her. Surely he wasn't angry enough with Effie to stand by and let her be cheated.

"Why?"

"It's not your concern. It's hers. Let her take care of it."

A thread of something she couldn't make out was in his voice. She felt herself being pulled by it, toward him, away from Effie.

"It is my concern," said Cecily softly. "I'm working for her."

Lyle & Co. was going to become a laughingstock because of this latest blunder of Orlena's. Jordan scowled at the knowledge and began another brooding circuit around his office. He was fed up with the complications caused for them by Cecily Catlow. He was fed up with Orlena's failure to deal with her. Their venture in Palm Beach should be off and flying by now, but instead they were facing a move, expenses, gossip. It was time he was running the business instead of Orlena. Past time.

"Jordan, for heaven's sake will you learn to sign these vouchers before you put them through?"

Of course it was Lucy.

Jordan looked at her with speculation. He'd woo her today. He might need her help soon.

"They're initialed," he said mildly. "It's just as good."

"Any idiot could forge initials—"

"Oh, for God's sake, Lucy. Ease off. You're starting to sound like her." He jerked his head toward Orlena's office. "You don't want to turn into the sort of bitch she is, do you? Look at those nasty hints she's always dropping about you taking that necklace of hers. It's criminal. And what's the point?"

He'd tapped into Lucy's sore spot. She forgot what she'd been fussing about and her mouth turned down.

"I suppose you think I took her stupid emeralds, too."

"Of course I don't. She's lost them somewhere. At the back of her safe, maybe. Or maybe she's made the whole thing up so she'd have something to rant about. How should I know?"

"Well, I'm glad she lost them." Lucy tossed the papers she'd been carrying onto Jordan's desk. "She let Vanessa get that emerald from William Lyle, but she never saw to it *I* had one—not one from him, not one from her. I know why, too.

She's never cared about me because I wasn't pretty enough. Well, that doesn't mean that I don't have feelings! Mothers are supposed to love their children, but the only one Orlena loves is herself!"

Jordan hadn't bargained for this. Grudgingly he started forward to calm her. Lucy stopped him with a backward step and an outflung hand.

"No, Jordan, I'm not in a mood to have my hair pulled or my arm twisted," she said petulantly and stormed out.

He shrugged. He'd found out how much support she'd give Orlena right now—which wasn't much. That was all that mattered. Feeling more satisfied he resumed the thoughts he'd been working through when she barged in.

It was time he started to take control of Lyle & Co., before Orlena made another blunder. The quickest way was to give Orlena a fresh reason to attack Cecily Catlow.

Walking to a nearby restaurant Jordan placed an anonymous phone call to a newspaper. Two days later a shipment of Israeli diamonds to Lyle & Co. were opened and photographed coming through customs. Except that the diamonds were clearly Russian, the bluish-white paper that packed them stamped with Cyrillic characters.

Customers and potential customers called, irate, when the picture appeared along with a short story questioning how many local jewelers used Russian diamonds. Orlena was hysterical.

"How? How could this have happened?" she lamented. "Why was *our* shipment opened when I pay every tariff? When I'm *scrupulous* to do everything by the book?"

Russian stones were thought to be unpatriotic if you cared about that sort of thing—and many of the customers Orlena had gathered and was trying to gather did care. This could ruin them.

"I see Cousin Cecily's hand in this," said Jordan, satisfied at how it was all turning out. "Why else would anyone finger our particular shipment?"

Orlena's eyes grew as hard and as green as the emeralds around her neck.

"I think I see a way out," continued Jordan blandly. "Let me take care of this."

And he did. His impassioned public statement vowing Lyle & Co. would never again do business with the supplier who had furnished such stones, and promising all profits from their sale to a group helping Soviet dissidents, won as much good will as the photograph had bad. Meanwhile, he'd insured that whatever he did now to Cousin Cecily, his mother could be counted on to look the other way.

Ben read for the third time the small, vicious hint of Cecily's old scandal, dropped into the gossip column that some of Effie's customers read as desperately as they popped diet pills—that Effie had conditioned him long ago to read to deal with those customers.

His face darkened. It had been another lousy day. Yesterday that fight with Effie over the sapphire and this morning a workman had upset a tray of the small diamonds used *en pavé* inside his studio. He'd been distracted by voices and noises for hours while the stones were tracked down. In the entire day he hadn't produced one sketch that held any promise. When he'd gone in to see Cecily a while ago, just wanting to hear her voice, she'd been in a meeting with Effie.

This was going to hurt her, damn it. And the fault was entirely Effie's.

The before-dinner drink he'd come down to enjoy sat untouched at his elbow. He crumpled the paper in his fist and started to hurl it away until anger stopped him. The paper still crushed in his hand, he strode up the stairs, too filled with the need to move to wait for the elevator.

There was no sign of Jenkins in the outer office. He swung the door open into Effie's bizarre and guarded cave. Good. She was alone.

"Have you seen this about why Cecily left Landis and Oxenburg?"

He shook the paper as he moved toward her. She looked up, disinterested.

"I see everything," she said shortly. "Who will believe it?"

"It's your goddamned fault, Effie! You know good and well Lyle and Company must be behind this. You've kept this alive for Cecily by buying that goddamned building of theirs!"

"Ridiculous! And what would you have had me do when I could buy the building? This has nothing to do with their building. It has come about because they were caught with Russian diamonds. It was not my fault the item ran. Whoever was behind it will pay for it dearly. I protect my own."

"Like you protected my mother?" Ben asked harshly. "Like you protected Marguerite, hounding her until she ran and used a car you knew she'd use? One that just happened to have defective brakes that day? Don't think I didn't find out about the fight

you started with her—the threats you made—the way you pressed
and pressed until she didn't know what she was doing. But you
did, didn't you, Effie?''

She wheeled explosively toward him, attacking as he attacked.

''Your mother loved what she did! She died because she was
hotheaded and addicted to little planes—just as you are. And
your wife Marguerite!'' Effie sneered as she came around from
behind her desk. ''She insisted on making that trip because she
had a lover she wanted to see. There is every likelihood the child
she was carrying wasn't even yours!''

The knife-edge of her words cut at him mercilessly. He hated
her. She'd known something he'd suspected and she'd meted out
her own justice.

Ben jerked open a cabinet and found she still kept liquor there.
He downed raw whiskey.

''You're not telling me anything I didn't know. We'd have
worked things out. We were happy.''

The words sounded flat. He'd forgotten how deadly Effie was
in battle.

''Happy. Ha! You could be happy with Cecily!'' she rasped
like the crone she was.

He felt something hit his belly. Maybe it was the booze.

''So you can destroy her, too?''

He swung to face her. She propelled herself toward him.
''Cecily is mine!'' Her eyes were burning. ''She is cut from the
same cloth I am. I know what is best.''

The feeling that had hit his belly spread through him now. He
knew it was fear.

''Christ but you're a monster! You think everyone on this
earth was put there to nourish you, don't you?''

They both were bellowing.

He wouldn't let it happen. Not to Cecily. He was going to
block Effie for once. She was too constricted by her chair, as
well as too sure of herself, to follow him. He stormed from her
presence, found Cecily's office deserted, and continued down
the hall to pound on her door.

''Listen to me!'' he said as soon as she opened it. The soft
shadows of her eyes seemed to close around him like warm
waters, like music, like the rushing vastness of space he knew in
the Peregrine. He caught her above the elbows, the softness of
her flesh tugging at the knot in his belly. He kissed her urgently,
then spoke. ''I want us out of this house!''

She fell back the half step his grip on her would allow and stared at him.

"Ben, what is it? What's the matter?"

"Nothing. I want us to set up housekeeping, that's all. Away from Effie. Miami or Heredia, I don't care where, but away from here!"

She was silent. He felt frustration, then anger. Why couldn't she see? Why was she so blind? He wanted to shake her. Instead his fingers moved restlessly up, measuring her slender neck, her square little chin. Some other emotion joined the fear inside him, but he couldn't give it a name.

"I'm asking you to leave my grandmother," he said harshly. "Because if you don't, you're going to end up like her. Or dead. Is that what you want?"

The tips of her fingers raised to smooth his lips. As though she thought he needed comfort. As though . . .

He shuddered.

"Ben—"

He kissed her violently, seeking to draw out something he could not find. Her voice became a whisper, her body a quivering particle of silver.

"Ben, I . . ." As though to hold something back, she closed her eyes. "I don't understand what's happened. And I can't leave Effie."

"Why not?"

"You know why not! Because of what she's done for me and Van. Because I want—I *need* to crush Lyle and Company! Because I'm not going to stop till I've made Duvall the most exclusive jeweler in the world again!"

The pale determination of her face made her look like a stranger.

She started to free herself from him and he saw the suitcase open on her bed. It was like cold water after being drunk all night. His senses came back to him. His arms fell away from her.

"Where the hell are you going?"

"To Harry's. Day after tomorrow. Effie wants me to see if some goods of his are as good as he claims before she brings them in. I was checking things out—"

"No."

"What?"

"No. You're not going. I won't let you."

Her mouth took on a stubborn look. "I don't belong to you, Ben!"

"Did you belong to him?"

"To whom?"

"The guy who left that look in your eyes. The one who ruined you for anyone else."

"This is ridiculous!" She turned away.

He yanked her back to face him. He could feel himself shaking. Business over emotion, over people. She was just like Effie.

"What is it you really want, Cecily? To live for power and nothing else like she does?" A new thought hit him, one that hadn't occurred even though he knew the greed with which Lynette and the others eyed the profits of Duvall. "Or has she promised you a share in the company? Is that what you're angling for?"

A translucent curtain was shimmering over her eyes. She struck his hand away.

"You don't understand, do you?" Her voice sounded odd, hurt and angry at the same time. "You don't *feel*. You can't see that I—" Her hand doubled into a fist and she struck the bedpost, turning her back on him.

"Just leave, Ben. Please!"

Ancient bitterness ate its way through him. He should not have come back here. He knew how Effie manipulated, yet he'd fallen victim to the part of her that chuckled, that had baked him cookies in childhood.

He heard Cecily speak his name but didn't turn back as he slammed her door.

TWENTY-FIVE

"Y OU WANT ME TO SWING BY MY ANKLE WITH DIAMONDS OR SOME-thing around my neck?" April snapped her gum and looked from Cecily to Effie and back again.

Van smiled at her. She thought maybe April felt a little uncomfortable here in Effie's dining room with china luncheon plates and water goblets whose stems were as narrow as drinking straws. She'd watched April's eyes move from detail to detail behind their spiky black lashes. And April had hardly touched the cold poached salmon, which was very good.

"Something like that," said Cecily, nodding. "We thought—because of that Ringmaster Necklace we showed you earlier and how Madame came to think of it—that maybe we could present an entire circus. Very small, of course. In a ballroom."

Cecily didn't sound as happy today as she had of late. Maybe it was because she was leaving for Bangkok tonight, Van decided.

Wesley hadn't heard the plan before and was looking interested. He seemed to come to the house a lot since Effie had hired him. Van supposed that was what lawyers did. She wondered why he was always bringing her presents, flowers and candy and books about history that always made her feel sleepy when she tried to read them. Ben had brought her a book last week that she liked. About advertising.

April's gum popped loudly. "Hey, that's pretty funny," she said. "A circus in some fancy hotel for a bunch of high-class women."

Effie laughed raucously. "It will be a bit scandalous. Rowdy. Just the thing for Effie Duvall." She wagged a suddenly commanding finger over her coffee cup. "No snakes and no freaks. The models must be attractive."

"If you think you can find people for us, we'll work out the acts next week," said Cecily. "We'll pay what they would get for a regular performance." A turn of her head sought Effie's confirmation.

"Twice what they would get," said Effie. "Their performances will be shorter, but they'll have to rehearse them in unfamiliar surroundings." Her eyes went momentarily hard. "They'll have to be bonded, too. And warn them I know how to deal with gypsies. My guards break legs at the first thought of theft."

April nodded wordlessly.

"Madame . . ."

Jenkins, who hadn't joined them for lunch, appeared in the door with a squat, unpleasant little man Van remembered seeing before.

"Ah, Ricki." Effie looked good-humored as she beckoned him to the table. "I have not done with my lunch yet. Let me see the goods."

From a chain around her neck she produced a key which she used to open the small case offered her. She grunted without comment.

"Here, Cecily. What do you think?"

She passed the case to Cecily and Van saw April's shoe-button eyes pop as she saw it held loose emeralds.

Van shivered. Great-Uncle William's wife had always worn emeralds. Van hated them.

But Cecily was shifting one on the back of her hand now.

"They look lovely, Madame. Better than we'd expected. Don't you think?"

Effie only repeated her grunt. She did that to keep from admitting when she pleased, Van knew now.

"Take them up to my office and wait for me," Effie said, locking the case again. "Jenkins will order you lunch—"

"Madame Duvall . . ."

Van looked around and saw Cecily's secretary hovering in the door. She was very pretty in her candy-pink suit and dark, glossy lips, but she always seemed terrified when she met Effie.

Now Effie glowered at her. "I am at lunch."

"I know, Madame. Forgive me.. But there is a man on the phone. Mr. Mortimer didn't know what to answer and Mr. Jenkins was away—"

"What is it?" Effie barked.

Thida's eyes were wide. She looked uneasily at Cecily, then back to Effie.

"He's from the paper, Madame. He's a photographer. He says they want a picture of Mr. Duvall before he takes off in his plane—"

"Takes off? Takes off where?" barked Effie.

Cecily made a gasping sound like a cry.

"The man on the phone says it's an incredible venture, depending on nothing except a computer to fly a plane between takeoff and landing," Thida said nervously into the silence. "And he wants to know, is Mr. Duvall still here or is he already at the airport?"

"With the weight of the extra tanks, you know you must make longer takeoffs, Ben."

"Right."

"No more playing the cowboy or you will find yourself in trouble."

"Sure."

"*Jesu Cristo*, man! Are you even listening to me? I am talking about your life!"

Ben, one booted foot poised for entry into the Peregrine, looked impatiently at his partner, Pepe Hilbrun.

"Longer takeoffs, no playing, and in case the fucking computer doesn't work, I'd better stay awake so I can pray. Did I miss anything? Do you want to come along and make sure I don't? Do you want to fly it yourself?''

Pepe put up his hands.

Ben felt bad for having snapped at him. He liked Pepe. He supposed if he thought about it, they were closer than friends. And Pepe, whose skill as an electronics whiz had been overlooked by family and prospective employers because he was slow to speak and slightly hunchbacked, had just as much riding on this flight of the Peregrine as he did.

They'd met at Purdue when Ben was finishing up his degree in aviation. It had been an invitation from Pepe that had first lured him to Costa Rica. Four years ago they'd formed a partnership to build and test their first invention, a stability augmentation device.

"Hey, come on up and give TRINA a good-bye pat," Ben said to make amends. "She tolerates it better than I do."

He didn't know what was causing this bad mood. Or rather he did and didn't want to face it. It was that goddamned last encounter with Cecily—knowing she chose Effie over him, watching her turn her back when his gut was burning with worry for her.

He'd been a goddamned fool to worry. He'd been a fool to care. Women like her and Effie would always land on their feet.

He wondered if Marguerite would have, if Effie hadn't interfered. He wondered if the unborn baby had been his.

"Shit!" said Pepe, aboard now and employing his favorite word. He was staring in dismay at the cockpit instrument panel where half a dozen dials had been removed, their empty spaces covered with black vinyl. "Shit! What have you done, Ben? You were just supposed to seal them off—have a switch you could throw to use them if the system fails!"

Ben patted a small computer console between the cockpit's two seats.

"TRINA's not going to fail."

They had nicknamed the system TRINA, Traffic-Radar Input Navigation Aid. If it worked, it would alert a pilot to any other aircraft in his vicinity, reducing the chances of midair collision to almost zero. It would take and process all radar readings necessary to keep a plane on course.

"Somebody'd be sure to say I'd used the switch and resealed it. This way there can't be any question," Ben said, wishing Pepe would drop it. He knew as well as his partner that he might pay with his life if TRINA didn't live up to expectations.

"You are an idiot," Pepe said bitterly.

Ben grinned and pushed a program cassette into the computer.

Three newly installed display screens on the instrument panel sprang to life.

"Stop worrying, Pepe," urged TRINA's voice synthesizer in nasal, nagging tones. The message was a touch Ben had put on just for Pepe, the whining voice instead of a breathless, sexy one an impulse.

His partner sighed and embraced him clumsily. "Be careful, Ben."

"Sure. Call you from San José."

Ben touched his arm and, as Pepe exited, closed the door of the Peregrine. Without extra fuel tanks, San José would have been just out of range for a nonstop flight at top speed. He and Pepe had solved that problem six months ago. Now he and this plane could make it from Miami to Colombia in a single hop. From Colombia to Joao's place, even.

His mouth settled into a grim line. He wondered why he was starting to think of things in terms of Effie's business. The important thing was that the Peregrine now had a decent range, allowing him to test TRINA in and out of a wide variety of airfields with an equally wide variety of traffic conditions. The collision avoidance capability of TRINA was, in his opinion, one of the most important aspects of the entire system. If the traffic display worked, he and Pepe would one day hook the whole shebang into an autopilot, creating a plane that could practically think for itself.

Ben relaxed to the feel of the thrust lever in his hand, the crisp communications with the Opa-Locka control tower, and finally to near quietness as the Peregrine soared. Its single fanjet was mounted above and behind the cockpit, so exhaust noise was never a problem. That was one of the plane's many beauties. The control tower here had refused to let him rely exclusively on his own traffic display during takeoff—too busy, they'd said. But from here on out TRINA was going to guide his every move.

Ben eased forward on the thrust lever. He could feel the plane's speed entering his blood. He looked down and could see only nothingness, a void where everything that had ever existed became mere particles of light hurling faster than he was. The Peregrine was heavier than usual because of the extra fuel. He could feel it pull a little. He could feel the pull of gravity.

And then he began to feel that other sense he always felt up here, that sense of oneness with all who had ever known these skies before him, that sense of attachment he never felt on earth. Up here he could feel his mother's presence. Crazy. But up here his solitude was not a solitude, it was a warm blanket spreading around him. It beckoned to him. He found he could urge the lever forward a little more now, and did.

A finely tuned tension began to take hold of him. His eyes strained at the navigational display waiting for the radar fix he knew should come next. Was it late in coming? Was the damned system not going to work?

It fluttered to life, accompanied by the voice synthesizer's nasal recitation of a fix. He sat back, relieved.

His legs already felt tired. He'd been born clubfooted, but from the time he was a toddler Effie had outfitted him in specially made boots with steel braces, determined to correct the problem. She'd succeeded—as she did in most things. His boots no longer had braces, but they gave him a welcome support while flying. Except that today he couldn't seem to relax.

Ben shifted the Jeppesen charts spread on his knees, one eye on the navigational display. They were on course. He waited impatiently for the traffic display that should be appearing. Nothing happened.

Oh, Christ. Either the bloody thing wasn't working or the commercial flight that had left Miami after he did, which he'd figured would cross his path just about here, had veered way off course.

The cavalier pose he'd adopted in Miami had left him a long time ago. By his third hour in the air the nav display still matched his Jeppesens and the traffic display was giving him random readings. *But were they right?*

"Check your fix," nagged TRINA's voice.

The screen told him they were passing over a fix called Radon. He'd flown this route enough to know the time was right, even without a chart. He was forty miles out of San José, time to establish contact.

"El Coco tower, this is Peregrine November eighty-four forty-nine Golf," he said. "I show two aircraft coming in ahead of me. Is that about right?"

"Roger, Peregrine forty-nine Golf. Congratulations, Duvall."

Ben grinned and ten minutes later made a perfect landing.

"Bloody Christ," he yelled to the ground crew that came cheering to greet him. "The damned thing worked!"

Most of them spoke English and laughed at the joke. He was stiff, bent like a pretzel from the time in one position. They thumped his back.

Photographers were waiting. He guessed he and Pepe were

going to have no trouble finding commercial backing for further modifications of TRINA. He also guessed from some of the types he saw hanging around that maybe a few people had laid bucks the system wouldn't work and he'd be shark bait by now.

Somebody shoved a microphone in his face. He muttered they ought to talk to Pepe. He recognized a reporter from *Aviation Week* he'd met at a banquet once and noticed a cute-looking girl with a notepad out. From the small crowd gathered on a patch of concrete watching the field, he judged his arrival had been turned into an event.

Then he saw a face half-hidden by others. A pair of brown eyes.

"Hey!" he called as she saw him discover her and tried to duck back toward the terminal. "Hey, stop her!" He bounded ahead.

He must be losing his mind. It couldn't be Cecily. All at once he was angry without knowing why.

He caught her and spun her. She looked angry, too. Furious. Her eyes were flashing.

"What the hell are you doing here?"

"Waiting to bring back your ashes!"

She tried to jerk away and he didn't let her. The stubborn set of her jaw was making him crazy.

"You sound disappointed there aren't any."

"Maybe I am!"

She made a savage sweep at her cheek with the back of her hand. "I don't suppose it ever occurred to you to say good-bye. No, of course it didn't! Funny how sleeping with someone for three months can make you feel near enough to them you need that—though it's obviously a female failing—"

"What the devil are you talking about? You were set to fly off to Harry's without telling me!"

He was yelling at her.

"You never gave me a chance!" Her volume matched his. "And I was going on a commercial flight—with tested equipment! You could have been killed!"

That glimmering curtain he'd noticed the other night was over her eyes again. She was quivering.

"Well, go ahead and be killed! People disappear out of other people's lives all the time. My mother did, and—and they didn't let Van say good-bye either—and it doesn't matter, because no one owes anybody a thing and you have to learn that early or get crushed and— This is stupid! I don't even know why I'm standing here—"

Ben heard the unassuaged grief of a lonely child mixed with a woman's passion. He felt his grip on her tighten.

"Cecily." His voice was rough because he didn't know how to ask what he was starting to understand, the knowledge bombarding him like a falling wall of bricks. "Are you . . . saying you're in love with me?"

Her breasts rose and fell. It seemed he could hear her heart beat.

"Yes. So there's your victory. If that's what you want."

His eyes scanned her face. "It's not. I don't know what I want."

To protect her, he thought. He kissed her with a desire so deep he could not explain it. He *had* to protect her now. He had to keep her from winding up like all the others.

And he would. He could. He wanted her.

"Damn Effie!" he muttered, but the words were muffled in the softness of the lips holding his. Ben felt a shudder wrack his body.

A flash went off. And another. He realized people were watching. But it didn't matter. Suddenly, just for that moment, the earth was more appealing than the sky.

In the bedroom in Heredia where they had first made love they undressed each other with shutters drawn against early evening light. The ride from the airport had taken forty-five minutes. Ben had been in the air for nearly four hours. Cecily couldn't imagine he'd want anything but sleep.

Her error became apparent immediately as his strong body took hers captive. His thighs pressed demandingly against the soft inner sides of her own and she gave feverishly, possessing him as ravenously as he possessed her. Her tongue, with a growing excitement, tasted the smoothness of his shoulder, the small, hard pinprick of his nipple. The hours of this afternoon had been filled with terror for her. Realizing she loved him. Realizing—hearing confirmed from those who knew about it—the risk involved in the flight he'd made.

Effie thought she had rushed off because of some sudden change in plans in getting to Bangkok. It didn't matter. Nothing seemed to matter just now except the reality of Ben, alive, holding her.

Cecily smoothed his hair, eyes tightly closed as she felt herself being swept toward completion. Nothing mattered except the fact she had not lost him. Even if he had not said he loved her. Even if she was only letting herself in for greater pain.

Afterward he took her hand and kissed it. They lay together without words, the room growing dark around them. There were no sounds here. Cecily heard only the tempo of her own heart.

Foolish. Foolish, it said.

Ben got up and opened the shutters. The upper part of one wall now was opened to the garden. She could see blossoms nodding on head-high, branchless tree trunks. By their shape she knew they were orchids, some large and fluttering regally, some no bigger than fingers, but in the moonlight all of them an identical silver.

"How the devil did you get here ahead of me?" he asked, his back toward her.

"Some photographer called the house. You were already at the airport. I had Thida call and get me on the commercial flight while I snatched up my suitcase."

He did not understand that she cared because he didn't. He desired her, perhaps. She inflamed him as he did her. But his old bitterness at Effie had filled him with a suspicion she did not know how to assuage. There were moments when they seemed to draw close to each other, when they seemed to think alike; yet in his eyes she would always be some trick of Effie's. It meant she could never touch the loneliness she sensed inside him. It meant she could never erase the scars she was starting to feel as sharply as if they were her own.

Overwhelmed by sadness, she reached out and touched his cheek as he returned to the bed.

"I suppose Effie thinks I'm on my way to Harry's," she said unsteadily. "I didn't have time to argue with her, so I just left. She was frightened when she heard you were making this flight, Ben. She's such a master at hiding emotion, but I've been around her long enough now to tell—"

"Oh, crap. If she was worried, it's because she was worried about her designs. She likes to think I'm some goddamned genius."

The cutting edge on his voice told her argument would be futile. He leaned across her and she lay in his arms for a moment. She wondered if he knew how much he was like Effie when it came to stubbornness and being closed. She wondered how deeply he'd buried the memories that scarred.

"Tell me about your wife," she said softly.

She felt his muscles stiffen. At first she thought he wouldn't answer, thought he might even get up and walk away, leaving her there.

He rolled onto his back.

"What's to tell? Effie's nephew was running the ruby mines into debt through mismanagement. Marguerite's father owned mines which he ran well. Effie saw the chance to bring good management into the family—I didn't realize at the time she already was laying plans, just went to consult with the man whose advice Effie said might help us, found the man had a daughter who was pretty and sweet and—

"Hell."

His arm, which had been touching her, moved rigidly to his side.

"After about a year Effie got dissatisfied with the new operation. She didn't like Marguerite, either. In fact, Effie hated her. When I was away they had a big fight. Effie baited her, bullied her, threatened to turn me against Marguerite if she didn't leave.

"So Marguerite ran. She caught a flight to Bangkok. We kept a car in a rented garage near the airport. Its brakes failed. She was killed."

Cecily heard the controlled passion of his words. She reached for the hand beside her, felt it resist but did not let go.

"I'm sorry." Her words seemed inadequate.

"Don't be."

He turned and the lines of his jaw were set and hard. His eyes were angry. Yet the heel of his hand rubbed up her neck with curious gentleness.

"Kiss me," he said, and the low softness of his voice was as compelling as the request itself.

His lips drew her close to him, softly at first, and then with a sudden savageness. His hands gripped her shoulders. He rolled, pinning her beneath him. His hands were unsteady.

"Marry me, Cecily. I'm not going to tell you I love you, but I sure as hell want you to be part of my life—I sure as hell want you waiting for me at airports." He drew a breath. "I need you, maybe."

He kissed her again. At the window the orchids were stirring. All she had ever wanted was to share her life, to not be alone and know that she mattered—a little—to someone.

"That's enough," she whispered, holding to him as she'd never held to anyone. "That's enough."

TWENTY-SIX

"YOU EXPECT TO HAVE A JOB WITH ME AFTER WHAT YOU HAVE done? Disappearing? Failing to keep an appointment I had set for you? Making a mockery of your work—"

Effie was furious. Thirty seconds ago, when they'd entered her office together, Cecily had thought the formidable figure in black might somehow rise from her chair to throw them both out. More unnerving still was the fact that Kim was sitting there with them, observing the scene with a sly look of interest while blotting himself with his handkerchief.

"There's a good reason Cecily didn't make it to Bangkok," Ben said. His voice low behind her, he rested his hands on Cecily's shoulders, steadying her against the tongue-lashing.

"There is no good reason for disobeying me," Effie said dangerously. "Now I have no rubies from Harry. My workers will fall behind. And you! Who gave you permission to fly off in that plane—"

"Harry can bring his own damned rubies," Ben interrupted. "Cecily's been with me. We're getting married."

The lids on Effie's eyes lifted slightly.

"Ah!" she snorted. It was less a comment, more an outrush of air. Her moment of gathering her composure was almost imperceptible. "And what has that to do with anything?" she demanded severely. "I thought I was running a business, not a dating service. I still do not have my rubies!"

Pressing Cecily's shoulder, Ben came around and hooked a leg over one corner of Effie's desk. He grinned, deliberately aggravating his grandmother.

"Thought you might be pleased."

"It is no concern of mine," said Effie blandly. "I have other things on my mind."

She looked sharply at Cecily. "There is no time for the nonsense of a fancy wedding. We will have it when the board meets. A little champagne, a cake, some flowers, and music—that is all!"

Cecily hid a smile. Effie was delighted. Her unconvincing brusqueness made it hard for Cecily not to laugh aloud.

It's going to work, she thought. *Ben and I are going to work! Whether he loves me or not doesn't matter, there's so much right between us.*

He held out his hand now. She went to him and leaned against him with a sense of belonging and happiness that brought a pain to her throat.

"I believe I'll excuse myself down the hall," said Kim with great formality. He did not look pleased.

"What's he doing here?" asked Ben as the door closed.

"A customer in Oman wants pearls." Effie shrugged. "You know how Arabs are. They will have only natural ones, and are willing to pay a great differential for them—which no one else is. It has taken me twelve years of hoarding to furnish a matched strand that might interest them, completed with one of three Kim brought me yesterday. He was not pleased being summoned, but he will be when I pay him."

She looked pleased with herself. "You see, while you two have been indulging yourselves, I have been accomplishing things," she continued. "An advertising man who used to work for Lyle and Company also came to see me. MacDonald's his name. They failed to pay him for his services—their money must be in quite short supply. I may hire him."

"Good," said Ben. "None of us here really knows what we're doing in that department. It sounds more efficient."

Effie waved a hand. "Of course it's efficient. I have always been. Now have the goodness to tell my household you're back so everyone won't be worrying. I will see you at dinner."

"Do you really think it's a good idea?" asked Cecily when they were in the hallway. "If he worked for Lyle and Company, I'm not sure I do. He could be a plant."

Ben shrugged, his gesture reminiscent of Effie's. "Plenty of time to check up on him. You can be sure Effie will."

"I suppose. Look, I want to see Van. If I don't tell her about the two of us before she hears it from Effie, she'll be hurt."

"Better run, then." Ben's lips twitched. "Effie's likely to roll through that door and go from room to room grumbling about our arrangements to everyone she can collar."

Cecily laughed. Their stolen days in Heredia had changed things between them. Ben no longer sealed himself off with anger and sarcasm. She watched him move quickly toward his studio and knew he had a design in mind.

"So. You will be a Duvall at last," said a voice breaking into her thoughts.

Looking up, she saw Kim and smiled thinly, feeling challenged without knowing why.

"Yes, it appears I will."

"Clever," said Kim, eyes glittering in his broad face. "Ben has finally assured his place as her heir. He's finally pleased her."

He paraded away, bulk swaying importantly, as Cecily felt a shadow pass over her heart.

"You are slow. Did you fall asleep?"

"No, Madame. Forgive me."

Cecily was out of breath from hurrying to answer Effie's summons. She could be cross at this criticism, but she had come to realize such grumblings were Effie's way of reminding those around her of her power. They meant nothing. This current display, Cecily decided, must be for the benefit of the man with a beak-like nose who sat on a bench before Effie's dais.

"This is Petrie. He deals in curiosities," said Effie. "What do you think?"

She shoved a stone toward Cecily, a square-cut canary diamond. Cecily picked it up with some surprise.

"It's a handsome size, Madame, and the cut seems good." She had never realized Effie bought stones not from her own mines. "Did you want me to inspect it for clarity?"

Effie made a sniffing sound.

"It is stolen. Petrie's goods are often stolen. It is a nasty habit of his."

Petrie looked completely undisturbed by the accusation. In fact he smiled.

"It will do you well to memorize the stone," Effie continued. "It and the blue diamond, too. Tell me, Petrie, are these two rubies also stolen?"

The flesh around Petrie's beak-nose creased as he displayed golden teeth.

"Ah, Madame. Stones of this size I would not attempt to pass off. They would be remembered. Even by a memory less formidable than yours. Do you want them? The color is perfect."

"The color is good, but not perfect," Effie said calmly.

Petrie stirred his shoulders indignantly.

"Perfect pigeon's blood! I should have known you would try to rob me!"

He reached for the stones, but Effie covered them with her fingers.

"Shall we test?" Her eyes glittered and she pressed the intercom on her desk. "Jenkins, send me a pigeon."

Cecily wet her lips. She had heard about the ancient test, but she had never witnessed one. She hadn't believed it was still performed. She wished there were some escape.

Effie's eyes slid toward her as though enjoying her discomfort, as though daring her to show weakness.

"You are going to be a Duvall," she rasped in a whisper. "I am going to make you into my own image."

Something close to fear pressed Cecily's stomach. She found herself wondering how much of her destiny Effie had already manipulated, and why, in this minute, the question disturbed her.

But the door was opening. A guard was bringing in a struggling bird. It was soft and gray and fought as though it too were resisting a force it already knew to be beyond its control. Effie pointed toward a sheet of white paper. Petrie's rubies lay on opposite corners. The guard held the pigeon over the paper, above Effie's desk.

There was a flash of silver as a knife slashed toward the pigeon's breast and Cecily's eyes flew closed. The piercing, desperate cries of the bird seemed to come from inside her own head. She did not know whether the creature was dying or would survive. She thought she might vomit. As she opened her eyes, determined to steady herself, they fell on a dark splash of blood.

"You see," said Effie, nudging the rubies near it. "Not bright enough. Shall we talk price, Petrie?"

Had the test been necessary, or had it been merely a flaunting of Effie's panache? wondered Cecily. Upset by what appeared to be her needless cruelty, and more annoyed with the woman than usual, she made her way from the room.

She needed tea to settle her stomach. For once she relied upon the elevator to take her down to the living room, then rang for Charlie.

"Here's your mail, miss. Your sister's is there too if she's coming to join you," he said, returning after he'd delivered a tea tray.

Cecily nodded. She would see Van. That would steady her. Out of habit she opened envelopes and inspected personal bills.

It never occurred to her the large manila envelope might be addressed to her sister, who never received anything but letters. Cecily tore it open without looking, then bent over it with a muffled cry. It was awful. Hideous. A grainy eight-by-ten photo of Van looking slack-mouthed, totally crazed and helpless, as a hand gripped her breast.

"You're down awfully early," a voice said. It was Ben. "Didn't think—" He broke off. "Cecily? What's the matter?"

She leaned back, allowing him to see the photo.

"Oh, Christ!" he said, dropping to one knee beside her. "From the guy who called you, do you figure?"

"Yes." She'd told him about the phone call only a few nights before. "Ben, what am I going to *do*?"

"Burn it," he said, shoving it back into the envelope. There was anger in the gesture. "And then tell Van about it in case he sends another."

"I can't!"

"Whoever sent it's sick. Why else would—"

"It's Jordan. Jordan Lyle. He's—" Suddenly the tears spilled out and Cecily ground her fists into the sofa cushion beneath her, unable to speak and scarcely able to breath as a fear held in for weeks—even years—burst from her. "Help me, Ben! Please— help me take care of Van. She's suffered so much. She—oh God, Ben—she matters so much to me! When we were little we had no one! *No one!* There's always been just the two of us. I can't even remember what my mother looked like. Van was the one good, happy thing I had when I was a kid, and now I'm all she's got! I can't let them destroy her!"

His two hands nestled her tightly curled fist. As though from a distance she felt their warmth, felt a strange protectiveness, the unfamiliar reassurance of another person waiting at her side.

"We won't let them hurt her," he said, and the certainty of his words was like bedrock. It allowed all Cecily's raw emotion to pour out still more freely.

"I want them dead!" she said savagely. "I want all the Lyles dead! It's the only way we'll ever be safe."

"Stop it." His voice grew suddenly sharp. "You're sounding like Effie."

"I don't care. It's true."

"It's not." He drew back, staring at her, then shook her once with passion. "Damn it, Cecily, you're not alone."

The words reached her in a way she could not explain. They comforted. And they were not Peter's words. She trusted this simple statement, and in its very clumsiness found something she'd never had before, an ally.

Silently now she began to cry again. She clutched the hand holding hers and Ben drew her head onto his shoulder and smoothed back her hair.

TWENTY-SEVEN

"THIS IS ABSOLUTELY THE MOST EXCITING THING THAT'S EVER happened to me!" Van smoothed at the puff of lilac chiffon that was her dress and corrected herself with a laugh. "Well, of course, it's happening to *you*, but I'm here to enjoy it, I'm even part of it. And oh, Cecily, I'm so happy for you!"

They embraced amid the clutter of what had been Cecily's room and from which she would depart in a few hours as Ben's bride. For an instant Cecily thought how quickly time had flown since that day little more than a month ago when they'd told Effie of their plans. Van, to Cecily's relief, wasn't the least upset about the prospect of remaining on her own at Effie's for a week or more. The two women—one bent with age and one more innocent even than her years—sat up every night playing canasta. They chuckled together and enjoyed each other's company.

"I'm happy for us both." Cecily smiled, more plagued by thoughts today, with Effie's board gathering downstairs, than she wanted to be. She squeezed her sister's hands.

They looked into each other's eyes and for an instant Cecily knew they both were thinking of the past. *Out. Out of our lives!* she ordered silently.

There was a tap and then the door popped open.

"Jeezus! Don't you two look great!" said April, staring.

"Cecily should have had a long dress, though. And a veil," Van fretted.

Cecily laughed a little nervously. She looked down at her fragile milk-white dress with its draped Grecian neck and flowing sleeves. Its hemline was irregular, layer on layer of tissue-thin silk cut in handkerchief points that rose in a cascade on one side, fluttering over a soft underskirt.

"I'll be just as married in this. And I can't stand things on my head. Doesn't Van make a gorgeous attendant?"

She tried not to let in the thought that had pressed her all morning. Was she only going through motions, playing a role that other brides had played in this house? Had her marriage been brought about to secure a part of Effie's empire—this time to Ben? Kim's words had troubled her ever since she'd heard them.

She touched the locket Effie had sent her that morning, a strange five-sided emerald set in a gold heart. This was a case of bridal jitters, surely. The fact that a truce had sprung up between Ben and Effie these last weeks and that Ben every day seemed to spend more time with Effie in her office was coincidental.

A loud rap jarred her from her reverie.

"You can't see her now! It's bad luck," Van cried as Ben opened the door.

"You been reading again?" He gave a teasing flick at the orchid pinned in Van's gleaming hair. "Go keep an eye on Effie before she drags anyone else in for this ordeal, will you?"

"Saw the organist, huh?" asked Cecily wryly. She tried to recapture the easiness that had started to grow between them, but just now it seemed to elude her. Despite Effie's comment about not having time for a fancy wedding, the downstairs was sprouting every trapping usually associated with that word.

"No, the orchestra," said Ben. He, too, seemed faintly on edge. He looked at her now. His eyes caught the locket around her neck and lingered, darkening.

"*What* orchestra?" asked Cecily in dismay. Effie couldn't do anything by half, it appeared.

"The one that came with the caterers—or was it the photographer?"

She could see that his humor was forced now. As soon as April and Van were in the hall, it faded.

"Did Effie give you that?" he demanded.

Cecily touched the locket, bewildered. "Yes."

"Take the damned thing off," he said shortly. "You belong to me now."

She stared at him. Something was pushing between the two of them, gnawing and threatening.

"I don't belong to either of you," she said, unable to believe her ears.

Ben turned away, cocking his foot on a chair. He looked troubled, hardly like a man about to marry at all in his white dinner suit and ruffled shirt.

"All right," he said, voice tight and not easily given to compromise, his back toward her. "My choice of words was poor. Take it off anyway. The stone's flawed. It's unlucky."

"All emeralds are flawed."

She didn't understand what was happening. She wanted to chide Ben for his superstition, but a moment came back to her: Louie at an auction, urging her not to bid for a black opal.

A flawed gem brings misfortune. Three sides means quarrels, four sides means terrors and fears, five sides means death.

"Ben, why are you marrying me?" The words burst from her, unrelated to the present moment, yet brought forth by the tension in it. She thought she couldn't bear it if he told her now it was all to please Effie. Being with him each day, confiding in him was healing some wound inside she hadn't even known was there.

He didn't look at her. "I don't know. Do you want out?"

"No."

She felt frightened, and utterly without defenses. An eternity passed before he moved and came toward her.

"Christ, Cecily. I'm sorry. Wear whatever you want. I just thought since you wouldn't have a diamond, you might have this."

He held out his hand and across it there lay a delicate choker whose whiteness was so exquisitely soft she could almost feel it. There was something old-fashioned in the design. Twists of antique gold held opals the size of a fingernail, and twining between the opals were an extravagance of glowing seed pearls and, here and there, the tiny teardrop sparkle of a diamond.

Cecily had never seen anything like it. She knew it was the intricate, quiet sort of piece that Ben, so vastly different from Effie, preferred above all others. She looked up, unable to speak.

"Ben . . ."

She could get no further than his name. Without being told, she knew he had envisioned this for her and made it with his own hands. She slipped Effie's locket off.

"Will you put it on me?"

As he did, she caught his head, urging his lips down to hers. For a moment she thought he held to her as tightly as she held to him.

"Let's get your flowers," he said.

They found Jenkins, Ben's attendant, who was beaming in his role.

"Madame is still wishing that the two of you would come in separately—you down the staircase like brides in the films she remembers," he said, handing Cecily a nosegay of bright yellow roses and baby's breath trimmed with long yellow streamers. Throughout the whole house there were sprays and table arrangements of similar flowers, touched here and there with lavender buds to echo Van's attire.

"Well, I'm going to disappoint her on that," said Cecily, smiling, her doubts reduced to an echo now with Ben here at her side and his gift around her neck. "Is Joao here yet?"

"No."

This would be her only chance to interact with any members of Effie's board. She and Ben were leaving before the meeting tomorrow. Cecily's eyes swept those assembled and saw that not one of the "family" had noticed her presence yet, for which she was just as glad.

"Margaux is, though," she murmured to Ben. "Do you mind if I have that talk with her?"

He gave her a slow look. "You're a hell of a bride, talking business when you're on your way down the aisle. Sure. Go ahead. I don't suppose we'd start till Joao got here, anyway."

His words were dry, but not disapproving. She moved quickly across the central hall, glad Effie's back was to her, and touched Margaux's arm.

"Oh! Don't you look lovely!"

Margaux's smile was tentative but genuine.

"Yes, lovely," echoed Lynette, but her expression, like her hair, seemed carefully arranged.

Maigrette was talking to Martin, whose appointment to the board had punished his father's treachery.

"Could I talk to you, Margaux?"

The girl's blue eyes seemed to flicker. "Of course."

Cecily led the way to a small room, the seldom used library. Margaux spoke first.

"I understand Joao—"

Cecily raised a hand, the cool petals of the flowers she held still imprinted on her fingers.

"Look. We haven't much time. I wanted to advise you, Margaux"—her lips had considered the word *warn* and discarded it—"that there are discrepancies in your records."

"Discrepancies?" Margaux sounded wary. "But Madame complimen—"

"On their thoroughness. But the number of good stones making their way to Madame has been slipping rather alarmingly."

Margaux's eyes fluttered to the floor.

"The soil plays out. We've been mining there for a long time—"

"No. I don't think that's it. The numbers for the overall mining operation still look good."

There was silence.

"I—I can check on it—" Margaux began.

But the door *whoosh*ed open.

"Cecily?" Van put her head in. "Oh, good. I thought I saw you come this way. Joao's here. We're ready to start!"

Cecily settled both hands on her flowers again. Her eyes met Margaux's. The other girl nodded. An admission of something, perhaps? There was no time to rethink their conversation. It was time for her wedding.

They stood amid sprays of flowers in Effie's large living room, she and Ben and Van and Jenkins plus a minister. Effie, in her eternal black dinner suit, with Bibi at her feet, sat nearest to them. As Ben slipped a wide gold band on her finger and kissed her, Cecily felt as though they had become part of each other in some mysterious way that nothing could ever end. She closed her eyes for an instant and the others in the room vanished into another universe as Ben kissed her publicly.

Then Effie was chuckling and everyone was laughing and Van was hugging her.

"Welcome to the family," Harry said.

For a second she felt Ben's hand tighten around hers.

In the dining room a three-tiered cake was waiting. There was chilled champagne and hot hors d'oeuvres and on the back terrace, under a canopy, a string quartet began to strike up the first bars of lilting music.

"Go on, go on. Leave them a minute," Effie urged the others.

But when they were gone she turned to Ben and Cecily.

"Joao is not well," she said bluntly. "He has gone upstairs. Let's see what he brought us. Then we'll join the others."

Effie's rasping voice made the world of her business suddenly more real than the celebration around them. Cecily knew, and felt confident Ben did, too, that they were being invited to view that world's inner workings. Two days ago Joao had called to say there were troubles at one of his mines. Last week a diamond courier had failed to arrive. Reluctantly, with a premonition of something being lost, she lay her wedding flowers on a table and hurried into the elevator with Ben and Effie.

Joao was waiting for them in Effie's office. A frail, white-haired man, whose proud carriage seemed at war with the trembling of his hands, he was sliding a pill beneath his tongue when they entered. He rose immediately.

"Sit down, my old friend," said Effie. "You look the worse for travel."

There was silence, and Cecily realized the man who had dropped back into a chair was laboring for breath.

He extended a hand.

"Ben. I am happy for you. May your marriage last a thousand years."

The men shook hands and Joao reached for Cecily.

"Much happiness and many children." His tired eyes gave the ghost of a twinkle. "Or is the latter wish out of fashion these days?"

"How is young Joao?" asked Effie. "I am surprised he is not with you."

"Young Joao!" A passion that made him hoarse was in Joao's voice. "Young Joao likes boys! He is no longer a son of mine. I have disowned him!"

He had to pause again to gather his strength.

Ben looked worried, and Cecily felt events in the room closing in on the two of them.

"Let's see what you have brought us," said Effie, wheeling toward her desk. She seemed unaffected by the pain so evident in Joao's voice. "Ah, Joao, these are very fine stones!"

He nodded. One hand had crept beneath his jacket to pat at his chest.

"The larger pile I carried in my hand. The import slips are there beside them. The three large ones by themselves—my faithful Pablo had some dental work done before we caught the airplane."

"Pablo's his bodyguard," Ben whispered.

"We stopped at a dentist here before we came to see you. Poor Pablo—such work on his teeth within two days." Joao stopped to breathe. "They match," he finished at last.

Effie already had a loupe to her eye and was clucking.

"They are wonderful, Joao, but you should not have made this trip. I can see you are tired."

"I could not trust those three to a courier. Too fine to come except as submarines. The courier who should have reached you last week was dumped on my doorstep. His diamonds—the ones you see here—were still with him."

Effie made an angry sound. "This is Aurelio's doing. He is the one who started these troubles."

Cecily watched Joao's eyes turn to her and Ben. As though to ask our aid in something, she thought.

"We are getting too old for such troubles," he said.

Effie looked up sharply.

"I have had another offer to buy my mines."

"And you said?"

Joao's hand was massaging his chest again. "What could I say? We are partners, you and I. But I am too old for war—"

"We will not sell," Effie interrupted. "I will take care of this. Now go and rest."

She pressed a buzzer and a burly man opened the door. Joao rose slowly and went out leaning on his arm.

"I will put these in the vault and see you downstairs," said Effie, sweeping the diamonds before her into a bag. The sternness of her voice warned she expected no argument on the issue Joao had raised.

"That's going to be a bucket of worms," said Ben when the two of them were alone.

Cecily nodded somberly. "I gather it won't be brought up at the meeting tomorrow."

"I gather." He looked at her, but his eyes were distant for a moment, perhaps contemplating the problems Joao's view of things might cause for Duvall. Then he stirred. "Well. I suppose we'd better go on down and go through our paces since we're the focus of this celebration."

Cecily felt the start of a wicked smile. Now that they were alone, the prospect of making small talk with Harry and Lynette and all the others seemed odious. Here, in this room, she felt for the first time totally Ben's wife. It seemed to free some long buried joy inside her—some impulsiveness from her youth.

"I was wondering what would happen if we didn't go down. If we just slipped away. I can't imagine anyone would even notice."

Ben slipped his arms around her. Her words seemed to please him. He kissed her thoroughly.

"You know, you're right? I can't for the life of me see how our skipping the thing could possibly matter a bit."

"I wonder where Cecily is?" Van looked around the room again. "She should have cut the cake."

Wesley touched her arm lightly. "Don't worry about it. April's doing a fine job with it. Everyone's having fun. And things have been hectic these last few days. Maybe Ben and Cecily just wanted to be alone for a while."

Van blinked at him. "Why?"

"Uh . . ." He started to blush. With the hand that wasn't holding a plate of cake, he straightened his glasses.

"Excuse me, but has anyone told you you make the loveliest bridesmaid that's ever been seen?" interrupted a voice.

Van turned to see a handsome man with silvery-gray hair and piercing eyes. He held out his hand.

"You're the bride's sister, aren't you? I'm Trace MacDonald. Mrs. Duvall has hired me to consult with her on some advertising matters."

"Oh . . ." She didn't know how to answer him. It seemed too late to thank him now for his compliment. Anyway, she'd never had a man say anything like that to her. She thought maybe she was blushing like Wesley had been a moment earlier.

"It's wonderful with those doors open to the terrace, isn't it?" Trace MacDonald asked.

Somehow they had turned away from Wesley.

"I think it's perfect." Van laughed shyly.

"Would you like to dance?"

She looked quickly toward the terrace where Lynette was dancing with Harry and Maigrette with Martin.

"Oh I—I'm afraid I don't know how to dance. . . ."

She'd been hoping secretly that Wesley might ask her.

"I don't either, very well," said Trace MacDonald. "To tell you the truth, I went to boys' schools all my life and it's been a terrible handicap. I probably didn't even ask you the right way, did I?"

"I thought it sounded just right," Van reassured. She couldn't imagine Trace MacDonald worrying about what he'd said. He looked like an ad from a magazine in his pearly three-piece suit, and his smile was so attractive she found it hard to look away.

She glanced back at Wesley. He was standing where she'd left him. Van gave a little wave.

"We can both just sort of walk around and try not to step on each other's feet," Trace was saying. He'd offered his arm just as they did in movies and was moving her onto the terrace. "Unless . . ."

He had turned her toward him and taken her hand. He was about to place his hand on her waist, but now he halted. Concern seemed to dampen his polite expression.

The music washing around them produced a giddiness in Van. So this is what it's like to be on a dance floor! she thought.

"Unless?" she repeated.

Trace was frowning toward Wesley.

"You're not engaged to that man you were talking to, are you? I'd hate to intrude."

The question amazed Van. It had never occurred to her anyone might think of her as engaged, with plans and a future like Cecily had. It was very flattering.

"Oh, no," she said. "Wesley's awfully nice, but we're just friends."

She suddenly felt older somehow, and the experience was very pleasant.

TWENTY-EIGHT

"BEN, I DON'T UNDERSTAND. I THOUGHT WE'D LIVE WITH EFFIE."

The condominium on a private island off Palm Beach was spectacular, a retreat in the clouds. Sun through sliding glass doors bounced off white walls and carpeting; low, modern furniture. Each room, with its wraparound balcony, gave a panoramic view of the intercoastal waterway. But as they'd returned from their honeymoon, even as they'd picked up their car at the airport, she'd supposed they'd return to Effie. Ben's surprise had shocked her.

"I know," he said, leaning against the balcony rail, looking out at the blue Atlantic. "I should have asked you. But damn it, Cecily, can't you see living away from her is our only chance?"

Our only chance at what? she wanted to ask.

Ben had grown progressively tense as they'd returned to Miami. It puzzled her. Their ten days in Heredia had been so wonderful, filled with a peace and contentment such as she'd never known.

She went to him and put her arms around him. "Ben, what is it you're afraid of?"

"Christ. Can't you see? Don't you know?"

"Effie's fond of us. Of both of us."

"That won't stop her from using us. Maybe she already has."

"Don't—"

"She's so bloody dangerous!" His voice was despairing. "You don't understand that, do you? You don't want to believe it." He stared at her, caught her by the shoulders, suddenly savage. "Why don't you want to admit it? Why did you marry me?"

Cecily's mouth felt dry. His mood was frightening her. He was as suspicious of her motives as she was of his. He thought she had married him for gain, as everyone seemed to do who stood in Effie's shadow.

Some desperate need drove Ben to possess her, just as Effie was driven to own and dictate Duvall. Such a need was wrong, yet she was starting to see it was the symptom of some deep wound—in Ben, in Effie, perhaps in everyone. Didn't the need to own something indisputably come from fear? From the need for something to cling to like a magic charm that would keep away evil?

"I married you because I love you, Ben." Her voice was barely audible in her own ears.

"Don't. Don't say that."

Thrusting her hands aside he moved away from her.

Cecily was bewildered. Behind his gruffness she heard an aching longing. Hesitantly, half-fearing rejection, she went to him and touched him.

He turned, his arms devouring her.

"Oh, Cecily . . . Cecily . . ." His whispered repetition of her name sounded curiously like a prayer.

He held her and for a moment they were ageless: children giving each other courage. They wound together like branches of a single tree. Like best friends.

"My mother was her favorite child," Ben said against her hair. "But Effie used her anyway. She conned her into flying to pick up some stones when the weather was bad and she never came back."

Cecily heard his grief, muffled for years by the sound of it. She pressed his bent neck in sympathy, gathering him to her, being the strong one for a minute, yet not daring to give verbal comfort for certainty his pride would drive him away and end this moment of trust.

She felt closer to Ben than she ever had felt to anyone in that moment. At length she brought his hand up to her breast, an invitation that usually led to making love.

Instead, as if to shift the mood, Ben swung her into his arms with a sudden laugh.

"If we're going to stay here, let's christen the place. I've had something special put in just for you."

So rapidly that it made her dizzy he carried her into a sun splashed bedroom, then on into an adjoining bath where he turned in a circle. Cecily caught glimpses of a greenery and mirrors, yards of sparkling white tile and finally the gleaming, sensuous lines of a sunken black marble tub.

"Oh my God" she said laughing, too. "This must fall in the same category as black garter belts. Have I married some kind of a kink?"

"You should know by now," he said with a grin. With one foot, still booted from their flight, he nudged a handle on the tub. Nothing happened. "Well, hell," he said, setting her on her feet.

Cecily tried unsuccessfully to control her merriment. Clearly Ben had meant to do this with a flourish; undress her and ravish her in the water or some such.

"I know this is the one that's supposed to fill it," he was muttering as he knelt by the tub.

"Maybe the water's off," she said, spotting a valve handle in the wall.

"When Rudolfo came up yesterday to get things ready for us?"

"Maybe he forgot."

Cecily turned the handle. There was a yelp behind her. She turned to see water spraying out at what was obviously an incorrect angle. Ben had gotten the full force of it and was trying to duck the unplanned fountain.

"You did that on purpose!" he sputtered.

"No—"

He slipped in a puddle, grabbing for her to pull her down on top of him.

"Come on in. The water's fine."

"Ben! Let me turn it off! The place'll be flooded!"

She was laughing so hard she could not pull away from him. Water rained down on their faces. Ben kissed her, rolling her deeper into a puddle. They were both soaked to the skin.

"Actually, this is how it always works," Ben said over her giggles. "That's why they put it on sale."

Cecily staggered on her knees back to the cut-off valve with him behind her. She turned off the water. They collapsed and looked at each other. Ben grinned.

"Glad I didn't marry a daddy's-girl who waits to have everything done for her."

Out of breath, Cecily propped an arm on the wall and leaned against it, rolling her eyes.

"That'd be pretty hard when I don't even know who my father was."

"How about that? We've got something in common." His grin grew slowly rueful. "Hell, isn't it?" His finger traced her cheek. Leaning forward he kissed her with a seriousness that blotted out their lighthearted romp. "Cecily . . ."

She silenced his lips with her fingers, aware that the tension that had filled him during their earlier argument was still a part of him.

"Nothing's going to go wrong for us unless we let it, Ben. And I'm not going to end up like your mother or Marguerite. I promise."

"Oh, Christ!" he said, and there was a fervor in his voice she didn't understand.

Two hours later they were at Effie's.

She sat with sapphires spread across her desk as Jenkins showed them in.

"Ah, good. You are here," she said, putting down the loupe she held in her hand. Without further word of welcome she began to reel off the progress of various projects.

"Lyle and Company has opened a branch in Paris." She shoved a pile of newspaper clippings toward them and did not look pleased. "It is brazen. Stupid. They cannot afford such a move."

Cecily glanced at Ben and found him waiting for her look. Did he feel the same stir of worry she was feeling? The expansion by Lyle & Co. *was* brazen, but if they had good designers, if they had money behind them, the publicity generated by such a move might spur Lyle's growth.

"And Vanessa. . ." she began while she could get a word in.

"Vanessa is out. She went for lunch with MacDonald . . . MacDougal . . . the advertising consultant I told you about." As she digressed to deliver the information, she shoved a stack of clippings about a party marking the new location of Lyle & Co. into Cecily's hands.

Cecily was surprised. "You mean he took her to lunch?"

"Of course that's what I mean." Effie sounded irritable.

"But—" Cecily bit her lip. Maybe she was too protective of Vanessa.

"And now there is the matter of a wedding gift for the two of you." Effie bridged her fingers. "If you hadn't run off from your own reception, I would have told you then."

Her eyes, impenetrable as ever, moved from Ben to Cecily.

"As Cecily's a part of it now, I am giving her ten percent in Duvall."

"No!"

Cecily heard the word burst from Ben's lips the same instant it did from hers. A cold and nauseating billow moved through her stomach. Was this what Ben had feared? Did he think she'd been bought by Effie?

She wet her lips. "Effie, please, I—we don't want that!"

Effie made a growling sound. Her eyes were sharp. "Ridiculous! You act as though I meant to poison you."

She began to move her chair toward the window in agitation.

"Very well! I will make it a gift to Van. She is more appreciative than either of you!"

Cecily felt herself suspended, not wanting Ben to believe this had been any sort of pact between her and Effie, leery, though she could not say why, of what Effie was hurling out as the alternative.

"Ben, wait!"

He was already leaving the room.

This instant, this single encounter, seemed confirmation of all his doubts, not only about her motives in becoming his lover, but about how easily the equilibrium of their marriage could be destroyed by Effie. By what they each could get from Effie. Ben was suspicious of her, just as Cecily, because of that small uncertainty Kim had planted in her mind, had been suspicious of him.

By the time she reached the hallway Ben already was disappearing toward his studio.

"Is your meeting with Madame over?" Thida asked from another direction. She was standing in the door to the small office next to Cecily's. "There's a gentleman waiting to see you."

"A gentleman waiting to see me." Cecily heard her own voice repeating the words and the sound was hollow.

Thida didn't seem to notice.

"In your office. About insurance." She gestured and smiled. "You looked beautiful at the wedding. Was your trip nice?"

"Yes, thanks."

Nothing's going to go wrong for us unless we let it.

The words she'd spoken only hours ago came back to her and made her shiver. She opened the door to her office. A man stood up. Her voice came out in a thin quiver.

"Peter!"

TWENTY-NINE

"**F**ORGIVE ME FOR TELLING YOUR SECRETARY. I WAS HERE ABOUT insurance." His voice sounded almost foreign after all these months. He spread his hands in a helpless gesture. "I was afraid you might not see me if I gave my right name."

That little-boy look was there on his face. His hazel eyes coaxed her to understand.

"You're right about that, Peter."

Cecily managed to push free of the doorknob behind her, against which she'd been supporting herself. Her legs felt weak as she crossed the floor. She was being crushed by images from the past. The first time they had made love. When he'd asked her to marry him. How when she'd needed him he hadn't been there.

"How did you find me, Peter? What is it you want?"

Her words sounded crisp, almost curt, but her heart was pounding. Gratefully she sat down in the fawn leather chair behind her desk and touched its arms.

Peter stood before her earnestly, the uncertain charm of his smile merely intensified by the perfect tailoring of his suit.

"I. . ." He looked with slight apology down at his hands. "I came to confess to being an idiot, Cecily. I paid someone to trace you. Naturally."

"Naturally," she said dryly. She'd forgotten how much for granted Peter took the privileged status money had bought him. If a whim for something occurred to him, he had only to pay.

Anger and pain she'd thought long vanished churned through her. Speech was impossible. Why had he had to come back into her life?

"You've done very well for yourself." He looked around her office, smiling cautiously.

"For a thief?"

He winced. "Cecily, I never believed—"

"Of course you did!"

"No—"

"All right. You were worried about your precious status, then."

"Yes." He held up a hand. "Yes, I was. I admit that now. I was shallow, and stupid—but I want you back. That's why I've come—"

"I'm married, Peter."

His eyes shot to hers, measuring her in a way she'd never seen before.

"You're serious."

Cecily nodded. Unconsciously she was fingering the beautiful choker of opals and seed pearls Ben had made for her. She raised her other hand, showing her broad wedding band.

"See? No gaudy engagement rings this time. None needed. Though I suppose I should thank you for favoring me with as fine a one as you did. It kept me from starving when I couldn't find a job—"

"Cecily!" He leaned across her desk. "Please—you can't despise me any more than I've despised myself. I want you back!"

"You said that, Peter. But it's too late."

Cecily swept a folder to the center of her desk and started to read it. Another report from Margaux. Sapphires. No big stones listed.

"It's never too late." Peter straightened, composing himself. "I'll wait for you. I can run my business from Palm Beach as well as from anyplace else. Maybe your marriage won't work."

Her head shot up. She looked at him, appalled at his self-centeredness. Appalled at his almost childish stubbornness.

"Get out."

Peter drew himself up indignantly. "Cecily, I love you! I have—abased myself completely coming here. Are you just going to throw me out?"

His knuckles were white with determination. She felt the tug of emotion. A pain for him, perhaps. A sympathy. She could not wrest her eyes from the pleading in his. With an effort she lowered her gaze to the folder from Margaux and rose.

"You don't even know what love means, Peter. Now please leave."

"Does he know? Look me in the eye and tell me you love him and he loves you! Then I'll leave."

She found it hard to control her breathing. Could Peter *see*?

"Yes!" she said fiercely.

Their gazes locked. The past swirled between the two of them. Cecily thought dizzily that except for the day when they'd parted they'd never quarreled like this.

Peter managed to smile. Even now it was engaging.

"I think you've made a mistake," he said lightly. "I think you know it, Cecily. I'll be around."

He turned to leave.

The door opened.

"Oh . . . Ben! Come on in."

She was grateful for the sight of him, so darkly handsome and capable-looking. She could not even chatter out some explanation about insurance. She wanted to hide herself inside his arms and cling to him.

There was a pause that seemed to last forever. The two men eyed each other as Peter walked out. Ben closed the door with a definite shove.

"That was him, wasn't it?"

Cecily tried to recover balance.

"What do you mean?"

"You know what I mean. It shows on your face. It showed on his. Why play games?"

"All right. His name is Peter and—"

"I didn't ask who he was!" Ben's voice was violent with anger. "I just wondered why you were lying about it."

"For God's sake, Ben! Give me a break!"

Her hand flew at a bud vase, knocking it to the floor. With fingers still stinging, she kneaded her forehead, pushing, pushing against the fear that was engulfing her, the anger, the despair.

"I didn't ask him here. He found me. I told him to leave."

"Noble."

"Damn you, Ben—"

"You lied about why you married me!"

He'd crossed the room and leaned on her desk now as Peter had done. Only Cecily couldn't see him for her thickening tears. He loomed more solidly, more formidably than Peter had. He seemed about to reach across the narrow space and seize her.

"You wanted to forget him, didn't you? And you wanted a piece of this bloody company!"

He was hurting her so deeply that she could only strike back.

"Yes!" She flung back her head. "Effie told me a woman has to use both mind and body to get what she wants—so I did!"

He drew back as though she'd struck him.

"Don't think that's a game for women alone," he said tightly. "If I play my cards right, I'm going to be Effie's heir."

She was sobbing now, weak with unhappiness. She wiped shaking hands across her face and fought for reason.

"Ben, let's please not fight. I didn't mean what I said just now and you know it. I'm upset. It was a shock walking in to find Peter waiting for me. That's all there is to it."

He was silent. No answer was forthcoming. Cecily fumbled in a drawer to find a tissue and blotted her face.

Business, she thought. Turn it back to business and this would pass. It could be healed later.

"I need to go to Sri Lanka," she said, glancing back at Margaux's report. "How do you suggest I get there?"

Ben's mouth set and he turned away from her desk.

"Any damn way you want!"

The hot, humid air of the tropical island off the southern coast of India pressed in upon her. Cecily fanned the lapel of her light gauze shirt, wishing it were cooler. On the road to Lynette's plantation she'd passed slow-plodding elephants, drab, utilitarian-looking beasts that bore no resemblance to the bejeweled replicas sold in the souvenir shops of Colombo, the capital city. Now she crossed the raised wooden porch of a rambling, pagodalike building. The door stood ajar. Cecily knocked on it as she stepped inside an indifferently furnished front office.

"May I help?"

The girl occupying the foremost of several attractively worn wooden desks looked up with commendable courtesy. She wore a sari, and jewels upon jewels. Strings of tiny topaz, ruby, and emerald. Strings of diamond, sapphire, and amethyst, all of them set in gold. The quality of the stones was less than spectacular, Cecily guessed. Nonetheless she was intrigued by the way in which the women of the island weighed themselves down with their treasures.

"Yes, will you please tell Mrs. Duvall or one of her daughters that Cecily Catlow is here on behalf of Madame Duvall?"

The secretary upset a stack of letters she'd been typing.

"Sit down, please," she said, rising quickly, eyes stretched to bursting. "I'll tell her at once."

But rather than sitting, Cecily leaned one elbow cautiously against a paneled wall.

Damn, she thought. This heat is miserable.

It wasn't the heat, though, that was making her irritable. She faced the knowledge almost against her will. It was the rift with Ben . . . was it only two days ago? He hadn't spoken to her since that argument in her office after Peter had left. He hadn't returned to the condominium that night until she'd fallen asleep.

And because she'd been hurt, and angry, she'd gone ahead with this trip—though God knows it would have to have been made sooner or later.

The side of her fist tapped lightly against the paneling. She wished she hadn't come. She wished she hadn't been pigheaded and were back with Ben, attempting to talk things out. An ache permeated her throat. It still seemed impossible the trust that had slowly grown up between them had been destroyed in a single day back in Miami.

Back with Effie, her mind whispered traitorously.

She tried to ignore it.

She'd think about other things. How she must talk to Van about Trace MacDonald. How she must caution Van to move more slowly and not get too involved.

"Cecily?" a voice said nervously. "Oh, my God . . . we didn't know. . . ."

All at once Margaux was standing before her and, not far away, Maigrette. Cecily pulled herself from her reverie.

"You have a very efficient looking office," she said.

The compliment didn't put Margaux at ease. She looked edgy.

"I'm afraid my mother's not here—"

"That's all right. Better, in fact. Are you going to ask me in?"

"Oh, yes. My—that is, Mother's office is this way. Why didn't you let us know you were coming? We'd have met you when you came in."

"Did you have a nice honeymoon?" Maigrette asked eagerly.

Cecily nodded. Their footsteps echoed in a wooden hallway. Margaux opened the door to a large office with a Cézanne lending a sense of coolness and tranquillity to one wall. Overhead a ceiling fan stirred muggy air.

"Meg, why don't you go see about some tea for us," Margaux suggested.

She looked unaffected by the heat. The spring green of her light cotton dress wasn't even wrinkled. Her blond hair was neat. But Cecily could see the faint lines at the sides of her mouth. Margaux was worried. Her eyes observed her sister's departure, and Cecily wondered whether Margaux had been wise enough to know the two of them should be alone.

In the strangely old-fashioned office Cecily sat back. Yes, Margaux was wise and there was no reason for wasting time between them, she decided.

"I've just seen your latest records. Again, there's not one stone of even two carats."

Margaux lifted a hand. "They don't come along that often. I can list only what the mines have produced—"

"Where's Lynette?"

"In Paris. She . . . likes to spend time in Paris."

Something flickered in Margaux's blue eyes. Anger, Cecily thought, perhaps at being left in this situation.

"I want to see the contents of your safe."

Margaux's face paled. "I . . . don't know the combination. Mother will be back Monday—"

"I have the combination, Margaux. Open it or I'll do it myself."

It was purely a bluff. In theory, at least, Effie had the combination to every safe controlled by members of her far-flung family, but Cecily hadn't told her the reason behind this trip. Instead she'd invented stories . . . about how Margaux had mentioned an adjacent parcel of land might be for sale and about how certain officials in the government needed wooing.

Because I don't really believe Margaux is behind this, she admitted now. She kept her expression hard.

Margaux held to the arms of her chair for a moment, then ran fingertips across her lower lip.

"All right. I'll open it. But first you have to listen to me—"

"Who's responsible for the doctored books, Margaux? You or Lynette?"

She knew she'd been on the right track. The safe would yield sapphires that had been held back. She needed to wring the confession from Margaux now, before the girl could think of a defense.

"I guess we both are," Margaux said dully. Her mouth turned suddenly stubborn. "I never wanted to do it. But Mother—I told you she likes to spend time in Paris—she hates it here. She wanted money for tickets, hotels, clothes. She said it would be just a stone now and then—I couldn't talk her out of it, you see. And I was afraid of Effie—afraid we'd lose everything—"

"And how much do you get from all this?"

Margaux's eyes flew wide. "Nothing! That is . . . I don't know it if I do. I've gotten a salary since I started working in the company, but . . ."

Her shoulders slumped. She rested her head on one hand, eyes tightly shut. "We're—we're going to be ruined, aren't we? Effie will throw all three of us out for this!"

"Not if I don't tell her."

Margaux's head jerked up. There was relief in her expression, then disgust.

"Do you want a cut? It that what this is all about?"

"No, I don't want a cut."

"Why wouldn't you tell her, then?"

"Because I think you—*you*, Margaux—are running a fairly efficient operation here. Because changing management here after all these years would be one more disruption we don't need." She sat forward in her chair. "And because I think you're smart enough to know heads will roll if this doesn't stop now that I've warned you!

"Now. Get your mother on the phone. I'm going back to Miami and I want her to meet me there."

"You aren't going to—I wouldn't want Mother hurt! She's— she's been unhappy here for so many years, but she didn't have any other way of making a living. . . ."

"She won't be hurt," promised Cecily grimly. "Not as long as she cooperates."

"Señora Duvall!" Rudolfo, Ben's houseman from Heredia, who had come to manage things in their new home, opened the door to the condominium as Cecily stood fumbling with her key.

"Hello, Rudolfo." She tried to smile. She hadn't been sure she'd find him still here, and now she wondered if she would find Ben.

He took charge of her luggage.

"I did not know you were expected. Señor Duvall is at Señor Hilbrun's. A company is very interested in their invention if it continues to work on test flights."

"How nice."

"Shall I fix you some dinner? There is some very good chicken."

She shook her head, flipping through the mail awaiting her. "No thanks. Just a sandwich, maybe, as soon as I've had a bath."

"A sandwich, then. No mustard," he said agreeably.

Cecily shot him a look. "I don't remember telling you I don't like mustard."

"Señor Duvall did. He said he would fire me if I ever gave you a sandwich with mustard."

From his tone she knew he was not much worried by the threat. She gave a tired smile. She remembered telling Ben how one foster home she'd lived in had used only mustard on sandwiches because it was cheaper than mayonnaise, and how she hated it.

"Leave the tray in the bedroom, if you would, Rudolfo."

Continuing into the bathroom, she began to run steaming water in the black marble tub. After the heat of Sri Lanka she could not even think why a hot bath appealed to her. She discarded her clothes. Every bone in her head ached dully. She lay back, closed her eyes, and tried to think about meeting Ben.

Afterward, as she wrapped a white robe from her wedding trip around her, she was almost too weary to plan. What else could she say but that she regretted the explosion between them . . . that Peter meant nothing to her . . . that the trip she'd departed on in anger had been a chain of self-recriminations and sleepless nights?

She swallowed down half a sandwich. Rudolfo had fixed her a lovely fruit cup, too—pineapple, strawberries, cataloupe, all of them fresh. She picked the strawberries out.

"Cecily?"

The sound of Ben's voice made her whirl. Every word she'd meant to say flew from her mind and she stood mute. He'd opened the door and stood half leaning against the frame. She searched his face and could see nothing, no clue, to what he was feeling.

And then he moved. Words seemed unnecessary. She was in his arms and their mouths were meeting. Her heart, which had been small and heavy inside her, expanded with new life as she let go of fear, let go of loneliness, let go of all pretenses to simply press against him.

"You're back," he breathed. "Oh, bloody Christ, Cecily, I wasn't sure if you'd *be* back!"

His face rubbed against her hair.

The humility in his voice touched her and flooded her with the need to ease the pain she heard there. For an instant Ben was hers.

"I've hated myself every mile of that stupid trip!" she whispered. "Oh, Ben, you made me so damned mad! Why couldn't we have *talked*?"

"Talking's not one of the things we're good at," he said dryly. His fingers traced the shadow of her collarbone, moved down, unfastened her robe.

She let him carry her to their bed, her body awakening to the knowledge it was theirs, that this whole room was theirs, that they were safe in a world of their own making.

"Back in a minute," Ben said, kissing her and moving toward the bathroom.

Cecily watched the rhythm of his body, the perfect set of his shoulders. Emotion swelled in her chest. She realized what a precious thing it was to memorize the shape of a back or the sound of a voice when they were dear to you.

Most people, she supposed, took such things for granted. She, though, remembered the years when the only warmth in her life had come from her memories of Van. She would conjure them up at night when there was no hand to pull up the covers and smooth back her hair. She would summon them when other children her age laughed about pranks with parents.

Now she had not only Van but Ben—both real and in the flesh. Tears of gratitude slipped down her face. Somewhere deep inside her there was an abiding fear that anyone in her life might walk out of it. Her mother had. Peter had. Even Van had, through no fault of her own.

The phone beside the bed rang. She put out a hand.

"Cecily? Look, I lost my temper the other day. I'd like to see you again—"

"No!"

It was Peter. Fear swept her. Swiftly, guiltily she pushed the phone back into its cradle, held it there, praying it would not ring again.

"Who was it?"

Ben was back in the room now, moving toward the bed. Did a question lurk in his eyes, or was she imagining it?

"A wrong number."

He slid in beside her. The phone rang again.

A fear so great she could not even breathe swooped down upon her. Her hand flew numbly out.

"Cecily?" Van's voice sang out at the other end, excited. "Oh, Cecily, guess what! I'm getting married!"

THIRTY

"I DON'T SEE WHY YOU CAN'T BE HAPPY FOR ME. I WAS HAPPY FOR you when you got married!"

Van felt an unfamiliar anger pushing at her stomach. As usual, Cecily was treating her like a child. Last night Trace had come to dinner at Effie's, along with Ben and Cecily. She'd been so sure Cecily would like him. He always made conversation so easily. And he'd bought this lovely big box of chocolates.

But Cecily had said afterward that he seemed awfully worldly. Van knew it wasn't a compliment.

Now Cecily sighed and stood up from the chair on the terrace where she'd cornered Van first thing this morning.

"Van, I didn't say I wasn't happy for you. I just said—"

"You didn't *sound* happy. You haven't all week—ever since I told you about it!"

"All I said was that I wished you'd wait a little."

"For what?"

Van stopped, a little embarrassed to realize her words were almost a yell. They sounded like some howl of Bibi's. But anger—and hurt feelings—nudged out the embarrassment. Here she'd met this perfectly wonderful man who was perfectly wonderful to her, who had taken her to movies and dinner and even a nightclub and all kinds of places no one else had ever taken her; who had asked before he'd kissed her and showed no inclination to go overboard in that direction, which she'd worried about a little. All that and no one seemed excited that he loved her. Cecily least of all.

They don't think I know enough to get along on my own, she thought. They don't really believe I'm well.

Tears crept into her eyes, but she ordered them sharply back.

"Vanessa . . . dearest . . ." Cecily touched her arm and the pressure made Van feel better. "If you're happy, I am, too. Truly. It's just that you haven't even met that many men yet. There's plenty of time." She took a breath. "You haven't been out on your own that long, Van. And you only met Trace, what, a month ago? At my wedding. It's so fast. And it's such a big step. I just don't want to see you make a mistake. I don't want to see you get hurt."

"But I *love* Trace. And he wants to marry me!"

Why couldn't anyone understand what that meant to her?

"Do you need some coffee?"

Thida rose from her desk to pour it before Cecily, passing through to her own office, even answered.

"Heavens, yes. I took a cup out with me when I went to say good morning to Van, but I don't think I touched a drop of it."

Cecily continued to her desk, sat down, tried to dislodge the frustration lodged inside her. Why couldn't Van be reasonable? She was worried. Her sister was moving too fast. But she couldn't live Van's life for her. The very fact of freedom brought with it the possibility of mistakes. So which was better, being swaddled and safe—and maybe happy—or living life to the fullest, scrapes and all?

Maybe Trace MacDonald was touched by Van's innocence. Maybe he wanted to protect it. There were men like that. She settled into work determined, in spite of all the 'maybes', that this wouldn't be the last talk on the subject she would have with Van.

The top of her desk was in perfect order, phone messages arranged down one side, a folder of letters awaiting her signature on the other. And under her paperweight, a fist-sized but impossibly flawed clump of amethyst crystals, were clippings from the morning's paper. Thida was exceeding her expectations as a secretary. Cecily smiled at her as she appeared with the coffee.

"A shipment from Colombia arrived this morning," Thida announced. "I expect you'll be sorting emeralds."

"I expect. And thanks."

Of late Effie often gave her the initial sorting of colored stones. Then they would argue about them—though Effie found fewer chances than she'd like to quibble over the sorting, Cecily suspected. She appreciated how Thida noted the comings and goings in the atelier and was able to anticipate, sometimes before she was, what daily chores it might create for her.

Thida continued to stand before her. There was little resemblance, now, between the girl who had worked in the kitchen and this trim-limbed young woman who wore her stylishly cut hair and yellow gauze dress with ease.

"Was there something else?" asked Cecily.

"I thought you should know . . . Madame had another of her headaches last night. I was here finishing some letters and heard her tell Mr. Jenkins he should stop fussing."

Cecily sat back and let her breath out explosively. "I suppose she was in a rage about something."

"Yes, I think so."

"I'll get Van to talk to her . . . make sure she's been taking her medicine. I think she pays more attention to Van than she does to Ben or me."

Already it seemed like hours since she and Ben had left their sunny apartment. In fact it was less than one. Cecily sipped coffee, grateful for the chance to catch her breath, then buzzed Thida and asked her to start dialing calls.

The day began in earnest when Effie wheeled into the room.

"At her age you would think the Countess di Crichi would be beyond birthdays," she grumbled. "But no, I am invited to a party for her, no less! What nonsense. I suppose I must send a gift. I have never known of anyone beyond the age of twelve to have a birthday party. What do you suggest?"

Though still half-lost in her own thoughts Cecily felt her fondness for Effie teasing her lips into a more pleasant shape.

"I'll have to think," she admitted. "I'm afraid I've never had a birthday party myself." It was something she'd longed for wistfully as a child—a full-blown party with friends invited and tantalizing packages and a store-bought cake.

"Hah! You see, we are very much alike." Effie rolled closer and stopped. "I have never had such a fuss made over me. A waste of time."

But Cecily wondered if she didn't detect a certain envy beneath Effie's growling. She filed an idea away.

"You look preoccupied," Effie observed.

"Yes."

"It has nothing to do with the show—not a clown sick or a tightrope walker who has broken a leg or—"

"No, no," Cecily reassured her. "Everything's fine for the show."

It was still a month away, the kickoff of the social season for the Miami–Palm Beach area. Already people were buzzing about it. The French and German press were coming, as well as representatives of a dozen U.S. publications to whom Cecily had granted invitations. By restricting the number of press in attendance, they had sparked a wild curiosity—which had been Effie's plan.

"It is your sister, then," Effie guessed shrewdly.

Cecily turned up an expressive palm. "Effie, I don't know what to do. I wonder if she just wants to copy me, and then I wonder if I'm being awful, conceited or something to think it. But she's been so sheltered—good grief, she was in a mental hospital less than a year ago! She's never even dated a man before. I just think she's rushing it."

"Of course she's rushing it," Effie grumbled, stroking her chin. "And I shall be left with no one to play canasta. People move in and out of my house as though it were a hotel!"

Cecily's gesture turned impatient. Fond as she was of Effie, the old woman did have a tendency to see things in terms of herself.

"Look, Effie. I know you didn't like it when Ben and I moved out, but we needed some time to ourselves."

For the first time, and though she didn't mean to, Cecily found herself wondering whether Effie had built this large house meaning to fill it with family . . . whether it had ever been filled . . . whether Effie had paid a high price for the matches she'd made for her offspring or had paid it as gladly and indifferently as it seemed.

What is the price of loving? Cecily wondered. The cost of not loving? The chance of betrayal and heartbreak with one, loneliness with the other. Which was the easier cost to pay?

"What do you know about Trace MacDonald?" she asked, her voice grown calmer.

Effie grunted. "He was with a good agency. He was not assigned to Lyle and Company very long. When he grew disenchanted with them and decided to offer me his services, he also made the decision to strike out on his own. He has a modest income of inherited money from his father, an Englishman, a fact I checked." Her upper lip raised as she grinned at her own cunning. "He also admitted to me that he is the one responsible for the cancellation of my ads. He is very anxious to please me so I will not harbor grudges."

Cecily's intercom stirred to life.

"Miss Catlow, Lynette Duvall is here to see you," Thida announced.

Effie's eyes stirred curiously.

"Is she." Cecily assessed the situation quickly. Lynette must have thought to throw her off balance by showing up unannounced. And if Effie were present, Lynette must either go free or everything must explode.

She swiveled her chair.

"Effie, I want you to consider transferring Lynette's five percent of the company to Margaux's control. We should have discussed it earlier, but there's hardly been time."

Effie's gaze was unnervingly level. "Why?"

Did she suspect something? Cecily moved smoothly ahead. "Because I think Margaux will be far more dependable should we ever need her vote. She has more enthusiasm for the work in Sri Lanka than her mother does, too."

"Lynette would never agree to such an arrangement."

"I think she will—if you make it clear it's not a punishment as it was with Aurelio. If you open a branch of Duvall in Paris to

compete with Van Cleef and Arpels—and Lyle and Company—
and put her in charge."

"Hah!" Effie's scrutiny was like the touch of a knife's edge.
"You have thought of everything."

Cecily sought to match the challenge in her voice. "I hope so.
I have some figures. . . ." She opened a desk drawer and took a
folder out quickly. "The company could easily bear the expense.
You have many customers on the continent. Why give Lyle and
Company even a hope of sharing them? Lynette knows Paris
well—"

"Ask her, ask her if you want. But I warn you, Lynette will
still want to cling to her shares." Effie waved the folder away.
"A branch in Paris," she said with a chuckle. "I have always
wanted a branch in Paris. I was born there."

She left through the connecting anteroom and Cecily pressed
the intercom.

"Send Lynette in now."

A moment later the widow of Effie's first son stood before her.
Lynette looked sure of herself. Morning sunlight danced on the
champagne contours of her feathery hair.

"I understood Effie was with you," she said, eyes narrowing
slightly as she looked around.

"Not anymore." Cecily stood up and pointed to a chair. "Sit
down, Lynette."

At first the woman hesitated. Then, with studied arrogance,
she took a seat and crossed her legs.

"You're a troublemaker, aren't you?" she asked. "Coming
when I was gone and poking around. Is that why you married
Ben? You thought it would give you the right to meddle in
family affairs?"

Cecily controlled herself at the implication.

"Looking out for Effie's interests gives me all the right I
need."

"I'm not scared of you, you know. And there's no proof I've
done anything wrong."

Cecily rested one hip against the front of her desk. She
intended the posture would communicate who was in control.

"Lynette, I don't have time to fool with you—or the inclination.
I'm offering you a chance to have this stop with me instead of
Effie.

"I've had papers drawn up. You can sign over your control of
the business in Sri Lanka, and your vote on the board, to
Margaux—Maigrette, too, if you wish—"

Lynette's outraged gasp nearly interrupted her, but she continued.

"—and in exchange you'll be put in charge of a new branch of Duvall that's opening in Paris—"

"I won't give up my place on the board! I earned it! I spent years stuck on that stupid, stinking island, rotting away when I should have been having fun. *I earned it!*"

Lynette sprang from her chair. She was breathing quickly. Her eyes were glittering.

Cecily regarded her calmly. She was not sure yet how formidable a foe Lynette might prove, but she was counting on being stronger.

"If you refuse, Lynette, I've acquired certain gambling debts of yours which I intend to call due. I don't think you'd like that. I don't think you'd like being thrown out on your ear, either, which is what's going to happen if I tell Effie you're cheating her.

"Now. You can save face. Draw a nice salary. Live in Paris—which should be enough in itself to satisfy you—and manage to make it all look like a promotion if you have any sense at all. Either that or I pull the plug on you. Here's the paper to sign. You've got thirty seconds."

Lynette wet her lips. "I'll go to Paris, but I want to stay on the board—"

"I'm counting, Lynette."

"You have no proof—"

"If Effie cuts you off, what are you going to do for money, Lynette? What kind of job could you get? Where could you live?"

Lynette's face hardened into lines that betrayed her age.

"I'll get even with you for this!"

"I hope not, Lynette. Someday you may even think you've struck a very good bargain."

Lynette slashed her name across the bottom of the paper offered her and threw down the pen.

"Effie won't live forever, you know. And when she's gone you'll see how little Ben cares about anything but getting his hands on this company so he can destroy us all! You're a fool if you think he married you for any other reason!"

Muscles jerked tight in Cecily's stomach. She thought she might retch from their contraction. Turning on one needlelike heel, Lynette stalked from the room.

Cecily sat down and pressed her forehead against templed fingers. *There was nothing but anger behind Lynette's words!* She wouldn't be upset by them. And yet they echoed Kim.

She couldn't let herself think about it. Wouldn't let herself. Going to the small safe that had been installed for her, she put Lynette's transfer of ownership inside. Effie could have made the transfer abitrarily, of course, but this was better. It made the new arrangements look voluntary, reduced the chance for dissent among other members of the board, made the changes look like part of a long-range plan. She had won a fight. She should feel pleased. Instead her stomach burned and her head ached so violently that the room rocked around her.

"I'm going to the workroom," she said, leaving her office without even slackening her pace as she passed Thida. Her steps were quicker than she wanted them to be. *She had to see Ben!*

Even though what Lynette had hinted at about him wasn't true.

The workroom covered most of one wing in the second story. It was running at peak capacity now. Three goldsmiths worked at separate tables, one hammering, one polishing, one bent near a flame as he worked with flux. Mortimer hovered about another table where the last of the diamonds were being set in his snowflake necklace.

But it was Ben's dark head she sought. She saw it bowed above a work surface while one of the stone-setters squatted at his elbow conferring with him.

"It's the eyes that are going to make us or break us on all of these," Ben was saying, a graver moving deftly and delicately between his fingers. "A fraction too much and the contours of the face are gone. A fraction too little and the stone falls out. . . ."

As Cecily approached she saw he held the first of his golden Foo dogs, bracelets in the shape of the mythical Chinese temple guards that always appeared to her half dog, half lion. There were to be eight of them, each with bulging eyes of a different gemstone, each with different detailing, each holding beneath one uplifted paw a round ball symbolizing the world—and made of one round and perfect-faceted gem.

Effie had approved the designs for them just days ago, the morning after Ben had left his bed at two A.M. and started drawing them. Things seemed to come to him in flashes, and they were coming with increasing tempo. Cecily watched his hand move again, turning up another sliver of gold to anchor the ruby currently held in place by sealing wax. The flesh around his eyes was taut with concentration. He cared about this work. He would never harm Duvall. Lynette had been lying.

He saw her now and glanced up, though with only partial attention.

"Hi," he said.

"Hi."

His eyes were on his work again.

"Nice," she said, looking from the bracelet in his hand to the eight sketches spread out nearby. "And not a female in the lot, I see."

He flashed her a grin without looking up.

"Can't cut a stone to look like a cub. The sphere's bad enough. Want something?" He reached for the small wooden handle of a beading tool.

"No."

Her throat felt very full. She loved him so. And in spite of this sight of him at his work, Lynette's last words kept ringing in her ears. She needed a reassurance from him he could not give her. She was desperate for Ben's love with a secret, guilty longing she could never admit to him or Effie.

She let her fingertips brush his shoulder, then took them away. Ben looked up.

His attention was all on her now. His eyes held hers. And for an instant she seemed to see her own struggling fear reflected there. He brought her hand back against the curve of his neck and held it against him.

"Everything okay?"

She nodded. In all the crowded workroom she had an overpowering sense of only the two of them, and she knew the moment was fleeing even as she experienced it.

The door opened. Here came Thida, beckoning to her.

"If you could spare ten minutes for fitting a dress to wear for Madame's show . . ."

"Oh, good grief! I'd forgotten about a dress!"

"I know. I went last week and selected some for you to try. If none of them pleases you—"

"I'm sure one will. Thida, what would I ever do without you?"

Ben was already turning back to the bulging eyes and grinning mouth of his Foo dog.

There was so much to do, thought Cecily, threading her way past a tray of arriving aquamarines, a concession to "lesser stones" Effie had made just for the Foo dogs. So much to think about.

Effie's show.

Effie's headaches.

Those words of Lynette's.

And most disturbing of all, the prospect of Vanessa's marriage.

THIRTY-ONE

JORDAN LEFT THE BAR WHERE HE'D PAID A MAN TO MAKE THE ADJUSTments on Cousin Cecily's car. Half now and half when the job was finished. That was the arrangement.

It was obliging of Cousin Cecily to leave her small brown Audi where it was easy to get at every day when she took the boat over to the island where she worked. It was going to make things very simple, the man he'd met with had told him. Orlena was likely to suspect, but she wouldn't say anything. Not with the Duvall show just a few days away and pulling all kinds of publicity. Not after that flap about the Russian diamonds.

Jordan smiled. If something got in your way you got rid of it.

It would have been so much simpler to let old Madame Duvall have a boating accident on the way to that first fashion show. Then Cousin Cecily would never have had the chance to become a nuisance to them. But Orlena never listened to his suggestions. She thought he was stupid. But after this she'd be afraid of him. He'd be the one running Lyle & Co. from now on.

He wondered if in the split-second that it was happening, Cecily would have time enough to realize that she was being repaid for making a fool of him?

He slid into his car. A package on the seat beside him held strips of new leather. Their scent excited him.

Too bad he'd never have a chance to tie up Cousin Cecily.

That's what he'd *really* like to do to even the score.

He imagined her biting and struggling, unable to humiliate him ever again. His breathing quickened. But no. He had to be practical.

Of course there was always the chance that Cecily's husband would be with her. Sometimes they rode together. Pity.

Terrible what the hot sun could do to the tiniest leak in a gas tank down here.

*   *   *

Cecily had thought if she sat in the dark she would disturb no one. The light switching on in the tranquil nightscape of the living room startled her, and she looked up to see Ben, a wrap thrown around his waist and hair rumpled with sleep.

"What are you doing out here?" he asked. "It's two in the morning."

Her hand had gone up to protect her eyes from the light.

"I couldn't sleep. I had a headache."

"Take some aspirin and come back to bed."

"I did take something. It—takes a while to work. I've had these before."

He was beside her now, and stifling a yawn.

"That what that prescription's for in the medicine chest?"

A glint of amusement pushed its way through the ache in her head.

"You really do an audit, don't you?" she said, squinting at him.

He grinned.

"You worried about the show day after tomorrow? Is that what's the matter?"

She sighed.

"I guess so. Among other things."

The upcoming show, in fact, had been peripheral to other thoughts: The nagging, often-present doubts Lynette and Kim had planted about why Ben made her his wife. Van's insistence on marriage. The possibility that the plan for a Paris branch was a major blunder. What if it lost money? The last two topics, she shared with Ben.

"It's a gamble," he agreed. "But the timing's good, what with the show to stir things up. Let's face it, Effie's whole attempt to make a comeback in a big way is a gamble."

One I'm responsible for, thought Cecily.

Ben rubbed the back of his hand against her cheek. "Why didn't you talk to me about it tonight if it was worrying you? You like being left on your own with your worries, Ms. Prickly Pear?"

She smiled. It wasn't the first time he'd used that name for her.

"No. Not a bit."

"Well, then." He drew her to her feet. "Come back to bed." He lifted her and carried her gently back to cool, lace trimmed sheets. "Now about these headaches," he said. "Are you defective or what?"

She laughed at his teasing. The squeezing at her temples was almost gone now.

"It's happened for years." She felt suddenly playful, and wide awake as she lay on her back with Ben leaning slightly over her. She twisted to face him. "Do you want to know what I think it really is?"

"As long as it's not syphilis or something equally inconvenient."

His voice came from the darkness. She could scarcely see him. The sense of the two of them alone and drifting endlessly made her feel incredibly merry, incredibly free.

She began to laugh before she could get the first words out.

"I think it's because of my teddy bear. When Van—when I had to leave Great-Uncle William's I was so upset I didn't take it. And that first night at the children's home—it was so awful anyway, and I was used to having my bear, and I couldn't get to sleep. I just lay there thinking of things I didn't want to think about and I guess it was then that the headaches started happening. I had one that night.

"God. Don't I sound like a melodramatic waif? Marked for life because I lost my teddy bear."

She felt silly now, and laughed again.

"A sweet waif, though." Ben kissed her softly on the lips. His arms lay loosely around her. His manner, though, seemed far too serious for the discussion.

Cecily picked playfully at the square corner of his beard. Something magic and wonderful seemed to be happening between them.

"Let me guess. I'll bet you never even *had* a teddy bear. I'll bet Effie thought they were sissy."

He grinned.

"I seem to remember some argument between my mother and her over just that subject."

"Ah-hah. Thought so. And you weren't allowed coloring books because they'd stifle your creativity."

"Right."

"And you wore wee little custom-made boots instead of sneakers, so all the other kids made fun of you."

"Wrong. They were jealous. All except one kid. He always snickered at me. So Effie told me to punch his lights out."

"And you did, and got expelled for fighting, and Effie sent you to a better school."

"Are you kidding? I already was at the better school. As a

matter of fact, he mopped up the floor with me. Broke my little finger and loosened a couple of teeth. Effie made me practice throwing punches with one of the guards. Told me by the time my finger was out of the splint, she expected me to beat the pulp out of the other kid.''

''And?''

''He beat me to shit again, but I picked another fight and won it. *I* was expelled. But I got to go to Joao's with Effie. I'd been begging her to take me for a long time.''

They were shaking with shared laughter, locked in each other's arms.

''Oh, Ben!'' she sighed. It was all so funny, what they were talking about. Yet it wasn't funny. They kissed, and conversation came to an end.

The next morning Cecily was surprised to find Ben up and gone ahead of her. More surprising was the message he'd left for her to wait for him before going to Effie's. Often they went in separately as Cecily often had business in Palm Beach or downtown Miami in Effie's behalf. Ben's work lay almost exclusively in his studio. Now, today of all days, when there were details to check for Effie's big show tomorrow, Cecily found herself waiting at the apartment while it grew later. Finally Ben called to say he was already at the island. Vexed by the delay, Cecily drove quickly to the marina where she left her car and hurried to work.

She walked into her office, intent on a phone call she must make immediately. Halfway to her desk she halted, unable to believe her eyes. There in her chair, looking over her desk, sat a two-foot high toy bear with a red ribbon circling its neck. Between its spread, stumpy legs there were miniature dishes.

''Hello,'' piped a voice from beneath her desk. ''I'm Prickly Pear the Second. Would you like some tea?''

It was Ben's voice. He was scrunched down out of sight, his hand making the teddy bear nod agreeably.

Cecily choked on her own merriment. The fact he'd delayed her work day for this seemed insignificant now.

''Why, thank you, Prickly Pear. I'd love some. But only if there's gin in it, I'm so overwhelmed!''

''Gin? Of course.'' The bear turned side to side as if in search of something. ''Giles? Giles? That does it. He's fired. Never hire a rabbit to do a butler's work!''

She was gurgling now, holding her sides. The door to the anteroom opened and Effie wheeled in.

"What is going on?" she demanded. "Why is no one working?"

Cecily was unable to control herself.

"We're playing house," said Ben popping up from behind the desk.

The phone rang. It was April.

"Hey, this juggler and me have rented a big boat for this evening," she said. "How about if we pick you and Ben up after work? Good way to relax before tomorrow night's big do, don't you think?"

Covering the mouthpiece Cecily relayed the invitation to Ben.

"Sure," he said looking up. Having abandoned the role of Prickly Pear, he was bent to confer with Effie. "One of the guards can go over and drive your car back to the condo. We'll have April drop us at my car when we get back."

Cecily smiled and fondled the teddy bear's soft ear. Everything was so perfect.

THIRTY-TWO

"WESLEY, DO YOU KNOW BEN HAS A *GUN* UNDERNEATH HIS jacket?" Van gripped his arm, clearly a little concerned by her discovery. "I saw it just a minute ago, when we got out of the car!"

Wesley turned and looked at Ben, whose black-tie attire looked splendidly fitted regardless of what he might be wearing beneath it. "I hope he has a permit."

They were in the thick of the crowd assembling for Effie's show. Wesley's palms felt damp as he thought how near this had come to being a night of mourning instead of a night of celebration. That freak and violent accident with Cecily's car. A guard killed. Except for a miracle—that invitation from April—it would have been Cecily lost in the fiery explosion.

That was why Ben had a gun. At least Wesley supposed it was why; he'd never been involved with a family like the Duvalls before. But he knew Ben was worried. Although the police said most likely a small gas leak was to blame for the car going up in flames, Ben had confided to Wesley he thought it might be something else. Effie had made more than her share of enemies, and it was possible they'd try to get to her through Cecily.

Wesley shook his head. Readjusting his glasses he patted Van's hand and tried to reassure her.

"That's just how Ben is, Van. You know—sort of swash-buckling."

He'd come to like Ben. He wished he were a little more like him. Then maybe Van would have noticed him instead of Trace MacDonald. Wesley ground his teeth.

He decided he ought to change the subject. Vanessa was a little nervous in crowds still.

"You look beautiful in that dress," he said, feeling clumsy about it. "But then you always do."

She laughed and fluffed at the pleats of her long orchid gown.

"Thank you, Wesley. It's funny, isn't it, wearing long dresses and all to see a circus? Of course, I guess no one knows it's going to *be* a circus yet except us."

Wesley nodded gravely. This ballroom setting was so small for such a production, the surroundings so elegant, that the concept was starting to seem a little obscene to him. There were tables with white cloths and buckets of champagne, all lining the long stretch of floor that would serve as an intimate stage for the various acts and from which all those present could see every jewel.

He studied the setting briefly and tried not to think about the complications there could be to this. Since coming to work for Effie Duvall it seemed he was always thinking of complications that never would have occurred to him at Fitch, Fitch & Cromwell. If any of those performers tried to run off with jewelry, for instance, he was quite sure Effie would do something dreadful. Then he'd be stuck defending her. He held out a chair for Van and sat down beside her, thinking working for Effie Duvall made being a lawyer almost exciting.

Down the table from them lights were flashing as people took Effie's picture.

"Do you know, I've never seen her in a dress before," he whispered.

"Neither have I," Van whispered back.

It was funny, Wesley reflected. He knew the woman he worked for was rich and powerful, but tonight she looked the part. The top part of her black crepe dress was covered with hundreds of thousands of black jet beads, all shimmering darkly. The ruby she wore at her wrinkled throat was as large as the one on her finger, but faceted so that it shot fire.

"I wish Trace could be here," Van said in a small voice. She
looked wistfully down at the oblong diamond glittering at her
finger. "It's so special, and I wanted him to come with me. I
don't see how he could stand to miss it."

"Business." Wesley offered the word of explanation through
clenched teeth—and only because he hoped it would make Van
feel better. His blood boiled every time he thought of Trace
MacDonald. The man didn't care about Van the way he ought
to. Oh, he brought the right presents and took her to dinner
sometimes, but he only did things *he* wanted. He missed things
like this that were important to her.

"I can hardly wait to see April," Van was saying. "And Effie
says when the show's over she's going to make an announcement that will be a surprise to everyone—even Cecily!"

Wesley caught himself short of a groan. Now he'd sit here
wondering what she might have up her sleeve this time, and
what brushfires he might find himself stomping out tomorrow.
He wished Effie would be more predictable. But then things had
been predictable at FF&C and they'd been dull.

He watched Cecily catch Ben's hand and squeeze it. They
were so happy together, he thought miserably.

Then the lights went out. The room was filled with coos like
the perch song of birds as people whispered expectantly.

At one end of the room a spotlight came on. The old calliope
Effie had purchased for this occasion and secreted behind a
screen began to play riotously. A blonde in a black cloak and top
hat stepped into the spotlight.

"Ladies and gentlemen, *mesdames et messieurs*, welcome to
the exotic and the glittering from all parts of the earth—welcome
to the Circus Duvall!"

And then the lights were on again, and people were on their
feet and gasping, applauding feverishly as the blonde in the top
hat made her way toward the center of Effie's arena. She had
flung off her cloak, and above a strapless black camisole and
satin-striped tuxedo pants, the Ringmaster Necklace glittered in
all its black-and-white splendor.

"And for a matching set, the Ringmaster Bracelets!" a carni-
val barker's voice was announcing from somewhere as the model
pirouetted, cracking a whip, displaying two diamond bracelets
drawn out on the sides like French cuffs whose studs were large
black sapphires.

The audience was going wild. Effie was chuckling openly.
Jenkins, beside her, was gripping the table in his excitement.

But before the furor could die down, colored lights were circling the ceiling. Two trapezes had appeared there, and as the announcer's voice continued, a blonde with curly hair caught one with a hook and prepared to swing out.

"Oh, look!" cried Van in delight. "It's April."

The slightly scatterbrained woman he'd met half a dozen times was suddenly in the air above them, hanging by her ankles, swooping toward union with a lean young man on the other trapeze. Rubies, reaching down like great long fingers, hung from her neck.

And so it went, three minutes an act, with applause between, as people gaped and gasped. There were jugglers, dogs, a sword swallower with emerald cuff links, acrobats, and tightrope walkers. April appeared again to dangle by her foot from an aerialist's ring and juggle wooden hoops. There were belly dancers, sporting real gemstones in their navals and bracelets on their feet and arms—fifteen acts in all.

Before it was over, Effie's rich—and in some cases royal—audience was behaving like a group of children caught up in a world of clowns and cotton candy. Wesley sat wondering whether he'd ever witnessed anything so incredible.

Then people were on their feet with their applause. Effie turned her chair one way and then another, acknowledging their approval with a wave of the hand as television cameras moved in toward her.

Finally she was forced to leave her table, presenting herself in the ring that had held her circus. A microphone was passed to her. She looked around, commanding silence.

"The House of Duvall is only in its youth," she rasped. "Let no one doubt it. Next month we will open our Paris branch, and tonight I wish to announce the appointment of my grandson, Ben Duvall, as vice-president—the first in our history."

Ben rose to polite applause, but Cecily, staring at him, looked utterly stunned.

Wesley frowned. There was something very wrong about her ashen expression. And Lynette, who sat farther down the table with other members of Effie's board, was watching the couple like a hawk. Lynette's eyes, with a mean triumph in them, waited until they caught Cecily's. Her lips thinned disparagingly as Cecily managed a smile and reached dazedly up to receive Ben's kiss as he bent to her.

The whole brief moment was over before Wesley could reflect on it, yet it bothered him. It didn't seem very thoughtful not telling Cecily about the announcement beforehand. He wondered whether Cecily was hurt because she'd hoped to be vice-president herself. Or whether it bothered her feeling Ben had some sort of authority over her.

Neither of those possibilities seemed very much like Cecily. Besides, everyone looked happy now, and Effie was speaking again.

"I am giving the emerald dome ring seen here tonight to the cause of charity, to be raffled off in the interest of Saint Mary's Hospital. . . ."

"Isn't it wonderful? Isn't Effie wonderful?"

Van sighed and rested her chin on her hands. Her eyes were large with all the sights around, but they were wistful, too.

"Oh," she said, "I do wish Trace could have been here."

Impossible.

Impossible that his plan could have succeeded just as he'd planned and yet have failed.

Jordan laughed automatically at a supper club act. The people he was with were tedious, but good contacts, Orlena said.

Orlena. Now he'd have to put up with her bossing; her insults. Already she'd made snide comments about the accident to the Catlow car, all the while giving him a sneering, sidelong glance. She wouldn't have sneered if Cecily Catlow had been dead.

A fucking servant of some sort.

How had it happened?

This bitch of a cousin was bad luck to him. She made everything go wrong. He was starting to think she'd been sent to test him somehow. She was his—what was the word?—his nemesis.

Yes, that was it.

Rudolfo had left a bottle of champagne waiting for them in the bedroom, but neither of them had touched it. Cecily adjusted a strap of the lace-trimmed nightgown she'd just stepped into, her back toward Ben, who was still undressing.

"Why didn't you tell me about the vice-president business?"

In her mind she'd rehearsed the question a hundred times, yet it still didn't sound as soft as she'd intended. It carried the hint of accusation.

"I didn't know for sure she was going to do it."

He dropped his tie across the back of a chair. He hadn't looked at her.

"But you'd discussed it?"

He shrugged impatiently. "Effie's mentioned it off and on for a long time—even ten years ago. What difference does it make?"

What difference does it make? thought Cecily. The violence of her heartbeats made it hard to hear. She thought of what Kim had hinted about Ben wanting control of things. She thought of Lynette's words. Ben still wasn't looking at her.

"I just would think you might have let me in on it," she said stubbornly.

Ben threw his pants down and there was irritation in the movement.

"For Christ's sake, what's eating you? I still have to have her stamp of approval on everything I do. The title doesn't mean a damned thing."

"Then why did you agree to it?"

"To make her happy."

Cecily felt a lump in her throat she couldn't swallow away. Ben's answers sounded too guarded. She didn't want to believe Ben had married her for gain. She didn't want to believe there were secrets between them. They had laughed together, talked together—and she'd thought for both of them it was talking as they'd never dared with another person.

This made it all false. This made it seem they'd only been living out some sort of lie. She knew she shouldn't pick, shouldn't ask the question, yet she had to.

"And what's Effie giving you in return, Ben?"

He froze in the midst of closing the lid on a leather box where he had stowed his cuff links, but still he didn't face her.

"Financing for another experiment with the Peregrine."

THIRTY-THREE

H E WAS SETTING A STONE ON THE SERPENT, FINE INTRICATE WORK JUST possible without a magnifier. Work that kept his attention from going elsewhere, Ben thought. All right, so maybe he felt guilty over that tiff with Cecily. Maybe he should have told her about the vice-presidency. The problem was, the moment he'd given in to Effie it had made him uneasy.

Why had he given in?

He picked up another stone with tweezers, enjoying the early morning solitude of his studio. He squinted at how the pale green stones on the table before him were taking shape.

Because of this, he thought. Because sometimes there was magic in working like this. Just like there was magic in Effie sometimes. The grit she had. The biting humor. The audacity.

"Ah! And why are you here so early? What are you doing?" the woman he'd been thinking about demanded, rolling in so suddenly and stealthily he dislodged a stone.

Ben stifled a childish impulse to cover his work and hide it from her.

"I couldn't sleep," he said shortly. Maybe if he looked busy and sounded out of sorts she'd go away.

But Effie continued toward him, the glint in her eyes less agreeable than it should be this morning after her show and the praise that was being heaped on her by all the media.

"You signed for an order of peridot last week," she said in a threatening voice. "I want to know why."

"Because of this." He made an impatient gesture with his hand. He was caught. Might as well get on with it.

Rounding his table, she looked at the stripes of diamond and peridot shimmering before him.

"What is this creation?"

"A serpent, Effie. A snake. It's a necklace. Look."

More eagerly than he wanted to, he reached for the sketch. There would be no clasp on the piece he was creating. The sinuous tail of the serpent itself would hold it on the wearer's neck, while the narrow head of the serpent, with topaz eyes, twined wisely and erotically down toward the wearer's bosom.

"How have you made it thus? Flexible yet rigid?" Effie demanded with sharp curiosity, sliding a finger beneath it. "Ah, the links of the chain themselves. Yes?"

Ben watched it glide over her finger. It looked, he thought, like a real goddamned snake, all bright and darting.

Effie let it fall back to the table. The lids on her eyes were motionless.

"Suspend work on it. I will not have such an item come from Duvall. It is too brazen. Too suggestive. What woman wants a serpent crawling down her breast?"

Ben couldn't speak at first for the rage inside him.

"You approved the idea! I told you about it!"

"You did not tell me it would be in peridot. You did not tell me the stones would be so small—"

"Why the hell make me vice-president if I can't make one goddamned decision—"

"Because you are my flesh! Because it is your destiny!"

He walked out on her. That was the only way to end an argument with Effie. It always had been.

When she woke up, Ben was already gone.

When she got to Effie's, things were in chaos.

"Telegrams keep arriving," Thida said, shoving a pile of those already recorded toward her as they met in the upstairs hall. "And the phone is ringing constantly—people wanting to buy things, people wanting to interview her. She's with Lynette now, and the moment she's free a TV man from Hollywood is waiting to see her. Mr. Jenkins has run out of message pads. I promised I'd take some over."

Cecily's head ached. "Where's my husband?"

"I haven't seen him this morning. I don't believe he's come in yet."

Tension flashed in hot needles from Cecily's head to her jaw and back again.

Kim heaved himself from a bench outside Thida's office.

"If she can afford a branch in Paris, she can afford to pay me more than she did for that Muslim's pearls," he began in huffy tones.

Cecily's jaw pressed tighter together.

All three lines into her office were ringing. Someone wanting to reserve a bracelet. Someone wanting Effie to speak at a college of art. Someone from *Vogue*.

By the time she finished with one call another was waiting. Effie's show had taken the world by storm. Her clock read eleven A.M. and already she'd done a full day's work. She hadn't had coffee.

A complaint from a customer whose dearest friend had not received an invitation to last night's event. A complaint from an animal welfare group over using Bibi in photographs.

A magazine wanted to interview Ben about his dual roles as pilot and designer, but a call to his studio and the workroom turned up no trace of him. Nerves jangling, Cecily went down by the back stairs, got coffee in the kitchen, and escaped with it to the terrace.

Why hadn't Ben told her about Effie's offer?

She reached to set her cup on a metal patio table, but a wave of vertigo rocked her. The cup slipped from her hands and crashed on flagstones. She grabbed at the edge of the table.

"Cecily!"

It was Ben behind her. His hands were on her waist, supporting her.

"Cecily, what's wrong?"

The sound of his voice made the vertigo loosen its grip on her.

"Nothing. Just a headache making me dizzy. It'll pass in a minute."

His face, as he shifted her gently to look at her, was taut with alarm. That, and his being here when she needed him, made things suddenly right between them.

Cecily tried to laugh. "It's—happened before. I was scared I might have a tumor or something, so I saw a doctor. He says it's just . . . the way I clamp my jaw down does something to my inner ear."

Ben still looked worried.

"Christ, you must lock your jaw up two dozen times a day. When you're mad. Or determined." He grimaced with a trace of humor as his hand began to smooth at her temples and then down to her chin. "To tell you the truth, I always kind of liked to watch you do it. Want to sit down?"

"No. Where . . . where were you?"

"Just walking. Down at the cove. Effie and I had a set-to. I was just starting up to find you when I saw you come out here."

He hesitated, then held her against him. He started to speak but was interrupted by the sound of Effie's irate voice.

"I have told you, I am not interested in discussing this further. I am not interested in compromising myself! Now leave, before I summon my guards to throw you out!"

She rolled through the door to the terrace as she said the last. A pudgy man in bright yellow pants huffed in pursuit of her.

Effie whirled her chair to face him.

"But Mrs. Duvall," he pleaded. "The necklace would be featured on three episodes—maybe four. Think of the exposure! And magazines, fan magazines, newspapers—"

"You refuse to meet my price."

"But you don't understand. We don't *need* anything near a flawless stone! Just one that looks good to the eye—and has your name."

Cecily, watching, thought Effie might run him over with her chair as she lurched toward him.

"I do not put my name on something that merely looks good to the eye! I deal in costly pleasures for people who can afford them, not window dressing for those who cannot. I will not sell short my reputation for free advertising—that is what you're suggesting!''

Again she made a charging motion and the man in yellow pants retreated. Effie lingered a moment, noticing Ben and Cecily.

''I thought he must want to see me to discuss a film of my life!'' she said indignantly.

She shot back into the house. Ben began to laugh at the same instant Cecily did. It bridged any gap left between them.

''Damn, but she's vain!'' he said beneath his breath.

''Has she just missed a chance, do you think?'' Cecily asked, recovering.

Ben shook his head. ''Oh, judging by the sound of it, she's missed out on some hoopla—designing something for a TV series, I gather. But if that guy was wanting her to compromise on quality to get the spot, then I agree with her. To hell with him.''

Van appeared with one of the kitchen staff.

''What's all the yelling?'' she asked.

''Effie's found out she's not going to be a movie star,'' Ben said dryly.

''Oh. Well, I've decided we're going to have lunch out here today. It's the only way to get away from those phones!''

A bright linen tablecloth was now in place, on which Van set two baskets of round, brown, hard rolls.

''How about a game of catch while we're at it?'' said Ben. ''Make up for all that good behavior yesterday.''

He pitched a roll at Van, who gasped and caught it. She looked at it, looked at him, mischief lighted her eyes, and she pitched it back. Then Cecily found herself drawn into the game. They circled the table, laughing. For an instant Cecily had the sense of all of them being children. Van grabbed two handfuls of rolls from a basket and began to pelt Ben with them. Cecily joined in.

''Miss Cecily . . .'' Charlie spoke from the door of the house, eyeing them uncertainly.

Ben caught a roll and deflected one with his elbow. Van ran laughing back toward the kitchen.

''A Mr. Peter Kemp's on the phone,'' said the butler. ''He says you know him personally, and he'd like to speak to you about buying a bracelet.''

Cecily's heart fell. She wanted to fly at this moment and tear it apart. She could hear Ben's angry silence.

"Ben—it doesn't mean anything. I swear—"

But Ben's hands, with a single motion, crushed the hard roll. It fell to his feet.

"Save the pretty words, Cecily," he said bitterly. "I expect we both knew pretty much what we were bargaining for when we got married."

"Stop sulking, Jordan!"

Orlena watched her undeniably handsome son kick a footstool across her office. He'd done the same thing as a child when he was out of sorts. He'd always had a wretched temper.

"I intend to sulk until doomsday," he snapped back. "And you can't stop me! Just look at what we're up against!" He waved a hand wildly toward the papers and magazines spread on her desk.

It was time for her massage, and Jordan knew it. But here he'd come at the end of the day, spewing and howling, dragging Trace and Lucy in with him. Did he really suppose she hadn't seen these periodicals? Why couldn't he learn to be calm and think things through?

"Not only has Effie Duvall's show gotten coverage for more than a week, but now her—her hole-in-the-wall operation in Paris gets written up in *Vogue Paris* before it even opens! We *advertise* with them and we got one lousy column!"

"That happens, Jordan. And our trade here seems to be picking up in spite of it."

"Picking up!" He was getting red in the face. "You call 'picking up' getting a customer here and there, while *she*—or that little bitch Cecily, rather—announced one afternoon a week to receive new customers like it's some royal audience?

"Oh, sure, it looked as though we were doing all right in the beginning. She'd kept such a low profile for years that plenty of her customers were just plain waiting to be wooed away. But what happens the minute her show hits? The minute her ads hit? A good dozen customers who looked solid with us have gone straight back to her."

Orlena twisted an earring. Sometimes the weight of William's emeralds made her ear sore. But she'd never tell Lucy that.

"Well, what do you suggest, Jordan?"

"We could run them out of business. Undercut their prices. Offer some of their best customers our things at cost—or below cost."

"Absurd! You might run us out of business."

Jordan narrowed his eyes. Orlena found it unpleasant, as much because it made him look cunning and she wasn't used to that much cleverness in him as for any other reason.

"We could cut off the supply of some of their stones. There must be someone out there who hates the old lady—"

Lucy interrupted her brother.

"Even if we did knock our prices down, I'm not sure we could steal any customers from Duvall." She was bent over pages cut from the latest issue of *Town & Country*, their ad and Duvall's, with Trace MacDonald looking over her shoulder. Nearby were ads from the last two months. She straightened and, clearly exasperated, looked at Orlena. "Effie Duvall's designs are very good. And the panther, lying there with things between his paws as though he's guarding them, it's—it's fiendish how quickly she's going to imprint herself on people's minds!"

For an instant Orlena felt a tingle of something like affection for the girl. Poor Lucy was able to see things clearly and knew what they were up against.

"Those designs—at least some of them—are by a grandson," Orlena corrected. "Cecily's husband now, I believe."

She glanced at Trace and he nodded. "Yes. That's true."

Her children knew Trace was planted at Duvall Inc. They did not know the rest.

"Who cares whose designs they are?" Jordan snarled. "The fact is you've botched this whole thing from the start, Orlena. If we don't have money to maneuver with, it's because of that Paris branch—it was too much too soon. And I'd hate to think how much this last move cost us—all because you didn't check the lease!"

"The Paris branch will pay its way by next year—"

"You play at being a businesswoman, Orlena, but that's all you do—play! You don't let anyone else advise you and you don't have the guts to wipe out a competitor."

He was taxing her patience. Orlena's fingers pushed against the edge of her desk.

"Our gross receipts have tripled since we expanded out of New York. Our client list has doubled. And I assure you I have my own plans for dealing with Cecily—"

But Jordan, as usual, wasn't listening.

"This is business, Orlena! We find Duvall's source of rubies—or diamonds—or whatever—and we turn them—"

"Do you know what you're risking?"

"Duvall's going to make Lyle and Company look second rate.

They already have! And I'm sick of romancing socialites over lunch so you can flatter yourself you're getting new clients—''

"It's all you're good for!''

Orlena rose, hot with her fury.

"I know your limitations, Jordan. I know exactly what you're capable of. It's certainly not planning, or anything else that's useful, or you'd have come up with donating an item for charity and getting all that nice, warm publicity as Duvall did with that ring!''

"That's Lucy's department,'' he said sullenly.

"It's time for my massage,'' she said, unable to stand his foolishness any longer. "There's a TV producer coming to see me tomorrow. Trace tells me Effie Duvall has turned him down. We're not going to. He wants something for a nighttime soap. Vast publicity. We'll see he gets it.''

Lucy, who had followed the argument with Orlena and Jordan like a ping-pong game, sighed and turned to Trace.

"I've heard about a place that's fun in Coconut Grove. Let's go there and forget about this.''

Trace avoided her eyes.

"Love to, Lucy, but I've got something else to do tonight—a meeting.''

His glance caught Orlena's. He'd been quick to agree to marry William's unstable great-niece in exchange for stock in Lyle & Co. Orlena almost felt sorry for Lucy. Now by Trace's tone and glance, she judged all was going well.

By Christmas Jordan was going to see just how well she could crush a competitor. By Christmas Cecily Catlow would be too frantic about her sister to think about business, Orlena thought smugly. From then on, Duvall Inc. would pose much less of a threat.

THIRTY-FOUR

"GEEZ, THAT WAS SOME CROWD AT THE AIRPORT!'' APRIL SAID, curling up comfortably on a chaise in Vanessa's room as Vanessa poured tea for the three of them. "I couldn't believe it when I heard they were all there watching for Ben.''

"TRINA's big news,'' said Cecily, trying not to grit her teeth.

She already had a headache. She didn't need an attack of the dizzies, too.

Barely a week had passed since the day Ben had worked the tension from her jaw so tenderly. He hadn't touched her since—had barely spoken. She hated Peter for causing this. She hated Ben. She hated TRINA and the Peregrine most of all. They had a hold on Ben she would never have. They gave him escape. They beckoned him to a savage recklessness that—

She closed her eyes, trying not to imagine how Ben's wild flights could end if he wasn't careful.

Was he careful? She didn't know. Her heart pounded, hollow inside. A part of her had died when she'd learned he'd gone off again without telling her. And this time it had hurt even more than the first. This time, she'd resolved, she would not be there waiting. She couldn't bear it. Not her pride. Not her nerves.

Now at least she knew he was safe. April had been at the airport when his plane had come in.

"You look pretty fancy," said Cecily, forcing all her attention back to her friend, who sat with a gorgeous lynx jacket thrown casually back as she grinned and mauled her gum. "What have you been up to?"

"Nothing much. A little traveling." April's eyes, bright behind their stiff lashes, danced with mischief. "I . . . uh, met this real gentleman at that show we put on for Effie. He was there with his sister. He's shy, you know? But awfully sweet. He wants me to meet his family tomorrow, and says I should make a nice impression because they're social and all. Gave me money to blow on clothes and all, so what do you think? I got it in Paris."

April fidgeted happily, and Cecily realized, with some dismay, that she was being invited to comment on the dress that April wore. It was obviously expensive, but more suited to a night on the town than meeting a male friend's family. The skirt was too short and both hem and neckline were trimmed in beaded fringe.

Before she could think what to say, April flourished a hand.

"And look. I thought I'd put all the rest of my money in one really good piece of jewelry. So I'd look like quality, you know? Knew I couldn't afford Effie's stuff, but this girl I know who used to swallow swords before she got married put me in touch with this guy who sells nice things secondhand. He said the color was light for an aquamarine but the size made up for it. And it didn't seem too flashy. What do you think?"

Cecily had no choice but to take the ring being offered her. The blue was indeed very pale, but the stone was uncommonly lively for an aquamarine. Its brilliance bothered her.

"April, I don't think—"

"It is not an aquamarine," a voice cut in from the door and Effie joined them. Van had called her when April arrived, saying they were about to have tea. Now she took April's ring and held it up as April's face fell. Her words were addressed to Cecily.

"Do you not recognize the stone? It is Petrie's blue diamond, the one the scoundrel tried to sell me months ago. You must remember such things."

Cecily nodded, sick inside. She hadn't remembered Petrie, but she'd had a hunch she was seeing diamond.

"The stone is stolen," Effie said bluntly.

April looked on the verge of tears. "But I *paid* for it! All that money . . ."

Cecily looked uncertainly at Effie.

"It's important April have a nice piece of jewelry. I don't suppose we could extend her credit . . . ?"

She would not have asked it for anyone but April, who had been a friend to her and Van and deserved one small crack at happiness.

The lids hovered low over Effie's eyes. She held out her hand for the ring.

"I will make a trade. I have a nice strand of pearls in the vault, with sapphire rondels."

April slumped on her chaise. "Jeezus, Madame Duvall, I don't know how I can thank you—"

"I am doing it for Cecily."

As Effie's eyes moved toward her, Cecily felt a prickle, as though, all unspoken, she'd incurred a debt.

"I will bring the pearls," said Effie, and left again.

Cecily spoke into silence. "Now, April, if you really want to make an impression, you've got to get a suit instead of that dress—I'll lend you the money."

Ben muttered an acknowledgment of Charlie's greeting.

"Everyone at work, I suppose?" he said, moving from the hall to the living room without waiting for the butler's answer.

Of course everyone would be at work. It was only midafternoon. Nothing ever interfered with routine for Effie or Cecily, he thought darkly. Cecily hadn't even bothered to be at the airport.

"Ben! You're back. Congratulations!"

Wesley Bell was sitting in a wing chair sipping a drink and reading a paper. He sprang to his feet.

"Oh . . . yeah." Ben put his hand out halfheartedly to shake the one Wesley extended. He hadn't expected to find Wesley here.

Poor bastard. Still coming around when Van was already lost to him, sitting here all alone, waiting. Ben peered at him from eyes that had grown weary monitoring TRINA's screens. He felt angry for the lawyer. Angry for himself.

"Hell of a day to be sitting inside, Wesley."

"I suppose."

Wesley gave a good-humored smile. He was so damned patient, so damned easygoing and quiet in spite of his large physique and considerable brain that Ben found it impossible not to like him.

Ben's legs ached. He was tired and out of sorts. The voice on TRINA had failed this trip—a faulty connection. The crowd at the airport had been an annoyance. And Cecily hadn't been there.

Not that it mattered. He knew he was a damned idealist the way he sometimes saw her and he knew he'd probably set her off, leaving without telling her. He'd been fed up with himself, annoyed with how he couldn't bring the things that were eating at him out in the open with her. Still, she might have gone through the motions of behaving like a wife.

"What's been happening here?" he asked, moving toward the bar. He couldn't remember the last time he'd had a drink except at dinnertime. Not since he and Cecily had been married. Not since before that, maybe. It seemed like there was always something else to occupy his interest.

"April's upstairs visiting—buying something, in fact. I guess she's come into money. She looks very nice." Wesley tapped his glasses lightly back toward the bridge of his nose.

"Fix you another of whatever you're drinking?" Ben asked, pouring one for himself.

"No thanks." Wesley sounded less than buoyant. "Well, maybe I will."

He brought his glass to the bar and held it out. "Whiskey and soda." He watched Ben freshen it with ice. "I . . . uh, I had business to tend to with Effie. I thought I'd just loaf a minute and look at the paper before I started back."

Ben struggled to control his anger. "Christ, Wesley, why do you keep torturing yourself? Why do you keep waiting around just to see Van?"

Wesley looked startled. "Am I that obvious?"

He smiled a little, sadly, yet with a directness Ben found unnerving. "I love Van," he said simply. "I can't stop loving her just because she doesn't love me. Isn't that how it is with you and Cecily?"

Ben tipped his head back, letting the contents of his glass spill down his throat, avoiding an answer, avoiding what it was he felt for Cecily.

Among other things, she was becoming Effie's accountant. Cecily bent grimly over the ledgers spread in front of her. In order to help Effie set the prices of Duvall's creations, it was necessary to see what gems and gold had cost them, the expenses of the Paris branch, the salaries of Mortimer, Jenkins, even the household staff. She reached for a cup of coffee Thida had brought her to find it already empty. Had she been here that long? It seemed she had barely said good-bye to April and dragged herself back to work.

She wondered if Ben would come here when he left the airport. No, he would more likely go to the apartment. She wondered if things were ever going to resolve themselves between them. Her door opened and she looked up to find him standing there.

Rage rose inside her, but it was intertwined with pain. He doubted her. He thought she still loved Peter. Maybe that was because he didn't want her love. By rejecting her Ben could keep his distance, live within himself, not have to care.

He could enjoy the terrible chemistry between them with no investment on his part, she thought, looking up coldly. He could take control of Duvall as Lynette had suggested, while caring for no one. Her heart shrank from the thought.

She waited for him to speak.

"Figured this is where I'd find you," he said with a sarcasm she didn't understand.

"Where else did you expect to find me?" she asked tartly, rising to drop the ledgers back in her file drawer. "Not chasing after you again, I hope!"

She slammed the drawer closed with a metallic thud. His eyes were dangerous as he moved easily toward her.

"Why not? Are you tired of being a wife already?"

"You think you've treated me like a wife? You no more told me you were taking the Peregrine up or said good-bye to me than you did the first time!"

"You could have read in the papers when I'd be back. Tell me, which is it you were looking forward to most if I didn't make it, inheriting my shares of Duvall or having a clear road with someone else?"

She struck him across the face, so hard his head snapped back. All the rage and the hurt and the terrible, aching doubt inside her spilled out in hotness. She could feel it in the warmth of the blood from his lip that coated her fingers. She could feel it in the silent tears burning her cheeks.

He caught her hand, but there was no violence in his touch. Cecily saw in his eyes only pain now—a pain that matched her own.

Her fingers trembled as she rubbed them over his mouth, shocked at what she had done. "Ben . . . I . . ."

His head curved downward, offering itself to the touch of her two hands.

"Don't, Cecily. Don't say anything. Just let me hold you."

She shuddered, terrified, as if something were tearing the two of them in opposite directions even as something else drew them together. Her arms clung tightly to his neck. She could taste the blood she had drawn as his lips sought hers.

She needed him. As elusive as he seemed, as changeable as his moods, she wanted him as she'd never wanted anything else. In this moment, in his arms, revenge, even caring for Van seemed unimportant. She wanted fiercely to live only for the two of them.

"I'm sorry," he whispered, and taking her by the hand, never lifting his eyes from her face, he led her toward the bedroom still kept as his. Stripping her clothes from her he lay her gently against cool sheets and made them one again, all wordlessly.

A long time passed before he left her. With drowsy contentment Cecily lay savoring the weight of his body, the deep, steady sound of his breathing. Her eyes, opening languidly, sought shapes in the room, came to rest on his discarded boots, and closed again.

"There's liquor on your breath," she said with effort. "Please don't drink when you're flying, Ben. I couldn't bear to lose you."

His index fingers teased lightly down her cheeks, balancing her face between them as he kissed her slowly.

"I had a drink downstairs with Wesley just now—the first in a couple of days. Don't worry."

He rolled onto his side and studied her with a perplexity that was also pleased.

"You have a hell of a temper, you know that?"

Cecily turned her face away, embarrassed. "Ben . . . you made me so mad saying that about inheriting . . . that about Peter . . ." She swallowed, tense with fear now that she'd brought the name out into the open. Her ears strained for a movement. "He means nothing to me now. No one ever could but you. I swear it!"

A second passed before he spoke. "Okay."

The word was cautious. She turned to him. Did he believe her? Was this the end of his doubting? She searched his face.

Before she could guess at what he was thinking, the phone at the bedside rang. She could hear Effie's strong voice as Ben picked it up.

"I thought I would find you there, as you were not in Cecily's office. Put on clothes and come down—both of you. There is a photographer here."

"Tell him to go away," said Ben. "Tell him to talk to Pepe."

"It is not about your airplane. It seems something of yours has been selected as a finalist for the Prix Internationale."

The phone clicked down. Ben sat up. Cecily saw a stirring of the corner of his mouth that she realized was satisfaction. She gripped his arm.

"The Prix Internationale! Ben, I didn't know you'd entered anything!"

"I hadn't. Effie took it on herself to do it."

She could hear his delight. He reached for his pants.

"I had something in the semifinals once before, twelve years ago," he said. "Effie doesn't give up easily."

And you've been back at designing less than a year, thought Cecily. Effie's right about your talent. You've inherited her touch, whether or not you're ready to face that.

"What did she enter?" she asked. "Do you know?"

"I've got a hunch."

She fastened her dress and they started out of the room together.

"Oh, my God!" said Cecily, suddenly horrified as he grinned down at her. "Your lip—it's swelling!"

Ben stopped, touched it, looked briefly sheepish. Then they began to laugh as one.

"I'll just tell them the road to fame is not without its bruises," he said. "No, I'll say you hit me with your teddy bear."

"Or maybe they'll ask me if I've stopped beating my husband," Cecily said, rolling her eyes.

"Or we could give a convincing demonstration of how I got it."

Ben grabbed her and kissed her intensely. In the hard pressure of his lips she felt a second of undiluted caring. Her eyes misted over. His hands held her arms, firm and steady.

"I'm glad we got together, whether it was by Effie's design or not." His deep voice was soft.

"Me, too."

They moved as one toward the stairs.

"Your Foo dogs are a success," pronounced Effie in a strong voice as they came into view.

There were, in fact, two men with cameras waiting, and a businesslike man with a notepad. Raoul and another guard were standing by as Jenkins displayed the ornate, heavy bracelets on a tray lined with velvet. The golden temple dogs, one done in ruby *en pavé*, one delicately enameled, held ominously to the precious globes beneath their feet. And, Cecily realized with a start, one of the eight was now a female. A cunning cub done in rosy gold rested beneath her uplifted paw.

Looking quickly up, she caught the amusement lighting Ben's eyes. He'd been watching for her reaction.

"The ad for them has not even run, and already every one is sold," said Effie in triumph. "One order came from Buckingham Palace."

One of the men with cameras scribbled quickly on a pad of his own. The one without a camera began to talk with Ben.

"This is wonderful," Jenkins said gravely. The guards had taken charge of the case now. He and Cecily stood on the edge of things. He smiled at her. "You know you are responsible for Ben's success."

"Me?" Cecily shook her head. "I talked him into coming back to work. That's all." It seemed like centuries ago.

"You've given him something he needed," Jenkins insisted. "You've brought him a peace inside himself. I'm even gladder for that than I am for this accomplishment—"

He broke off as Charlie appeared.

"Madame, forgive the interruption, but your Christmas tree has arrived."

Cecily could see it behind him, carried by three men. Even with a foot or more cut off, it was going to reach from floor to ceiling.

"Is Vanessa—ah, there you are," said Effie as Van appeared, pink-cheeked with excitement. "Advise them on where to place the tree, will you, Vanessa?"

Van, her excitement overflowing, hugged her sister.

"Isn't it spectacular, Cecily? What's going on here?"

"Ben's Foo dogs have made the finals for the Prix Internationale. It's very prestigious."

"Oh, Ben! Congratulations!"

Reaching out to touch his sleeve, she planted a light kiss on his cheek. Ben gave her a broad smile.

"You look like the angel for the top of the tree, Vanessa. Make sure the thing's done right. Effie hasn't had one in years."

Van spun, catching Cecily's hand.

"Are you busy here, Cecily, or do you want to come watch?"

A sudden happiness washed through Cecily.

Van sounded so strong. So sure of herself. And Ben . . . Cecily turned and found his eyes on her. They caressed her as his hands had caressed her only a short time ago. He seemed to share the moment with her. He showed pleasure at his success and it was so different from the dark mood of the man she first had met that her heart threw off all its worries.

"I want to come help!" she said with a laugh.

Van squeezed her hand. "See, Cecily, we'll keep having good times even with both of us married. Trace and I will be back in time for Christmas and it'll be just like coming home. The two of us, and you and Ben, and Effie and Jenkins—just like a family!"

Why not? thought Cecily. Maybe Ben at last believed she loved only him. Maybe there would be no more walls between them. Maybe everything would work out exactly as Van dreamed it would.

Why not?

THIRTY-FIVE

EFFIE'S EYES SURVEYED THE COLOR AND LAVISHNESS OF VANESSA'S wedding. The trappings were a bit ridiculous in Florida—poinsettias and holly, April and Cecily marching in solemn beat down the staircase clad in long dresses of bright red velvet in which they looked slightly uncomfortable, fur muffs beneath their bouquets. Ah, but it gave things an exotic feel, and she liked the exotic. It pleased her, too, to indulge the fairylike young woman who had come into her life almost like another child. Impatient for the bridesmaids to finish their descent of the stairs so she could see Vanessa, she drummed her fingers and thought about other weddings this house had seen.

Her eldest daughter had married in a suitably elegant ceremony, full of anger. Effie cast her gaze on Kim, who was blotting at his fat forehead. What a waste that he had survived while his wife had perished. She had always found him the least appealing of the children-in-law she'd acquired.

Her thoughts jumped to Ben's mother, who would have made a lovely bride but had refused to marry at all. The girl had been stubborn, shrugging off her involvement with a Scottish laird, a Jewish banker, coming home to announce she was pregnant and meant to let nature take its course and that was that.

"I won't give you another connection, but I'll give you another Duvall." She'd smiled, shaking back her black curls with the spirit that had governed her. And she'd taken the legal surname of Effie's first union, the name under which her mother had worked and amassed her empire. She had given that name to her bastard son, insuring that he would be part of her, part of Effie, part of no one else. A gift.

Effie narrowed her eyes against the memories. As a wedding march started to play, Van appeared at the head of the stairs, a vision in white. Her gown, too, was velvet, trimmed with fur along a trailing hem and long, flowing sleeves.

Effie grunted satisfaction. The main hall of her house made an excellent wedding chapel. She and the others could watch from the chairs set up in the arch of the living room just beyond in perfect comfort. They could hear every word.

Wesley Bell was watching as though he were facing a firing squad. Perhaps he didn't like weddings. The others looked bored. They would not lack animation when she announced her gift to the bride, Effie thought, suppressing a chuckle.

She had worked all her life for power. Now it amused her to use it. She could not remember enjoying life as she had these last months with her new plans, spawned by a brown-eyed girl who sometimes seemed a carbon copy of her younger self and was the ready student she had always longed for; with her grandson back and elevated at last to the place she had years ago chosen for him; with a sense of her family doing her bidding—not because they anticipated her demise, but because they feared her.

At last the words were spoken and Vanessa's handsome young husband was kissing her. Not so ardently as Ben had kissed Cecily on a similar occasion, Effie noted.

With a chuckle, she started forward. Bibi stretched and rose to his feet.

"Now, before we move to the reception, an announcement!" Effie commanded.

Everyone paused obediently: Lynette and her two daughters, one of them a giggler; Harry; young Martin. Joao had not made this trip. His health was failing. And there was to be no board meeting this time, as there had been with Cecily's wedding. These members of her family had come this time because she'd told them to—because they found her unpredictable these days. She would not disappoint them.

"I am very fond of Vanessa," she said bluntly, turning her chair so she rested beside the girl in white and faced the others. "As her sister is related to me legally now, I believe Vanessa must be, too. And she has contributed a great deal to this renaissance of Duvall—the idea of using Bibi as our trademark— playing canasta with me."

There was muted laughter, some affectionate, some indulgent.

"So," continued Effie, "you will understand why I am making Vanessa a wedding present of ten percent of Duvall. She has earned it. She and her husband will advise us well on matters of advertising, I have no doubt."

There were gasps, at least one of them hot with anger. Effie ignored them. She was enjoying the look of utter, disbelieving joy on Vanessa's face at this gift that made her now dependent on no one's charity. She was noting with pleasure the sparkle of dampness in Cecily's eyes that told her this was, as she had expected, a gift to both these close sisters.

"Effie! You're too wonderful! I don't know what to say. . . ."

Van's arms went around her neck in a hug much more pleasant than the Countess di Crichi's.

"This is unbelievable!" Kim was muttering. He was not happy that with a single stroke she had given a newcomer more than his piddling five percent, but he would grow used to it.

"Come! Let's toast the marriage!" Effie announced. She led the way toward the dining room feeling full of energy.

Vanessa and her husband looked like the bridal couple from the top of their cake. MacDonald was cognizant of the size of the gift she had given his wife. He would be very careful to stay in both their good graces.

Effie's eyes traveled over him. She hoped he would please Vanessa in bed. That was not necessary in a husband, but it was agreeable and Vanessa had led too confined a life to think of looking elsewhere.

She watched as Vanessa and the ad man cut their cake. She liked intelligence around her. And MacDonald, by courting Van, had displayed his. He had shown his interest in allying himself with Effie Duvall. He understood how business was run. It would be a good match, too. He would take care of Van.

As to love, well perhaps it would come. She was not sure she would wish it on Vanessa any more than she did on Cecily. Love was costly. It was far more costly than the jewels she sold, and the investment less reliable. It led to trust, and when you trusted you might not live to a ripe old age.

She must teach Cecily both those truths. Or did Cecily already know?

Effie looked at Cecily, in her red dress, and thought how different these two sisters were.

"Cecily . . . can we talk?" Margaux's voice was low, a murmur in passing. She picked up a plate of cake and laughed, though her words kept their private pitch. "It's warped, isn't it, always talking business at weddings?"

Cecily picked delicately at the neckline of her velvet dress. She was roasting in it.

"Do you want to go into the library?"

"No," Margaux answered swiftly. "No, I don't want the others to know we've spoken privately. Let's just pretend it's social conversation."

She took a bite of cake, blue eyes alert and appealing. Cecily, feeling some clue had been given, smiled for anyone who might be watching them.

"Okay."

They had managed to turn away from the crowd in the room a bit. The others present seemed to be talking to Van or drinking champagne.

"It's—" Margaux's eyes flicked to Lynette, to Harry, and found them occupied. "Maybe it's nothing. But I thought you ought to know. Aurelio has been to visit Harry."

Cecily felt her eyebrows raising. She gestured toward a table holding gifts.

"Pretend we're looking at those. How did you find out?"

Margaux swallowed nervously. "I was at Mother's. In Paris. Harry called her there. I listened in another room. He wanted her to join them, but Mother said no." The newest member of Effie's board, save for Van, drew a shaky breath. "She doesn't exactly like you well enough to tell you. I figured I owed you one. You've been generous with both of us—even though Mother's still pretty steamed that I've replaced her on the board. But you see, she's loyal now. She wouldn't have any part of their plot—"

"What is it they're plotting?" Cecily interrupted.

"I don't know. Only that Aurelio was at Harry's."

Margaux's words came to a stop. Her eyes were grave. *"Aurelio!"* she repeated in a whisper. "And after Effie threw him out!"

Cecily nodded.

"Don't worry about it."

The quiet privacy of their balcony made the bustle of Van's wedding seem more distant than the few hours that had passed. But Cecily's eyes were fixed on the distant water. Ben knew she was brooding.

"Ben, how can I not worry? How can you not? Aurelio's a snake."

"They all are. And it's not worth the toll it takes to live in the midst of them. Look at you. You have a headache, don't you? I can tell by the way you've tightened your eyes."

He slid from his lounge chair onto the edge of hers. He found the tightened muscles of her jaw. He could feel her tension.

"Cecily. Let's leave. Let's get out before we're destroyed by the rest of them—or become just like them. Let's start our own company."

Her startled eyes moved up from her distant thoughts to see if he was serious.

"I *care* for Effie! I care for Duvall." She sounded shocked. "Don't you feel anything for her? She raised you—she loves you, for God's sake!"

Ben ran a hand back over his hair, exasperated. Sometimes he wondered whether Cecily knew her own mind. Sometimes he wondered if he did.

He felt caged in. Confused. What he'd said just now had been half impulse.

"I don't know what I feel for her sometimes—for her or Duvall either. There are things I remember about her. Good things. But she robbed me of the two people in the world that I—that I loved."

He rose and paced.

"She's obsessed with Duvall. It's twisted her. I want there to be more for the two of us than that. I want us to have a normal life. I want . . ." He hesitated, wary of even saying it to her. "I want a child."

Steeling himself, he looked at her. He felt as though he'd revealed a part of himself he shouldn't have. She'd never mentioned children, maybe she didn't care about them. And he didn't want her producing them as Effie had, because they seemed obligatory to the marriage contract.

Her brown eyes were solemn. The dimple in her chin trembled slightly.

"I want that, too," she said in a small voice. "I just didn't know if you . . ."

He reached her side in three swift steps. She held to him tightly.

"I've never had a family, Ben—not even like you did. And I—I want that so much it scares me. When I was little—after Van was gone—I used to have this sort of dream I put myself to sleep with, about being part of a family out on a picnic, laughing together. And there was a merry-go-round. And sometimes I was the little girl on the merry-go-round, and sometimes I was the mother watching . . ."

She tried to laugh at the silliness of it, but he saw she was choked with emotion.

"Maybe that's how it's supposed to be," he said softly. "Not forgetting how it was to be a kid. One blending into the other."

She nodded and leaned against him and he felt a strange relief.

"But we don't have to walk out on Effie to lead our own life, do we?" she asked.

Ben sighed. "I guess not."

"You're nervous, aren't you, Vanessa? I shouldn't have surprised you like this. I shouldn't have brought you here, so far from your sister."

Van smiled quickly at her husband.

"Oh, no, Trace. It's lovely! A honeymoon in London—it's a wonderful surprise! There'll be so much to see. The changing of the guard . . ."

She knew she was chattering. But she wasn't nervous, only excited. And tired—the plane trip had been so long on the heels of their wedding, and she hadn't been able to sleep, even though the seats were nice.

She squeezed Trace's arm to show him everything delighted her. They'd planned just a few days at a Palm Beach resort, and that had seemed romantic enough to her, but then when they'd left Effie's island and reached the mainland, Trace had produced the airline tickets. He'd told her he wanted to give her a honeymoon she'd never forget. Now they were standing here at this tall house on an elegant street, and a butler was opening the door.

"Good morning, Mr. MacDonald. Did you have a nice trip? And this would be Mrs. MacDonald."

The man had a pinched expression, but he bowed to her.

"I love it when someone calls me that!" she whispered to Trace as the butler lifted their bags and turned away. "But Trace, I don't understand . . ."

"What don't you understand, Vanessa? It's my house. We're going to live here. Don't you remember?"

"Remember?" Vanessa frowned. She couldn't recall Trace ever mentioning London. "Oh . . . yes," she lied. "Only I thought—since you're working for Effie, I assumed we'd be living there—on the mainland, I mean."

She chewed her lower lip, searching her mind with determination, certain she was not forgetting in this case as she spoke again. "We never talked about where we would live. Not about it being London, anyway. I know we didn't!"

He looked at her for a minute, then smiled suddenly.

"You're right. We didn't." He folded her hands together and covered them with kisses. "I'm so sorry, dearest. I guess I just assumed . . ."

Van loved it when he called her "dearest." She sighed and leaned her head against him. It had frightened her when Trace had asked if she didn't remember—terrified her. She didn't want Trace to think there was anything wrong with her.

There wasn't. She was just so tired. The wedding had been fun, sort of like playing dress up with Effie and everyone watching, but now everything was so new. She found herself wondering if every move she made was the right one. She wanted Trace to hold her.

"If you don't like it here, we'll buy a place in Palm Beach," he soothed.

She nodded, reassured.

Trace was so good to her. He kissed her gently on the forehead and looked at her as though he were being naughty, with eyes all narrowed.

"Now, Mrs. MacDonald. I think it's time we go up and slip into bed, don't you? The arrangement on the plane wasn't very comfortable."

Vanessa laughed, feeling shy but happy. "Yes, I think we should."

He took her hand and led her up a dark, polished staircase.

The bedroom where the butler had laid our their luggage was very attractive. Not pretty like the one she'd had at Effie's, Van thought, taking in the long velvet curtains that closed out all light, but terribly rich-looking. A fire burned on the hearth. She was glad of that, because she was chilly.

She was nervous now, too, though she didn't want to be. The psychiatrist she'd been seeing since coming to Effie's had talked to her about her wedding night, about what to expect. He'd talked to Trace, too, and said he was sure Trace would be very gentle. Cecily had tried to tell her things, but she'd been cross with Cecily for always wanting to give her advice and hadn't listened. Now Van wished she had.

There were pills in her overnight case. She took one and it calmed her almost at once. She slipped into a long white nightgown trimmed with rows and rows of lace. It had been a present from April.

It's going to be different, Van. It's not going to be like those times when boys at the hospital pushed you into a corner and scared you. It's not going to be like that time Jordan came to the hospital, either. You're well now, and Trace loves you.

Her eyes had fallen closed. She opened them and smiled into the bathroom mirror. She *wanted* this to happen. She *wanted* to know what sex was like. It shamed her that she had been afraid of it for so many years. It made her feel childish. Crippled. Incapable in some way, even though the doctors said she was well. And sometimes when Trace had kissed her in these last weeks, she'd wanted more of something. She knew what that something was, too. She understood that.

Suddenly she felt ready. She felt happy. It was like the wedding all over, and scarcely able to control her eagerness she returned to the bedroom.

Trace had changed into a velvet robe. His chest was bare. She liked the look of it, the silver hair like that on his head only very curly.

He came toward her and put his arms around her. They felt

different with so little covering her. Harder. His kiss felt different, too. "Get into bed," he said.

She obeyed, removing her thin robe and shivering a little. She'd thought this part would be different—that he'd lead her or just keep kissing her until she was there without knowing how.

The sheets felt cold. She reached for the bedside lamp.

"No." Trace spoke sharply. "Don't turn it off. I want to look at you."

He was smiling at her. The way the lamplight fell on his face didn't make it look nice.

Trace moved toward the bed, toward her side. His hand moved out and he seized the top of her gown, ripping the filmy fabric.

Van gasped. "Trace, don't! Don't act like this—"

Her gown ripped again. Her breasts were exposed. She began to struggle but Trace knelt astride her now, holding her down.

"What's the matter, Vanessa? Don't you like being married?"

His voice was taunting, like a stranger's. He stripped off his robe. He was big in front, and ugly. It brought back memories.

"Stop it, Trace! Turn off the light! You're upsetting me!" She could hear herself sobbing the words.

Something was all wrong.

Close your eyes!

She tried to obey her mind's command, but her eyes seemed frozen.

The hideous shaft of flesh stabbed toward her, touched her face, her mouth. Trace was laughing.

She began to scream and the scream became a tunnel, sucking her in.

THIRTY-SIX

Cecily FELT LIKE ONE OF Effie's DISCARDED OPALS, BRITTLE AND HARD. Hunched on the couch in their apartment, she listened without really hearing as Ben completed a telephone conversation in the adjoining study.

It seemed there had been so many calls since the one about Van. She heard Ben enter and looked up, fighting, even now, against despairing hopelessness.

"Van's resting," Ben said somberly.

"Sedated," she corrected, biting out her bitterness.

They'd had two phone calls from Trace, the first informing them with insufferable calm that Van's mind had cracked, the second that she'd been admitted to a private clinic near London.

Ben came and sat beside her, shifting her wordlessly into his arms. They were all that steadied her now, all that kept her from following Van into madness. She longed to rage, scream, rail. Van had been here. Van had been well. Now she was lost again. Lost!

"I want her out!"

She tore herself from his arms and stood looking blindly out toward blue water. She could not bear a comforting touch. She ached as though she and Van were part of a single entity, a single body, and she was feeling half her own bones crushed by a giant press. The old fear was back, mauling her, taunting her, telling her it would always be like this. The people she loved would always be snatched from her.

"I promised you she wouldn't be hurt." Ben's voice, behind her, sounded low and strangely subdued.

He was blaming himself. He was hurting, too.

"It's not your fault."

"We'll get her out," he said. "We'll go to her as soon as she's able."

Her dully moving eyes stopped on a new shape in the room, a Christmas tree. Rudolfo had put it up sometime since yesterday. To cheer them, she supposed. A sob burst from her.

Ben's arms encircled her. His breath brushed her cheek as she wept and it seemed the only warmth in the world to her.

"The tree—Van was counting so much on Christmas! We—we trimmed that one at Effie's and she was so full of plans . . . so happy. . . ." She shuddered and the grief inside her turned to anger. "Van was well! I don't understand!" She twisted to face him. "Trace must have been a jerk—a brute! Their first night together, for God's sake. He must have approached her like a—an animal!"

"Don't think about it!" Ben's words were sharp, his own concern echoed in them.

"What were they doing in London?" she persisted. "Van thought they were going to Palm Beach!"

"He wanted to surprise her. He said she'd talked about how much she wanted to see London someday. She'd read about the Tower of London, the changing of the guard—"

"And you believe that?"

"I don't know."

Ben released her and pushed his fingers through the high crest of his hair. Once, when she first knew him, the agitation and anger she felt simmering in him would have sent him toward a liquor cabinet, Cecily realized dimly. Somewhere along the line he'd changed, become a man who had stepped from darkness to offer her, if not love, a wonderful and rarely failing sense of belonging.

"It'll be all right," he said. "Bloody Christ, Cecily, if there's any sort of plan or design to the universe, it'll be all right!"

He took her hand. His strength seemed to flow from his fingers to hers. He was standing beside her as no one ever had. He was sharing her anguish. He was wrapping her in a tenderness she'd not known he possessed.

"We'd better call Effie and tell her what we learned," she said around a rawness in her throat.

"I'll have Rudolfo call her."

A single heart seemed to beat for the two of them. She loved him so. Suddenly, desperately, she flung herself into his arms and held his head between her hands.

"Ben—don't ever leave me! Let someone else fly the Peregrine from now on. I need you so!"

She had spoken it at last, all the fears she still bore because of Peter's faithlessness, all her need.

Ben's eyes swept back and forth, capturing every nuance of her face, and something seemed to change between them.

"Sweetheart," he said, drawing her against him. "Sweetheart!"

"I hate her!"

Lucy's small eyes were swollen from crying and vaguely disgusting. She had never been much of a looker, Jordan reflected, but she had always recognized his cleverness, which was more than their mother had done. And now, by God, Orlena had more than overplayed her hand with both of them.

"I told you she was a bitch," he said furiously, squashing out the cigarette between his fingers and stalking the length of his bachelor apartment.

Lucy sniffled.

"I told you what she was like, but you never listened," he continued with relish. "You've been too busy licking up to her. You thought you were her darling—"

He ducked as Lucy hurled an ashtray at him.

"Hey, stop it! The things on that table cost a fortune!"

She flung an ormolu clock to the floor and tugged at a lamp before collapsing with fresh, messy tears.

"Trace and I were going to be married! Trace loved me! Orlena knew that!"

"Yeah, sure," Jordan said.

Some love affair, that Orlena could buy the man's marriage to someone else with stock in Lyle & Co. Which was exactly what Lucy had discovered had happened. Not that she saw how it affected anyone but her.

He'd guess their mother had taken great pleasure in depriving Lucy of Trace—of anything—just as she took pleasure in making sure he didn't have a scrap of power in a company where he should have plenty. Now this bastard MacDonald owned stock in Lyle & Co. and would be telling *him* what to do, and he, Jordan, hadn't even been consulted about Orlena's latest scheme. As usual. He and Lucy had both been treated like flyspecks.

His lips curled. He wanted to tell his sister again what a fool she'd been. Only something stronger than anger was seething through him. It made him think quickly, think of the future, think of possibilities.

Yes. It was time to change his tactics. Time to stop wasting time. And Lucy could help.

"Let me fix you a drink," he said with sudden sympathy. "It'll make you feel better." He moved toward a drop-front bar. "Poor Lucy. It's a terrible thing to have dropped on you the day before Christmas."

His sister stopped wailing, hiccuped, and blew her nose.

"It's a terrible thing to have dropped on me *any* time," she said pettishly.

Jordan set his teeth. Did she always have to correct him? Couldn't she manage to be even marginally tolerable?

He brought over a couple of good stiff drinks for the two of them.

"She only cares about herself," he said. "It's all she's ever cared about. She's never shared her emeralds with you. She's never shared the company with me. She wants to keep us children all our lives."

Lucy slugged down half her drink and nodded morosely.

"I think she's jealous of you," Jordan said, and waited to see if Lucy would buy that. "She's jealous because you're good-looking. She wanted to hurt you. That's why she set this up with Trace."

Lucy's nose and cheeks were red. Her black hair puffed priggishly behind her ears.

"I hate her!" she repeated.

He knew she would follow him now—just like when they were kids. Reaching cautiously out, he gave her shoulder a brotherly pat.

"She could have an accident, you know." Lucy's mouth dropped open and he spoke quickly, catching her while she was weakest. "You could have your emeralds. And I could *really* rid myself of Cousin Cecily."

Cecily turned at the sound behind her. Though she stood at the window, her eyes had seen nothing. Now, brought back to the reality of her office, she searched for a smile.

"You should not be up and around with that cold, Madame."

Effie, absent from her routine for nearly a week now, moved her hand impatiently.

"It is not my cold that lingers. It is age. Besides, work is the best medicine." She scratched Bibi's head. The hoods on her eyes looked heavier than usual. "For you, I think, the prescription is to see your sister this weekend. It will put color back in your cheeks."

Cecily's brown hair stirred in disagreement.

"There's no point. She barely recognized us ten days ago, and when she did she started to cry. I don't want to upset her more."

Effie sat in silence for a moment.

"We will wait, then—but we will have her back. Now. Call Raoul and tell him I am expecting a courier from Joao. He should arrive within the hour."

Cecily looked at her in surprise. She had heard of no expected shipment from Joao.

"My old friend is worried," Effie added as though aware of her puzzlement. "There is trouble at both mines—strikes. He thinks it prudent to move what goods he has on hand. A decoy courier set out earlier. This is the real shipment."

Cecily frowned. "If . . . anything happens to Joao, who will control the mines there? Will he make good his threat to disinherit his son?"

"He has already done so," Effie said darkly. "But nothing is about to happen to Joao. He has been frail for years."

Her seeming blindness to the truth stunned Cecily. Surely Joao's death was imminent. He had seemed conscious of it himself when he'd come for their wedding.

"I will not be scared out of my own mines by strikes or dead couriers or any other maneuvering of the cartel," muttered Effie, her chair rocking back and forth restlessly. "Perhaps we should have explored The Farm more closely years ago, had another location to turn to. Ah, but Joao and I were never greedy. And all this is hindsight."

Her mood was not good, and Cecily sensed she wanted questions asked. Perhaps she wanted only a chance to share her worries, or maybe companionship.

"What farm?" asked Cecily.

Effie made a dismissing gesture. "A piece of jungle. We thought once to sink a mine there. Our initial reports from the geologists looked promising." She began to wheel with stubborn energy toward her own office. "Spilt milk. That is all such thoughts amount to. I must get to work. I see Ben has not remembered today is my birthday and is still away talking about his plane. Not that I have ever believed in silly celebrations, but he might at least pretend respect as I advance in age."

Cecily hid a smile. So that was what was nettling Effie— Effie, who had never had a birthday party in her life. Well, today she would. Cecily and Van had laid the plans for it months ago. A lump filled Cecily's throat.

Van. Locked up. Missing everything.

And maybe, Cecily thought, the fault is mine. If I hadn't been so wrapped up trying to sort things out with Ben . . . If I'd paid more attention to my sister and less to rubies and sapphires . . .

But Effie had gone. This was not the time to wrestle with personal guilt. Hours later Jenkins called to say that Effie was satisfied with the goods Joao's courier had brought and was ready for lunch.

April greeted them in the dining room where the table was set with balloons and a small pile of gaily wrapped gifts.

"Some surprise, huh?" she said with a pert grin for Effie. "And you haven't seen the half of it!"

"What nonsense," Effie pronounced. "And for someone my age!" But her fingers reached greedily for a package with curling green ribbon, which she unwrapped to reveal a monogrammed canasta deck, a gift from Van.

"She'd ordered it before she left," said Cecily, her throat tight on the words.

Ben hadn't come. His place sat empty. Cecily shared Effie's disappointment as she watched the older woman's eyes slide toward it. Had he stayed away deliberately? Sometimes she thought there'd been healing between them, sometimes she thought he cared for Effie, but perhaps it was only part of that strange accommodation that made the very warp and woof of Effie's world.

Then, amid much merriment, Effie opened a crystal wine decanter from Jenkins, a gold pen from Cecily, and a flask of extravagant bubble bath from April, the latter gift eliciting more than a few teasing comments.

They had started on their luncheon plates when Ben strode in.

"Sorry I'm late," he said, a sparkle in his dark eyes. "Had to stop off for your present."

Effie let out a sound of pure amazement. Cecily gasped.

"Oh, Jee-zus!" breathed April.

Walking beside Ben, tugging somewhat against the leash restraining it, was a small female panther.

"So that's why you said Bibi's blanket must be replaced and brought him a new one!" Effie said as the male, alert and wary, approached the female.

"Yep. So the scent was familiar. But I have a feeling the two of them had better be let outside to get acquainted. The new one's nervous."

Ben opened the patio door and slipped the female's leash. Effie came to the door and watched as the animals disappeared.

"He has needed a mate." Effie's voice was dry with meaning as her eyes met Ben's. They regarded each other as though the others weren't there. Her face seemed to lose some of its wrinkles and soften slightly. Ben grinned at her and slid into his chair.

"Chicken salad?" He made a face.

"I like chicken salad. Cecily remembers such things," Effie said grandly, returning to pick up her fork.

Ben took several bites.

"Oh, yeah. Another birthday present for you, Effie. Jenkins, do you have the box?"

Jenkins produced a cardboard box and Ben reached into it.

"Couldn't explain this too well with a drawing, Effie, so I made models. The shape's called a Möbius strip."

He was taking out two identical shapes, not quite ovals, not quite triangles, made, Cecily realized, by turning one end of a long rectangular strip facedown and hooking it to the other end. What might have been a hoop was twisted instead. Its curves glided over each other with lithe and complex grace. Its planes never touched. To trace it completely would require going twice around its perimeter.

These were to be necklaces, Cecily saw, and the shape alone was fascinating. Ben had covered the models in sequins. One was all in silver, no doubt to indicate diamonds. The other flowed color to color, vivid blue like sapphires on one edge to the deep purple of fine amethysts and then to a glittering, robust ruby red.

"They are cunning!" Effie crowed, dangling one from her forefinger. "Cunning!" Her eyes grew feverish. She watched the movement of the strip of paper. "A rigid shape. It will stand out from the bosom—be a frame. Ah! Sophisticated. *Moderne.*"

Abruptly she put the models down and looked around the table. "We will enter these in the Paris Prize competition."

Jenkins nodded.

"Yes, I thought so," Ben said calmly. He looked at Cecily and the smile of pride he'd been trying to hide broke through.

"And now the cake!" Effie demanded. "There *is* a cake?"

Everyone laughed merrily.

It's wonderful, Cecily thought. The most wonderful time we've ever had around Effie's table. And she's enjoying herself. She's like a child.

A pang that came so often sliced through her. *Van should be here!*

The cake arrived, two layers iced in white buttercream with lavish trim, pink roses and nine candles—one for each decade of Effie's life plus one for the extra years.

"And now what?" asked Effie when the singing was over.

Her eyes fanned stealthily to Ben. Cecily suspected she knew very well what came next. Cecily suspected she was remembering birthday parties she'd given for a small boy.

"Make a wish and blow out the candles," April prompted.

"Ah. My wish will be for the Paris Prize, then. Duvall has never received one. *I* have never received one!"

Leaning forward, she blew out the candles, then raised the glass of champagne she'd insisted on having served over everyone's protest.

"To Paris," she said.

"To Effie," Ben answered, voice ringing.

For a moment Cecily's eyes filled with the emotion she felt in the room. Then the cake was being served and eaten and people were talking.

"So, have you backing for production of your flying device?" asked Effie.

"Looks like it, as soon as I make half a dozen more runs." Ben tipped back his chair. "Pepe and I both figure the company's hoping for an investment write-off. They're going to hate it when the damn thing works."

More coffee was being served. Effie nodded agreeably.

"Enjoy yourselves. I am going to go out on the terrace and watch for Bibi and his consort."

"Was she miffed when it looked like I wasn't going to show?" Ben asked as she disappeared.

"Yes, and I'll bet you planned it that way."

Beneath the table Cecily felt his leg brush hers. The silence between them was happy. Jenkins was attempting to explain to April something about the mining of emeralds, while April, who'd confided to Cecily she was trying to eliminate her gum-chewing habit as it wasn't "classy," bit thoughtfully on the tines of her fork.

"Ben, tell me—"

Cecily broke off at the sound of footsteps. She turned as Wesley stalked in. His hair was disheveled. His face was grim. He seemed oblivious to the glasses slipping down his nose.

"Van signed over all her affairs to MacDonald!" he exploded. "We can't do a thing to free her!"

"What?"

Cecily felt her breath squeezed out of her. Wesley jerked a chair out but stood as though too agitated—or too angry—to make use of it.

"They went to a lawyer before they were married. She made him responsible for her in case anything ever happened."

"No!"

Cecily was on her feet, trembling, and now Charlie was in the room.

"Madame . . . Oh, has she gone up to her office? Prince Karim is on the phone."

"She's—she's on the terrace. I'll get her."

Cecily had to escape, had to steady herself against the reeling fear of this latest news. She lurched out blindly.

"Madame . . ." She saw Effie at the edge of the terrace. Effie would know how to handle this. If Wesley's legal means couldn't free Van, Effie would. "Effie . . ."

Usually the creator of Duvall turned at once, alert to whatever was happening. This time she didn't. Cecily called her name again, moved closer, saw the slump of her body, and began to run.

"Effie!" she cried.

The woman who had hired her, trusted her, taught her how games of power were played, and much, much more sat crooked in her chair. Her eyes were rolled upward. Her lips were working, twitching, but no words came out.

Cecily fell to her knees beside her, shouting for help.

"Effie," she gasped in terrified disbelief. "Oh, my God, Effie!"

THIRTY-SEVEN

"THEY'RE STILL NOT SURE IF THERE'S BEEN ANY BRAIN DAMAGE, April. And all they seemed concerned about at the moment is the paralysis, damn them."

Cecily rubbed her forehead, cradling her desk phone on her shoulder. It had been a week since Effie's stroke, and the weight of running Duvall was suddenly resting on her. At least the hourly calls from the vultures who sat on Effie's board had stopped, she thought, Thank God for small favors. Except for Joao she'd almost smelled their disappointment when, one by one, they'd come to the realization Effie wasn't going to die.

"Do me a favor, will you, April? Call Van and chat. It's been four days since I talked to her, there's been so much to deal with here. . . . No, there hasn't been time to explore this legal mess she's made for herself, and frankly I'm not sure I trust myself to. I'd like to kill that bastard Trace."

As she spoke the words she realized they were true. Despite the chaos over Effie, one thing she had managed to do was set a private detective agency combing through Van's husband's past. They *had* to find something she could use as leverage against him. There *had* to be some way she could regain her guardianship of Van.

Thida knocked and opened the door.

"A customer, Miss Catlow."

Cecily nodded understanding. With Effie sick she would have to deal with customers as well as the business details to which she was more accustomed. She wished Ben hadn't had to be away this morning signing the contracts for production of TRINA.

"I've got to run, April. Thanks for calling." She looked up at Thida. "Who is it?"

"Mr. Kemp. He bought a bracelet a few months ago, and some earrings—"

"Yes. I know who he is."

She realized she had snapped at Thida without reason. She felt trapped. Peter had become a customer of Effie's. She had to see him. But if Ben came in, he was sure to take it the wrong way.

In a distant corridor Bibi was yowling plaintively. He did not understand his mistress's illness and he missed his mate, who preferred to spend more time outside than she did in the house. The sound wore at Cecily's nerves.

Poor damned animal. He was lost without Effie. *She* was lost. Effie's absence was turning everything upside down. Her secretary waited.

"All right." She knew there was no other decision she could make. It was hardly her place to turn away paying customers because of Ben's jealousy. "Show him in. But then stay with us. You can—you can look through my files for anything you think ought to be retired."

Thida looked curious for an instant. Then she obeyed. A moment later Peter, a tentative smile on his face, stepped into the office.

Cecily stood behind her desk but did not offer her hand. "Peter. What can I do for you?"

He moved easily into a chair, adjusting the crease of his cream-colored suit as he crossed his legs. In spite of the confident movements there were traces still of a boyish anxiety on his face. He looked at her hopefully, shyly, and Cecily felt resentment loosening its hold on her. Peter glanced at Thida.

"You're investigating your brother-in-law," he said. "Funny, I never even knew you had a sister. I . . . ." He lowered his head in humility. "I understand now what you said a long time ago about having responsibilities," he said softly.

She nodded.

"If I'd known . . . but I suppose that's water under the bridge now. I understand your sister's a patient in a mental hospital, recently married, and that you've hired people to ask questions about her husband. Why?"

His knowledge shocked Cecily. She couldn't reply for a moment. "How do you know?"

"Let's say I've got friends in the business community." He gave a wry smile. "I've heard. Why?"

She could feel her jaw tightening.

"Because he refuses to get Van out. Because I want her here. Where I can take care of her."

"And he's got legal control of her? That's what I thought. I've come to help."

Her heart began to beat with more hope than it had in days. Peter's hazel eyes had always been so gentle and so earnest. They clung to her now.

"How?" she asked.

His smile came easily, and with faint reproach. "Don't you want to know why?"

She shook her head.

"No, Peter. That's finished."

His eyes regarded her for a minute, their quiet acceptance touching something inside her.

"I can get your sister released. By the end of the week." His gaze traveled pointedly to Thida. "May we talk privately?"

Something quivered inside Cecily, hesitation.

"I trust Thida completely. You can speak in front of her."

Peter looked worried.

"I'm sure I can. However since what I'm suggesting involves a certain risk to my reputation and . . ." He paused, his next words deliberate. ". . . since we mean nothing to each other now, I'm unwilling to have anyone else be privy to any part of it. Should I go now?"

Cecily felt her mouth growing dry.

"No. No. Thida, will you leave us, please?"

She had to hear him out if there was any chance to help Van. A closed door had nothing to do with being disloyal to Ben.

"What makes you think you can do what you're saying?" she asked when they were alone. "I've had two attorneys working on it, one here and one in London. They both agree it will involve a court hearing—time—"

"Not if you buy the right people," Peter cut in bluntly. "Which I already have." His manner turned apologetic. "I know you don't like to think things are done that way, Cecily, but the fact is that they are. The fact is I still love you, and when you love someone you want to do something—anything for them. Isn't that how it is with you and your sister?"

Reluctantly, she nodded. Blood drummed in her ears. Peter had already laid the groundwork. Van could be freed.

"What would I have to do?"

Peter lighted a cigarette.

"Be ready to meet a businessman I know at the airport on short notice. Fly to Grand Cayman and wait for your sister and her traveling companion. Bring her back here."

"A female traveling companion?" Cecily cut in quickly.

"If you like we'll arrange that, yes. There may be problems at immigration if your sister's papers aren't in order. If so you're on your own with those. I want my part in this mentioned to no one. And I want your assurance these plans will be kept absolutely secret. Do you agree?"

She thought rapidly.

"I want Ben to know. I have no secrets from Ben."

Peter rose.

"No. Impossible."

"Why?"

"Because he'd be a liability." He seemed to be hedging. "Someone else helping his wife—he might take it into his head to improve on our plans and ruin everything."

"No."

He looked at the carpet.

"He . . . Cecily, there's a chance he might be just as glad to have your sister where she is. I've heard he had lunch with MacDonald a couple of times before the man married your sister." He looked up quickly. He seemed embarrassed by what he'd said. "Of course that could be unreliable. The person I heard it from could be mistaken."

Her stomach contracted as though from a blow. She could feel it churning inside her, a bruised, painful mass.

No! What Peter said wasn't possible. Ben was fond of Van. He wouldn't . . .

Yet Effie, by all accounts, had been as fond of Ben's mother as she was of him, and still she had lain schemes for both of them. Ben had grown up in the midst of scheming. He'd known it all his life. And he hadn't told her about being named vice-president of Duvall until Effie announced it. *Why had he kept that secret?* How well did she know him?

"I'm sorry . . ." Peter was saying.

"It's—all right. You're wrong, of course, but it's all right."

She pressed at the side of her tightly set jaw. Her head was reeling. It was so hard to think. She wanted to believe in Ben. If Peter was wrong and she did this, she risked whatever beginnings of trust there were between Ben and her. If she said no

. . . oh, God, if she said no she condemned Van to months in an institution—months that might make real recovery more elusive with each passing day.

"I can let you think about it," Peter said.

"No. I—I want to do it."

She made the decision and looked at him with a shiver of apprehension. She *had* to do this. And when this was over she had to confront Ben, ask him questions she'd been afraid to ask, know once and for all exactly what lay between them.

Peter smiled sadly.

"All right. Sit tight till you hear from me. I hope this atones a little for the times I've hurt you, Cecily."

She came around and gave him her hand. "Thank you, Peter."

He held her fingers for a moment as though to cherish their feel.

Let his plan work, she prayed as he left her office. *Let it work!*

"Three times I've drawn this bracelet and still you're not satisfied! I'm sure I don't know why I continue to work here when I could go to Tiffany!"

Mortimer threw down the pencil in his hand and stalked out of the workroom.

"What the hell's the matter with you, Cecily?" Ben asked, scowling at the sketch left behind. "It's a good design."

Good but not great, Cecily thought. Adequate for Tiffany but not for Duvall.

"I'm not sure Effie would like it."

"Effie's not running things right now. You are. Do *you* like it?"

Cecily dropped the sketch onto a bench. Two days had passed since Peter's visit and every hour she was growing edgier. The worry about Van. The uneasiness inside her at the possibility that Ben might have lunched with Trace. Something must have gone wrong. And now, when she didn't need it, Ben was hounding her.

"I've got enough to do this morning without standing here arguing," she said in a tight voice. "If you want the design, put it through. I can't stop you. You're vice-president of Duvall."

"Oh, Christ! We've finally come back to that, have we?" He crumpled the sketch and flung it toward a wastebasket, glaring at her. "Let's forget the damned business for a few days. Let's go to Heredia."

The suggestion was so irresponsible, so indifferent to concerns surrounding them, that she hated him.

"You expect me to enjoy myself while Van's locked up? While Effie's sick?" she asked sharply.

Ben rounded the bench in a step. "I expect you to have a life of your own, goddamn it—"

"Miss Catlow . . . a call on your private line."

Thida's voice came to her from the other end of the room. With Ben's eyes still blazing at her, Cecily turned.

Every thought had spilled out of her now except one at the pit of her stomach: Perhaps it was Peter. That was why she couldn't go running off with Ben, though part of her longed to. That was why she flashed at him while weakening to the thought of orchids and no pressure less appealing than the feel of his arms around her and the peace of their own private world.

Perhaps it was Peter. And because of that possibility, she had to quarrel with Ben. She had to put distance between them because of the guilt she was feeling.

"Cecily?"

It was the voice for which she'd been waiting. Her tightly curled fist unwound. She'd been right to keep this one secret from Ben. Van was going to be free!

"Your flight leaves at five tonight. The tickets are at the check-in counter. My businessman friend you'll be traveling with will be ticketed as Mr. Fox. He'll meet you there."

"Peter, thank you. I—I don't know what to say."

"Don't be late."

"No. I won't."

She hung up and smoothed her hair. Just a few more hours— half a day—and it would be over. She walked back toward the workroom.

Ben raised an eyebrow in question. She avoided his eyes.

"It was just a customer. About a broken clasp." What a fine line between lies and truth, she thought with irony.

"You may be right about the design," Ben said. "I fished it out of the trash and looked at it again. It's pretty ordinary."

She forced a laugh. "I'd just been thinking it's not so bad. And you're a better judge of design than I am. . . ."

Would his body always affect hers with such force? The faint heat he gave off made her want to fling herself into his arms and tell him everything. His closeness made her so aware of her love for him she wanted to cry.

Ben took her hand. "We don't have to decide today. You've

got enough on your mind. I guess it was crazy to think about Heredia, but let's at least get away for dinner somewhere quiet. We could use that."

Temptation pulled at her so strongly she couldn't speak. She shook her head.

"I've got things I've got to do, Ben. As a matter of fact, I'm thinking of leaving early tonight and checking into a hotel somewhere—so I can't be bothered by the phone. I won't be home tonight."

She saw the surprise in his eyes and turned away quickly. Just hours. That was all she must endure. By tomorrow Van would be here, in Miami, safe. Then she would tell Ben everything and he would forgive her.

The hands of her wristwatch seemed glued in place. She took lunch on a tray in her office, immersed herself in work, rose finally at three for the trip to the mainland and the airport.

"I'm hiding away with some work," she said to Thida. "I may not be in till noon tomorrow. Call Wesley Bell and ask him to be here first thing in the morning. I'll want to see him the minute I come in."

Thida looked up and nodded. Was there something disapproving in her eyes?

Cecily fled into the pleasant warmth of the afternoon. It was right, what she was doing. Anxiety welled up in her, but that was only because she feared something yet might go wrong. Her progress from Effie's dock to the municipal marina and finally to the sprawling efficiency of Miami International Airport seemed interminable.

She had no luggage, looked strange, she thought as she approached the ticketing counter.

"Oh, yes," said the agent as he produced her ticket envelope. "Mr. Fox is waiting for you in a private conference room, if you'd care to join him there until your flight is called. I'll show you the way."

She was glad at the thought of privacy. Corridors and people blurred past as she followed the agent.

He threw open a door in the sleek wall of a corridor. Cecily stepped in and gasped.

"Sorry if I'm not the Fox you were expecting."

Ben's voice was the scrape of steel against steel. Arms crossed, he lounged against a gray metal desk. All the warmth that had been in his eyes that morning had been replaced by something cold and deadly.

"Surprised to see me, Cecily? Seems there's some guy who makes a living off tropical infidelities—checks travel agency tickets to see who's traveling with whom and oughtn't to be. He called this afternoon. For five hundred bucks to a post office box he told me about the tickets Kemp bought for your little tryst—"

"No! That's not—"

"Like hell it's not!"

He was off the desk coming toward her. The ticketing agent had vanished.

"You going to stand there—after that lie about holing up with your work in some hotel room—and tell me you're not meeting Kemp?"

His breath came in deep, threatening bursts. Cecily fell back a step.

"Yes! That's exactly what I'm telling you!" She could not take her eyes from the fury in his, and the aching beat of her heart jarred words from her she hadn't meant to say. "I don't know what you think you've caught me in, Ben, but I'm not meeting Peter! I lied to you because—because I had to. For Van—"

Her voice was crushed out of her as he slammed her back against the wall.

"Goddamn it, Cecily! Don't try and use Van!" The violence that had lurked in the set of Ben's mouth leaped into full view now. He shook his head, face white and grim. "I'd have bet my life you were above using her, at least. I see I was wrong there, too!"

His fingers bit into her shoulders so deeply her eyes swam with tears. The pain made rational thought easier.

"You're right." There was still a chance she could throw him off, get to Van; she mustn't jeopardize that. "I—I'm meeting a man Peter knows. There's a good chance Trace MacDonald's been laundering money on Grand Cayman. Mr. Fox can help me gain access to the information. But I knew you wouldn't approve—just because Peter helped me."

A rap sounded at the door. Ben didn't look away from her, but the pressure of his fingers had grown less.

"Cecily . . ." Another voice intruded.

Pinned into place against the wall, aghast, disbelieving, Cecily could move no more than her eyes as Peter entered.

"There's been a change of plans," he began, then stopped at sight of Ben.

Suddenly she was free and Ben's fist was swinging toward

Peter's mouth, sending him staggering. His hand caught Peter's vest front. He struck again.

Peter, unconscious, hit the floor of the small private room. On trembling legs Cecily hurled herself toward Ben's arm, pulling back with all her strength as he bent to strike again.

"Stop it, Ben! Have you gone mad?"

He shoved her against the desk, then whirled to face her. His voice crashed off the metal walls around them.

"Mad? No. I was mad when I fell for you—when I trusted you! How long's it been since you cried in my arms and begged me never to leave you, Cecily? You put on quite an act!"

"Ben, please!"

Tears cascaded down her cheeks.

"Did you think I'd be your security blanket, Cecily? Somebody to dry your tears and puff up your ego? Bloody Christ, I suppose there are men who'd be content with that for a woman like you, but I'm not one of them."

She put out a pleading hand but dared not touch him. Van. She had to think of Van, didn't she? Anyway, if she told the truth now, he'd hardly believe her.

"It's—it's not what it looks like! I swear it. *I love you, Ben!*"

He drew back as she took a stumbling step toward him. His words were a sneer.

"Love? You don't know what that word means any more than Effie does. You wanted a piece of Duvall, you wanted to be as much like her as you could, and I was your ticket. Try Harry now, or Martin—maybe they won't mind a wife who cheats. Or if it's Kemp you want instead of Effie's blessing, I'll make it easy. By the time you two get wherever you're going, I'll have all the paperwork in for a nice fast divorce."

He left. The room tried to reel around her. She held to the desk.

Plans. Peter said the plans had been changed. She had to act, find out what to do next. As soon as Van was safe she could think of herself.

She knelt above Peter and fought her thundering fear. *What if she lost Ben?* She couldn't believe, had never been able to, that he was in any way involved with Trace MacDonald.

"Peter?" She rubbed his cheek briskly, efficiently. "Peter?" His lip was swelling and blood still trickled down both sides of his chin.

He opened his eyes and as they cleared she drew back from something she saw there.

Then it was gone. Illusion.

"I—I'm sorry," she said. "What are you doing here? Where's Mr. Fox?"

Peter sat up. He put his hand to his mouth and brought it back bloody. His hazel eyes were as brilliant as ill-colored aquamarine. There was on his face now no trace of anything remotely boyish.

"Fox isn't coming," he said. "I tried to reach you to tell you, but you'd already gone. That's why I'm here. I'm afraid there was a last-minute hitch in London. Your sister never left. You'll be glad to know, I'm sure, that the information was apparently wrong about your husband and MacDonald. But it looks as though, for the moment at least, the plan to rescue your sister is off."

THIRTY-EIGHT

CECILY STOOD AT THE WINDOW IN SILENT ANGUISH, THE DIVORCE decree in her hand. Should she have fought it? She'd asked herself that question every hour of every day since the papers requiring her signature had come and she'd put her name to them.

Her heart had counseled her to oppose what was happening. But not her pride. If she'd fought, Ben would have thought it was only because, through marriage, she longed to be part of Duvall. She'd prove to him how wrong he'd been. She'd prove to him she also didn't need to lean—not on him, not on anyone. But the cost of it . . . the cost . . . an unceasing ache tore every nerve ending, every fiber of her body. She had shared things with Ben that she had never shared with anyone, not even Van. Doubts and fears. Dreams. A rare and special laughter. And it was gone, its absence making her sense of isolation more pronounced and painful than in the days before she learned how a single spark between two people could be nurtured almost magically into a fire by which both could warm.

The day's mail lay on her desk, all of it neatly opened by Thida save this. Thida must have known what it contained. Sometimes she thought she could not have kept going these past few weeks without her secretary.

Thida had brought her food, made her eat, kept her aware of

business details that might otherwise have escaped her distracted mind. Meanwhile Cecily had put on a calm, if hardly cheerful, front of Effie. Though rallying from her stroke, Effie had been hit hard by Ben's departure. He had been in touch with his grandmother, Cecily knew. He had given reassurances he would complete the Möbius strips. Still, though Effie hadn't raised the subject of his leaving, she clearly was stunned.

And I could never explain what happened, thought Cecily, tracing letters on the windowpane. Such a disaster. Yet maybe from the very beginning I knew it would end like this. Ben never trusted me. And he never loved me.

She looked at the letters her fingers had traced. B-e-n. Hot tears rose in her throat, but she fought them back savagely.

Peter had called once, twice, apologetic. There seemed to be no hope of freeing Van quickly now. The risk she had taken— the sacrifice of her marriage—had been for nothing. A door opened and she turned in surprise to see Effie.

She had not expected to see the durable woman up for a day or two yet, and certainly not outside her room.

"You will overdo, Madame," she murmured with no animation behind the words.

Effie moved slowly, propelling herself with one hand now.

"Why do you stand at the window? You stand at the window when there is bad news."

"No bad news." Cecily drew a breath. "Just thinking."

Effie's eyes slid to the paper in Cecily's hand and she grunted. She began a slow, wobbling progress, circling the room.

"Thinking," she rasped. "That is the hardest of all. That is why it is good to work. There is no time to think."

A strange conversation, Cecily thought. But she understood what was being said—and so did Effie.

"While I have been sick, my thoughts have hung around me like vultures," Effie continued. "Vultures from the past, all picking at me." She drew up abruptly. "Why did Ben leave?"

Cecily looked away, the pain sharp in her throat. "He thought I was unfaithful."

"Were you?"

"No."

She could feel Effie's sharp eyes boring into her, uncommonly hard. For a moment something in their assessment frightened her.

Then Effie nodded wisely. "You will live. Just as I lived when William Lyle left my bed for someone else's."

Even through the grief enveloping her Cecily felt disbelief. Once before Effie had denied this. Now she sat admitting it.

"Ah, yes," said Effie. "Your great-uncle and I were lovers. And when he left me, I felt I had been burned with a white-hot poker, here, inside." She thumped her breast.

Bibi was pacing restlessly. Cecily watched him, trying to escape something, trying to outrun some pain.

"He is lonely," said Effie. "His consort has disappeared into the woods and will not return to him. He howls for her in the night.

"You see, that is how the world is. An animal like Bibi howls its grief. A man hides his in drinking, as Ben does. But a woman . . . what is a woman to do?"

She moved closer and held out a trembling hand, inviting Cecily to come to her. For a moment, as Cecily felt herself drawn along on invisible strings, she had the sense of the two of them moving through the intricate steps of some grand ballet, planned out for them, as Ben's departure had been, from the dawn of their lives.

Half-mesmerized, half-captive of that thought, she knew it was not true. She and Effie were not pawns of fate. They had invited their own destinies by the choices they'd made. They had chosen, suffered, and half a century later she was following the same road Effie had.

Strength poured into her as she clasped Effie's hand. They had never touched before. And as they held each other in that simple gesture, a nearness that was bitterly comforting seemed to flow between them.

Effie's heavy old ruby glittered. Her fingers were firm.

"Work, Cecily. Wed yourself to business. It is the only thing worth loving. The only thing that will never betray you."

"Oh, Wesley, it's just such a mess! Why did they get a divorce? Ben was here last week, and he looked so unhappy!"

Tears welled in Vanessa's eyes. They made Wesley apprehensive.

"Van, it's just one of those things." He patted her hand. "I mean, sometimes a marriage just doesn't work."

He paused, watching closely for any sign Van saw what he was saying might apply to her. There was none. Only the loveliness of her upturned face as they sat on the hospital terrace, Van with a blanket tucked around her though the apple trees were budding. Only the concern for Ben and Cecily he saw hovering there.

"I wish I could be with Cecily . . . just be there *for* her," Van murmured. She shoved her hands into the pockets of her coat and watched a robin in the tree above them, her face drawn into a frown.

"I've messed up my whole life!" she blurted out suddenly. "Right from the start! And I hate it!"

"No!" Wesley sprang to his feet and drew her up with him anxiously. "Van, that's not true!"

"It *is* true! I have."

He had never seen her like this—never heard her say such things. It alarmed him.

"Come on, Van. Let's take a walk."

"Damn it, Wesley! Stop treating me like a—a child!"

As her voice rose she sounded strangely like Cecily. Wesley blinked.

"Ben's the only one who's ever treated me like a grown-up human being. I may be crazy, but don't you think I at least deserve that much?"

"You're not crazy!" Wesley bellowed, then stopped, shocked by his volume.

He and Van stared at each other. She looked as amazed at him as he was at her.

"Uh . . . okay. If you don't want to walk, then let's get down to business. I'd have brought it up last time I was here, but I wasn't sure you felt up to it. If you want to get out, you're going to have to help, you know."

"All right. Let's walk," Van said grimly.

They started out under the apple trees. She was pale from the mindless, sedated days when she'd first come here. Wesley felt like a bully. Was he right to press her? All the endless books on mental illness he'd read and he still didn't know. He just knew he loved her. Blindly. And that he'd do anything to make her well and strong and able to leave this place and never come back.

"We can't get you out, Cecily and I can't," he said. "Not since you signed those papers."

He hadn't meant to bring it up even though it hurt, Van going to some other lawyer, not trusting him. She wouldn't be in this mess if she'd let him advise her.

"I . . . just wanted to stand on my own feet for once," she said in a small voice. "Trace was going to change his will so that I'd be taken care of, and he said I could come and have one drawn up, too, if I never had. It seemed like a good idea. And when Trace's lawyer suggested provisions in case I ever got sick again, I . . . well, I thought if I did it, maybe it would be like a charm. You know . . . how you sort of plan for something and that guarantees you never need it?"

She bit her lip.

Wesley gave every bit of discipline he possessed to not softening.

"Well then. Either Trace has to get you out or you can divorce him so Cecily is your nearest relative again. It's as simple as that."

He could see her shrink.

"It's not Trace's fault I'm in here. How can I divorce him?"

Wesley felt himself fuming with irritation. Like hell the fault wasn't Trace's. But Van seemed to have no recall at all of whatever had happened to send her here.

"I want to be a good wife," she said, her voice going bleak. "I haven't even had a chance."

"Do you love Trace?" he persisted stubbornly.

She looked at the ground. Her hands were pressing into her pockets so hard Wesley was afraid the cloth might rip.

"He comes to see me every week if he's in London. And he calls all the time to ask the doctors how I'm doing."

Wesley sighed with frustration.

They walked in silence. Van kicked a stone.

"I've made a fool of myself, haven't I? Cecily said I couldn't handle being out on my own—and of course she was right!"

Twin spots of angry color burned on her cheeks. Her vehemence worried him.

"Don't be mad at Cecily," he pleaded.

"I'm not. I'm mad at me!"

She was trembling now. Wesley put his arms around her. It seemed so natural. It had been so hard to resist. And she leaned against him. He could feel the wonderful softness of her hair. His fingers smoothed over it as though they had minds of their own and his lips touched it tentatively.

Then, emboldened, he pressed a soft kiss to her forehead. Van drew back. Her eyes were startled, yet some other reaction hovered there, too. Her mouth was parted and very close to his.

He knew she was innocent, knew she trusted him, but Wesley could no longer fight against such nearness. He kissed her lightly, lingeringly, his muscled frame quivering with the sweet sensations the act unlocked.

For a moment Van accepted him, but then he could feel her resistance.

"Wesley, I—I don't think you should do that!"

"Why not?" he asked, suddenly bold. "I—" He caught himself. "I care about you, Van. I don't like to see you unhappy. And I'll do anything to help you. Always. Don't you know that?"

She looked confused. Wesley cursed his blundering.

"You're . . . so good, Wesley. Such a good friend. I don't know what I'd do without you. But I don't think you ought to kiss me."

Wesley sighed and started to draw her along the path again.

"Okay," he said darkly.

He felt a small guilt that he was spending an extra day here when maybe Cecily needed help. He entertained thoughts of Trace MacDonald drowned, shot, crushed by a runaway automobile.

"You've really got to start thinking about your future, Van. About what you want to do." He knew he sounded stuffy now and changed the subject. "What did Ben have to say?"

"Nothing much. He brought me a dirty novel." She gave a self-conscious laugh. "And a book on Amelia Earhart and an autobiography by Stanley Marcus. Eclectic, huh? I think Ben tries to stretch my horizons."

She fell silent, and Wesley could sense the rapid shifting of her mood.

"Wesley, is Cecily going to be okay? I'm worried about her. Ben's gone. Effie's sick. There's so much competition in the kind of work she does—there's so much nastiness."

"That's silly." He adjusted his glasses, glad to be on safer ground. "The only nastiness has been from Lyle and Company and I think they've learned their lesson. Orlena Lyle must know by now she'll get burned if she tries to take on either Cecily or Duvall. Believe me, Van, there's nothing to fear."

"Have another drink, Orlena. We flew up here to relax, after all."

Orlena looked suspiciously at her daughter. It wasn't like Lucy to be so solicitous—especially since Trace MacDonald had been married off. The girl had been an absolute stormfront for days on end. She'd put on weight, too, Orlena observed with distaste as Lucy put a coaxing hand down for her glass. The problem with Lucy was that she lacked willpower. When things didn't go her way she sulked and indulged herself. That was dangerous, indulgence, Orlena thought. Fingering her emeralds, she tried to fathom what had made her children wax suddenly enthusiastic over spending this weekend in Marblehead.

For at least six years they had thrown annoying tantrums when she went to William's house to escape the heat of August and expected them to come with her. "Dull," they had called it. "Stuffy." Now they'd turned nostalgic, wanted to come here in spring.

It was some plot of theirs, she thought shrewdly. Were they trying to make her feel old with all this talk of resting? Was Lucy trying to make her think she *looked* old? It would be about the level of the girl's rather childish spitefulness.

"I find I've grown to rather like martinis," she said as her glass was returned to her. "I find I don't need to watch my calories as much as I did when I was your age—but you should, Lucy. You're looking rather bloated."

There had been an almost hidden smirk on Lucy's mouth. Now it jerked down at the corners.

Had the girl hoped to make her gain a few pounds this weekend? Was that her game? How ridiculous.

Orlena sipped avidly at her martini even though she did not particularly like the taste. Jordan had prepared a pitcher of them before going down to the dock and some silly surprise he kept muttering about. The drinks seemed to go to her head faster than she remembered this evening. Especially this one. Orlena tried furtively to make the pattern of a nearby lamp come into focus and found it difficult.

"That's great," Lucy snapped. "We're stuck with another disgusting dinner of broiled lobster because everyone knows you're *always* counting calories, and now you say you're not!" She cracked down her empty glass. "Come on. Finish your drink. Let's go see whatever it is Jordan wants to show us and get on back. I'm hungry."

Hate glared at her from Lucy's small ratlike eyes. They really looked quite feverish, Orlena thought. They were watching her raise her glass again, following her every move. If they had belonged to someone besides her own child, they might have made her shiver.

Lucy, her own daughter, was sitting there wishing misfortune on her . . . wishing *pounds* on her, or age, or something. Orlena felt her vision mist. It was so unfair.

She had been a good mother to Jordan and Lucy. She had

worked her fingers to the bone; she had spoiled them both shamelessly. This was the thanks she got. Both of them always glaring at her. Both of them resenting her because she was clever and skillful and didn't waste time on fits of temper like the two of them. Because she knew it would make Lucy seethe, she let the martini slide down her throat before standing up.

The room shifted slightly around her. The walk in the wretched night air would sober her up, though, and next week she would diet like a fiend—out of Lucy's view—to compensate for the small excesses she would flaunt this weekend.

She hugged a linen jacket around her as they started out.

"I cannot imagine what your brother's found to attract him down at that old cabin cruiser. I hope he's not hatching some wild scheme to restore it. He'd look like a fool back in Palm Beach—and that's assuming he ever learned to manage it properly."

"Maybe he needs a hobby," Lucy said as though pouting.

Lucy took her arm. It was dark on the path to their small private dock, and that last martini was having alarming effects on Orlena, so she allowed the gesture.

"Maybe he's not happy," Lucy persisted. "Have you ever thought about that, Orlena? About whether Jordan and I were happy?"

It was such a ridiculous question that Orlena ignored it. She tried to shake off Lucy's hand, but Lucy was shoving her down some steps onto the cabin cruiser.

"For heaven's sake! Will you stop shoving me?" she snapped. "Jordan? Where are you? Get some lights on before someone breaks an ankle. Haven't you any sense?"

Her green eyes, slow in focusing, spotted a rowboat down below. Someone in it. Blond hair. Jordan.

And then the push came from behind her, hard and vengeful. The low side of the cabin cruiser became, for an instant, the pivot over which her body rotated.

Cold water. Her clothes and the heavy emeralds at her throat and wrists were pulling her down as understanding rushed in. Her son. Her daughter. *They were doing this to her!* She knew pain, outrage, then panic.

She struggled, but something was holding her down from above. An oar, she thought in disbelief.

Water surged into her lungs. A calm voice filtered down:

"Ten minutes, Jordan. Make sure she's under for at least ten minutes."

THIRTY-NINE

"LOOK AT THIS! HOW CAN HE WASTE HIS TIME WITH FOOL-ishness? How can he turn his back on his destiny—his real genius?"

Effie waved the newspaper strangled in her hand, her break-fast coffee untouched beside her as she sat at the terrace table.

"His plane. Cutting off its tail to make it go faster." Effie spat the words. "When am I going to have his Möbius strips? When am I going to have the entry for my Paris Prize?"

Cecily let her breath out patiently. She did not know why she eternally came to work in time for breakfast. She did not know why she had come this morning, especially, having already seen the wire service story on Ben. It was too much to bear on top of the front page photo of what was being billed as "Lyle & Co.'s Superstar," a necklace for the pudgy producer whose business Effie had refused, a necklace unveiled last night on network TV and scheduled for viewing on talk shows and the cover of *TV Guide* this week, according to the paper.

Yes, she did know why she'd come here so early. She'd come out of loneliness. She'd come because her lovely apartment seemed like a shell. Yet she couldn't bear to vacate the special place she had shared with Ben, and which still bore both their imprints. It was haven to her as often as it was hell.

"You know he'll start on the necklace as soon as Joao's shipment comes," she soothed.

The arrangements had been made weeks ago by Ben and Effie. Ben would work at a studio in Palm Beach. He would not come here.

"Joao. Hah! Another thing to annoy me," Effie fumed. "Joao has turned into a dithering old woman. He is afraid to ship my diamonds."

"Effie—" She did not like to see Effie grow as angry as she was becoming. The stroke had shortened her temper, and now, with her good arm, the old woman whirled herself across the terrace, her breakfast untouched.

"He's afraid!" Effie cut her off. "Last week they were to come . . . three days ago. What work does he think I can do without my diamonds? And Ben—what work does he think *he* can do if he kills himself?'' She stopped at the edge of the terrace and scowled. ''Even Bibi deserts me more and more, running off to play with his consort, who will not come to my house!''

''He's with you now,'' said Cecily gently as the panther padded after Effie's chair and sat down beside it.

She could feel Effie's impotent anger. For nearly two-thirds of a century the woman had wielded power and now, today, it seemed beyond her grasp.

Cecily was far more concerned than she wanted to show that they hadn't heard from Joao. She poured another cup of coffee and tried to think. She didn't know what to do. Though she'd learned a great deal about the running of Effie's business, it was still the judging of stones she knew best, not how to acquire them.

It seemed harder to keep Effie focused entirely on business these days, too. Personal grievances, like this one about the new panther, kept nudging in. Did that mean Effie's mind had been affected by the stroke? The thought made Cecily shiver. Effie *had* to be all right.

''I think you must give some thought to acquiring another diamond source, Madame.'' She brought discussion back to where it had been before Effie had opened the paper. ''I think it's time to diversify, to explore that other land Joao owns in case the old mines are lost.''

Effie gave her a long look and then wheeled back. ''I will not lose my mines,'' she said stubbornly.

Subject closed, locked, sealed, thought Cecily in frustration.

''Prince Karim wants earrings. Rubies.'' Effie chuckled, more like her old self now. ''He came to me last night. I suspect he had been comparison-shopping and no one else could deliver. It seems he is soon to acquire a daughter-in-law, and this will be his gift to her. Of course, it will be photographed. Look over our stock this morning. See if we must call Harry.''

Cecily nodded. Mortimer would undoubtedly be drawing the design. She would have to check with him on the size of stones needed.

She started to rise, but Jenkins came hurrying out of the house. Two spots of angry color burned on his pale face.

''Madame!'' he burst out. ''Your—your grandson Harry—he's just announced he'll no longer be affiliated with Duvall. He's been named an associate vice-president of Lyle and Company. Phone calls are coming. I've checked. It appears to be true!''

The lids stirred over Effie's eyes. Her good hand curled into a fist.

"Fool!"

Cecily held her breath.

But Effie began to wheel back toward the table with her old vigor. Resolve and an ironlike certainty of her own power molded her face.

"He has just given up his share in my profits, which he will regret. I set him up in the ruby trade. Does he think I can't replace him?"

Jenkins, too, let out a breath. They'd both been worried about Effie's temper, Cecily thought. Only Effie seemed less fragile now. Perhaps she thrived on challenges.

"Being part of Lyle and Company will soon count for nothing! The last of William's wives is dead—drowned with her emeralds. The business rests in inexperienced hands. We will make sure everyone is aware of that. We must have a war council."

She gave orders as Charlie appeared to clear away the breakfast dishes. "Jenkins, pull the inventory sheets so we can estimate how long our current stock of stones will last us. Cecily, you will fly to Bangkok. At once."

"Yes, Madame."

"Madame . . . perhaps you should rest a bit before we deal with this," Jenkins ventured. "It has been a shock."

"Treachery is no shock," Effie snapped. "Not to me. This is bothersome, in view of my promise to Prince Karim to supply him with earrings. But nothing more. I do not need rest." She turned her chair away from them. "I will make some phone calls—see if any of my old friends in Asia are still alive."

"Who's been calling?" Cecily asked Jenkins in a lowered voice.

His expression was worried. "Papers. The Countess di Crichi, who always knows everything."

"Damn! And she's got a bracelet on order with rubies in it."

"Lynette called from Paris just after I'd confirmed. There were rumors there, too."

"Did she know in advance it would happen?"

Things were moving too quickly for Cecily to feel any impulse toward subtlety. Jenkins shook his head.

"Well, let's—"

She was interrupted by a cry from Charlie.

"Help me! Come quickly! Something has happened to Madame!"

Cecily knew, before springing the few steps to Effie's chair, that it was another stroke. Effie's eyes were turned up, almost lost behind drooping lids. Her whole face was twitching.

"Get the doctor!" Jenkins shouted.

The smell of sickness was on Effie's breath. As Cecily knelt beside her, near animal sounds struggled out over Effie's bunched tongue.

"Stones . . . stones . . ."

Cheeks wet with tears, Cecily caught her quivering hand.

"Don't worry, Effie! We'll get your stones. We'll take care of everything. I promise!"

It was morning. Midday. A day had passed since Effie's second stroke.

"You shouldn't be here," Jenkins said as they sat in Effie's living room. "You should get some rest. You were up all night."

"I should be upstairs," said Cecily grimly. She blew at coffee Jenkins had just poured for them. "I should deal with some of these problems so she'd have less worrying her, but I don't know how. Put some brandy in this for me, will you, please?"

Jenkins frowned at her even as he complied. "Food and rest would do you more good, Cecily. Don't ruin your health."

She gave a wry, tired smile. "Coffee with milk for breakfast has kept Effie going for eighty-five years. This'll do me for this morning, at least."

Jenkins sat down with a sigh he tried to hide. He must be tired, too. Cecily wondered when he'd found the time to shave. She was glad of his company.

"Madame was foolish to insist on staying here," he said. "The hospital would be much safer."

"This is her home." And maybe she knows she doesn't have much longer in it, Cecily added silently.

"You haven't reached Ben yet?" Jenkins asked.

"No. Thida's still trying."

In the hallway the sharp click of high heels sounded and April came in.

"Jeez, those two nurses are like wardens!" she exclaimed. "The way they hover, poor Effie's likely to croak from lack of oxygen."

She threw a hand across her mouth. "Oh, Jeez! I shouldn't have said it that way, should I? I mean, Effie looks *okay*. Not serious or anything."

Cecily grinned. "Sure, April. I'm glad they let you see her. And thanks for coming."

The news of Harry's defection to Lyle & Co. must have made the papers last night, though Cecily hadn't looked at them. But April had and called and had learned about Effie. Through a long, tense evening and into the night she'd kept vigil with them, departing reluctantly, returning first thing this morning.

Now she dropped a warm hand on Cecily's shoulder in passing.

"Going to log some more beauty sleep now, but you need anything, you give me a call. Okay?"

The phone rang.

"Karim," said Jenkins, answering it and handing it to Cecily.

She took it, heard the prince's questions, answered with no certainty of truth behind her answers. There had been a dozen other calls already this morning.

"Yes, Your Highness. . . . Expect the earrings as promised. . . . Yes, Madame Duvall had everything well in hand before her attack.

"No, of course this will not affect her ability to supply rubies. Or their quality."

She hung up. The droop of Jenkins's shoulders seemed more pronounced as he leaned against the mantelpiece. He seemed lost in thought.

"The things I would have missed . . . the things I wouldn't have seen without working with Madame," he said at last. "I guess I can forgive her now for keeping me here."

"You didn't want to work for her?" asked Cecily in surprise. It was nice to talk about something, anything, other than the problems of the moment.

Jenkins smiled gently. "No. I wanted a life of adventure, you see. I'd trained as a geologist. But Madame brought me here, to this job, when I'd been only six months with Joao."

He drained his coffee cup. His eyes gave one of their cautious twinkles. "I've had an adventure of quite another kind. I know that now."

This time the doorbell interrupted.

Cecily turned in time to see the entrance of an obese figure in white linen.

"Kim!"

His fat eyes looked greedy. Hopeful, at least.

"How is my mother-in-law?"

She fought back revulsion. It seemed unlikely that Kim ever thought of Effie in such affectionate terms.

"Alive. Her vital signs are good. Her speech has been badly impaired."

Why had he come? Martin had merely called. The vultures were circling already.

And why haven't you called, Ben? Why haven't you returned the messages? She needs you!

Ben's leaving had hit Effie so hard. Ought she to bear part of the blame for Effie's latest stroke on her own shoulders? she wondered in anguish.

I need you, Ben—but I know I've thrown the right to that need away. She hasn't. Please come. Please!

"So it's true Harry has cut off our source of rubies," Kim said, sitting delicately on a love seat, which he filled. "And Effie is ill. It seems we should make some provisions for the future of Duvall."

The phone again.

"Joao," announced Jenkins, passing it to her.

Cecily looked at him, looked at Kim, thought desperately. A courier had not yet brought the expected diamonds. This had to be bad news.

"I'll take it in my office," she said, hurrying toward the elevator.

She answered out of breath. "Joao? It's Cecily. I'm sorry I took so long."

The wire crackled faintly.

"Where is Effie? Is she out with those tigers of hers?"

He hadn't heard.

Closing her eyes, Cecily sat down in the cool leather of her chair. "No, Joao. I'm afraid she's had another stroke. And I assume you've heard by now we've lost our ruby source."

There was no sound on the other end. She pictured him slipping a tablet under his tongue, gathering breath to speak. Or worse still, having a heart attack himself.

"My news is also bad," he said with effort.

"I thought it must be."

"It is madness—subterfuge—the government says there is something wrong with our taxes. No stones of ours may leave the country until all the records are checked. It may be months!"

"Offer a bribe."

"I have. It has been refused."

Her arm pressed the edge of the table. It wasn't right for this to happen to Effie. If these were the last of Effie's days, they mustn't end like this.

Joao spoke again. "Cecily . . . I have stones for you . . . some I have been putting back against such a happening. But I have no way of getting them to you. Not even as submarines. I'm sure my couriers . . . will be watched."

He was losing strength. She raced her thoughts.

"I'll get them out, Joao. Let me think of a plan."

He gave her the number of the friend's phone he was calling from, a precaution in case his own lines were tapped, and they hung up.

Cecily rested her head against one tightly curled fist. What am I doing? she thought. Who have I become? I used to think smuggling was terrible. Awful. Wrong. But I love Effie. I can't let everything that she's built be destroyed.

Ben had warned her she would come to this in Effie's world. She hated him for his accuracy, just as she hated him for doubting her, for leaving her, for leaving this ache in her heart. Most of all she hated him for abandoning her to the same weary question that had shadowed her most of her twenty-eight years: What was wrong with her that she had never mattered enough to anyone for them to stand at her side and fight for her?

Her door opened. Jenkins stood there, eyes filled with question.

"The government has slapped an embargo on all Joao's goods," she said in a tight voice. "He can't send anything out."

They looked at each other. She faced what she didn't want to.

"We could lose her, Jenkins. We could lose Effie *and* Duvall—everything there is!" The words burst from her lips.

Pain crossed his face. He looked aside in agreement. "She's been asking to see one of us. She needs some word of encouragement."

"Tell her . . . tell her that the diamonds were delayed but will be here shortly. Tell her we will have rubies."

"How?"

"I don't know! Just tell her, Jenkins."

She spun in her chair, looking out the window until he had left. She thought of happy times, the day Van had been freed, Effie's triumphant show, the feel of Ben's arms. Effie had been the catalyst in all.

She turned her chair again and dialed, a number once memorized, never forgotten.

"This is Cecily Catlow at Duvall," she said. "I'd like to speak to Teddy Landis."

*   *   *

It was like the past rolling back on her, the sight of Teddy's red, wiry hair. Only now she sat behind a desk far grander than that once occupied by Jacob Landis. Now humiliation was buried, in part by sadness for friendship lost.

"Sit down, Teddy," she said, gesturing to a chair. "Thank you for coming."

He nodded awkwardly. "It's good to see you, Cecily—good to know how well you've done."

She longed to say something sharp, but the words wouldn't come.

"How are things at Landis and Oxenburg?"

He answered with a rueful gesture she remembered, that pass at his circus-clown hair.

"Okay. I always knew I'd have trouble filling Uncle Jacob's shoes." His smile was pinched.

"Are you and Terri married now?"

"She is, I'm not. She left about a year ago."

"I'm sorry."

"Yeah. Me too." He propped elbows on his knees as he had when they'd talked in their cubicles as contented underlings. His eyes were sad. "What's up, Cecily? It surprised me when you called me yesterday."

"I'd like to do some business, Teddy. If you trust me."

He looked down at his hands. "Cecily, I never believed . . . I mean . . ."

"I need rubies, Teddy."

It took him a moment to see her direction.

"You mean you want to buy them? From Landis and Oxenburg?"

"You must have heard that Effie's source has walked out on her. There's nothing that says we have to sell our customers new stones. Only good ones."

He tapped his fingers together, his expression wistful. "You always had such a head on you, Cecily. You're running things here since Madame Duvall's had her stroke, I take it."

"Yes, I have some rubies. A bracelet. Seven stones. What do you need them for?"

She shook her head. "Will you sell it? I'll pay you in cash."

The good humor she remembered as part of Teddy danced in his eyes for a moment. "I'd be glad to have it, C. C. To tell you the truth, I'm afraid we've made a couple of not-so-smart purchases lately."

Cecily's intercom lighted.

"Miss Catlow, I've finally reached Mr. Duvall. Will you talk to him?"

"Yes."

Cecily spun her chair away from Teddy and picked up the phone.

"Ben?" She poured her relief in hearing from him into anger. "We've left messages for you halfway around the world. Why haven't you called? Effie's had another stroke."

"Is she—" Whatever he'd been on the verge of asking he choked off. His voice turned bitter. "And you want me to come hold her hand? You do it. You're good at that. Get Kemp to help you."

Her teeth clamped with irritation and she had to speak between them, voice modulated because of Teddy.

"You're a fool, Ben. And you always were." She drew a breath, determined not to let temper get ahead of her. "Effie needs you, Ben. And she needs something else. Joao's shipment is hung up. She doesn't know yet, but she's worried about it. The only way I can see to get it is if you'll fly it out."

"Why the hell should I?"

She lost control. "Because we've got to have it for your damned necklace. Because you promised her that and God knows how much longer she may be around—"

"I'd think you'd feel like an idiot, coming crawling like this. There must be other men who'd do the job for a roll in the sheets with you. You could save your pride."

"Damn it, Ben, stop! Do you think I like asking? I know what you think of me."

Her hand pressed the receiver against her head so hard her ear hurt. There was silence on the other end.

"We're talking outside goods," Ben's voice said, the edges harsh. "If they're watching Joao, they'd watch me, too. They'd pick me apart at customs."

"I know. You'd have a passenger." She paused. "Are you willing? If you are, call me back in two hours and I'll have details."

Their briskness now hurt almost more than his insults earlier. There'd been feeling in that. Hurt. Anger. This was cold and uncaring. The knowledge hurt like a great, tearing gash ripping over the surface of their life together, disfiguring everything that had ever been between them.

"There'll be a price," Ben said.

She could hear the taunt, the narrow contempt.

"All right. What?"

"Meet me and we'll talk about it."

Across the miles she could see the bitterness of his eyes, the challenge in them. It made her tremble. Wanting him. Loving him. Stung by her pride for admitting that. Knowing a door had been closed between them that could not be reopened.

"Agreed," she said.

She hung up, wiped tears from her face with the back of her hand, aware Teddy had heard more than she'd like and yet not caring. As she turned back she saw the sympathy in his eyes. He seemed about to speak. His lips had shaped a word.

Instead, at last, he looked down at his hands. "I can have those rubies to you this afternoon, Cecily. We'll talk about price then."

She could feel the old friendship between them warm the room. Teddy wanted to say something comforting, but he couldn't quite, because of the past.

She nodded, said good-bye, and then, alone at her desk with its amethyst paperweight, dissolved in despair. She had gotten the rubies for Prince Karim. She was holding Duvall together. Except now, when his hate for her matched her love for him, which she could not admit, she would have to face Ben.

FORTY

"GODDAMN IT, THIS IS AN EXPERIMENT. AND THE SCHEDULE'S important. Can't you understand?"

Ben waved a sheaf of papers and clippings about TRINA beneath the nose of the Recife customs agent, wondering if he'd buy the story.

"Boots." The customs agent pointed.

"Oh, bloody Christ!" Ben sat down on a chair in the tiny cubicle he'd been ushered to and began to haul them off.

Was this a fluke? he wondered. It had been years since he's undergone a search like this. Could it be that every airport in this bloody country was watching for the least connection with Joao? Or had the surname Duvall on his own passport alerted someone along the line? That would mean they'd been expecting him— and that Cecily had better have one good plan.

He steeled himself against her name and watched, fuming, a
the heels were pried off his boots. So they thought he'd try tha
old trick. The customs man's assistant threw the heels aside wit
clear disgust. They were solid, not hollowed out. No hidde
diamonds.

Christ, how *was* Cecily expecting to get them through? Sh
hadn't told him that much, only what time to be here and tha
he'd have passengers.

To hell with it. They wouldn't nail him for smuggling, and h
didn't care what happened. He was here for Effie, not fo
Cecily. He figured he owed Effie something. He'd grown u
learning to think like Effie. If he'd been toughened and mad
quick and shrewd, it was by her rearing. After all these years h
couldn't hate her as much over Marguerite, and anyway, the ol
autocrat was probably dying. He'd let her go in peace. The scor
would be even between them. He remembered how she'd chuck
led with him when he was a boy . . . those damned suga
cookies she used to make. He thought she knew he remembered
This would show her he did. Everything would be square.

"Spread your legs."

The customs agent's heavily accented English intruded o
him.

Great. They were going to do a body search. Brazilian cus
toms had always seemed like a remnant of the gestapo anyway
in his book. He submitted.

Five minutes later he was out of the cubicle, watching as th
customs assistant, still determined, jabbed into the middle of hi
disassembled heel with a long stiletto. Ben felt foolish in hi
socks and annoyed by the predicament.

"Hey! You the American? You the one with a private jet?"
voice vaguely familiar called through the general crunch of th
customs area.

Ben turned. His eyes flared. But then, he realized as h
swiftly controlled any other expression, every man around hir
was now gaping, too. For here came April in a circus costume
blue silk and sequins topped by a long flowing cape. She wa
chewing gum and a long-limbed man in a costume similar to he
own accompanied her. He was juggling three plastic rings whil
balancing two softballs on a stand in his teeth, and bystanders, a
he passed, burst into delighted applause. April was juggling, too
three glitzy balls sparkling with clear glass stones.

Only Ben knew he wasn't looking at glass. He was watching

April keep a few million dollars' worth of Joao's diamonds in the air as she walked along chewing.

Christ but it was crazy. Instead of trying for something unnoticed, Cecily had seen to it every eye would be on her courier. With people busy gaping at April and her act, the balls wouldn't get a second glance.

The grin that started across his face, his enjoyment of Cecily's cleverness, gave way to a hot inner burning. Of course Cecily would be good at this. She was nothing but a goddamned schemer. She'd never cared for him—enjoyed him in bed, perhaps, but not much more. She was a master of illusion.

"You the one with a private plane?" repeated April.

"Yeah," Ben snarled, knowing instinctively how this scene must go. "So what?"

"The circus we were with went bust. We need a ride somewhere."

"I don't take passengers."

"Hey, please, mister." April stashed the balls in one hand, catching his arm with the other. Her shoe-button eyes were wide, with no hint of recognition. "We haven't got a thing but the clothes on our backs. When they closed us down, the creditors took everything. But we got the promise of another job. We can pay you when you get us there. Show him the telegram, Ollie."

The man who was with her fished in a pouch at his waist. He held out a telegram saying the Circus Faisal in Gibraltar would welcome them.

"I'm not going to Gibraltar," Ben said shortly.

"Yeah, but you're going the right direction," April persisted. "How about it?"

Ben threw up his hands.

"Am I free to go?" he snapped at the customs agent. He got a nod, and his boots—in pieces—were handed back to him. "I want these fixed," he said, returning them. "You got any glue in this goddamned airport?"

He shot a look over his shoulder to April. "Okay. If you're cleared and ready to leave, I'll take you as far as Freetown."

"Jeez, we're some actors, you know it?" April grinned.

They had flown across Africa and finally to India, touching down for refuelings and once to sleep. Fortunately no one had looked a second time at the glittering balls April stowed in a cardboard box with the other juggling paraphernalia. Now they had cleared the last hurdle, Bangkok.

A pedicab was pulling them through the streets. April had changed into a silk dress bought at the airport. Cecily was trying to stomp out a lot of brushfires, he gathered, coming here to try and find a new source of rubies. Okay by him. If he'd been watched in Brazil, this looked like a less suspicious direction to head than Miami. Besides, having lived here off and on, he'd known the perfect place to meet.

"That fellow who was with you know what you were doing?" Ben asked. He had, at April's instruction, paid the man the price of a plane ticket home plus a little extra and they'd parted.

"Nope," said April brightly. "Ollie's not real fast on his feet. I told him it was a bet you and me had made with some friends. He got to do some real traveling, so he was more than pleased." She thought a moment. "If he'd known these were diamonds I've been toting, he might have gotten nervous—or killed us both. There's no telling what people'll do for a buck, huh?"

The pedicab stopped. Ben led the way to the door of the address he'd given Cecily, a private gambling club.

"Someone waiting for us?" he asked the sleek and dangerously beautiful Thai hostess who met them in an inside hall.

"Welcome, Duvall. Long time no see," she purred, stroking breast-length black hair and looking him up and down. "Yes, a woman's upstairs. The end of the hall. I see you've brought another one. Don't we amuse you?"

"Business," he said shortly. He motioned April ahead of him.

"Hey, this is some place," she said with admiration, looking down at doors curtained with beads and up at an eight-foot gilt mirror as they climbed the stairs.

The upper hall was deserted. It was lined with carved doors, all of them closed. Ben knocked on the farthest one.

"April's here," he announced, loath to call the other name he once had spoken so easily.

There was movement inside. Then he was looking into the soft, shadowed pools of Cecily's eyes. He stepped past her with feelings exploding inside, a desire to punish her.

They had entered a vestibule. While April halted to stare at great framed impressionist murals, Cecily followed him into another room, which held a bed. Her expression was tense. A little angry.

"Is this hotel your idea of a joke, Ben? There's no phone in the room, no sign of a restaurant—"

"It's a whorehouse, Cecily. Seemed appropriate for meeting you. That's what you've become for Effie, isn't it?"

He saw her pale.

"Hey, this place is *exotic*," April said behind them.

Cecily turned. He could see she was trembling and it gave him a strange satisfaction.

"April. Thank God you're all right! I've been sitting here all day thinking I should never have asked you to do this—imagining what could go wrong."

April grinned. "Piece of cake." She took the balls from a camel-skin bag she'd bought in Africa and tossed one to Cecily. "Looks just like junk, huh? Another performance here and in Miami and then they're yours to keep."

Cecily shook her head. She went to the room's only table and held out an envelope.

"No, April. You've stuck your neck out more than enough. Here's a plane ticket back, and cash if you want to stop off in Hong Kong and do some shopping. Miami customs could be tough, and I won't have you taking risks that ought to be mine. If anyone gets caught with these, it's going to be me."

Ben saw April swallow. He could see she was touched. Goddamn Cecily.

"Jeez," April said. "After all you've already done for me? You're the best friend I ever had. If you got caught, it'd hit the papers. With me—"

"No, April. Thanks. Now head for a good hotel. You must be beat."

"But how're you going to . . ." April looked doubtfully at the balls.

"Easy."

Cecily flicked open a parcel on her bed and held up a brightly jeweled elephant, a common tourist purchase, Ben knew, in Sri Lanka.

"I stopped at Margaux's on the way here. For a few hundred dollars I got three of these—with customs receipts to prove it. I have glue. By the time they hit Miami, each elephant will hold a ball in his trunk."

April shook her curls in admiration. "Boy oh boy!"

"Now run on. Don't worry." Cecily crossed the room to embrace her. When they were alone, she turned to face Ben.

"All right," she said in a cold voice. "Now tell me what your price is going to be. I'd like to be on my way."

Ben liked this cat-and-mouse game, this sense of her being in his power as she'd never been before. He took a step toward her.

"Can't you guess, Cecily?"

He saw her pupils contract. He had never seen her soft chin look so square, its dimple a last, lost contradiction to its hardness.

"Forget it," she said in that same freezing voice. "You should have stuck around if you wanted that."

A rage consumed him. He almost wanted to kill her—anything to break her composure, anything to drown out the jeering, mocking possibility that what she said was right.

"Hedging on a business deal?" he drawled. "Effie wouldn't. She bought a business deal with her body each time she married—maybe more."

He began to circle her. In the harsh light of the room her skin had the milky iridescence of an opal. He had hungered—starved—for the feel of that skin against his every night in his dreams.

Her breasts were pitching. She was afraid of him. He wanted to hurt her, to use her and discard her as she'd used him. Still, he didn't touch her.

"The fact is, you're not as much like Effie as you'd like to believe," he sneered. "You're not as hard. You don't have her guts."

Her eyes had become small brown pools of anger. They clashed against his without faltering. Before he could speak again, before he could move toward her, she caught at her dress and stripped it off over her head, standing before him defiant and steely of posture in bra and panties.

The fabric was silky. He could see the dark fields of her nipples, the faint, curly swelling at the front of her panties.

"If you want your payment, you do the rest," she said, head rising with arrogance.

His own swelling need made him curse. He reached her in two swift steps. Lace ripped beneath his fingers as he pushed her back on the bed. His own clothes were an encumbrance.

Without undressing, he wrapped his thighs around her. His feverish hands slid over her back, moving up, then down her vertebrae, pushing her into him, into him. His tongue raped her mouth. It plunged deep into every crevice. And she clung. Her coiling limbs, her quickening breath, no longer transmitted the wild, sweet giving of the past, but a hard and angry hunger that matched his own.

Ben felt alone on the face of the planet, alone with her in his arms. He shoved off his pants. His mouth had moved to her breasts now and she gasped beneath him. He shed his shirt. For a split second, even now, he was loath to hurt her. Then he thrust in brutally and found the way already satin.

He felt lost, savage, caught in a vortex he did not understand. Her warm seas pulled at him, sucking him toward a destination he could not control. His being moved in hers and it was like the battering of sea on boulder, fierce and futile, wild and inevitable.

All the forces of nature were unchained between them as the collisions came. Ben, hurtling with her toward a bitter pleasure, knew he should never have touched her.

The tides that swept the two of them toward each other were dark tides. They would destroy. If ever again he embraced her, they would both be dashed into sand.

FORTY-ONE

"MADAME, YOU MUST RUN THE MEETING!"

Cecily bent anxiously above Effie's bed. It was piled high with pillows. Lace-trimmed pillows. The sight of them had amazed Cecily the first time she'd set foot in Effie's room.

Now she frowned, all her concentration on getting Effie's attention. Yesterday Effie had been up, in her office, asking questions. Today she seemed frail, hardly aware of where she was. It had been like this for a week, this seesawing, ever since Cecily had returned from Bangkok and found the indomitable woman up despite doctor's orders.

"I shall die at my desk," she had rasped.

But her speech was so slurred these days Cecily could scarcely understand the words. When she was up, in her chair, Effie's stout body slumped precariously.

Jenkins stood at the head of the bed, out of Effie's sight.

"She must chair the meeting," he said. His face was grave.

Effie's absence would tell her board how fragile her health was. There was no telling what they might do.

"Please, Madame," coaxed Cecily. "It will only be for twenty minutes—long enough to show them you are still in charge— long enough to tell them we have a new source of rubies, and an entry for the Paris Prize. . . ."

She let her voice trail away. Mention of the Paris Prize had made her think of Ben and the bruising, explosive sex between them that afternoon in Bangkok. Oh, but she'd been a fool!

When she'd lifted her dress she'd wanted to show him she was immune, that she could be as ruthless as Effie and give him no satisfaction. But they had satisfied each other, she thought bitterly. They had parted exhausted. They had drained each other and without a scrap of tenderness, without any pretense of love, had reached for each other like two people feeling the hated, destructive jerk of narcotic cravings.

In the single flash of Ben's eyes as he'd left her, silent, she'd seen he'd loathed his own weakness as much as she had hers. Yet even now a treacherous surge inside warned her that if the two of them ever stood alone again, that same risk would be there.

"Miss Catlow?"

She and Jenkins turned as one as Thida slipped in. They were working very well as a team, the three of them. Cecily knew the scope of Effie's business, knew how things were managed; Jenkins, almost equally informed, consulted with her; Thida kept everything organized.

"Mr. MacDonald is here," her secretary announced now.

Cecily disciplined her thoughts. First Effie. Then Trace.

"Tell him to wait in my office." She turned to Effie as Thida slipped out again. "Please, Effie. You must run the meeting. We have to buy time. . . ."

She looked helplessly at Effie, lost in her lace pillows, and then at Jenkins. She felt guilty over this hounding, and Jenkins's face said he felt the same.

Effie's eyes looked weary beneath their shrouding lids. She struggled to speak.

"Arguments . . . if arguments come . . ."

Cecily understood. She herself must run this meeting of Effie's board. Effie was counting on her. As a last resort Effie would make the effort of coming, but Cecily knew that if she cared for Effie, she could not let that happen.

"All right." She pressed Effie's fingers. Then, avoiding a curious look from Jenkins, she went out to confront Trace MacDonald.

He was waiting in her office, smoking and looking vaguely wary as she entered.

"Thida said you wanted to see me before the meeting," he said in greeting.

"That's right." Cecily, brushing past him, took her place behind her desk and sat back with a brief, coldly pleasant sense of power. "You married my sister to get into this company, Trace. When you were at Lyle and Company, you were dating

Lucy Lyle. Sleeping with her, by the looks of things. I have times and places."

He let out a thin stream of smoke and regarded her blandly. His face beneath his attractively silvered hair betrayed no emotion. "So?"

An anger she'd been holding in check began to mount. He was not even going to deny it—not even going to offer some excuse.

"I'd heard you'd hired someone to ask questions about me," he said. "Frankly, Cecily, I don't see the point. Van looks well, by the way. I saw her just yesterday."

Cecily's temper gave way and she leaned forward, gripping the desk.

"Of course she looks well! She wouldn't be where she is if it weren't for you!"

Trace looked insolently at his watch. "The others will be waiting. Did you expect this discussion of my past to serve some purpose?"

"Yes. And I won't be disappointed." Cecily's voice had grown as hard as diamond. "I'd hoped to find something I could send you to jail for, Trace. I didn't. So I'm serving notice now that I want my sister out of that hospital.

"You were clever, getting control of her, but two can play games about legal competency. Effie's very sick. As a matter of fact, we think—her attorney and I—that she probably wasn't competent when she gave Van that stock in Duvall. Someone outside the family . . . after all these years . . ."

His lip curled. "You'd never make it stick."

"Oh, wouldn't I?" She eyed him with a slow satisfaction. "I'm sure the board would agree—the whole board, if Van's ten percent were to be parceled out among them. You've met them, haven't you, Trace? You've seen their greed."

His bland assurance slipped. "You'd rob your sister of that?"

"I would."

"You're crazy!"

"Van's not, Trace. And I want her out. You can either leave for the airport right now and sign papers for her release before another day passes, *or* you can come to this meeting and watch me carve up Van's holdings right from under you. Which will it be?"

The ash from his cigarette fell on his fingers. Trace jerked.

"Which will it be, Trace?"

"You're bluffing!"

"Try me." Her arms were spread, palms resting lightly on the desk. It gave her a feeling of strength and of hardness akin to Effie's.

Trace's lips had tightened. Deliberately, he dropped the butt of his cigarette into her carpet and ground it out.

"I'll go to London," he said shortly.

She nodded once. His face was seething with rage as he walked out. And now to face the board, thought Cecily.

Two hours later it was over.

"Shall I bring you something?" Thida asked, following after Cecily as she returned to her office.

"No." Cecily kicked off her shoes. Her head was splitting. She took two aspirin from a drawer, stood undecided for a minute, then went through to Effie's office where she poured a glass of watered Scotch with which to wash them down.

The room, with its dais and statues and glittering Byzantine walls, seemed cavernous without Effie. She would have to go to Effie soon. Report. But not yet. Carefully, so as not to increase the hammering in her head, she made her way back to her own desk and with eyes closed tried to relax as images from the board meeting just concluded raced through her brain.

There had been only three members present: Kim; Margaux, whose vote could be counted on to cancel his out; and Martin. The two men were already pressing to carve up Duvall. If Trace had been present, they might have succeeded. Trace would be present next time—Martin had demanded another meeting of the board next month. And Joao might be dead by then. His daughter had called this time to say he was confined to bed, unable to come, so apparently he was weakening even past the point of making phone calls.

Cecily pressed her palms together and blew between them. Something had to be done at once, if Effie's empire was to be kept together for her. She would mend, of course, but it might take time.

Or she could die tomorrow.

Cecily silenced the voice attempting to whisper inside her. Effie wouldn't die. Not yet. She was all that Cecily had. She couldn't die now, when all she had built was collapsing around her. Things must be rebuilt. Her last days must be content.

And Cecily must be responsible for insuring that. She was the one who had come here, drawn Effie back into the fray of competition, disturbed her peace.

Now, for these past weeks, she had held the reins of Duvall.

She had lain awake nights seeking any way out of the problems pressing closer on every side—the loss of their ruby source, the squeezing off of Joao's flow of diamonds.

"Get Joao on the phone for me," she said into her intercom. "Not his daughter—I must talk to Joao. And tell Jenkins I'd like to see him."

It was a wild and daring thought she'd had. Effie might find fault with it when she was up and in control again. Yet to wait might mean to lose a possible out for Duvall.

Cecily had time to finish the contents of the glass in front of her before the call went through. Joao's voice was frail, a whisper barely strong enough to span the miles.

"Joao, don't try to speak," she urged. "Just listen, please. There are problems here—many problems. Duvall may have to move in new directions to survive. Effie wants you to sell her The Farm, Joao. It would be off your hands completely. Do you understand?"

She waited.

"The Farm . . . and what of my mines here? My daughter . . . her inheritance."

He feared Effie would turn her back on those mines, cut him out of Duvall, perhaps. Cecily thought desperately.

"She'll have every penny of it, Joao. Your seat on the board, too. I guarantee it. Sell us The Farm and in one year's time Effie will sign over her interest in your mines. Your daughter's inheritance will be even bigger."

She wondered how she would ever get Effie's agreement to those terms. She'd find a way.

"The cartel . . . I could sell . . ."

"Yes, Joao! You could sell to them. You could be very rich. No more strikes, no more worries."

"Yes. . . ."

A door opened. Jenkins stepped in quietly.

"You'll do it, then? Shall I send the papers?"

"Yes. . . ."

"Bless you, Joao. Effie will be pleased. I hope God will grant you both the health to shake hands over this one day."

She knew that would not come to pass. They were both old and sick. The hint of a lie left a taste on her tongue.

Hanging up, she looked at Jenkins and tried to smile.

"Trace MacDonald went back to the airport before the meeting," he said in surprise.

"That's right. I figured the only way I'd get through that meeting without Effie was to stack the odds in my favor."

Jenkins smiled, but she thought he did not completely believe that explanation. He was an intelligent man, that fact too often hidden by his quietness.

"You wanted to see me?"

"Yes. I need help, Jenkins. I think we've got to fight, and Effie's not able."

He was silent, inviting her to speak. She waved him toward a chair. Then, as he listened, she told him about Joao's parcel of land and the deal just made by phone.

Jenkin's round shoulders seemed to curve further still. He pulled at his lip.

"Am I crazy, Jenkins?"

"To make such arrangements without Madame's agreement? Yes. She'll never consent. She'll never give up those mines."

"She's going to lose the mines, Jenkins. One way or another."

"Yes. I believe so, too."

"Well, then?"

He shook his head. "It's a bold step, Cecily. One like she herself might have made once. But it's going to take money. For the land . . . for financing the *garimpeiros*—those are the free-lance miners who technically would be selling to us. You say there was a geological survey done?"

"Yes. Years ago. The results looked promising."

"Has the board agreed?"

"The board doesn't know. The board *mustn't* know until we've found diamonds. It'll be a card up Effie's sleeve."

"Then back to my first question. How will you talk her into this?"

"I don't have to—yet. Before she got sick this last time, she'd made arrangements with Wesley. I can enter agreements in her name. If she doesn't agree with what I've done when she's herself again, she can fire me—just like when I let Mortimer stay."

They shared a grin.

"Then what do you need from me?"

Cecily rose and rounded her desk to lean against the front of it. She regarded him somberly.

"Effie's plan of relying on family may have broken down, but her idea was right. A mine—or any other operation—has to be in the hands of somebody you can trust. Someone has to be in harge of this new venture, someone who understands it and will ush at it night and day to get it going. Will you do it?''

"Me?''

She could tell he was stunned.

"Cecily, I'm sixty-one! My entire life's been spent behind a esk. Be practical.''

She dimpled. "I am. You're a trained geologist. You've even vorked with Joao. And I seem to remember you telling me how ou'd wanted a life with adventure.''

His mouth was ajar to argue, but suddenly he looked amused.

"Adventure. It would be that all right. The oldest white hunter o ever go up the Amazon.''

"There's another thing, Jenkins. To be really safe, the venture vould have to be owned by a Brazilian citizen. Are you willing o make that change?''

He studied her for a moment.

"I think you're offering me a great deal,'' he said in a kind oice. He stood up. "You're offering me trust—and riches. I'll lo whatever you ask.

"But I have reservations. Not for myself so much. For you. 'm afraid more and more the running of Duvall will be on your houlders. If I go away, who will you have to help you? Who vill you have to advise you?''

Cecily's throat tightened on her answer.

"No one.''

FORTY-TWO

"'T HE OLD GOAT IN RIO'S GOING TO CROAK SOON.''

Harry lounged back in his chair and propped his feet on the corner of Jordan's desk. Jordan's eyes narrowed.

He despised this man, with his smell of hair oil and assumptions of equality. He'd put the bastard in his place someday. But Orlena, bitch that she was, had taught him a few things. He knew what mattered now was consolidating his power. That was why he suffered Harry's arrogance. That was why he endured Lucy's whining and scheduled this meeting to placate both of them just because Trace MacDonald had blown into town.

"I just had the phone call," Harry continued, lighting a short cigar with a cloying scent.

"From whom?" asked Lucy instantly.

The man with his feet on the desk looked absurdly cocky. "A friend."

"Who gives a good shit about somebody dying in Rio?" MacDonald, usually all calm and polish, sounded curt as he paced back and forth. "I want to know what I'm supposed to do about a lunatic wife? She's not only alive, she's going to be released soon. That wasn't part of the deal I made. She was supposed to stay locked up!"

"I didn't make the deal," said Jordan with satisfaction. "You and my mother did."

"Well, you might do something, Jordan!" Lucy's petulance dragged at his nerves.

She looked silly in Orlena's emeralds. They made her face look fat, her eyes too small. Maybe she was too short, Jordan thought, observing how the necklace and heavy earrings seemed to pull her head toward her shoulders. Then again, maybe she simply wasn't as attractive as Orlena had been.

Stupid of her to side with MacDonald. MacDonald had thrown her over for a measly ten percent in Lyle & Co. Now he'd screwed up trying to hang on to an interest in Duvall and was stuck with crazy Vanessa.

Jordan was going to destroy Duvall. At least Harry had sense enough to see that much.

"Trace made his bed. Let him lie in it," Jordan said. "As a matter of fact"—he lounged back, enjoying the thought this was *his* office where the four of them met, *his* desk covered in its entirety in soft white leather—"that's probably all that's needed to send Cousin Vanessa back wherever he wants her."

MacDonald went red with anger and stopped his pacing.

"Sure—and then I'm up against Cecily Catlow!"

"Oh, Christ! I'm sick of hearing about Cecily!" snapped Jordan. "Who cares, when Harry's telling us Duvall's about to lose its source of diamonds?" He paused. "That is what you're telling us happens when the old man dies?"

Harry blew a stream of smoke. "Yep. His heir's his daughter. Single. Sheltered. Never had to make a choice beyond which dress to wear. She'll sell before the body's cold, what with their current troubles."

Jordan tried to make sure his first thought didn't show on his face. But Lucy was interrupting now.

"You're such an ass, Jordan!" She flounced to her feet. "You might give Trace a civil reply! After all, he married Vanessa to help us all out."

Her virtuous sound set his teeth on edge. Orlena had always thrown it up to him how clever Lucy was, but the fact was Lucy could be incredibly stupid.

"He married Vanessa to line his own pockets," Jordan said ruthlessly. "Isn't that right, Trace?"

Now Lucy was livid. "You can't stand for anyone else to do something right! You never could. Well, let me tell you something, Jordan! If it weren't for Trace—and Harry—you wouldn't have a company left to run.

"Every triumph Duvall's had has been a setback for us. They had that show—and we lost customers. They opened their branch in Paris—and now ours is almost in the red. Vanessa was Cecily's weak spot, and Orlena saw it and knew what to do, and Trace agreed. If Cecily hadn't had that to distract her, God knows what else she and that old woman might have accomplished. It bought time for you to make contact with Harry, too, I might point out."

"I'd already made contact with Harry," Jordan said coldly. He'd had the idea a long time ago. Orlena had tried to make him out a fool when he'd suggested it—had said it was too risky. "I told you both the Paris branch would be a disaster, too."

He felt smug. His mother and sister had always wanted to think he was incompetent, but he'd proved otherwise. Look how he played the two of them against each other, and neither one had ever suspected.

"If you're so clever, how come you didn't succeed in cutting off Duvall's source of rubies?" Lucy asked nastily. "I *assume* you saw the photograph of those earrings in this week's *Time*—"

"All right!"

She was always nagging, always arguing. She seemed to have gotten worse with Orlena gone.

"So *that* plan didn't work, Jordan. What are you going to do if this man with the diamonds takes his sweet time dying? What if—"

"I've got ideas!"

He allowed himself a moment of pleasure at how well they were laid.

"Oh?" Fondling her emeralds, Lucy looked at him scornfully. "Let's hear them, then."

What the hell business was it of hers? He was the president of
Lyle & Co.

"We're starting to pick up sales because of the splash we
made with that TV necklace," she droned on relentlessly. "We
need to keep up the momentum. We need to keep up the
visibility. I think we should hire a new designer. Her name is
Pêche. She's the love child of a French count and some Hollywood actress. Perfect for gossip. I think she'd jump at the
chance . . ."

Jordan wished he could shut her up. He wished he could run
his company by himself once and for all.

"This is a magnificent stone—incredible color. I want it set
higher, so it catches the light. And I want it done by tomorrow.
Mortimer. A client's coming in who's partial to emeralds—"

Cecily broke off, halting her midmorning pass through the
workroom.

"My God, are they still working on that spiral bracelet?"

"You're as bad as Madame!" exploded Mortimer, at her heels.
"Things can't be done in a minute."

Her smile was shadowed. "We're having a show. Remember?"

It would not be large, owing to Effie's still delicate health, but
it would be important. It would kick off the Miami–Palm Beach
social season, give everyone cause once again to talk of Duvall.

"You are worse than Madame," amended Mortimer, snatching back the ring she'd criticized and squinting at it. "I see
nothing wrong with this!"

"It is set too low," rasped a voice behind them.

Cecily twisted.

Effie was making her way toward them, and where once she
had sat erect she now leaned heavily against the pillow propped
beside her. A whirring sound accompanied her. She'd been
forced to change to a motorized chair to conserve what strength
remained in her one good hand, but, loath to capitulate completely.
she had had the motor installed on a high-backed, black-lacquered
chinoise chair with traces of gilt. Even now her ambience was
one of flair.

"It requires light." Effie bit the words off.

She must be feeling well today, thought Cecily. Her speech
was almost clear.

"Incite them to speed, Madame. They will not perform for me
as they will for you."

Effie didn't return her smile. She glowered instead.

"I am not in a mood for cleverness. I have seen my paper today. My grandson arrested for brawling in a nightclub—drunk, I am sure! And he has given me nothing from his workshop, nothing but two necklaces conceived long ago. No designs.

"He will kill himself! He will waste his talent. It is all your fault!"

Her mood changed even before her barbs could lodge in Cecily.

"You could win him back," she said with sudden, childlike wheedling. "He could not resist. He would come if you asked. You could do that."

I love you, Effie. Even now, with you doing this to me, I love you, Cecily thought.

"You are wrong, Madame," she said in a calm voice and turned away. She could not tell whether there'd been cunning in Effie's eyes or a childlike hope.

She fled and knew that word defined how she felt about the workroom even apart from this conversation—how she felt when in it, how she longed to leave. Even without mention of his name, this place was filled with Ben. She could see his dark head bent to discuss a design. She could see him at his own table. Sometimes, when the door opened, her heart lurched upward in expectation.

Ben.

She could not clear her mind of him. Only by working incessantly, having no time for other thoughts, could she escape the longing that ate at her.

Not love. Not after all this time. Ben had never loved her.

"Cecily . . ." Jenkins had appeared, coming toward her as she walked unaware. "Thida says to tell you your sister's on the phone—and Mr. Kemp is here."

"Oh . . . thanks."

Her thoughts cleared, and now there was happiness to push aside the longing. She picked up a phone by the door.

"Cecily?" Van's voice bubbled over. "Oh, Cecily! I'm out! It's wonderful! I knew you'd make Trace see how well I've gotten—"

"Is Trace there?" interrupted Cecily.

"Why, no. He's—he's away on business. I thought he must be with you."

"On the way, I'm sure," Cecily lied. She was glad Trace wasn't around. If she had her way, he wouldn't be under the same roof with her sister again, but she supposed it was too soon to raise that subject. "Wesley's with you, though? And the woman I hired?"

"Yes. But really, Cecily! I don't need a nurse—"

"I want you to have somebody with you, Van. Just for a while."

"Are you coming over this weekend?"

"Oh, Van, I thought I'd be able to manage it, but now I can't. There's so much going on here. . . ." She looked back at the workroom. Jenkins had joined Effie and Mortimer and was listening as they argued passionately. "I'll come as soon as I can. Look, I've got to run. I'll call you tonight."

"Okay. Oh, Cecily, it's so good to be free. I *knew* I wouldn't stay locked up with you for my sister!"

Cecily blinked back a tear as she turned down the hallway. Van's confidence in her made her desperate to insure Van would never be hurt again.

At the moment, the number of things needed to guarantee that frightened her. She needed Duvall to be stronger than Lyle & Co., but Effie's illness and the Lyles's involvement with that movie-star necklace had cost Duvall business. Duvall was fairly rotting away with internal problems. Jordan was heading Lyle & Co. now, since Orlena's death, but she had no idea at all how he was going to prove as a competitor.

All she knew of Jordan was perversion and violence. She shuddered, remembering the phone call and that picture. There had been no reason at all behind them. He had not tried to blackmail her. Was he sick? She'd suckered him at that auction over the emeralds, but she had an uncomfortable feeling he'd never prove so careless again. She tried impatiently to push aside the sense of threat that had hung above her since Orlena's death and hurried toward her office to meet Peter.

She couldn't remember seeing Peter's name on her morning's schedule. Perhaps he'd had an appointment with Effie and Effie had forgotten it and Jenkins had tried to cover. Effie did forget things of late. Cecily tried to quell uneasiness. It didn't matter. Effie still was competent to run Duvall.

Peter sprang to his feet as she opened the door.

"Cecily, I won't stay a minute. I have an appointment shortly with Madame Duvall, but I wanted to see you first, see how you were doing . . ."

He had seized her hand with the old youthful eagerness. She didn't withdraw it at once. His touch was warm and familiar and—she admitted it—charmingly hard to resist. There was always something so pleading, so engaging in Peter's eyes.

Peter made her feel guilty. He'd sent her flowers regularly, had called and asked her to dinner a few times only to have her say no. Now here he was asking about her, overlooking her rejection.

"I'm all right, Peter. Thank you."

"You look tired."

"There's a lot of work just now."

He looked sadly at the floor.

"It hit you hard, the divorce."

She hesitated, then nodded.

Her intercom buzzed.

"Miss Catlow, your next appointment is here."

"I'll be free in a minute," she said, and then to Peter, "Was there anything else? Effie isn't quite back to her old self yet, so if there's any problem—"

"No, no. We get along famously. She's a wonderful old dragon—plays the role with class. I love watching her. I wanted to see her today about a pendant, a promotional gimmick, actually. Everyone who signs up for a hide-away weekend at one of our hotels has a chance to win—you know the idea."

He reached into his pocket.

"I . . . just had a little present for you, Cecily. To cheer you up a little. For old times' sake."

He offered it on one fingertip, a narrow gold bracelet like the one that had been his first present to her.

Cecily's breath caught. Her eyes met his for a second. His still shyly boyish gaze held a hesitant ardor. Sweet memories from the past. And Ben was gone.

He pressed the bracelet into her hand, his fingers just brushing hers.

"I haven't given up on asking you to dinner yet," he said.

No! Peter had abandoned her when she needed him. Yet he seemed different now, and his words fanned the loneliness inside her into an ache. Before she could sort through her rush of feelings, he was gone.

That afternoon there was a new name on her schedule. S. Chantharangsy. "Prospective customer," Thida had noted, and this was the afternoon set aside for them. Nevertheless, the name bothered Cecily. It didn't sound familiar, and Effie was so insistent on her reading the social columns that Cecily saw names in her sleep.

When the door opened, she looked up to see a rather tall man with Asian features. Thai, she guessed. He was young, maybe thirty, and smoothly good-looking. His pocket held several cellophane-wrapped cigars.

"Miss Catlow? How nice of you to see me." He extended his hand.

"Sit down, Mr. Chantharangsy. I see you're interested in seeing something from our collection. Did you have anything particular in mind?"

He sat down, dragging his chair so close to her desk that Cecily frowned. With a measured and strangely confident smile, he reached for a cigar.

"I'm interested in doing business with Duvall—but not in buying."

His wrists moved deftly, twisting in two the now unwrapped tobacco. On the edge of Cecily's desk, bright lumps of red spilled out amid brown bits. Caught unaware, she nonetheless fought off the impulse to suck in her breath. She tried to keep her face impassive, as Effie would.

"You've lost your source of rubies," the man before her said bluntly. "I can supply them."

Now, at last, she allowed herself to scrutinize the small pile before her. The color was good. Only one pink stone, and it was of a size to make it choice despite its lightness.

"Madame Duvall does not buy stones," she said slowly, sitting back. "Duvall is a family business."

Chantharangsy opened a second cigar. It held only five stones, but the diameter of one of them was that of a gumball.

"I'm quite willing to become a part of Madame's family," he said with a smoothness that shocked her. His gaze flickered over her with no hint of apology. "You are without a husband, I understand."

Cecily felt herself stiffening. An outrage out of all proportion knotted inside her. She felt defiled by his casual words—defiled that after Ben anyone could suppose—

"I am not of Madame's family. And I am not for trade."

She swept his rubies back toward him so that some of them almost fell. Chantharangsy reached for his last cigar, and as she watched, hypnotized in spite of herself, he put it in his mouth and lighted it.

"Terms can be discussed later," he said. "I wish to show my

stones to Madame Duvall. You cannot afford to throw me out without permitting me. You were in my city recently, but you failed to reach an agreement with anyone regarding the stones you need. My family has owned the mines these stones came from for three generations. They are legal goods. Here. Look at the papers. Look at what I can supply. Here are mining reports.''

Without wanting to, Cecily took the papers tossed toward her. Not one word of what this stranger said could she dispute, and the knowledge rankled.

''I'll speak to Madame Duvall,'' she said in a voice of ice. ''Give me a stone to show.''

He dropped one the size of a pea into her hand. She passed through into Effie's office. The knot in her stomach persisted. A pressure she tried to ignore seemed to follow her, pushing and threatening. Effie wasn't in sight.

She moved on to the outer office.

''Jenkins, get Margaux. Tell her I need to find out everything I can about Chantharangsy Mining out of Bangkok. Where the hell's Effie?''

''Resting . . .''

She was out of the door before his word was complete. Reaching Effie's bedroom, she found it in darkness, the draperies drawn.

''Madame . . .'' She waved away an objecting nurse, always in attendance now. Effie lay on her pillows. ''Madame, forgive the disturbance, but a man is here about rubies. He owns mines. The stones look good. He wants to talk to you about supplying them.''

Effie's eyes had opened with effort. She listened.

''Rubies,'' she repeated. ''Why should I talk about rubies? Harry supplies them.''

A chill climbed Cecily's spine. Now she knew Effie couldn't see Chantharangsy.

''Harry left you, Madame,'' she said, fighting back her own dismay. ''Don't you remember? We need a new source. . . .''

Slowly, carefully, she went over details. She described the Thai's arrival with his cigars, the main facts of his mining reports, his desire to be part of Duvall.

''Do you want to consider, or shall I send him away?'' she asked.

Effie seemed to study the air.

''I am tired,'' she said at last, turning her head away. ''You decide.''

There was no recourse. Though a protest lodged in her throat, Cecily stood mute, then turned away. Haunted by a reality she could not avoid, she retraced her steps down the hall to Effie's office.

She stood in it, trying to breathe in vestiges of its occupant's strength. Chantharangsy wanted to join Effie's family. That was out of the question. Yet they needed stones badly. And she herself was going to have to make the decisions—on quality, among other things, and without a test set. Effie, in one of the fits of possessiveness that seemed to come over her lately, had locked them all up only yesterday.

Cecily touched a button on the intercom.

"Raoul. I am in Madame's office. Send me a pigeon."

She set the motor in motion, opening the draperies. Light flooded the room. Deliberately she emptied her mind of everything but this, of everything but survival. By the time a guard appeared with a bird struggling under his arm, she had placed a square of plain white paper on the front of the desk.

"Cut," she said, steeling herself.

She remembered the horror she'd felt the one and only time she'd seen this done. How long ago that seemed! Plaintive shrieks and the beat of a wing filled the room as the pigeon's breast was slit. Gouts of bright red fell on the paper.

Cecily shoved Chantharangsy's ruby between them. Not perfect pigeon's blood, but very good.

The guard took away the dying pigeon. Alone, she sat down on the dais as she had sat her first time with Effie.

In her stomach the knot created by Chantharangsy's blunt bid to join Effie's family was tightening with fear, and yet with strange resolve. Ben was gone and had never loved her anyway. What did alliances matter?

Survival. That was the important thing.

Had Effie been right that business was the only thing worth loving? Worth struggling for?

She could strike a deal for rubies. She could make Duvall invulnerable. She had lost Ben already, was losing Effie, could lose Van, too, unless she was strong enough to protect her.

You decide.

FORTY-THREE

VAN FROWNED BENEATH HER SUNGLASSES, RECROSSING HER LEGS IN their crisp white shorts and watching her sister. It didn't make sense.

Here they lay on the terrace of a lovely resort in Portugal, enjoying sun while the rest of the world was freezing, and Cecily, instead of relaxing, seemed on edge. Oh, she'd smiled a lot since they'd arrived here two days ago—Van from London and Cecily from Miami. The smile seemed strained, though, and her eyes were shadowed. Right now she was staring off with a tense, uncertain look about her face.

"What is it?" Van asked in a low voice.

Cecily stirred. "What? Oh. Nothing. Business."

Van waited.

But she was given no further clue to the nature of Cecily's thoughts. No one ever shared worries with her, Van thought unhappily. They treated her as though she must be kept in cotton batting, as though because her mind had potholes her capacity for empathy must be equally faulty.

"You ought to have some time away from business," Van scolded. "That man you came with—Chantharangsy—you said you have business with—"

"I didn't come with him! I came with Wesley!"

Cecily's interruption was so cross, so explosive, that it made Van swallow. She stared at her sister, puzzled. Why was Cecily so upset?

"I only meant in the cab from the airport," Van amended. "But you *have* had several meetings with him—"

"I didn't intend to have anything interfere with our weekend, Van. He insisted on seeing me here. It's—important."

"I wasn't complaining. Only . . . maybe you're working too hard. You're not yourself." Van bit her lip. "You know what I think's the matter?" she asked in a burst of bravery. "I think you're unhappy. I think you're still in love with Ben!"

"Don't, Van!"

Cecily's voice held a tremor despite its warning. Van persisted.

"He's in love with you. I can tell when he comes to visit me.

327

He doesn't joke like he used to. He tightens up if I say your name. And Wesley says he's drinking a lot. Can't you give it another try, Cecily?"

"Damn it, stop!"

Cecily swung her legs from the lounge chair. A door closed behind them and Wesley came out of a bungalow, but Cecily halted neither words nor movement.

"I'm not responsible for what Ben does! I can't carry the world on my shoulders!" She snatched up a blue cotton jacket that matched her shorts. "I'm going for a walk."

She stalked toward the shore.

"Van? Is something the matter?"

Wesley's tentative question made Van's frustration spill into anger. She flounced to her feet.

"Only that Cecily's stubborn and pigheaded!"

She shoved a chair aside and began to walk rapidly back toward the bungalows, past Wesley, who reversed directions.

"What do you mean, she's stubborn?" He sounded bewildered.

"I mean I tried to talk to her about her and Ben—but of course she wouldn't listen! Why listen to Van when her brain's been fried by all those shock treatments?"

She glimpsed Wesley's face as he caught up with her and it was stricken.

"No, Van! That's not fair—not to either of you. She didn't listen because it hurt too much. You shouldn't have brought it up."

When she reached the whitewashed bungalow she shared with Cecily, Van shoved the door open. Indignant tears bit at her eyes. Sometimes to get through to people you had to hurt them a little, and that's what she'd done with Cecily—tried, anyway.

Couldn't Wesley understand that? Couldn't anyone see that Cecily was afraid sometimes? Unsure sometimes? She just hid it, that was all.

"Yes, I should have, Wesley! *You* should have! Why haven't you tried to talk to her? Oh, of course she's smart and—and strong—but don't you suppose she can make a mistake just like anyone else?"

Wesley frowned. Van sensed an argument brewing. Suddenly she had an awkward thought, an embarrassing one that could explain all too well why Wesley hadn't done those things—that could explain why he was here now with Cecily without good reason.

"Wesley . . ." His name squashed out in a whisper. She

could feel herself staring at him. "Are you and Cecily lovers? Is *that* why? I mean . . . it's okay if you are. I just didn't . . ."

An incredible look came over Wesley's face.

"*Damn* it, Van! Are you blind?" He howled as though he'd been injured. "Of course I'm not Cecily's lover! How could I be when I'm in love with you?"

Van fell back a step. She thought for a minute she hadn't heard it right. Then she saw the set, accusing, hurt look of his mouth and knew.

She looked at Wesley, sturdy yet gentle, shy yet unfailingly good. Knowledge flashed in her. About her and Trace. About the mistakes she'd made. She felt sad and weary and endlessly bleak as she faced the future.

"I . . . wish you'd said that a long time ago," she said with difficulty. "I always thought . . . you were just being nice to me because of Cecily."

She knew the fault was hers, not his. She tried to turn, but Wesley had caught uncertainly at her cheek and was turning her back.

"Van—you don't love him, do you?"

She shook her head, squeezing back shame that the knowledge had come so late, and that she'd known for a long time, maybe always, Trace didn't love her.

Before she could keep her voice from breaking, before she could tell him to go and leave her alone with the knowledge of her own stupidity, Wesley was kissing her. And it wasn't like the other time, or the times with Trace. Wesley's mouth had grown hard without losing its gentleness. It parted hers, seeking something from her which she gave willingly.

She could feel Wesley's warmth. It had always been there, she realized, but now it was made incarnate in the hardness of his arms, the breadth of his chest. The change between the two of them confused her, yet she was swept along, made certain, by the startling, deepening floods of pleasure unlocked by Wesley's lips.

Other feelings began to stir in her. Slowly, instinctively, Van began to recognize what they were.

"Wesley." She leaned back from him slightly. Her brain felt swirly, like when she'd been on medicine. "I want you to take me to bed," she said.

His own eyes looked unfocused, then stunned. "No!"

He thought she would splinter. He thought she couldn't be whole.

"Yes!" she said fiercely.

"Van . . . you've got to trust me. . . ."

She pressed forward, raising her mouth to his, and Wesley groaned.

This time, as he kissed her, he fastened them together down their entire length. His lips moved to her neck, stirring a faint alarm in Van at their intensity. His hands moved toward her waist. Suddenly he thrust them apart.

"No, Van! I'm damned if I'll lose you again by rushing things!" His voice was strained.

"But—"

"Don't argue," he said, catching her hand and kissing it. "For God's sake, Van, don't argue!"

FORTY-FOUR

FOR THE LAST TIME IN HER LIFE SHE WAS BACK IN PARIS. PERHAPS she would die here. Effie looked at the hall around her. Large. Too modern for her taste. Filled with press.

"Are you all right, Madame?"

She heard Cecily's voice before she saw her, a vision in sheer, long georgette patterned like leopard's skin. It made the girl's brown eyes seem larger. Darker, too. Her hand squeezed Effie's.

"I am hot. Ben has gone to get me champagne."

Effie often heard people before she saw them these days. Sometimes they seemed to waken her from a dream, though she knew she wasn't dreaming. Inconsiderate of them to steal up on her that way. She must bark at them. The trip on a huge jet plane with meals and movies had been long. That was yesterday, of course, but she was tired. She would feel better after champagne. She would feel better when she knew she had won the Paris Prize. They had tried to talk her out of making this trip, but she would not be cheated of her moment of glory.

"My old friend!" cackled a woman she could not remember. "Ah, but you are elegant!"

Effie grunted. She was old. Crippled. It was stupid to put on a dress. And yet she had a reputation to maintain, so she had worn the one with black jet beads and around her neck a creation of hers not seen for forty years, a great golden dragon. Its eyes were rubies. It had been photographed a hundred times since her arrival. Effie grinned to herself.

Duvall. The name still brought people scrambling, hoping for a glimpse of her, a hint of scandal.

William Lyle's concern was not even represented here tonight. Their entry had not made the finals.

"You okay, Effie?"

Now Ben was kneeling on the other side of her. She looked at him slowly. He should be little more than a boy, yet he had grown older.

"Where is my champagne?"

He looked down guiltily, then exchanged a glance with Cecily that seemed almost accidental.

"Their champagne's piss poor, Effie. Not worth drinking. But they've got some excellent Vichy water. I'm having that sent over."

A moisture came into Cecily's eyes that puzzled Effie. The girl turned her head.

Ben's eyes, as they rested on Cecily's gleaming brown hair, grew momentarily softer. They had seemed so angry of late.

Ah, yes. Now Effie remembered. There had been some difference between Ben and Cecily. It had not turned out between them as she had expected. Just like her panthers, they had not bred.

Disappointments, Effie thought. Perhaps they were the price one paid for mistakes. Mistakes and pleasures. Both so costly.

"*Mesdames et messieurs . . .*"

Someone was calling the crowd to order. Men with diamond shirt studs. Women in sapphires and emeralds. Perhaps all the glittering trinkets in the world were paid for with disappointments.

The Vichy came. Someone put a glass in her hand.

"Anything you want me to say for you when you get your prize?" Ben asked with a grin.

She chuckled. He was as certain of the prize as she was. Merriment rose in her. What a place she had carved for herself in the world, and all because William Lyle had refused to credit her with a few designs!

Darkness. Images of a bracelet flashed on two giant screens while a model pranced down a runway. A finalist. Effie tried to concentrate, but voices from another darkness were whispering to her.

Her last child. Her daughter. Unplanned. Effie Duvall had borne three children, all of them tedious, all of them bored by her presence and squalling if she disciplined them. She'd needed no other.

Then came Lisette, a child with a mind of her own. Always stealing into her mother's presence with no invitation and no fear of reprimand. Sitting on Effie's desk. Causing chaos at dinner by mimicking her brothers' arguments about which one of them would someday run Duvall.

"I love you, *Mère*, but I won't be fed to the octopus," she'd said in her firm, breezy way.

She, Effie's favorite child, wanted no part of the business. Effie was furious. Effie cut her off.

But Lisette shrugged and made her own money and came back often, her sweet temper as much a part of her as her stubbornness. She became enamored of little planes. Perhaps, if she'd had a better one, one bought by her mother's almost limitless money, she'd still be alive, Effie thought.

She had loved that child. Why did the acknowledgment come only now? Why had her heart not softened?

The golden dragon around Effie's neck felt heavy.

Maybe she had made a mistake with Ben, too. Maybe she should have let him have his head, not punished his unfaithful wife. And maybe she should have spoken things she'd felt. . . .

The announcer's voice was booming now.

"Duvall! For the incredible innovation of Ben Duvall's Möbius strips!"

So they had won. Out of her own blood there had flowed the genius to capture this long coveted prize. Out of her lineage and her empire had come another like her.

Pleasure spread from her like a whirling skirt. Her heart thundered a frenzied vision of her name, her cachet, enduring for centuries. The crowd was going wild.

On the runway a brunette with high color and billowing hair was making her second appearance in the starkly elegant red-into-dark-blue creation that would be a standard of design for years to come. Ben bent to kiss Effie's cheek. At nearby tables men rose to bow to her. Effie acknowledged their tribute with a wave of her hand.

"I want champagne now! I do not care how poor it is," she commanded as Ben moved toward the stage.

Cecily sighed. "Yes, Madame," she said reluctantly, and turned to summon a waiter.

Ah, but this one was the best of all, thought Effie. Dearer even than Lisette, for this one obeyed.

Before she could even say so, before she could turn her attention to the public comments her grandson now was making, Effie felt the treacherous, cheating hotness of a river bursting inside her brain.

"Goddamn it, Wesley! How could you let her do such a thing?"

Wesley pushed his glasses back on his nose. "She's dying, Ben. She has a right to die where she wants."

His calm and the unwavering certainty of his words startled Cecily. Wesley had always surprised her a little with the grit that sometimes showed behind his quiet facade. But that he'd been in on this scheme of Effie's before she'd left for Paris, that he'd given legal clout to her demand that in case of illness she be brought home, to her own house, seemed impossible.

"If she'd gone to a hospital there, there might have been a chance!"

Ben looked ravaged as he killed a drink in the sitting room adjoining Effie's bedroom. Out in the hallway, forbidden entrance, one of Effie's panthers again took up a high-pitched, mournful howling and he grimaced.

Thida hurried in.

"Mr. Jenkins is on his way."

Cecily nodded. She had cried herself dry in private, in the brief snatches when she'd pretended to rest.

Oh, Effie, don't die! Or are you ready to?

She could feel her own selfishness. Effie must hate the state of helplessness her body was reaching. She must know at times, and hate, the humiliation of her mental lapses. If Effie lived or if Effie died, Cecily grieved for her—for a spirit slipping away; for a boldness that had challenged anyone to defeat her; for a woman who, though she had spawned both success and descendents, believed herself unlovable.

I love you, Effie. And I think Ben loves you.

She wiped away a trickle of wetness on her cheek.

"Also, Mr. Chantharangsy just called from the airport," continued Thida. "He said with Madame ill he must see you tomorrow and have an answer about the business deal he discussed with you."

Cecily closed her eyes. With Effie gone, Duvall would be in chaos. No one else would offer to be its supplier of rubies. But with Effie gone, what would it matter?

It mattered because without Duvall intact she would have no job.

It mattered because without Duvall she might have no way of freeing Van from Trace MacDonald and keeping her safe.

It mattered because she needed something to live for. As Effie had needed it. And because it was wrong to think of all that Effie had worked for and fought for coming to naught.

She could feel Ben watching her. Did he guess what the business deal with Chantharangsy might entail? Did he care? He had already accused her of being a whore in Effie's service. Her mouth firmed with pride.

"All right," she said wearily to Thida.

The door to the next room flew open.

"Mr. Duvall, I think you had better come," the doctor said in urgent tones. "You had all better come. She insists on talking."

Effie had regained consciousness, then! Already Cecily was halfway across the room. On the long trip on the hospital plane, in the ambulance, Effie hadn't opened her eyes. Even earlier today, when they had fluttered open, the doctor believed they saw nothing. Now there was hope.

But as she stepped into the darkness of the other room, saw Effie on her pillows, it died stillborn. For an instant she felt so close, so like the woman in the bed, that Cecily knew these shallow breaths that Effie drew would be the last.

Effie lay lost in whiteness, her face as pale as hair and lace-trimmed pillows. She lifted a finger. Even by the dim lamp near her bed the heavy old ruby glowed.

"Effie? What can I do for you?" Ben knelt beside her, taking her useless hand tenderly between his own.

"I have dreamed . . . my genius has come back to me . . . one last visit."

Ben looked agitated. "I don't—"

"Draw!" Her outrush of air was a harsh command.

Ben lurched toward a desk in the room. Effie's eyes, in slow invitation, turned to Cecily. As Ben returned with paper, Cecily ignored the doctor's protest and sat on the opposite edge of Effie's bed, near her, caressing her fingers.

"You draw." Now Effie's meaning was clear and a faint fire burned in her eyes, though her cheeks remained pale.

Ben was looking down at her now and there was agony in his expression.

"Effie, for Christ's sake shut up and rest! We can do this tomorrow."

Their eyes met, and Cecily had a strange sense they were communicating, saying things that could not be said by words, at least by the two of them.

"I am dying. I have seen the Garden of Eden. Jeweled."

Ben's dark head bowed. He pulled up a chair. "Tell me, Effie."

"Like your serpent. We must have your serpent. The Eve Collection. . . ."

Her eyes were burning brighter. Her breathing quickened. "An apple . . . ruby and diamond with one bite out . . . one emerald for a leaf. . . ."

She was straining. Cecily couldn't bear it.

"Please, Effie! Don't!" She felt tears sliding down her cheeks, but Effie ignored her.

"A breast jewel . . . fanning down from a collar to cover one side . . . leaves. And a pubic leaf on a sling belt of diamond. . . . When shown it must be on a dress that's very thin. . ."

Ben's pencil was working rapidly. The creations Effie described took shape on his pad as though she herself were drawing them; as though, for an instant, they shared a single mind.

"Yes," she rasped, the heavy lids sinking across her eyes. "Yes . . . and more apples . . . a serpent bracelet . . . serpent ring . . . platinum. . . ."

There was silence in the room. The folds of skin from which she could still view life parted suddenly.

"I will sign," she commanded suddenly. ". . . Prove they are mine!"

Ben put the pencil in her hand, held the sketches before her. She seemed to hesitate in order to gather strength. Her hand moved slowly. A faint F and E marked the paper. The pencil slipped from her fingers. Her hand fell, too, but as Cecily cried out, thinking Effie's heart had stopped, the gnarled fingers clutched at her own in a burst of strength.

"Promise me you will see this collection finished! Promise me!"

Effie rose from her pillows.

"Yes!" Cecily's word was a plea, a sound of agony. "I promise you, Effie!"

They had no source of rubies, no diamonds since the ones smuggled out. She did not know how she would keep her word. She only knew, fiercely, that she must.

Effie sank back. A small sigh escaped her. With that barest

sound, the woman who had growled and raged and governed slipped from the living.

"Oh, Christ!" choked Ben and stumbled back toward the sitting room. The sketches were crumpled into a wad between his nerveless fingers.

Cecily, stunned, unable to believe Effie was no longer a part of the world they inhabited, sat a moment beside her before following after.

The sitting room was suddenly filled with people: Raoul, with his rifle, standing rigid inside the door; Thida with a notepad in hand; Charlie, come up from below; Mortimer and an elderly stone-setter. Word must have raced through the compound that Madame had revived—or that the doctor had summoned them. Each face was anxious.

Ben was slumped against a table, forearms resting on it. His head was bowed. He had not told them.

"Madame is dead," said Cecily in a tight voice. She saw tears on Mortimer's face.

Raoul let his rifle dip. In the hall the panthers were keening incessantly now, piercing wails of loss, as though they knew.

"I will notify the family," murmured Thida.

And then there was only Raoul left in the room with them. The poor, lost beasts in the hall seemed to echo all the grief in Cecily's heart.

Ben didn't move. She longed to go to him. She knew that at the end, at least, he had loved Effie.

She started toward him but he whirled, face contorted.

"Damn it, Raoul, give me that rifle!" he said crazily, snatching the weapon as he lurched out.

Alarmed, Cecily ran after him. Ben's dark side had always been pulling him to destroy himself. As she reached the door and flung it back, she heard two shots.

With a cry she reached the hall in alarm to see Ben sagging against the wall, staring down at the bodies of Bibi and his mate. He looked at her, his expression one of unspeakable pain. His eyes reached blindly for hers.

"Ben." His name was a thickness in her throat as she moved toward him. "It's all right, Ben."

She caught his arm between her hands and cradled it. His body yielded. For an instant the hard corners of his mouth were softened and he seemed about to speak. His hand came up to hers. Cecily, through grief and loss and the pounding of her own heart, felt the closeness of a chance to speak, a chance for healing.

Then his muscles grew rigid again. He pushed her hand away from him with a stranger's touch. Turning, he stalked into Effie's office. When she entered, he was pouring a drink.

"I'm finished with Duvall. Consider this my notice."

His eyes, as he glanced up, were as flat as onyx. Maybe the chance for connection had been only illusory.

"I . . . see."

His rejection hurt afresh. Even now, hard on the heels of losing Effie. Cecily walked numbly toward the desk.

She had promised Effie there would be another collection; that Duvall would survive. If she was to keep that promise, she must act immediately.

"Get me *Connoisseur*," she said to Thida.

Ben turned to stare at her.

She would mourn Effie later. Right now she must think as Effie would think. If this call didn't work, she would try *Town & Country*.

A light went on and she picked up the phone.

"This is Cecily Catlow. Effie Duvall is dead. If you care to do a retrospective, we'll make samples of her work available to you, including sketches completed just moments before she died."

To her relief the offer was accepted. Another call would not be necessary. She agreed to discuss arrangements the following day and then hung up.

Ben's face was grim with disbelief.

"My God!" he said contemptuously. "You are as hard as she was!"

Defying him, ignoring the pain inside that threatened to bring her down, she threw back her head.

"Yes! I hope so!" She infused the words with a violent pride. "Effie taught me I had to be—you taught me I had to be!" She could not avoid giving the last a twist of bitterness.

Like an angered bull, he started from the room as Wesley entered. Cecily searched for a chair. There was one nearby she had used for a conference with Effie scarcely a week ago. With weakening legs she sat down behind Effie's desk.

"You'd better catch up with Ben, Wesley." She thought she sounded calm. "Decisions will have to be made and he's vice-president of Duvall. We need to know where to reach him."

Her palms were flat on the desk before her. She tried to draw strength from it. Wesley looked at the open door behind him but shook his head.

"No. Beyond his title, Ben has nothing but the ten percent he's always had. It's you who's in charge now, Cecily. I witnessed Effie's will. Except for some cash to the others to prove she wasn't crazy, you're her exclusive heir."

She thought even Effie's desk could not hold her upright. What she was hearing threatened to pull her down. Effie's heir. The head of Duvall. She couldn't speak.

And on the heels of shock came both wonder and fear. That Effie had cared for her—loved her—there could be no doubting. This proof of it, now that no words could pass between them, made her want to cry. Effie had given the thing she'd loved most, had entrusted it to one not even of her blood, and Cecily would cherish that trust. But the others—they would hate her. If she couldn't prove herself as strong as Effie, if she couldn't quickly solve the problems of Duvall, they would destroy it.

"Thank you, Wesley. I'd like to be alone." She feared her voice might break. That she might break.

"Cecily—"

"I'm all right, Wesley. Really."

For a minute after he left she sat erect, behind Effie's desk, on Effie's dais. Then slowly she curled forward to cling to the wood before her.

The only person, except frail Van, who had ever returned her love was dead.

This alone was left.

If Jenkins found diamonds, they might survive.

If Chantharangsy was married into the business, they would have rubies.

Straightening her back, she rose and walked out to find Thida. The girl looked up.

"Harry's ten percent is mine to dispose of now," said Cecily. "It's yours if you're willing to marry Chantharangsy."

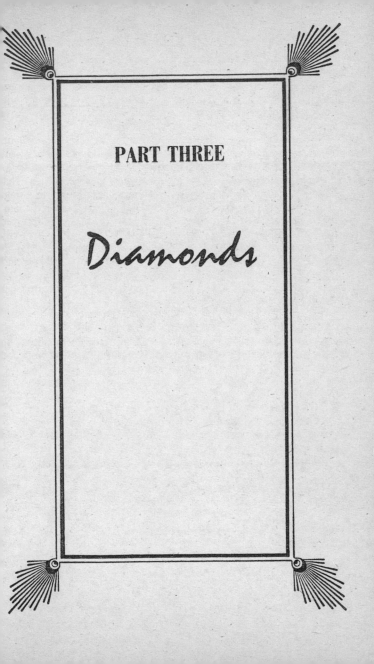

PART THREE

Diamonds

FORTY-FIVE

*T*HEY WERE ALL IN PLACE, TURNED OUT FOR THIS BOARD MEETING AS they had not turned out for Effie's funeral. Thank God Effie had made that provision with Wesley that her will not be read for one month afterward, Cecily thought. It had given her time to assuage her own grief a little. It had made it possible for her to prepare, as best she could, for this confrontation. What it had done to the greed and impatience of Effie's descendants, she hated to speculate.

Not half an hour ago Wesley had read the will. There had been howls of fury. Now, looking down the conference table, she could feel rays of antagonism stabbing into her.

Martin. Kim. Maybe even Margaux, who with her twin and mother must have hoped for more than Effie had left them, for some larger share in Duvall. All of them had reason to want to pull her down. And Trace, damn him, voting Van's stock.

At least Van was present, and safe, and looking uncommonly happy, Cecily reassured herself. Her eyes moved on to Margaux, whose help she hoped she could rely on in a showdown, and to Wesley and Jenkins, both of whom would lend support of the moral sort.

"Shall we begin?" asked Martin, tight-lipped with anger and about to try a coup, she suspected. "We have much to arrange today."

"As soon as the lawyer leaves," Kim said pompously. "And the others who have no business here. There have never been observers at these meetings."

Cecily's open palm smacked the table, making a nearby water glass jump and spill half its contents. She'd made sure she delivered the blow with the hand that now wore Effie's ring.

"They are here because I asked them to be," she said in a warning voice. But she wondered if she could control them. She saw Trace look at Martin and Martin at Kim.

The ruby ring was so heavy it was awkward to wear it— another proof of Effie's determination and knowledge of showmanship. At the table every gaze had touched that stone, aware of the power it signified and eager to challenge that power, she had no doubt.

"Let them stay," Martin said smoothly. "We want witnesses that the disposal of Duvall was done in an orderly manner. I propose we agree today to offer the house's assets now—perhaps to Cartier—with the amount received to be distributed according to our shares in the company. If we cannot agree to that, well then, we are each free to sell our interest."

"Interest in Duvall cannot be sold," said Cecily tightly. "It was granted at the pleasure and on the terms of Madame Duvall."

"Contingent on good behavior," sniffed Kim. "The concept is antiquated. Our shares cannot be withheld from us—or taken from us as they were from Aurelio. I've checked with a lawyer. We have precedent on our side, and common law. Our shares are an inheritance. Nothing more."

Cecily glanced uneasily at Wesley. He was frowning.

"As for me, I want out while the prospect of profit is greatest," Kim continued. "I vote to divide."

"And I," said Martin.

Trace nodded.

Kim shifted his bulk for dramatic effect and spoke again. "Joao wants out. If you insist, he will come and vote in person. Of course, if you do, you may have his life on your conscience."

Conscience! Cecily wondered if any of the three men had one. Uneasiness battered at her. She knew Joao undoubtedly did want out. She looked at Margaux.

The girl's face was filled with uncertainty. "I—I don't know. I thought Duvall would continue. But if Joao wants out . . . if we don't have diamonds *or* rubies . . ."

Her blue eyes pleaded with Cecily to understand. Cecily fought for breath. If Margaux didn't stand with her, she would lose.

"Wait!" Van was on her feet, looking agitated, yet in control of herself. "I don't want Duvall divided up! I know Effie didn't mean it to be. I know that's not what she wanted. I won't do that—not after Effie was so good to me! And—and it *is* my stock, Trace. I vote no!"

There was heavy, thunderous silence.

"Dearest, you're getting carried away by sentiment," said Trace between his teeth. "You're not in a state to make decisions."

"Like hell she's not!"

Wesley's voice erupted with a force that Cecily had never heard. For the first time she was aware of how solidly built he was as he moved to stand beside Van.

Cecily sat paralyzed. She'd not meant for Van to be drawn into conflict. She'd not meant for her to be upset.

Trace gave a murderous glance around the room, pushed his chair aside, and stalked from the room.

"Now that we're finished talking division, there's one more item of business," said Cecily, her voice betraying nothing of her inner tension. She pressed the bell in the carpet. The slim man who'd been waiting for her summons entered. "This is Sam Chantharangsy. He's supplying our rubies now—and he'll have Harry's ten percent."

"You can't do that!" Kim howled.

"Do you want to vote on it?"

Martin had pushed back his chair as though he, too, might walk out in anger.

"He's not from this family!" Kim continued to protest. "*You* are not of this family!"

"I do run this board, though," said Cecily on a note of hardness. "Now. I will hear your reports."

"I didn't think we'd come through this as well as we did," Jenkins confessed as he fixed a drink for them. They were in what had once been Cecily's office, now converted to an upstairs sitting room.

She ran her hand over the arm of the low, nubby couch where she had thrown herself.

"Kim and Martin think they'll win next time around. That's why they insisted on another meeting in two months. If I can't get Van to stay here, I'm going to hire a guard for her. I wish Effie'd never given her that damned stock! Look what it's drawn her into."

Jenkins nodded. "What kind of cash reserve will you have after paying those dividends you promised?" he asked, handing her a glass.

"Not much. I hated doing it, but I hoped it would buy me some time—make some of them rethink what they'd lose if Duvall no longer existed. You think I'm an idiot, don't you?"

"I think you're in good company," Jenkins said with a twinkle.

He settled himself in a chair and Cecily smiled at him.

"How is the oldest Amazon explorer? You look just wonderful, Jenkins. Tan . . . fleshed out a bit . . ."

"I'm finding I don't feel nearly as old as I did." He looked at her shyly. "In fact, I've slept with a woman for the first time in thirty years. Several times. Who knows, perhaps I'll even produce another generation for Duvall.''

She laughed, but his words made her think of Ben and her own missed chances. The feeling of loss that was always with her drowned her. She drank deeply of bitter Scotch.

"And what about you?" Jenkins asked. "You look thin."

"I'm up the creek, Jenkins. And the rest of them are so busy jockeying for power they don't realize how much so. Effie left a lot of bills I didn't know about—insurance for that Ringmaster Necklace, which we may never find a buyer for, in view of what it's worth. And of course we've lost customers since her death. People don't have confidence in me . . . are waiting to see what happens . . . I don't know.''

She sighed. "Let's face it, my background's as an appraiser. I've learned how to run a business and play for power, but I'm not creative. I don't have Effie's imagination. I'm not a designer.''

"There's no chance you and Ben—"

"No. We were never right for each other."

Jenkins shook his head. "Poor Ben. His first wife unfaithful. So many angry years. I'd hoped things might work out—for both of you.''

Cecily stared at him. "His first wife . . . cheated?"

"Why, yes. I thought you knew."

She slumped back in the couch as though from a blow. What Jenkins had told her explained so much. It explained Ben's jealousy of Peter, and why he hadn't believed her there at the airport. Stupid. *Stupid!* If she'd known, she would never have taken that chance, not even for Van. She would never have lied to him.

"Cecily?"

She realized Jenkins had asked her something.

"Tell me about The Farm," she said in a monotone.

He didn't respond. She knew he was studying her, suspecting too much of what she felt, perhaps.

"I'm optimistic." Regardless of what his mind might have been on a second earlier, enthusiasm overcame him now. "I've followed a stream back, found soil that looks promising—I really think it's possible to find a diamond pipe, the same as they have in Africa, instead of relying on panning. As soon as I get back we'll start drilling a core sample.''

"Then what?"

"Then we'll need equipment—crushers, if we're to automate.

Cyclone baths. An X-ray machine. It could wait until we're certain, until we've seen our first ore.''

"But that would mean delays."

"Exactly."

"We can't afford to wait. I need a source of diamonds."

"And the money?"

"Between Duvall and my own savings I'll scrape it up somehow." She rose and walked to calm herself. "I have to. This is my only chance of saving Duvall, isn't it?''

''And if I don't find diamonds?'' Jenkins asked gently.

The sky outside was growing dark. Van turned as the door to her old room opened. She smiled, seeing Wesley, and half ran toward him. His lips caught hers as they embraced. Each time they met it was better. They pressed to each other.

"Van . . .'' He drew back, caressing her hair as he always did with a look of wonder. That expression touched Van in a way she could not explain. It told her how gentle and unselfish Wesley was, and that he was the best of men.

"Van, what's this Cecily tells me about you wanting to go back to London? You're here—you're safe—''

"But if I *don't* go back, there's a chance Trace could say I'd deserted him. He could try to get part of my share of Duvall if he filed for divorce. Couldn't he?''

Wesley looked thwarted. He pushed his glasses up. "It's very unlikely."

"But not completely impossible."

"Well . . . no."

"I won't do that to Cecily."

He caught her face. His hands were warm and large. "For God's sake, Van! Think of yourself. I thought you wanted a divorce. I *love* you!"

He kissed her so fiercely that Van felt dizzy.

"I love you," she whispered.

She anticipated the feel of his hand against her breast. She'd drawn back the first time he'd done it, but now she welcomed the warmth his touch sent flooding into her. It came in a slow arc, spreading pleasure.

"Wesley, let's not stop like the other times. We've got more privacy here than we do when you come to London. And Cecily's talking about sending someone back with me—someone who may not be as nice as the nurse was about just letting me go off with you to see the sights.''

"Oh, Van." He sounded in pain.

He'd been fiddling with her blouse, and now Van gasped to feel his lips against her naked skin. This hadn't happened before. As the first shock passed she felt restless. Wonderful. His mouth touched the tip of her breast and she wanted to groan, but feared he would misunderstand. Driven by an instinct she'd never encountered, she thrust his head against her closer. His kisses trailed quickly down to her waist, her belly.

Abruptly Wesley turned her, drawing her back against him so she could not see him. She could feel his swelling. It pressed her backside. It made her feel strange.

His kisses hadn't ceased. Each one seemed to speak his love. His hands moved more quickly, more erratically than they had before.

"Unfasten your skirt, Van."

His voice was a caress against her ear. Van's heart began to pound. She thought he would push her skirt down now, but instead he merely slid one hand beneath it. It rested on her belly, rested there so long Van thought she would go crazy with unmet need. Then slowly it began to move, stroking lightly down, first outside her panties and then, like a slowly advancing river, beneath them.

Wesley kissed her neck. "Shall I stop?"

She shook her head.

Wesley's fingers parted her. They were gentle. They made her feel suddenly weak. She leaned back against him. All at once her body was contracting of its own accord, contracting, releasing. Wonderful sensations. More wonderful than frightening. Wesley was holding her tightly, whispering in her ear.

She was still faintly bewildered, still in awe as he turned her toward him.

"Next time," he whispered, kissing her happily. "Next time."

"I'm tired of having to grovel for them and you both. I want a bigger cut." Trace MacDonald paced in Jordan's apartment.

Jordan leaned back, torn between a smile and irritation. He rather enjoyed how Orlena's great plan was backfiring.

"Nothing doing. You knew what you were bargaining for," he said.

It was stupid of Lucy to have brought him here. In the first place, Jordan didn't like surprises. In the second, MacDonald ought to see the danger if Cecily Catlow learned they'd been together. Why did the white-haired idiot think Jordan tried to

arrange their meetings in New York? MacDonald was miffed
because he hadn't been able to vote his wife's shares. Big deal.

"I didn't know she'd ever get out," MacDonald snapped.
"That wasn't part of the plan."

"Here, Trace. Have a drink," Lucy soothed.

Jordan wanted to puke. She looked silly fluttering around in
Orlena's emeralds, making cow eyes at a man who didn't care a
fig for her.

"So get her back in the loony bin," said Jordan blandly.
"That's what you're supposed to do. That's the whole idea.
Don't you remember?"

"Stop it, Jordan." Lucy glared at him. "Trace is doing the
best he can. And *you* aren't doing anything! You *said* you'd
deprived Duvall of their rubies, but they got stones for those
earrings!

"As far as I can see, you've accomplished nothing by stealing
Harry Duvall. Now you're just sitting around hoping some old
man will die so Cecily can't get diamonds. That's some plan,
Jordan!"

Jordan looked at her with hate. "I have a plan."

"Oh?" She was sneering at him as Orlena had always done.
"Let's hear hear it, then."

"No."

"Why not?"

He was tired of her constant nagging, tired of her always
butting in, telling him what to do.

"Because I'm president of the goddamned company!" he
howled. "I don't have to ask your approval! Because maybe—
just maybe—I think it's a good idea to keep what I'm doing
secret instead of parading it all over like the two of you apparently want to—coming here together, for Chrisake!"

Lucy's puffy cheeks and piglike eyes were squeezing into a
temper tantrum. No wonder she'd never been able to land a man.

"I'm leaving," said Trace with heat. "I trust Lucy can find a
cab so the spies on every corner don't see us together."

"Now see what you've done!" cried Lucy as the door closed.
"Honestly, Jordan, when will you grow up and learn to discuss
things?

"What you *ought* to do is let Trace out of this stupid marriage.
Let him get a divorce. Let him come back to work for us and
plan an ad campaign. Pêche has made quite a splash with her
designs *and* her romantic parentage—she's practically royal, for
God's sake. You need to be promoting her more. That's the *only*

way you'll be able to crush Cecily. Because frankly, Jordan, I think she's smarter than you!''

Jordan seethed. There she went again, trying to run his business. She thought he was stupid. Just as Orlena had.

Lucy was in his way. She'd been nothing but trouble these past months, preening as though those emeralds she'd wanted so badly gave her some kind of power, cooing about this designer he'd had to hire to keep her quiet.

"Maybe if you'd called instead of just showing up I'd have been more inclined to discuss it," he said hiding his feelings. "Come on. I'll take you home."

"You don't *have* to, Jordan."

For once he enjoyed her crossness. She was such a bitch.

"We'll rethink things," he said. "Maybe discuss this tomorrow."

He picked up his keys and a pair of expensive driving gloves. Lucy, still sulking, whined nonstop the thirty blocks to her high rise. There was underground parking. The security guard on duty did not look up as they walked by.

"Can I look at your telephone book a minute?" asked Jordan as his sister stopped at her door. "I've forgotten the address of a girl I'm supposed to pick up."

"Honestly, Jordan! Why didn't you write it down?"

Lucy shoved the door open. Jordan closed it. He put his foot in front of her and she went sprawling

Jordan was on top of her, catching her heavy collar of emeralds and twisting it tight before she could scream. It seemed appropriate. She'd been so greedy for those emeralds. He could hear her make small choking sounds. Too bad he couldn't see her little pig eyes wide with fear.

And suddenly he knew he *had* to see them. He had to do something else, too. He was getting excited.

The fear in their eyes. That was what he liked. Their silent, helpless acknowledgment that he was the one in control. And because he knew what was going to happen this time, he knew it would be the best time ever. Even with Lucy. Especially with Lucy. Bossy, bitching Lucy who'd always thought she was smarter than him.

His knee was in the small of her back. It took only one hand to control her, cutting off her air. He eased his other hand down toward her breast and whispered in her ear.

"It's a game, Lucy. Like our other games. Women like it.

When you feel like you're choking you'll come and you'll come. You'll see.''

He was long as a pole when he left off diddling her to undo his fly. Her kicking and the flailing of her arms was subsiding. It was taking less strength to control her. He twisted her onto her back, still holding her necklace.

"You've wanted this for a long time, haven't you, Lucy?"

She tried to deny it.

He pulled her necklace tighter. The fear was there on her face.

"Yes you have, Lucy."

He'd forgotten her panties. As he reached to rip them, she tried to scratch him. Jordan butted his knee against her crotch. A whimper. A terrified, gurgling whimper. Her face was growing red now, her eyes bulging out.

This was the game they'd played with Van on the cliff all those years ago. The chain around Van's neck had been flimsy, though. It would have broken. Jordan looked at the three catches holding this one, watched flashes of green, and realized, dimly, it was taking less effort to hold her down.

He shoved into her and felt himself about to lose control. When he finished he'd have to take her necklace, bracelet, ring—make it look like a robbery. He rode her. He battered into her with increasing violence, watching her eyes.

She was in his power! Her life was in his hands.

He came in a frenzy, pouring into her, pissing into whatever woman lay beneath him.

When he'd finished, he couldn't even remember the instant at which she'd died.

FORTY-SIX

CECILY'S STOMACH GROWLED. SHE HADN'T EATEN BREAKFAST. SHE hadn't had time; hadn't wanted to. Every morning she told Hester she wanted her toast well browned and her coffee hot. Every morning the toast was pale and the coffee warm. Today she had simply spared herself frustration

Pressing Effie's desk against her midsection she fought hunger and tried to smile.

"What was it you wanted, Peter?"

She wished she'd said no when he'd called and asked to stop by her office. She almost wished she'd never begun to see him again. But the first time, a month ago, she'd been drowning in loneliness. She had no real friends except April, and April had been out of town.

"To see you," he said with the irresistable smile she had come to know anew. "To see if you'd have dinner tonight."

She shook her head. "I can't tonight. I've got a million things to do here."

No matter that April was coming to have lunch with her, she thought guiltily.

She'd had dinner with Peter twice, then had needed to represent Duvall at a social event and had asked him to accompany her. You're seeing Peter because he's useful. You've become that sort of woman, she accused herself scornfully.

Well, what did it matter? She knew what Peter was. He was spoiled. Weak. Used to buying both things and people. Knowing that, what danger was there in enjoying his companionship? In laughing a little? Besides, Peter was a man of considerable influence in the business community. That might prove handy someday. Cecily shifted in her chair, vaguely ashamed of herself for even thinking it.

Peter came around her desk now, so close it made her uneasy.

"I think you use work to avoid me," he said, his hazel eyes reproaching her. "You did it in New York; you're doing it here."

Cecily looked down. "Peter, that's not true—"

Her phone rang, saving her.

"It's Mr. Landis," said her secretary.

"Teddy, hello." She felt slightly puzzled and slightly wary. At the same time it was nice to hear from someone who once had been—no, even now was—a friend.

"Am I catching you at a bad time, C. C.?"

The old nickname brought a smile to her face. She could picture his rambling red hair.

"No, it's okay. What can I do for you?"

"Well . . ."

His hesitation made her frown.

"It's this way, Cecily. I need a loan. Sales haven't been as good as they should have been this quarter. They'll pick up in a month or two—Christmas coming and all. But I'm in a bind till they do. I was wondering if maybe I could fly down and talk to you about it?"

She cradled her head on her hand. "Oh, Teddy. I can't."

The bills were coming in from Jenkins. Purchases had fallen off since Effie's death. And those dividends to the board . . . She couldn't afford to make an unwise investment. Moreover, Teddy must be in dire straits if he couldn't get the help he needed from a bank.

"I'm sorry," she said.

Poor Teddy. He'd always joked about how he wasn't cut out to succeed his uncle. She wondered just how bad his situation was.

"Sure, I understand," he said with unfailing cheer. "How are things going for you?"

She wondered whether he did understand, or whether he thought this was her retaliation for being fired from his company. They chatted another minute before hanging up.

"Damn," she said.

Peter was watching. She'd all but forgotten him.

"Another invitation to dinner?" he asked lightly.

She stood and stretched. "No. An old friend needing a loan. And I can't help him." She couldn't keep frustration from her voice. "Every cent in this company's tied up. I don't even know how I'll put together the show I promised Effie."

Peter studied her, then caught her hand. "Why don't you give it up?" he asked. "Why don't you marry me?"

It was like the past folding back on her. Her heart was startled to a faster beat.

"Why worry about all this when you didn't even create it?" Peter asked, waving his free hand.

Cecily pulled slowly away from him. "I get the same thing from my work as you do from yours," she replied. "Satisfaction. A sense of accomplishment."

His smile was no longer boyish, but cynical. "Don't be absurd, Cecily. I get satisfaction from the profits—not what leads to them. And those profits are more than enough to give you anything you ever want. I could help out this friend of yours. Give him his loan. What about it?"

Cecily rubbed her hand. It felt bruised somehow. Out of some vague panic, some instinct it wouldn't be right, she answered.

"No."

Beneath his perfectly tailored suit Peter straightened. Surprise swept his face. No, more than surprise. Consuming disbelief. Then anger.

"April's here, Miss Catlow," the intercom interrupted.

Peter's eyes had grown hard. They seemed to dwell on her refusal, not leaving her.

"Very well. I don't know what it is you find fault with in me. God knows I've tried to humor you!" he said stiffly.

"Oh—I didn't know I was interrupting!" April poked her head in.

"It's all right," said Cecily.

So much for my illusions about a useful alliance, she thought as Peter, his look of displeasure heightened by her welcome to April, departed. Cecily moved forward to squeeze April's hands.

"My God, am I glad to see *you!*"

April's grin was full of mischief. She looked as though she'd stepped from the pages of a fashion magazine: hemline discreet, suit of expensive silk, only a heavy gold charm bracelet and her eyes irrepressibly her.

"Got a big surprise," she said. "I'm married."

"What? To *him?*"

April nodded delightedly. "Yep. In Monte Carlo. Can you believe it? And we saw his family after, and they were grand. Well, maybe not *warm*, but not nasty, either. And it's you I've got to thank, Cecily, helping me when I bought that hot ring and seeing I got my clothes and my manners spiffed up.

"I told him I wouldn't want a diamond from anywhere but here, so he said pick out what I wanted while I was out today. Only right now I'm hungry."

"So am I. Starving!" Cecily laughed. "April, I'm so happy for you!"

"You don't look like you've been happy about very much," said April bluntly. "Haven't you been sleeping, or what?"

"There's just lots to do."

"Hey, I read about that Lucy Lyle being murdered. Two of them dead in a year! I think it's some kind of sign, you know? The wicked being pun—"

Cecily's telephone interrupted. Cecily caught April's arm, urging her toward the door.

"Let's go on and let it ring!"

But Felice, Raoul's daughter and Cecily's new secretary, looked up as they escaped into the outer office.

"It's Martin," she said, putting the call on hold. "He's in Miami and wants to talk to you this afternoon."

Cecily hesitated. She'd hoped to take the bulk of the afternoon off, just visiting with April. And Martin had voted against her—would again, she suspected. What could he want?

"All right. I suppose I might as well see him at half-past four."

After all, she thought, things couldn't get any worse.

Wesley fingered the lock on his suitcase, unpacked on the bed.

"Van . . . are you sure you want to do this? Maybe I ought to go."

Van came to his side and took his hand. Wesley was always so serious, so concerned. She loved him for that.

"It's our perfect chance, Wesley," she said in a soft voice. "Maybe our only chance. Trace knew you were coming. Not that he was pleased, especially, but you have stayed in the house before. I think he's afraid to make Cecily mad by saying you can't.

"Anyway, I'm sure it's never occurred to him I might . . . *do* anything. And that ex-policewoman—bodyguard—whatever she is that Cecily hired for me was glad enough to have two nights away. She even called Cecily to make sure it would be okay, since you'd be here."

Wesley smiled, but he still looked uncertain. He drew her toward him and kissed her hair tenderly.

"If you're sure it's what you want, Van."

She drew back, hurt by his hesitation, wondering if he was starting to have second thoughts—which she could understand. After all, her mind *wasn't* as perfect as everyone else's, her past hadn't been as normal.

"If it's not what you want, Wesley . . ."

She could see tears come into his eyes. He held her tightly.

"It *is*, Van. You don't know how much I want it! But not if it's not right for you. And not if it might make trouble."

She sighed and settled against him. "There won't be any trouble. Shall I go and put my gown on now?"

He nodded soberly. Van slipped through a door to her own room, where she'd laid out a new gown of rosy-pink silk. There wasn't a robe to go with it. That had seemed right. Less to wonder about taking off. Less to make her feel nervous.

She *was* nervous, but not like she'd been with Trace. She trusted Wesley. She knew he'd be gentle. Since he'd declared his love for her he'd shown her, increasingly, the wonderful sensations his caressing hands could produce. More than that he'd talked, sharing all his ideas and listening to hers the way no one had ever done with her before. She knew how that mattered, too, that closeness. She closed her eyes and prayed.

When she stepped back into his room, her hand a little fluttery on the knob, she found it almost dark. Wesley came toward her shyly wearing a long wine-colored dressing gown. The dimness and the way he looked was the way she'd always thought it should be.

"You look beautiful," he said, and took her hand. "You *are* so beautiful, Van."

It felt like dancing. She seemed to turn into Wesley's arms and then he kissed her.

Through the single layer of her gown the feel of his body was startling, then electrifying. When at last they drew apart, Wesley was smiling.

"I love you," he said tenderly.

She caught his face in answer, returning his lips to her own. This time Wesley's hands moved slowly down, fitting them together. She liked the feel, yet her heart was pounding. What if something went wrong?

"Relax, sweetheart," Wesley said in her ear. "I'll never, ever hurt you."

He eased away and immediately she was hungry for the nearness. Wesley turned her away from him, kissing her neck. Arms wrapped around her, he lifted one fingertip to her breast. His touch was not unfamiliar, nor was the surge of her blood that followed it, yet all seemed different tonight with her so nearly naked and the knowledge that tonight they wouldn't have to stop.

Then Wesley's hand moved down, stroking her stomach, and every movement seemed to tell her he loved her. As it moved lower Van felt trembly, and sharp, small pains pulled at her. It had only been the last time that he'd touched her like this, and she'd felt them then, too.

"Wesley," she whispered, finding speech took incredible effort. "Don't you think it's time we get into bed?" She pressed his hand closer against her.

Wesley laughed softly. "We've got all night, Van. And I like this so much . . . just kissing you . . . looking at you."

He allowed her to slip around in his arms and their lips joined hungrily. She could feel his swelling—a great deal of it—and a little of her initial nervousness returned.

She tried to calm herself. That's how it was *supposed* to be. Then Wesley was moving her out from him, an arm's length away. The back of his free hand began to stroke up and down her body. Now there was no time for thinking. Van's mind could scarcely keep pace with sensations.

"Oh, Wesley—that feels . . . don't stop!"

She gasped the words.

The wonderful male feel of Wesley's hand was swinging out to fill the front of her breasts with tormenting sweetness, moving in almost between her legs.

"Maybe we'd be more comfortable on the bed," he said, reaching back to extinguish the single lamp left on in the room.

Van could scarcely see him now. She felt slightly dizzy. Wesley eased her down beside him. All at once she almost cried out as his moist tongue curled around her unprotected nipple, then moved in widening circles. He had not ripped her gown, not even seemed to touch it, yet this was happening. Van seemed to melt inside, a warm pool spreading out like the circles of Wesley's tongue.

She tried to urge him down on top of her. Somehow Wesley turned her, curling around her and holding her tightly.

"Van . . . Van . . . I've dreamed of holding you like this . . . of going to sleep with you in my arms like this," he whispered.

He was kissing her shoulders and neck. He was easing her gown up toward her waist, exploring her bare flesh. Van, still with that sense of dizziness, wondered when he would remove the gown from her, worried that it might frighten her even though she expected it, but forgot the questions as her body fell captive to a crescendoing, restless pleasure.

Wesley's hand smoothed over her thighs, again and again. Wesley's fingers parted her. They made Van understand she wanted *more*. She longed to turn to him, tell him it was time. But these present sensations were too exquisite—Wesley's fingers stroking back and forth across moist parts of her she hadn't known existed, Wesley's hand caressing her breasts.

Then there was a sudden shove, something breaking through all the pleasant feelings, something frightening. Van jerked, panicked, tried to pull away.

But Wesley was holding her so quietly now, just whispering her name.

"Van . . . Oh, Van . . . I love you so."

Dazed, Van realized that Wesley was inside her. She could feel his love, and a swelling, a stirring. Something wonderful had happened. Wesley was inside her and it wasn't painful, wasn't ugly, wasn't anything to fear.

Her hand reached back to him and she felt the tears on his cheek as he kissed her palm.

"I love you, Wesley!"

He began to move and release was blinding. Where his flesh was caught by hers, Van felt flash after flash of shuddering, freeing completeness.

"I trust your sister is well," said Martin, sitting down without invitation and crossing his legs.

"Yes, thanks." *She'd better be!* thought Cecily.

"Quite surprising, her recovery of health."

"There's nothing wrong with Van that divorce wouldn't cure."

He looked surprised, then shrugged. "I wouldn't know. I don't mix in such matters."

Cecily eyed him dryly, wondering what this was about.

"Why did you want to see me, Martin? I didn't expect to hear from you or Kim until you had your next chance for a power play."

Now she regretted replacing the hard, backless benches on which those who had sought an audience with Effie had been forced to sit. Martin would not have looked so comfortable on one of those benches. He smiled and that slow act made Cecily's heart thump with a sudden uneasiness.

"You don't like games of power? Pity." His aquiline features sharpened with pleasure as he leaned back. "I saw from the beginning the old lady was making a mistake putting you in charge. You haven't the strength to hold us together as she did. I think, very shortly, you are going to see the end of Duvall.

"So if you want emeralds from me, you will have to pay the market rate now—the rate I choose. Otherwise . . ." He shrugged. "I intend to sell on the open market."

"You bastard!"

Cecily pressed fingertips against the glossy surface of the great black desk before her, hiding the agitation that made her want to form fists. Despite all efforts, the question paining her throat burst from her.

"Why, after what Effie did for you, do you want to destroy Duvall?"

"Because I prefer to work for myself than come crawling to this island," he said blandly. "Because I don't care to ask a woman's permission to pee."

"How Latin! Your shares in Duvall were given in exchange for providing stones."

"Ah, but with Madame's will those shares have become ours legally. They no longer can be withdrawn by a wave of a hand. Duvall, of course, has an interest in my mines—but I'm quite confident the others will be glad to receive an appropriate share in my profits. The prospect of regular payments instead of shows and branches in Paris and other nonessentials has great appeal. Or shall we strike a bargain?"

Cecily's jaw clenched. Martin had trapped her. She couldn't afford to pay the rate he'd asked for emeralds, and Duvall, with its other troubles, couldn't survive without them.

"Of course, if you cannot afford to pay me in cash, we could make some other arrangement," Martin said smoothly. "Increase my share to twenty-five percent. We'll control Duvall together. I can manage better than you. I can keep it intact."

Cecily rose and walked toward the window to hide her fear. Effie had trusted her. Effie had believed she would see the Eve Collection presented—a last, and perhaps the only fitting memorial to Effie Duvall.

And already Cecily was losing everything.

No! I won't lose it, Effie!

"You've got a hell of a concept of sharing control, Martin— you getting the lion's share."

He had come up behind her without a sound. "Only five percent more than you. We would be on the same side. Our alliance might prove satisfactory in many ways. You're an attractive woman. Are you interested?"

One finger traced deliberately and brazenly down her arm. Cecily was filled with loathing. She had to buy time. She had to be able to think.

"All right," she said, moistening her lips. "I'll have papers for you before the next meeting."

"All right," he said insolently, enjoying his victory. "You'll have your emeralds then."

As soon as the door closed behind him, Cecily swept her hands across the desk in blind, despairing fury. One arc to the left, one arc to the right, and everything—papers, calendar, amethyst paperweight—was hurled to the floor. Still the rage inside her wasn't abated. She flung the console telephone. This was how she'd wanted to lash out at Martin—at the others who wanted to see Duvall destroyed—but her hands were tied.

Had Effie ever gambled, buying time with no thought of how to use it as she had just now?

Of course she had.

Cecily's small fists curled with determination.

Stooping to the carpet, she retrieved the telephone.

"Charlie," she said sharply, "bring back those damned benches!"

FORTY-SEVEN

"IF YOU'D LET ME KNOW YOU WERE COMING, I'D HAVE PLANNED A wonderful breakfast for you—a brunch!" Van fretted, drawing Ben into the small informal sitting room that was her favorite place. "But I'm glad you're here, anyway!"

Ben ducked his head to avoid a hanging basket filled with ferns. Plants were everywhere.

"Bloody Christ, Van, you've turned this place into a jungle!"

She laughed. "I know. Some cushions even got mildew from all the humidity and had to be thrown out. Trace was furious! But it makes me think of Effie's—and it makes it seem sunnier. I don't much like London

"Oh, good. Here's some coffee, anyway, and some sweet rolls."

She paused while Trace's butler set a tray on a Queen Anne coffee table and gave her a glinty look. Van didn't like him, either. Sometimes when she couldn't stop herself, she thought he'd make a perfect ward attendant in some nasty state hospital. Now she smiled sweetly. It was such fun knowing she was the boss and not he.

"You look awful," she said to Ben as she poured him some coffee. "Were you flying all night?"

"No. Got in late."

He gave a smile but it didn't have his old sparkle. Van wished she could take him and shake him and tell him whatever had happened between him and Cecily could be worked out. Only being with Wesley had made her see how private things were between a man and a woman.

Ben sat down, stretching out his long legs. It was only ten in the morning, and Van, still wearing a long ruffled dressing gown of polished cotton, stuffed her hands in the pockets and looked down at him, delight bubbling out of her.

"Guess what?" she said. "I'm pregnant."

Except for Cecily, and maybe April, there was no one else with whom she'd rather share her secret. It was fun, too, knowing the best of it was yet to come.

"Oh?" said Ben. He looked a little surprised. Stunned, actually. "Is Trace pleased?"

Van grinned, anticipating his reaction. "Trace doesn't know. It isn't his baby. It's Wesley's."

Ben's coffee spilled as the cup he'd been lifting toward his lips slipped back against its saucer.

"Wesley *Bell's?*"

She nodded, breaking into a merry laugh at his expression.

"You mean you . . . Van, are you serious?"

Van dropped onto a stool nearby him and hugged her knees. "Yes, and he's wonderful, Ben! Not just as a lover—I mean, not just physically—"

"Christ, you *are* serious!" Ben thrust his cup aside, leaning back and staring at her with dark, sober eyes as though in shock. "Wesley. For how long? And what the hell are you doing still here?"

Van could hear his concern. She reached forward and pressed his hand. "It's all right. Really. I'm so happy about it, Ben! It's proof to me I've overcome so many things, and that Wesley and I can have a life together—a *normal* life.

"I'm going to divorce Trace, of course. I've known for a long time I would. But I—well, Cecily's had so much to deal with, losing Effie and trying to see Duvall's not broken up. I didn't want to add to her worries. And you know she would worry."

"I think you ought to think of yourself." His words reminded her of Wesley's, months ago. "Goddamn it, do what you want. Cecily's made of steel."

She could see the unhappy twist of his mouth.

"That's not true. You know it isn't," she said softly. "That's how she seems sometimes, not how she really is. I remember when we were children she could be such a terror, hitting and biting, but only because she was afraid—only because she had to defend herself against somebody bigger, like Lucy or Jordan. . . ."

Van stopped and shook her head. "Anyway, the doctor just confirmed this yesterday. So I've got time. And as to how long Wesley and I have known we cared for each other, it's been for a long time. This isn't just a whim."

Ben gave a teasing, one-sided smile. "Knowing the two of you, I didn't figure it was. But look, Van. You'd better clear out of this place. I don't trust Trace worth a damn. And where's that guard you were complaining Cecily had hired for you?"

Van felt faintly embarrassed. "I made her take the morning off. Trace was going to be out anyway. Oh, Ben, can't you understand? I've had somebody watching me all my *life!* What can a few hours here and there hurt when I'm here in a house full of servants? She's always here when Trace is—and he's not here very often. She sleeps in the room next to mine, and you can believe I leave my door open—just in case he tries anything. I just . . . I just like being on my own sometimes."

Before he could answer, the door to the sitting room opened. Trace stood there for a moment and Van could tell he wasn't pleased about seeing Ben. He resented it whenever anyone who knew Cecily came to see her.

"I don't remember hearing you were expected, Ben," he said, an edge perceptible in his voice's habitual smoothness as he came into the room.

"I like the unexpected," Ben said acidly.

A muscle in Trace's neck knotted. Van knew it was a sign he was displeased. It rather amused her.

"I think it's reasonable to know who's going to call at my own house," insisted Trace. "After all, my wife isn't always up to com—"

"It's her house, too," Ben snarled, eyes crackling. "And I used to be her brother-in-law. I'll stop by to see her whenever I damned well please!"

Trace was stiff for a minute, then shrugged. Ben got to his feet.

"I'll be on my way, Van. Hate to intrude on your domestic routine."

He bent to peck her on the cheek. "Be careful," he said in a low voice.

She nodded, understanding his meaning. The pleasant little room seemed dull when he'd left it. She wished Trace would go away, too. He was studying her through narrowed eyes.

"You were rude," Van said, breaking the silence. She'd never said anything like that to Trace before. She stood to go upstairs and change.

"Rude!" He looked as startled as Ben had when she'd told him she was pregnant. His face grew dark. "You've got some nerve to criticize me after what I put up with for you! Making sure you're never upset, letting you have your way, keeping up the pretense of marriage when we've never even lived like husband and wife!"

Van lifted her chin. Her cheeks felt suddenly warm with a triumph she dared not hope for.

"So leave me," she said.

Jordan hung up gloating. He'd almost deprived Cecily of her emeralds *and* her diamonds. Word was old Joao was about to leave his lovely young daughter an orphan. With any luck at all, Jordan would get a showing of his own from the cartel from that.

And Orlena and Lucy had thought he couldn't do without them! He'd done better on his own. Even Trace MacDonald, who was maybe more suspicious than he should be over Lucy's death, had just come crawling.

Jordan adjusted ruby cuff links and buzzed to summon him.

MacDonald looked impatient, as usual. He had not taken kindly to being left to cool his heels in the outer office.

"Make it fast," said Jordan. "And start by telling me why you came here to see me when we'd agreed—"

"I came because it suited me," MacDonald interrupted. "What's the point in slipping around, anyway, if you're so confident Cecily Catlow's going to fall on her face soon? Or aren't you confident?"

Jordan balanced a pen between his fingers. Should he tell MacDonald how he was tightening the net around Cecily? Should he tell him how, when Joao died, he would pull it closed?

First, though, he was going to see her on her knees. He was going to make her pay for that trick with the emeralds back in New York when she'd made him look like a fool. He was going to deprive her of two people she cared for and see how she suffered.

Women were easy marks for that kind of thing. He remembered how Lucy had bawled when MacDonald had jilted her. He let his eyes close slightly in anticipation. It was something like wondering when a woman was going to start to beg, anticipating the moment when the bonds restraining her grew a little too tight and she got scared.

"The danger's in being *over*confident," he said mildly. "If we move too quickly, there might be rumors we'd had some part in Duvall's demise."

"Bullshit." MacDonald flicked the pen from Jordan's fingers and sat on the edge of his desk, leaning near. "If you have a plan, I want to hear it. If you want me to keep putting up with that frozen blonde I'm married to, you're going to make it worth my while.

"Fifty percent, Jordan. Otherwise, stuff that contract I signed with Orlena. I'll go to Cecily and tell her about the arrangement myself—let her buy me off. Maybe I'll also tell the cops they ought to look a little more closely into Lucy's death and that I saw the two of you leave your place together the night she was murdered. Pity—cabs were hard to find that night."

Jordan hadn't planned on anything like this. He kept his face emotionless. He had to stay on top. He was close—within six months at most—of having it all. The end of Duvall and a chunk of what was left of it as well. He couldn't let that slip through his fingers.

"What's wrong?" he mocked. "Got horns and pretty Vanessa won't let you near?"

But MacDonald was as calm as he himself was trying to be.

"She's let somebody near her. I'd put down money the little broad's pregnant. She's putting on weight in her belly, and for going on two months now she's turned into a tiger. If I say tit, she says tat. I've put up with her all I'm going to—and I'm not going to have some squalling brat on my hands. You either move fast or I'm pulling out."

Jordan made a decision.

"All right. I'll cut you in for a third." He'd still have control. "You deserve that much, I guess." He didn't believe it, but he wanted the kind of help that Trace could give.

"Give it another month," he continued, planning as he went. "Then we can get her off your hands and with no fingers even pointing at you."

MacDonald looked marginally interested for the first time. "How?"

Short on guts, thought Jordan. That meant MacDonald was never going to be a real threat to him.

"The baby," he said, wondering how MacDonald had failed to think of that himself. "We see that she loses the baby."

When Thida looked around the house in Bangkok she felt like a princess. Servants waiting at table—*her* table, silk dresses in the closet, satin sheets on the bed. And sharing the bed with her . . .

She turned and looked at her handsome young husband, lying beside her. He was lean, polished in touch as well as manner. He adorned her with jewels. He ignored the fact her roots were those of another country. He breathed sweet words in her ear. He made her body sing.

"Are you happy we're to have a child?" she whispered.

The news of it had not affected his ardor. They lay even now amid dampened sheets.

"I'm more than happy," he answered, rubbing his hand across her belly. "I'm a man twice blessed—by you and by this."

He kissed her breasts, the still flat house in which their child grew, and the place between her legs.

Thida cried wildly. To think she had come from scrubbing pots and pans to this! To a life like people she had envied. To a man who loved her even though she had come to him to seal a business deal.

"You're a goddess!" he whispered, his fluid hands caressing her. "I want to give you everything, Thida. I want to give you all you deserve. It would be so easy—a few synthetic stones in our next shipment. With you here she'd never suspect—never check! Once, perhaps twice, and we'd be independent for the rest of our lives. We'd no longer have to dance to her tune, nor to anyone's. Think, Thida! We'd be as rich as she is. We could build our own empire, sell stones in New York and Paris. After slaving for her and the old woman, don't you deserve that? Can't you taste it?"

He was holding her close. His electric excitement poured into her. Thida knew it was wrong, what he was suggesting. Cecily had been kind to her. Yet she found herself remembering old resentments. She found the taste her husband spoke of invading her own mouth.

FORTY-EIGHT

"I WANT EMERALDS," SAID THE COUNTESS DI CRICHI, PUTTING HER china teacup aside and folding her hands. She sat very straight on the tapestried sofa in the small room where Cecily, as Effie had done before her, saw clients. "A high collar of them. Very simple. Perhaps five large stones."

She described what she sought with crepe hands under sagging jowls.

Ben would die, thought Cecily. No, this wasn't his kind of jewelry, it was Effie's. For dinosaurs, he'd said once. It relied on size instead of beauty. He wouldn't care who wore it. Why was she thinking of him?

Cecily passed a hand in front of her eyes and hoped the countess didn't notice. It hurt to think of Ben. Yet sometimes a memory of how he had joked about something was all that got her through the day.

"Yes. I'm sure I can find just what you want," she said. "It may take time."

"Time?" The countess arched a painted eyebrow. "At my age one doesn't have time. How long?"

Cecily's tongue was knotted. If she didn't get stones from Martin, if she lost that source, she wouldn't be able to get them at all.

"I want them for my Christmas party," the countess insisted.

"But—"

It already was November.

"Madame—excuse me." Felice, rather out of breath, put her head in. "There's a man from a New York paper on the phone. He says unless you take one minute to speak to him he'll tie up all our lines until you do!"

Now what? wondered Cecily. She didn't feel much like "Madame," though even Mortimer seemed to call her that these days.

"Excuse me, Countess," she said, and rose to move to a corner where a table held a phone and more private conversation was possible. "This is Cecily Catlow," she said briefly.

The caller on the other end identified himself. "I wonder if you'd care to make a statement about Teddy Landis?" he said.

"About Teddy?" Her brain raced. She was completely mystified.

"Perhaps you hadn't heard. He's been arraigned for passing stolen goods."

"I don't believe it!"

"A large yellow diamond. It was stolen ten years ago along with other items—"

"No comment."

She hung up shaking. The square-cut canary Effie had turned down two years ago. She'd almost bet on it. But Teddy didn't have Effie's eye for stones—or her years of experience. Poor Teddy!

"When would I have my necklace?" the countess persisted, indifferent to everything else.

With effort Cecily looked at her. Joao had died two weeks

ago. The board, no doubt taxing itself with the decency of waiting so long, had demanded a meeting tomorrow. She didn't even know if Martin would come. She didn't know for sure what would happen if he did.

"I . . . couldn't say for certain, Countess—"

The countess had a formidable circle of acquaintances. If she took her business elsewhere, others would follow.

"Perhaps I will try Lyle and Company," the countess interrupted, rising. "I understand they may have emeralds soon."

Cecily felt her blood become like ice. *Where was Lyle & Co. going to get emeralds?*

"Or perhaps I will have their Pêche design something for me in tsavorite. She is so innovative in her choice of stones. Have you seen her work in this last issue of *Bazaar*?"

Because one had to smile at a customer, Cecily smiled. How quickly the glory of an award like the Paris Prize was forgotten! How easily loyalty faded.

"I . . . might be able to get you emeralds tomorrow, Countess."

She could not afford to lose this customer!

The countess gave a haughty look. "You have forty-eight hours."

As the door closed Cecily buried her head in her hands.

Damn the magazine spread touting this girl Peche as a fashion find. Damn her great ugly stones. Damn the fact that Effie had never let Ben use them.

If she lost the Countess di Crichi, she could probably not keep Duvall afloat.

Tomorrow.

Everything depended on tomorrow.

"I think I need to see a doctor."

Van pushed back her chair from the table set for luncheon, unable to eat. She felt hot. Light-headed. Awful.

"Nonsense," said Trace, looking up from his paper. "You're perfectly fine. It's only your nerves."

"There's nothing wrong with my nerves!"

Except that you're home, Van thought crossly. He had been for almost a week, expecting to go with her to the board meeting— and to try once again to vote her shares for her, she supposed. Only Cecily had called two days ago while she was resting and left a message that the meeting was canceled.

Van was glad. She didn't feel up to anything today, least of all listening to those people trying to carve up Effie's business.

"I'm going to see the doctor. I think I'm coming down with something." She stood up.

She'd felt so wonderful with the baby growing inside her, so *healthy* until two days ago. Now she was scared. And she couldn't call Wesley because Trace was here, and because Wesley was away anyway on some errand for Cecily.

She looked at the guard-companion Cecily had hired for her.

"Now, don't upset yourself," the woman murmured automatically.

They thought she was just imagining it. They thought that underneath it all she still was crazy!

Trace had risen, too.

"You're not resting, that's all," he said in such falsely agreeable tones it strained her patience. "Take one of these pills the doctor sent you and lie down for a while. If you're not feeling better when you get up, we'll call him then."

Disgusted at this show he was making of caring, when he'd married her only to please Effie and had all but abandoned her since, Van struck away the vial of pills she'd taken all day yesterday and through the night.

"I don't want another pill, damn it! Maybe they're what's wrong with me."

She hadn't meant it as an accusation. Or had she? Her own words seemed to trigger uneasiness, and a stirring memory, too buried to catch, of something unpleasant that had happened on their wedding night.

A devious look had come into Trace's eyes.

"It's you who'd be more likely to try and poison me," he said in a voice like silk. "After all, you're the one who has a lover."

Van's hired companion gasped.

Van was startled. Then she felt sure of herself. He'd thought he'd frighten her. He didn't understand she meant to leave this house and never come back!

She folded her arms in front of her and faced him squarely. "That's right! I do. And he's ten times the man you'll ever be! So find somebody else to pick on, Trace. Find somebody else to treat like they're feeble-minded, because I'm le—"

A sharp, jerking pain in her belly cut off her breath.

Van doubled under the force of it, her hand flying out for the back of a chair. Another pain followed, a storm of them. Van felt something warm begin to spill down her leg.

"No!" she cried in terror at what she knew was happening. "My baby! No!"

"Oh, My God!" gasped the voice of the woman in the room with them.

Trace was smiling.

Van tried to hit him, staggered, caught at another chair.

He'd had something to do with this. Those pills he'd given her . . . And Van knew now she'd never been as smart as other people.

No. Smart was the wrong word. She'd never be as wise.

Too many years locked away . . . and she'd never be able to catch up . . . never be able to hold her own.

Never.

Never.

She heard a shrill wailing scream filling the room around her and knew it was calling her back to a world where there was no pain.

The news about Teddy had made today's papers. Another reporter had hounded Felice all morning and into the afternoon, but Cecily was refusing to talk to him.

"Has my sister arrived yet?" she asked through the intercom.

"No, Madame."

That was strange. She'd expected Van soon after lunch and now it was almost four. The rest of the board was arriving. Perhaps Van's flight had been delayed. She'd have Felice call and check.

"What about Teddy Landis?"

"I've left messages, Madame. Several times, as you instructed."

"All right, then."

She wanted to let Teddy know she was on his side. She knew how it felt to be disgraced.

"Martin," Felice announced briefly.

Cecily drew a breath. She opened a desk drawer and pushed a button, making sure all was ready. So much depended on this next encounter—on this whole afternoon.

"Send him in."

As the door opened she sat higher in the chair she'd chosen to go with Effie's desk. It was huge, towering two feet above her head, lacquered in black with great rearing dragons at arms and headposts—lucky dragons, Cecily told herself as she saw Martin's step lag for a second.

She folded her hands on her desk, Effie's great ruby outward. It was hard to equal Effie's skill as a showman. At least she'd look uncringing in her dress of rich wine red

"I see the benches have returned," Martin said, casting a careless glance at them as he approached. "Do you have the papers?"

His eyes dismissed her as already vanquished. He was sure of himself.

"Of course. May I see the emeralds first?"

He drew two pouches from inside his coat. Still with that look of winning, he emptied them on a white-lined tray before her. One pouch held smaller stones, half a carat and less. The other held eight larger emeralds, five of which might do for the Countess di Crichi though light in color.

They looked clean to the eye. Cecily felt the dampness of relief on the back of her neck.

"Forgive me if I take the precaution of looking at them more closely," she said.

She carried the tray to the nearby infrared inspection light and microscope she'd moved in now that this office was hers. Quickly she looked through the stones. They all were real.

"Do you have the papers?" Martin asked again.

Cecily was grateful he was not restating the threats that had led to this meeting.

"Yes. Do you have the customs receipts?"

He produced them insolently, dropping them on her desk. Cecily could hardly lift her eyes from them. They were as she had anticipated. She was safe.

"This lists only half the stones," she said, looking up at him in feigned surprise. "What about the others?"

He stared at her, then began to smirk. "Surely you're not so naive? I didn't report the others."

She forced a frown, hoping she looked properly stupid. "Are you telling me you smuggled part of these emeralds, Martin?"

"I'm telling you I brought them by the same arrangement I've always brought them in," he said impatiently. "Half and half. As Joao did. As Harry did."

"Joao declared all his stones. And Harry is no longer with us."

"What?"

They both knew it was a lie about Joao. Martin was coloring with anger.

"I don't approve of this, Martin. I won't do business like this."

"Why, you little fool—"

Cecily pressed the button hidden in her desk drawer. "Spare

me the drama, Martin. And get out of here.'' Her voice had grown hard. ''I'm annexing these stones just as Effie annexed a shipment from Aurelio, you may remember. And for the same offense. Treason.

''I've got everything you admitted to me just now on tape. I think the officials of your own government would take a dim view of how you'd been cheating them. For my part, I can say I've only recently come into possession of Effie's books and didn't know this was going on—that perhaps she didn't, either. If I come forward with this evidence, it'll make me—and Duvall—look virtuous. And you'll go to jail.''

He looked as though he might lunge at her.

''Raoul is in the anteroom with his rifle,'' she warned without moving. ''Now get out.''

He wavered, swaying on his feet, eyes flicking from her to the emeralds. ''I'll vote against you. I'll ruin you for this!''

''I think you would have tried to ruin me anyway,'' said Cecily lightly.

Twenty minutes later Felice edged in, looking worried.

''Madame, they keep coming into my office demanding to talk to you. I can't hold them off much longer. They're talking of starting the meeting without you if you don't come out at once.''

Cecily nodded. ''Is Van here?''

''No. The flight was on time, but she wasn't on it.''

That worried Cecily more than all the rest. Maybe Van hadn't felt well because of the baby and hadn't been able to get word to her because of Trace—who didn't know she was pregnant. She *had* to get Van away from there. She'd go over this weekend.

''All right. Get everyone into the board room. I suppose they're downstairs drinking.''

''No. In the hall up here.''

Cecily went out into their midst. Martin was lounging in one corner of the great central landing, Joao's daughter and heir, Ana-Sofia, next to him. Not one face looked friendly, not even that of Chantharangsy, whom she'd brought to power.

''Where's Margaux?'' asked Cecily, apprehension spreading in her.

''Delayed in New York,'' said Kim in tones of mock sorrow. ''A malfunction on the plane, it seems. A pity.''

A plot? No, just happenstance, probably. But she was all alone now, without Van, without Margaux. Jenkins, whose advice and encouragement she'd relied upon, was in another hemisphere. Even Wesley was gone, made privy to the mining

project in Brazil and there to advise Jenkins in some legal
matters, though that was starting to look unimportant if no
diamonds were found.

"There's no reason to go through the farce of a meeting,
anyway," Kim said, sniffing a rose in the buttonhole of his vast
white suit. "Duvall is breaking up. We need only to discuss its
accounts and how and when the money from its division will be
paid out."

"Perhaps Cecily wants to wait until she has Margaux to
support her in some vote," Martin mocked, looking at her in
challenge.

They all were looking at her.

There was no way out. Surely she could count on Chantharangsy's ten percent along with her own thirty-five. Martin,
Kim, and Ana-Sofia could manage only thirty percent. She'd
have control by a thread—she hoped. She pressed Effie's ring.

"Let's get on with it," she said grimly.

She moved, without waiting to see who followed, toward the
board room.

"All right," she said, flashing a look around the table even
before they were all settled. "Since I gather you have little
interest in reports today, I'll hear your grievances."

"There are no grievances," replied Chantharangsy in pleasant
tones. "As Kim expressed a few moments ago, we wish only to
provide for orderly division of the company."

She looked at him in disbelief. One meeting and already he
was with the others! Had that been his intent from the first? Too
late she realized the share she had given to him should have been
Thida's instead. With him on the other side they could bring her
down and he, barely three months with them, would share in the
profits.

Cecily felt betrayal, like a great canker on her lip. Its bite
made her ruthless, determined to win.

"There's no way you can stop us this time," said Martin.
"I'm finished supplying emeralds to Duvall. I'll sell on the open
market. And Ana-Sofia plans to sell Joao's mines to the cartel.
You have nothing left to work with. You have no power."

Cecily leaned forward slightly. "I have designs for an entire
collection Effie did on her deathbed—another source of emeralds.
If you and Ana-Sofia want out, leave. Sell your stones wherever
you choose—but expect no further share in profits from Duvall."

"If Ana-Sofia sells, where will you get your diamonds?"
Martin sneered, covering the hand of the girl beside him, who

looked young in her black mourning dress and dismayed by the war around her.

"Times have changed since Effie's day," Cecily said. "Stones can be bought."

"De Beers would never give Duvall a sight!"

"Perhaps I don't need De Beers." She shot a scathing look at Chantharangsy. "You'll recall I had no trouble getting rubies after Harry turned traitor—large ones, too. Effie left enough stones in her vault to supply this company for a solid year."

"This is wasting time!" snapped Kim. "I vote to divide."

"Yes," said Martin, eyes narrowing. "If this treasure trove of stones exists, we'll have our share of them."

"They're in my name," said Cecily softly. "Several of Effie's investments are in my name. If you choose to disband Duvall, I'll simply start my own firm, taking Effie's customers with me. You'll be the losers."

"A bluff," said Chantharangsy.

"I—I don't know," wavered Ana-Sofia, looking helplessly at Martin. "I know so little about my father's business. I—I want to think it over!"

A sound of irritation escaped his lips. "Ana-Sofia, *querida*, you're not being wise! She's not making sense, and you know you want nothing to do with running a business—"

"I'm sorry!" The girl beside him sounded on the verge of tears. "It is too soon . . . I am too upset . . . and you have these meetings what, quarterly?"

The intercom buzzed.

"Mr. Landis is returning your call," Felice announced.

Ana-Sofia was rising, hurrying from the room. Without her there could be no majority vote for division.

"I think there's no need for reports," said Cecily dryly, and wondered whether any of them would try to dispute the end of the meeting.

"Teddy," she said as she picked up the phone in her office. Then she didn't know what else to say.

His voice, as though he understood the calls she'd placed to him meant friendship, exploded in despair, the fragments of it lodging in her heart

"I didn't do anything, Cecily! Didn't know the damn stone was stolen, I mean. Now I know how you felt."

Cecily gave a bitter laugh. His bluntness seemed to heal some injury to the easy closeness they'd once shared.

"It was my great eye for stones you were supposed to copy Teddy. Not my blunders."

Though his chuckle was strained, he seemed to welcome he teasing. "Looked like a great stone to me, C. C. I was right on that part, at least."

"Courage, Teddy."

"Sure. Thanks."

She hung up to see April watching her from the doorway "Sorry to sneak in on you," she said. "Felice was leaving."

Cecily nodded. "It's okay."

"So, are you still the big cheese or did they gobble you up?"

She laughed at April's question. "A Swiss cheese. I've got a lot of holes in me."

In all, it had been a victory. Emeralds for the di Crich necklace. A few more months to get Duvall back on its feet Why did she suddenly feel so empty?

"Where's Van?" asked April, peering curiously about.

"Didn't come. I'd like to call and make sure she's all right but it's almost midnight there."

"Hey, don't look so worried. Probably just didn't feel up to i with the baby on the way." April came around and took he playfully by the arm. "Come on, now. Drop you off at the condo so you can change and then we'll have a night on the town."

"April, I can't—"

"You can and you're gonna. You need it today. Anyway, you think I made the boat trip out here because I've got some kind crush on Kim the Fatman?"

Worn as she felt, Cecily found herself laughing.

April kept her laughing for the entire trip back to the mainland "I know what we'll do," said the blonde as her cream-colored Lincoln swung into Cecily's parking garage. "After dinner we'l order three splits of champagne and drink them and then I'l teach you to juggle—they'll make great Indian clubs. Hi, Tony,' she added, passing the downstairs guard.

Cecily smiled. Money hadn't managed to change April much and she was glad. Her spirits felt lighter. But as they stepped from the elevator and opened the door on her maid's wringing hands, she knew other crisis waited.

"Oh, Miss Catlow!" wailed Hester. "There's some reporte from *Newsweek* inside. He tricked me—I thought he wa delivering flowers! He keeps asking questions about why you lost a job in New York and some man named Landis."

"Oh, does he," said Cecily, fingering the necklace Ben had made for her. It gave her more courage than Effie's ruby. Suddenly she jerked off a sandal.

"Well, I've had to put up with people I didn't like all day long! It's going to be a pure enjoyment throwing him out!"

FORTY-NINE

CECILY JERKED HERSELF AWAKE AND DIDN'T KNOW WHERE SHE WAS. Then it all came back to her. The reporter she'd chased from her apartment, Ben coming upon her in the tub, his grim news of Van's miscarriage. She remembered standing in the privacy of her room and crying. Now she drew the fringes of her lynx jacket closer around her, even though it was warm in the Peregrine.

"There's coffee in the thermos there beside you," Ben said without letting his eyes stray from the window in front of him and the dark sky outside.

"No thanks."

"Goddamn it, drink it, Cecily! And eat a sandwich. I've brought you this far for Van's sake, but I sure as hell don't want responsibility for you if you faint somewhere."

He bit off the words. Dawn was just beginning, and the darkness still wrapped around the plane seemed to lock the two of them together in solitary confinement. A punishment.

"Do you know where they took Van?" she asked

"Psychiatric ward of a regular hospital, the scrubgirl thought."

She unwrapped a sandwich. Her hand was shaking. "I hire a guard and hear nothing. You get a call from a scrubgirl. I don't understand."

"I told you," he said in hardened tones, as though he found the act of talking to her a chore. "I promised a bonus if ever she called me about any trouble. Of course, I'd meant *when* the trouble was brewing—*before* something happened."

She traced a design on the window, looking away from him. "I should have known when she didn't show up for the board meeting. I should have called." Guilt and grieving suffocated her.

Ben had been more alert to Van's needs than she had. He'd

been more constant. There'd always be so much of him she
didn't understand.

"Why are you helping me get to her?" she asked in a low
voice.

"Apart from liking Van? Sheer economics. If we keep her
from being sent back to the other place, MacDonald may not be
able legally to vote her stock. Believe me, I'm as eager to sell as
the others are, but I want to do it when the return'll be greater—
not now when the water's muddy from losing Joao."

She shrank from his emotionless calculation.

"Where are we?" she asked.

He flicked his eye at screens. They were flying on autopilot,
TRINA II now in its testing stages.

"Coming over into England. Land in about an hour."

They had made the race to Van and they had lost. Cecily
stared dully at a London paper as she sat on the edge of the chair
Ben had shoved under her in a room at The Savoy. A small item
on the international page told of Teddy Landis's suicide.

A gun in his mouth. Poor Teddy. The grief she ought to feel
for him was all but blocked by that she felt for Van.

Why hadn't she made Van leave Trace MacDonald? Then this
wouldn't have happened. But she'd been afraid of pushing Van,
afraid she wasn't strong enough yet to go through the ordeal of a
divorce if Trace contested it. Now she was lost again. And the
last time this happened, the doctors had said if it happened again,
she might never come out. She bent her head and tried to think
of something to do.

Behind her she could hear Ben tipping the bellman. There'd
been no luggage to bring up. She wondered what the hotel
thought of that. She wondered if Ben expected to share this room
with her. She didn't much care.

There were sounds in the room. He brought her a drink,
sliding it onto the table beside her.

"I'm sorry we didn't get here in time," he said, his voice
restrained and distant.

She nodded bleakly. "So am I."

Perhaps she'd hoped Van's mind hadn't given way in a single
snap—that if she reached her soon enough physically, she'd have
the ability to reach her on some other level, too, keeping Van
from madness. Like Ben, she'd hoped they'd find Van still in a
general hospital, not whisked back to the private clinic from

which only Trace could win her release. The hope had been futile.

Steeling herself against the bitter taste, Cecily drank deeply of the liquor Ben had given her. It was strong. It spread through her like white fire, dulling her senses. She shuddered slightly.

What a fool she'd been not to take charge of her sister again the minute Van was free. She'd been too caught up in her own problems—Ben leaving, Effie's illness.

She felt Ben's hand rest on her shoulder, offering hesitant comfort.

"Don't, Ben. Don't touch me, please," she said in a tight voice.

His sympathy hurt too much. She might give way.

He moved toward the window, the unyielding set of his shoulders highlighted by the daylight creeping in through the undercurtains. Studying her in silence, he tossed back the last of his own drink.

"I wish to hell I'd never met you, Cecily."

"Believe me, it's mutual."

"Looking at you now tears my guts out. I see things on your face and I know they're all lies."

Did he think the despair she felt over Van was a lie? Did he think the ache that was hammering at her just because he was in the room with her was a lie?

Too defeated to blink back the tears that blurred her vision, she looked at him

"Whatever you may think of me, I'm not a liar, Ben."

There was doubt on his face, and it didn't fade, but his hand reached down, drawing her to her feet. He crushed her unresisting mouth with his, then half released her.

His spread hand worked restlessly, smoothing through the short silk of her hair. He seemed to seek something in her eyes. But she was too weary to challenge that seeking or hide herself from this man who once had sheltered her.

"Please hold me for a minute," she whispered, her fingers against his shoulders. "Just hold me."

Their eyes seemed locked together.

"That all you want?" he asked, completely motionless.

She shook her head. "No. I want you to make love to me." Her voice caught and she thought how easy it would have been to say those words to Peter, how eagerly he might have complied. "And I hate myself for that!"

All the tears, all the tension inside her were sliding down her face now.

"Not half as much as I hate you for wanting it, too," Ben said.

They melted into each other and it was like the first time, only now there was a gulf between them, a chasm of pain and loneliness that kisses and even the feel of bare skin on bare skin could not span. Without even turning the spread back they held each other, caressing, twining, joining themselves to a remembered beat. Each movement was agony. And beyond the pain was something they couldn't quite reach.

Ben stood in the visiting room of Langhurst Clinic and looked out the window. They weren't going to let him see Van. He knew he should leave. The only problem was he didn't know where to go.

Not back to The Savoy, he thought, so restless he couldn't stand still. He thought he might go crazy himself if he saw Cecily again. He still didn't know what had gotten into him yesterday, sleeping with her. There hadn't been anger in it like there'd been in Rio, either. There'd been need. It was like black magic, damn it. Like flirting with something he couldn't control, going higher and faster the way he did in the Peregrine. He'd wanted to comfort her and feel her soft lips on his even if she'd slept with a hundred other men and everything she'd ever said was lies.

They'd both been exhausted, had fallen asleep after just that single time, and he'd slept till two in the morning. Then he'd gone to bars, a private gambling club that never closed, a hole in the wall that served breakfast.

He'd come here knowing Van would be the same yet hoping, anyway. He'd needed something to fill the empty time that had weighed on him even before this had happened.

He'd waylaid a nurse and flirted, then threatened. No visitors. Not even family. Not even during visiting hours. The patient was . . .

Ben knew what she was. Strapped down. Drugged into oblivion. Christ. Why did it have to happen to someone like Van, who just wanted to lead an ordinary life somewhere and have some kids and a husband like Wesley?

Damn it, Effie, you ruined everything you ever touched—even if you didn't mean to, he cursed silently.

If he waited around much longer, Cecily would be here. He jerked a venetian blind cord and watched the metal pieces clatter down to vent his anger. Only now there was some commotion out in the main hall.

"I'm sorry, Vanessa MacDonald cannot have visitors!" a nurse was saying in elevated tones, as though she'd been forced to repeat it.

"If you don't let me see her, this place is going to be knee deep in police in half an hour!" another voice challenged. "I'm her attorney. I also represent the business in which she's a major shareholder. If you don't let me see for myself the conditions she's being held under, I'm going to have investigators combing through this place right down to the bedpans!"

"Wesley?" said Ben, at the door now and staring at him in mild surprise.

The lawyer was rumpled and unshaven.

"Ben," he said crisply, then turned back to the matter at hand.

But a doctor was hurrying toward them, apparently being briefed by another nurse who trotted beside him.

"Mrs. MacDonald requires complete isolation now—no distractions at all," he said after brief introductions.

"She's sedated?" asked Wesley flatly. "Unconscious?"

The doctor hesitated. "Yes. I'm afraid so."

"Then it won't harm her at all, our seeing her." Wesley's face was unrelenting. "Or shall I get a court order?"

The doctor looked immensely displeased. Wesley's assertiveness touched Ben.

"All right," said the doctor. "You see her and leave."

Wesley nodded agreement. "This man's her brother-in-law. He's coming, too."

The doctor spoke in low tones to one of the nurses, then, with an attendant, accompanied them down a long hall. A door was unlocked. They moved past a nursing station and several rooms to stop at one with an open door.

"The restraints are necessary," the doctor said, stopping there to wait for them. "She might harm herself otherwise."

Ben didn't think Wesley heard. He was moving toward the bed, where a figure lay swaddled in white. It was love that had made the usually reticent lawyer fight so to see the woman who lay unconscious there, and even though it was mixed with agony now, that emotion was clear on his face.

Ben felt suddenly like an intruder. He stopped, feeling he should leave but unable to take his eyes away.

"Van sweetheart," said Wesley so softly Ben could hardly

hear it. "Van, I'm here now. It's okay. Come back to me."

Bending over her, he smoothed her hair, kissed her frozen lips, and kissed them again

"Sweetheart, I'm here," he repeated. "But I need you to get well for me. I promise never to leave you again. I'll hold you in my arms, where nothing can ever hurt you. We'll make another baby."

"I must ask you to leave now, so she's not disturbed," the doctor's voice said behind them.

Ben realized he'd blocked the son of a bitch's view and was glad of that.

"If the patient's to have any hope of recovery, she mustn't see anyone she knows for at least several weeks now," the doctor said as they left. "Please appreciate our concern for her and allow us to act in her best interests. Don't expect to stage a scene and be admitted the next time you come."

Ben grinned without much humor. He and Wesley continued outside in silence.

"Good job, Wesley," he said at last.

Wesley readjusted his glasses. He blinked back something, then looked away.

"I thought—hoped—if just maybe my voice . . ."

His willingness to lay himself bare for a woman he loved made Ben feel ashamed.

"Sure. I expect it did some good in that department. I expect she knew you were there. Some part of her did, anyway."

It seemed cruel to give too much hope.

Wesley nodded. The lines of despair pressed into his face made Ben want to do something for him.

"You have a car? I do. Get in. Bloody Christ, you don't even have a topcoat!"

It was cold. The lawyer was shivering. But his mind seemed miles distant—back on the woman inside, Ben had no doubt.

"I was in Brazil when I got Cecily's call," he said vaguely.

"Brazil?" Ben was surprised. He knew about Joao's death, but he also knew Joao's daughter should have been at the meeting day before yesterday. "What were you doing there?"

"Uh . . . fishing," Wesley said vaguely.

Ben glanced at him and knew that was a lie. What the hell. The guy was grieving. It made him think of Cecily and an emptiness eating him that would not go away.

Yesterday, in The Savoy, it had slept for a while, but now it was worse than ever. He needed to go somewhere, do something, not think. Maybe Wesley needed that, too.

"Hey, look. You're going through hell," he said bluntly. "No sense being there alone. The Peregrine should be ready. I'm going to head for Bangkok, see some places I haven't seen for a while. Do a hell of a lot of drinking. You want to come?"

Wesley hesitated. The hardness he'd put on for Van's sake was fading and he looked tired.

"I don't know . . . it's a bad time to leave Cecily."

Ben jerked the car into gear. Things he didn't want to recall from Cecily's face at The Savoy were haunting him.

"Don't worry. Cecily will always land on her feet."

FIFTY

THE SUITE AT THE RITZ MADE IT POSSIBLE FOR HER TO BE NEAR VAN. From behind a small Queen Anne table that served as her desk, Cecily glanced around the cream and muted apricot and gilded molding of her sitting room, wearily satisfied at how it had been transformed into a small but efficient office above bustling Piccadilly. Lyle & Co. might have cut into Effie's Palm Beach trade, but in the two weeks since she'd been here, more than a few English customers had been won back by this chance to shop through photographs of the Duvall collection on their own doorstep.

Two phones were ringing. Felice was adding new names to an appointment book. An assistant, newly hired, was restoring order to color photographs of bracelets and pendants through which a departing customer had been browsing.

"Three left to see before you're done," Felice advised, looking anxiously up from her book. "A friend of Vicomtesse di Ribes arrived while you were with the last one. And you haven't even stopped for lunch—again. Let me get you a sandwich."

"No. It wastes too much time. Send in"—she checked a card—"Lady Place."

Memories would have haunted her back at The Savoy. It was why she had come here—why she almost welcomed her twice-weekly flights back to Miami to care for customers there during this, the height of the social season. The schedule she was keeping left little time for sleep, no time at all for thoughts of anything but Van and business.

Jenkins hurried toward her. She didn't know what she'd have done if he hadn't arrived to help her, with Wesley having vanished right off the face of the earth when she'd needed him most.

"They've picked up MacDonald," he said in a low voice.

"Good. With luck I'll be able to finish with customers before he gets here. Take him into the bedroom in case I don't, so there's no commotion."

Jenkins looked worried. "Cecily, I wish you wouldn't do it this way—"

"How else do you think I could do it? He sure as hell wouldn't come to see me voluntarily."

"But having him picked up by a couple of musclemen . . . kidnapped—"

"He argued with Van. He may have given her something that made her lose the baby. That's what that woman I hired to stay with her said. Do you want me to coddle him?"

She'd seen Van. Jenkins hadn't. He didn't know what it was like, seeing no recognition, no glimmer of consciousness at all behind Van's glassy eyes.

"I don't know," he said helplessly. "I just wish you'd find some other way—not try to be judge and j—"

"Cecily? My God, you've got a full-scale operation going here!" said a familiar voice.

Startled, Cecily jerked her attention back to her surroundings and saw Lynette. Immediately she felt wary.

Lynette had hated her ever since Cecily had deprived her of her place on the board. Her turning up here could only mean more trouble. For the first time Cecily was sure of the wisdom of wearing black on a daily basis now, as Effie had. The severe color, and the flawless fit of her knit Capraro coatdress bespoke authority. She raised her head so that Effie's ruby, now set in a massive chain high around her neck, was unmistakable.

"Lynette? I wasn't expecting you."

The blonde, as perfectly coiffed as ever and expensively attired, was surveying the scene around her with mild speculation.

"I didn't know you'd have customers waiting," she said. "I won't stay a minute."

"I'll tell Felice to hold your appointments," said Jenkins, his face still showing disapproval.

Lynette watched curiously as he left.

"I'm sorry about your sister," she said, her attention returning to Cecily. "Is she better?"

"Some." Cecily knew she didn't sound cordial. "What brings you to London?"

"A man inviting me to a weekend houseparty." Lynette's tone was faintly belligerent now. She eyed Cecily as though about to engage in battle and tossed her envelope-sized handbag into a nearby chair. "Look. I can understand you not being thrilled to see me. I'd have scratched your eyes out if I could've for taking my shares on the board away from me. But it's turned out okay."

Her slim shoulders lifted in a shrug that was half impatience. "I'd have left things to the girls, anyway. I like being in Paris. I'd heard you were here, and I'd heard how the board was looking to pull the plug on you. I figured maybe you could use a break."

"Such as?" Cecily didn't know whether to trust her or not.

"The branch in Paris could move a lot more items with smaller price tags than it does now. Things in the two-to-five-thousand-dollar range—with smaller stones, or *en pavé* like a lot of Ben's things—only less of it, of course.

"I knew Effie wouldn't be interested, but the occasional pieces I have had like that have been gobbled up. People come in. Admire. They'd like to buy the Duvall name—the Duvall *myth*. But they can't afford the big-ticket items. Tiffany has boutique goods, Cartier does. Why shouldn't we? My receipts would triple, at least. And if you get squeezed for large stones—"

She was interrupted by Jenkins's breathless return.

"They're here."

"What?"

"Apparently they were only a few blocks away when they called."

It was hard to divide her thoughts. What Lynette was saying made sense, but this was more immediate.

"Lynette, I've got to go. Thanks for coming forward with this. I'll call tonight and see what we might already have on hand. We'll talk more later."

She began to move, past Felice and the new assistant, with Jenkins hurrying beside her.

"Cecily. Please—"

"Can't you understand? I want to make sure my sister's not hurt anymore!" She was near tears and drew a breath to compose herself. "This is exactly how Effie would have handled things, I think."

"I know. That's what worries me." Jenkins's thin lips pressed grimly together. "I arranged to have those passenger manifests checked for you because you asked me to. I hired those men to pick him up. I knew how to do it because I'd done similar things for Effie through the years, but I'd thought your ways would be different from hers—"

"See Lynette out, will you?"

Feeling the tug of his words but determined not to yield to it, she turned her back on him to knock on the door of one of the suite's two bedrooms. A slender but tough-looking man let her in. His companion stood over Trace MacDonald, his very presence, as well as the gun held casually in his hand, threatening Trace to rise from a straight-backed chair.

"So you're the one behind this!" Trace colored angrily at sight of her. "I'll have you run in!"

"Shut up and listen, Trace." Cecily rested her hands on the door behind her, not because she needed support but because the loathing that welled in her made her unsteady. "Don't try getting up. I don't have time to waste on you. I had you brought here because I want you out of my sister's life once and for all."

"You sure as hell won't get it this way!"

He stirred as if to rise, but the gun moving quickly in front of him forced him back.

"I want you to file for annulment," said Cecily, secure in the knowledge she held the upper hand. "I want that paper you forced Van to sign before you were married—all copies. You've got forty-eight hours. When I've gotten both those, you get this." From her pocket she drew and held out the glittering blue diamond from which Effie had rescued April.

"It's a diamond, Trace. Do you know what it's worth?"

Trace's eyes moved over it greedily, devoured it, then wrenched up to her. "No deal."

"You can keep her ten percent, damn it."

She'd hoped to avoid losing that but had been prepared to.

He smiled and the act sent a chill through her. Something was wrong. This wasn't going as she'd expected. Trace sat back easily.

"Ten percent of Duvall is ten percent of nothing—will be soon, at least."

He was bluffing. He'd married Van for less than ten percent, for the mere chance to ingratitate himself with Effie and handle her ad account. But Van mattered more than the company. If she'd paid more attention to Van in the first place, Van would still be well.

"I'll double it—give you twenty percent."

"Twenty percent of nothing's still nothing. I'm finished doing ads for you, by the way. I'm resuming my acquaintance with Lyle and Company."

Cecily's blood turned to sand and drained out of her. Suddenly she understood.

"You've been working for them all the time. You married Van and—and tried to rape her so they could use her as some kind of pawn!" She could barely keep her voice from shaking.

"That's right," he said calmly. "The ten percent was a nice windfall. Unexpected, and handy for Jordan taking over what's left of your company."

She scarcely heard the final word. For the first time in her life she felt flooding hate, engulfing violence. The desire to kill.

Power. The complete destruction of Lyle & Company. A vengeance as ruthless as Effie's. Only with those could she insure no one ever harmed Van again.

"Hey, lady," said one of the two men she'd hired. "You want us to fix him so he ain't capable of raping no one? We can. We'll bring you a picture to prove it—for that stone you're offering."

Cecily's fingers hardened around the diamond she was holding.

"Do it!"

"Mr. Kemp's here waiting for you. He's been here over an hour," Hester said, taking Cecily's bulging briefcase at the door of the condominium.

Cecily nodded. She hadn't expected Peter. As she entered the living room her eyes caught the vase full of roses from him that had greeted her on her return from London yesterday.

"Hello," she said.

He was reading the evening paper, very much at home. He rose and pecked her lightly on the cheek, his usual greeting these days.

"How's your sister?"

She shrugged, kicking off her shoes. "She knows me. I suppose that counts as better, though she doesn't know much more than that. I thought it was time to come home."

She was tired. She'd been bothered by nightmares for weeks now—the same dream. Of herself. At Effie's desk, with a river of blood around her. She didn't know whose.

It had started in London, just after her encounter with Trace MacDonald. She'd thought it might vanish back here in familiar surroundings. It hadn't. Last night she'd lain awake making decisions. She was going to take out a bank loan, using her own shares in Duvall as collateral, so that Jenkins could drill yet another hole. If she had the leverage of diamonds, all controlled by her, some of the board members would be greedy enough to ally themselves with her for the profits, which would be shared if Duvall remained intact, hers and Jenkins's exclusively, if she was forced to set up her own company.

"Would you like a drink, Peter? What did you want?"

Not dinner, she hoped, though she supposed she owed him that for the times he'd been her escort to holiday parties important to her clients: the Tiara Ball in Boca Raton, the Animal Rescue League's annual benefit.

"Don't you know what I want?" He was behind her and he slipped his arms around her waist.

She wanted to draw away, but she was tired. His arms had a familiar feel. Besides, it seemed pointless to struggle against a man who made her feel valued—cherished, even. Three times a week he sent flowers. He'd called her daily in London. He had tried to give her a sable coat for Christmas, but she had refused it. It was his efforts, more than the gifts themselves—his constancy—which was making it increasingly difficult to say no to him. Would that fact even occur to Peter?

"Cecily, you know I adore you," he said. "I've missed you. I don't want to be separated from you again! So marry me, won't you? Here."

He was holding up a ring with a marquise diamond, even handsomer than the one she'd almost thrown in the gutter years before.

"Say yes, Cecily, and I'll give you more than this ring. I'll buy out the other members of your board—give you Duvall free and clear."

Her heart leaped, hungry. Marrying Peter could solve all her problems. It would be no worse of her than what she'd done to Trace MacDonald for pure revenge.

Survival. Survival and power were what mattered.

And then Peter started raining kisses on her neck and she could think only of Ben's kisses.

"Don't, Peter. Please!"

Her skin felt oily.

Instinctively she knew even Effie had never married like this. Always Effie had been the strong one in a match, bartering her body for a little more power, perhaps, but only when the bulk of

that power was already in her hands. Never when she was unable
to win and defend it herself. Never when she could be made a
supplicant.

"Peter, stop it!" She pushed roughly away. His kisses, though
soothing and skillful, were smothering her. "I—I'm grateful.
But I have to have Duvall on my own terms. Then maybe . . ."

"You're a fool, Cecily!"

He was suddenly far angrier than the situation warranted, his
hazel eyes crackling with an expression she'd never seen there.

"You married that drunken test pilot for a drop in the bucket—to
insure a piddling job in his grandmother's company. I offer you
everything—everything you want! And you turn it down. Can't
you see the kind of business you'd do with my name and
connections behind you? What the hell's gotten into you?"

"I said I was flattered!"

His words about Ben stirred a rage inside her.

"Flattered! You should be! I've waited on you hand and foot
for months and you've acted like a goddamned robot. Like you
were doing *me* a favor! I'm out of patience—and I happen to
know this little enterprise you're so set on is almost out of
money. So what's it going to be? I'm not going to ask again. If
you turn me down now, you lose it all—me and your precious
company!"

Cecily studied him a long moment, wondering how it was she
had never before seen his arrogance.

"You're wrong about one thing. That's not the reason I
married Ben Duvall," she said, and left him standing alone.

FIFTY-ONE

"JORDAN LYLE IS ABOUT TO MARRY INTO DUVALL AND TAKE CON-
trol of it. He'll call a board meeting in the next couple days.
But he wants his cousin disgraced first. He wants to see her
flounder. He wants to see her reduced to second rate, at best.

"She needs the rubies she's trying to coax from you,
Chantharangsy—for a bracelet, to go with the earrings Prince
Karim presented his daughter-in-law. If she gets inferior stones,
she'll lose Karim as a client, along with all the other camel-
kissers once they hear her quality's slipping. Give me your good

stuff and Jordan Lyle will pay you half again what she offered. Ship her pink-purple stones, not these beauties. We'll do business again. What do you say?''

Thida took her ear from the door. That was Harry Duvall speaking. She knew by his voice, and more certainly still by the scent of the heavy cologne he'd always worn. She was glad she'd slipped back down the stairs to listen after her husband, on the heels of a phone call, had ordered her upstairs to rest and a car had arrived.

She needed the rest. Her pregancy was not going well. The doctor said she showed a tendancy to hemorrhage and should be hospitalized so she could get help quickly in case anything went wrong. The thought of being away from her handsome young husband, though, when he had brought her so much more happiness than she'd ever expected, had been unendurable. Now two huge and despairing tears slipped silently down her cheeks.

The husband she loved and had thought herself lucky to have had just said yes. He'd just said he'd betray Cecily.

Thida remembered a night in bed when she'd been tempted to agree to a similar plan. The riches of Duvall, which Cecily Catlow had inherited, had seemed so vast. Thida's part, her husband's part, had looked unfairly small in comparison. Then she'd remembered how it had been before Cecily had befriended her—fear, hard work, patched clothes, no dignity and no trust.

She'd remembered that day in the hall when she'd been beaten with a rifle, accused of theft. Cecily had intervened to save her, putting her own job on the line by crossing short-tempered Madame. Cecily had lied not once, but twice to save her.

Cecily had trusted her. Cecily had been kind to her and relied on her and ultimately given her this chance to be well married, even though it meant losing her services, and even though Cecily might certainly have made the marriage herself.

Thida would not betray such loyalty. Cecily was as good as Madame had been evil, yet everyone had failed her, even Ben.

"I'll pick up the rubies this evening," Harry was saying. "Do you want payment in dollars or in gold?''

She turned and climbed the stairs as quickly as the heaviness low in her belly allowed these days. What was she going to do? If Cecily needed these rubies, she must get them to her. And she must tell her about her cousin's forthcoming marriage. She lay down and waited.

Within minutes she heard a car drive away. This was the stifling time of afternoon when no air stirred, when even the servants rested and sounds were rare. Her ears strained, deciphering movement. Her husband was up here now, his footsteps growing fainter as they passed her door. He was turning into his study. In the brief time required to dial open a safe, put rubies inside, and close it again, he returned down the hallway.

Thida tried to think through the rising waters of her own unhappiness. Why had he agreed to do this? Why did he want more when they had so much? Why did she have to choose?

She sat up. Ben Duvall had called her last week. He'd rented a bungalow outside Bangkok—he and the lawyer. He'd given her the address. She hoped they were still there.

Getting the rubies was not a difficult matter. Her husband had long ago, in a moment of passion, shown her the combination to his safe. Her hand soon held six stones like round red peas. These, she was sure, were the ones her husband and Harry meant to keep from Cecily. They were larger than most of the others, rich in color, in a small tray by themselves.

She stared at them. A fortune. And her husband trusted her.

As Cecily had.

She closed her eyes, tears squeezing out.

I must do this. Where first there was goodness, there must loyalty first be repaid.

Downstairs her husband would be relaxing in the cool living room. She would say she was going shopping. But often, if she left alone, he searched her, running his hands over each curve of her body in a playful, amorous game he had invented long ago. "Just to make sure you don't escape with our future," he would tease. Now she began to wonder whether it had ever been a game at all.

Of two things Thida was certain: She could never return to him after what she was doing, and she could not let him find these rubies.

Thida dropped the six stones into a small plastic sack and twisted it. She wrapped it back on itself, then twisted again. With a breath she squatted and pushed the small parcel up in her. When she took her finger away, it was spotted with blood.

Ben was alone, staring at the chessboard he and Wesley had agreed to give up on the previous night. They both must have been right royally drunk, he decided. None of the plays in progress made any sense.

Now Wesley was in the other room reading and Ben was bored. He'd picked up a magazine, but the first thing he'd seen were the garish wares from one of the small jewelry shops that filled every corner and block of Bangkok. A country full of gems, yet they were never used with imagination. Yesterday he'd seen flowers—small red native flowers—and his fingers had itched for a paper and pencil as he'd imagined tiny, petaled earrings.

He shook off the memory.

All in all, he was almost as glad of Wesley's company as Wesley seemed to be of his. It had given him something to think about now that work on TRINA II was at a standstill. It had given him something to plan for, taking Wesley places and showing him things he'd never seen.

Ben grinned, remembering the lawyer's expression when he'd seen the woman smoke a cigarette with her twat. For all the surface stuffiness, he liked Wesley. He respected him, too. The guy was gritty. Wondering what the two of them should do tonight, he got up and went to the box of bottles that was serving as a bar.

Before he could even unscrew a cap the doorbell rang. The houseboy he'd rented along with this seedy bungalow came running in shouting something about a taxi driver and someone bleeding, his skittering English almost as bad as Ben's Thai.

"What?" Ben demanded irritably, but the houseboy was already dancing back toward the door. Ben supposed he should follow.

A bald little fellow, his face wild with anguish, stood on the doorstep. Lady in taxi coming to this number. Lady bleed everywhere in back of cab now. She not can get out.

Ben got that much of it, but it made no sense.

Goddamn. Probably some woman in labor and the driver had stopped here hoping for help because he'd heard there were Americans. Ben took some baht from his pocket and handed it to the driver.

"Take her to the hospital. Fast. If the police stop you, you pay."

His houseboy chattered but the taxi driver shook his head.

"No. You Duvall. You come."

The repetition of his name surprised Ben. He started down the steps wondering what this was about.

As he neared the taxi he saw a woman resting back against the seat. It was Thida. Perplexed, and a little annoyed now at this talk of blood, he opened the door and reached a hand to help her out.

"Thida, what the hell—"

And then he saw.

Her yellow silk dress was soaked with red. It spread across the seat on either side of her. It crept in a constant trickle down her legs. The handbag she gripped as though for support was stained with it.

"Good Christ!" he breathed, starting to straighten. "Get her to a hospital! Hurry!"

"Ben, no—"

She caught at him with a hand where the blood was already drying to brown. Ben held it tightly.

"I'll come with you, Thida. It's going to be okay."

"No hospital! Take me into your house. Please, Ben! I—I think I am dying, and I must talk to you. There is something you must do for me. . . ."

She looked chalky white. Ben hesitated, torn between what she was asking and what his reason prompted him to do, then scooped her into his arms.

"Call an ambulance!" he shouted to his houseboy.

He didn't know what was happening. The bleeding was from between her legs. Van had lived through losing a baby, so maybe it wasn't so bad, but Thida's skin felt cold

"Wesley!" he barked as he entered the house. "Get out here with towels! All you can find! Hurry, goddamn it!"

As carefully as he could, he laid Thida on the couch. His arm was smeared with blood. He shoved a cushion under her to elevate her hips and heard Wesley's voice behind him.

"Oh, my God!"

Thida had turned away and was reaching beneath her skirt by the time Ben had folded a towel. With a trembling hand she pressed something into his.

"Rubies," she whispered. "Without them Cecily will be ruined. And her cousin plans to marry someone with shares in Duvall. Tell her . . . my husband thought to cheat . . . Harry came . . ."

"Shut up," he said, alarmed now at how weak she was, and indignant at what had brought her here. "Just be quiet and hang on until the ambulance gets here."

"Please, Ben. If you don't help, they will destroy her."

"Who gives a good goddamn?" he snapped. Thida was hemorrhaging. He scolded her out of concern, because he had to speak or lose his mind.

Her smile was grave and pleading.

"I'm dying, Ben. Please let me speak."

"Oh, Christ," he said—bitterly, because he thought she might be right. He wrapped his arms around her, holding and talking to keep her hooked to life. "I'll do what you asked. But you're crazy, Thida, doing this for a woman who cares about nobody but herself—a woman who operates out of vengeance and power lust just like Effie did."

Her eyes rebuked him gently. "You're wrong. All that she does, she does from love of others. Love for your grandmother, love for her sister, love for you. . . ." Her voice trailed off. Her fingers dug into his sleeve. "When she met Mr. Kemp's friend to go to the Caribbean, it was because Mr. Kemp said he would have her sister freed and brought there—he said he would help only if she told no one, least of all you—that it would harm your pride, and that you might be involved in a scheme with Trace MacDonald. I listened. I heard."

She shivered suddenly. Her voice was growing faint. "She tries to care for so many others . . . and there's no one to care for her!"

Ben knew she was dying and the truth of her words sank like chisel blows into his brain. He felt a double loss, the woman slipping away in his arms and Cecily, lost through his own blindness—through the very pride of which Thida had spoken.

"Who, Thida? Who's Jordan marrying?"

He bent forward, ashamed of pressing her when her eyes were clouding. There was no answer. He fumbled for her wrist, for the side of her neck, and, glad of Wesley's presence in the room, looked numbly up.

"She's dead."

Sam Chantharangsy sat in a car at the airport. With the field glasses in his hand he could see the little jet owned by Ben Duvall take to the sky.

Jordan Lyle was very clever. Chantharangsy thought himself lucky that Lyle had chosen him to make the approach to Cecily Catlow and offer rubies before the old woman died. It had been very profitable and would continue to be. Everything seemed to work as Jordan Lyle planned.

For instance, Lyle had known Thida would refuse to betray her former mistress. He had known, too, Ben Duvall's restlessness brought him periodically back to the city where he had once lived. Knowing those things, Jordan Lyle had waited, staging the little dialogue Thida had been allowed to overhear. He had known she would try to make off with the bits of glass she thought were rubies, would take them to Duvall—along with her information, and Duvall would fly off.

The plane was a speck now. Chantharangsy put down his glasses. *He* had not believed his wife would show more loyalty to another than she had to him. It was disappointing. Still, he was pleased that everything was going as Jordan Lyle planned.

"It was wrong, going off and leaving her," Wesley said in a muffled voice from his side of the Peregrine.

Been shoved a cassette in, activating TRINA II and its autopilot, out of habit.

"She was dead. If we's stayed around, we'd have been tied up in red tape trying to explain it. We couldn't have done what she asked. She'd have died for nothing. Would that have been right?"

They hadn't spoken of Thida in the rush to the airport or their preparations for takeoff. Ben also felt vaguely guilty about just leaving her.

A woman he'd known in her childhood. Gone. Dead in his arms. He thought he would always feel the stickiness of her blood. He imagined he could, though his hands were clean beneath the insulated flight gloves a company had asked him to test. Yet he knew the same fierce desire to protect now burning in his heart had burned in hers. Her sacrifice, more than her words, had jarred something loose in him he hadn't wanted to face, the truth about Cecily and what he felt for her.

"Keep that on," he said as Wesley started to undo his safety harness. It was the one thing that annoyed him about Wesley as a passenger, always having to remind him of that.

"Why Rangoon?" asked Wesley, scowling as he obeyed.

It wasn't like Wesley to be this quarrelsome. He was upset. Ben figured he'd never seen anyone die before, at least so unpleasantly. He probably wasn't pleased, either, about the six red stones Ben had stuffed in his compass case.

"It's close, and I've got friends there. We can get a call through to Cecily and catch the first commercial flight back to the States. If we'd waited back there, God knows when we'd have been done with the complications."

For the first time ever he found himself impatient with the Peregrine's speed. He looked at the instrument panel, reassured himself he was pushing it all he could, and cursed to himself.

It was lucky he'd always made it a practice to have the Peregrine serviced and waiting. Lucky whoever showed up at the bungalow—ambulance, then police, he'd guess—hadn't moved in time to cut them off at the airport.

He'd been a fool where Cecily was concerned. A lot of times, he thought, as the plane reached maximum altitude, maximum cruise speed, humming along. Now he could do the one thing that might matter to her, getting stones to her, warning her, voting with her—all to keep Duvall intact.

It wouldn't make up for walking out on her, or things he'd said, but he had to try, anyway. Christ but he loved her. Only he'd been afraid to face it. Maybe he'd been afraid to face what he felt for his work at Duvall as well. Easier that way; easier than losing, anyway. Maybe for these past twelve years he'd been taking the easy way out.

"Check your input."

TRINA's nagging voice startled him.

Ben looked at the screens in front of him. He was getting a strange traffic display, one that couldn't be right. He swore, reinitialized the computer, and now the navigational display looked strange.

"Error . . . error . . ." droned the synthetic voice.

Ben grabbed at the computer console, to jerk out the tape and regain control of the plane himself, but all at once they were rolling, upside down. He heard Wesley yell.

"Pull up . . . pull up," warned TRINA as his fingers found the cassette.

But the engine was out. And all at once he realized the cassette hadn't been in its usual place when they'd taken off from Bangkok.

"Goddamn it, we've been sabotaged!" he shouted.

They were going down. A crash was inevitable.

I never told her I loved her! he thought.

FIFTY-TWO

MORTIMER LOOKED WHITE-FACED AS HE CAME INTO HER OFFICE. CECILY waited, her pen poised above a letter she was about to sign, to see what had caused this unexpected intrusion.

"Madame . . . Cecily."

His eyes were crinkling around the edges.

"Mortimer, what's wrong?"

He came toward her desk. "Ben's plane. It crashed in the jungle. Wesley Bell was with him. They're both dead."

Everything seemed to recede around her.

"No!"

Layer by layer the scar tissue over her heart was wrenched away, revealing the truth that lay there. She still loved Ben. She had never ceased to love him.

"No! I don't believe it!"

If he were dead she would know as surely as she would know if one of her own limbs had been torn from her. She would *feel* it. The pain of the past two years had come because they could not be completely severed, because some connection that couldn't be put aside kept pulling at them.

A dark undertow of terror, the most violent she'd ever known, sucked at her.

"Even if his plane is down, he may have survived. The Peregrine had everything—"

His tragic, pitying look cut short her words. "I'm sorry. Since Madame Duvall was dead and he wasn't married"—Mortimer looked down in embarrassment—"they assumed he had no next of kin to notify sooner."

"But—"

"Ben had friends—pilots—people familiar with searching. One of them is downstairs now. It took nearly four days, but they found the wreck. The plane caught fire when it hit the ground, Cecily. There was nothing left except metal. And part of a glove he'd been testing out of some fire-retardant material."

Mortimer turned away as though unable to face her and braced against the wall. "There were . . . remains in the glove. A left hand. The small finger was misshapen. The gold they found was melted, but the man downstairs brought this."

Reaching weakly forward, he dropped something on her desk. It rocked and clattered. Cecily cried out. She was looking at Ben's ruby, the stone that had once been part of Effie's, now reset and hanging around her neck.

"Ben!" she gasped. It was all she could manage.

She was aware of nothing except her fingers gripping the cold hardness of her desk, and her tears rushing out, and the sobs that shook her sholders, all without sound.

Jordan Lyle slid the knot into place on his necktie, nodding at the mirror to congratulate himself. The crash in the jungle had been tidier than he'd expected. Occupants reduced to ashes, or so he'd heard.

The little gook had carried out orders well. Now Trace Mac-Donald would think twice about ever taking on Jordan Lyle or accusing him of not having a plan.

Not that MacDonald was saying much these days.

Jordan grinned at his reflection

MacDonald was nothing but nerves since losing his manhood. Stayed in his place in London. Crept into restaurants as though everyone who saw him could guess. He was mad as hell now, of course, wanted vengeance of his own on Cecily Catlow, but was terrified of her. After what he'd lost, he was willing to jump to whatever tune Jordan played in order to get the shares he'd been promised.

Jordan picked up his toothbrush, tossed it into the suitcase lying open on his bed, and snapped the lid down over it.

Time was running out on Cousin Cecily. He was ready to go to Brazil.

How long had it been? Ten days? Two weeks? There was something she must do today.

Time had ceased to exist for Cecily since the news about Ben. She was going through the motions of living—the motions of running a business.

"Your designs are lovely," she said to a young woman who had come to beg a spot as workroom apprentice in hopes of advancing someday. "If an opening should turn up, I'll be in touch with you."

Cecily watched the girl close the door behind her and thought she would probably find a spot at Van Cleef, Cartier, even Lyle & Company. She was very good.

The fact was, Cecily couldn't afford to add another person, even an apprentice, to Duvall's payroll. Every cent beyond the bare-bones budget had been sunk in the venture in Brazil. There was nothing left to buy stones if Jenkins didn't find them; nothing left to buy emeralds when her supply was gone; nothing left to put together Effie's wonderful Eve Collection. These days, she scarcely cared.

Oh, Ben, I was afraid to trust. Afraid to love. But I loved you anyway, even after you left. There was never any way to stop myself.

Her curled fist pressed into her cheek. Ben's ruby, reset and on her finger, dug at her flesh. It was all that was left of him.

She treasured it, clung to it far more than she ever had Effie's.

She looked down at a tray of mixed stones she'd been studying before this interview. Their colors jumbled together and their confusion made her think of her own life.

First there had been New York and Peter and Landis and Oxenburg. That period had been like the black opal Louie had warned her against, shot through with so many colors she could see no one of them clearly, opaque as her own vision was because of her inexperience.

Then there was the part of her life since she'd come here. Her vision was clearer now, but always colored. As though she held an emerald before her eye, she seemed to see only one hue at a time: the need to help Van, unaware Ben had also needed her; the demands of the business, when she should have tended to her sister.

Was there ever a time of life, she wondered, when everything was as clear as a flawless diamond, sparkling, with nothing hidden? No colors at all, only radiant light?

Behind her eyes she felt a pressure, but no tears fell. They were exhausted. How long had it been? she wondered again.

She'd been moving, pretending, holding Duvall together, but all in a daze. Her own grief was raw. It had been all she could manage. But she'd been avoiding another grief, one she also must shoulder. Tonight she must be on a plane to London. Tomorrow she must tell Van.

Everything around her seemed softened in wisps of chiffon. She felt eternally groggy. The sensations felt familiar to Van after so many years.

She wondered why she had ever tried to fight them. Looking sleepily around a dayroom, she thought how much easier it was being here and letting her mind dart or even be blank. Outside you always had to be alert. You always had to worry that normal people would look at something you did and know you weren't like them.

She did miss Bibi, though. She'd like having an animal to watch. And she missed Wesley. Why hadn't he come to see her?

She hadn't been meant to live outside, but Wesley wouldn't care. He'd come to see her. They'd have nice times. Maybe that's who was coming to see her today. She *thought* she was in this room because she was going to see someone. She couldn't remember.

"You have a visitor," said a nurse, popping up in front of her the way they always did.

Yes, maybe it was Wesley.

But someone squeezed her hand and she knew it was Cecily. Cecily held her face very close and it didn't look gauzy like everything else. But it looked funny somehow.

"I thought maybe it was Wesley who was coming to see me," Van confided. "I can't remember things, you know."

Cecily held her hand between both her own. Van always felt so safe when Cecily was with her.

"Van dearest, I've got to tell you something. I—I've put it off for a long time, but I think you've got to know."

Even Cecily's voice sounded funny. She took a breath. "Wesley's dead, Van. He and Ben were in a plane crash."

Van knew it was awful, knew it was very sad. She thought she was upset, but the fogginess in her mind seemed to soak it up somehow.

"Oh, dear," she said. "I thought he was just here to see me. Is Ben dead, too?"

"Yes."

"I'll miss him. Won't you? Even though you weren't married anymore?"

She saw her sister was crying and couldn't answer her. Van struggled to focus better and make the fogginess go away.

Cecily was crying, and that wasn't like her, and that funny look when she came in was from hurting. Cecily was hurting down inside. Van felt sure of it.

She tried to think and was suddenly angry at herself at how stupid she'd gotten

"How's the business?" she asked. That seemed right, changing the subject.

Cecily waved a hand. "I'm probably going to lose it. It—it doesn't matter somehow without Ben."

Then Cecily, who was always so grown-up and so strong and who looked so important in her black dress, wiped her nose on the back of her hand like a little child. Something flickered in Van's memory. She sat speechless, trying to catch it.

But before she could, terrible, pained words burst from Cecily's throat.

"Oh, God, Van! Don't go off again! I shouldn't have told you about Wesley—I'm so sorry—I thought you ought to know. Van—please! Don't just sit there. Don't—don't let go of the present! Please, Van! You're all I've got!"

Van felt bewildered. She didn't know what to do.

"I'm tired," she said at last.

Cecily rose, fighting more tears. She looked frightened. "I'll be back," she whispered, kissing Van's forehead. "Don't worry, Van. I *will* hang on to the business. For you and me. So just get well."

Van watched her leave, then turned her attention slowly to a window. There were birds outside in a tree. There were no leaves, though. It must be winter. She hadn't thought about birds for a long time. She hadn't even remembered how you could look out windows.

Wesley was dead and she'd been in love with Wesley. She ought to cry. Maybe she *was* crying. Cecily had been—and she had always thought that Cecily was so strong.

Think. Think!

Some memory was trying to push its way into her mind. Van frowned fiercely, trying to help it through the fogginess.

Yes! Now she knew. It was the way Cecily had wiped her nose. Cecily had done that as a little girl and Van had always had to scold her. She'd been doing it that day at Marblehead when she was crying—and Van had protected her then.

But ever since, Cecily had protected *her*. The realization brought Van up short. That wasn't right. All those years . . . and she was older . . . and now Cecily had no one.

She *had* to get well, even though it seemed easier being foggy. She had to get well so she could help Cecily.

FIFTY-THREE

*J*ORDAN SIPPED CHAMPAGNE AMID SATIN SHEETS. IT WAS LATE AFTER-noon in Rio and he'd just had a good romp. Stretching lazily, he savored the considerable successes he was amassing. Freeing himself from Orlena and Lucy. Bringing in his own source of rubies. And his new bride . . . He surveyed with satisfaction Ana-Sofia's silken back, turned toward him as she drowsed.

She'd come to him a virgin, and the fun of deflowering her two days ago, of seeing her so eager to please him, almost compensated for the restraint he'd placed upon himself. This time he'd tangled the sheets around her wrists, told her she was his prisoner. She hadn't been scared, but she'd liked the game. He'd imagined what it would be like when he tied her down, how she'd plead with him.

"It's time to make that phone call to our cousin Cecily," he whispered. He felt the stirring of an erection now that the moment was here.

Ana-Sofia faced him, awakening quickly, and her expression clouded slightly.

"You're sure this is the thing to do, Jordan? She seems to run the business well. And my father liked her. . . ."

He kissed her fingers, heavy with a wedding band of diamonds and emeralds.

"I've told you, my darling, she's crazy. She and her sister both. When she grows irrational there's no telling what harm she'll do to Duvall with her judgments. You might lose everything.

"You must trust me, Ana-Sofia. And think of the business we're going to have! A sight of our own from De Beers for selling to them—do you realize how few are allowed those, my darling? And the burden of your father's mines gone from your lovely shoulders—gone at a profit that has made you nearly as rich as you are sweet."

He kissed her compliant lips. "Your father would be very proud of you, my darling."

He gloated silently as she began to dial the phone. He'd pegged her from the first as a daddy's girl. Tell her that her old man would have wanted something and she went along.

Good thing Martin hadn't tried to move in on her. He'd been so busy scheming with the others to cut up Duvall that he hadn't seen this chance to get a bigger hunk of it and a rich wife, too.

"Cecily, I—I have some news for you," Ana-Sofia was saying. "I'm married now. My husband wants to talk to you."

She handed her white French phone to Jordan. He felt a surge of his blood, a distinctive pleasure, as he put it to his ear.

"It's Jordan, Cecily. Remember me? The last time we met was at an auction back in New York." *He hated her more than he'd ever hated any other woman.* "Ana-Sofia thinks I should take over her dealings with Duvall for her," he said. "She's placed everything in my hands. I'm calling a board meeting."

Her voice was collected. That disappointed Jordan.

"I assume you're selling Joao's mines to the cartel?"

He hadn't surprised her. But then he'd supposed she was clever.

Ana-Sofia blew him a kiss, not much caring what happened as

long as she didn't have to listen to voices raised, Jordan guessed, and left the room.

"That's right," he said into the telephone. "You're going to have to get your diamonds somewhere else—if you can afford them. Pity. Then again, you may not even need them after the board meets. I've got a feeling there's going to be a vote to merge on a half-share basis with Lyle & Company."

He grinned, enjoying his power. "Martin likes the idea. So do Kim and Chantharangsy. Oh, and Trace MacDonald—he didn't much appreciate the surgery you had done to him in London.

"We've got an agreement, MacDonald and I. Once Duvàll's absorbed, with me in charge, he's free to do whatever he wants with your sister."

He thought of her squirming. He thought of her fighting and bringing her to her knees. He was fully hard now.

"When do you want the meeting?" she asked.

Her voice had faltered.

"Tell you what, I'll give you five days," he said.

There was no way out for her. Let it torture her. Let her sweat.

He'd waited a long time to get even with Cecily Catlow.

Everyone had gone from the workroom. Felice had departed. The kitchen was empty. Only Charlie remained downstairs and Raoul and the guards outside.

Cecily sat with her head in her hands, in darkness. She was still in shock at this latest turn of events.

Jordan had married Ana-Sofia. He had married into her own company. How stupidly simple. And now he meant to absorb Duvall. To swallow it up.

Like a harsh rock thrusting up, the news had slammed her back to painful consciousness, snagging her, bruised, from the dark and numbing sea of unending bleakness in which she'd been drowning for weeks. She struggled, resisting the pain and despair that had overwhelmed her since Ben's death.

Perhaps his death had been a punishment, because of what she'd had done to Trace MacDonald

No. She wouldn't believe that. She couldn't. She had to be hard. As hard as Effie.

The telephone rang, loud, endless janglings in the silence. She sat and looked at it. Perhaps it was Van. It had been a month since she'd broken the news about Wesley to her sister, two weeks since she'd last visited. Van was able to talk on the phone

now. She chattered, sounded much improved, spoke with bursts
of determination about getting out. Only Cecily was afraid to
allow herself this time the hope of Van ever really getting better.

Reluctantly she answered.

"Cecily?" It was Jenkins's voice. He sounded euphoric.
"Cecily, we've hit paydirt! Bucket after bucket! The stones are
coming out of the cyclones now. Some of them are as big as my
thumb!"

A surge of hope; then Cecily knew, bitterly, this came too
late. Yet how could she tell Jenkins? How could she snatch from
him this triumph that had come to him so late in life?

"That's wonderful," she said. "Oh, Jenkins, I'm so pleased
for you—for what you've accomplished. It really is incredible.
And I want you to enjoy every bit of it!

"There's a problem for me, though," she continued reluctantly.
"I siphoned off so much for the cyclones and such that last
month, what with insurance due and other bills and having to
buy stones, I had to take out a loan. I used my third of The Farm
as collateral—it was all I had.

"Now Jordan Lyle's married Ana-Sofia. He's called a meeting of the board for Friday. He plans to take over. If he does—if
I can't win the vote—the others can seize my personal assets to
cancel the debt."

There was silence. Jenkins understood what she was telling
him. As things stood now, she wouldn't see a cent of the riches
from their venture. Jordan Lyle and the others would reap the
windfall. And Duvall would still be wiped from existence.

"Can you win the vote?" he asked as though he suspected the
answer.

"If Margaux votes with me, there'll be a standoff. It's all I
can hope for."

"Buy someone's shares. Someone must have a price."

Cecily laughed bitterly. "Oh, I suspect they all have a price.
But I just told you, Jenkins, I don't have the money. I can't raise
it. There's no way."

His lack of answer, Cecily knew, was unspoken commiseration.

"Cecily, I'd like to be there with you," he said finally. "But
I think I'm better off here. I'll ship the first stones as soon as
they're polished. I'll send rough, too. You can put that up as
collateral. Just stall—or win that vote. There must be a way."

She hung up and sat lost in thought, aware how close Duvall
was now to survival, aware how close it was to disaster.

"Yes, there is a way," she said aloud at last.

Everyone she loved had been taken from her. Effie. Ben. Van lost in shadows. Even Thida, who had done so much for her, had died God knew why or how in Ben's house in Bangkok.

She wouldn't let them take Duvall as well. It was all she had left to live for, her child, into whom she had breathed a second chance for life when she'd come to work for Effie.

Ben was dead. Only survival mattered.

Slowly, methodically, she began to dial Peter's number.

"I hadn't expected to hear from you again," Peter said, swirling ice in the drink that Cecily offered him

They were in the condominium. She had reached it only far enough ahead of him to change from her severe black into a dress of slubbed green silk. Make the offer more appealing, but don't deceive. She'd been wearing green that first day they'd met, she realized.

Peter was eyeing her cautiously. His little-boy look had long ago vanished into another one that had always lain behind it, but Cecily ignored the new shape.

"I've been wondering, Peter, if you still want to marry me," she said with a breath.

He looked at her blankly, then with dawning shrewdness. Was the shrewdness new, or had she failed to recognize it in the past?

"Why?" he asked.

She looked at him a long moment. Honesty had never been an element between her and Peter, she suspected. Yet that was the course she was choosing.

"Because of exactly what you said last time, Peter. There'd be advantages in it. Advantages for my business, and maybe advantages for my sister, too. I'm ready for those."

She stood before him with a terrible sense of not being able to turn back once this was spoken.

"Jordan Lyle of Lyle and Company has just married into Duvall. On Friday he's going to try to make it part of his own business—and the members of my board are likely to support him. I want to keep control.

"Buy out one of the shareholders. Give me the votes I need to keep Duvall entirely in my hands, Peter, and I'll marry you. I'll try very hard to make you happy."

Peter's face took on an incredulous look. He put his glass aside and rose, all in one motion.

"You're selling yourself? Is that the idea? What kind of begger—what kind of taste do you suppose I have?"

He had colored. His words were cutting, sharpened by an underlying indignation. Cecily shrugged.

"It's the same offer you made me last time, it seems to me," she said, annoyed by the sudden morality he seemed to be trotting out. "Better terms for you, in fact."

He stared at her, his hazel eyes hard with anger. Angered equally by his reaction, Cecily stared back at him. Slowly the hostility guttered out behind his eyes, replaced by something else impervious to her gaze. He took a step toward her.

"The minute I put somebody else's shares in Duvall in your hands, you marry me. Is that what you're agreeing to?" His voice grew coaxing.

Cecily nodded.

He smiled, the effect not altogether pleasant as it was lost behind his narrow mustache. His arms closed around her, forcing her against the smoothness of his three-piece suit.

For an instant Cecily, obeying something inside her, resisted the contact. Then she acquiesced. Peter's lips, with a cool, almost frightening, possessiveness, began to move over hers.

"All right," he said. "I've never made a bad investment in my life."

FIFTY-FOUR

"C ECILY? THE DOCTOR SAYS I CAN HAVE A WEEKEND PASS IN A month or so if Trace will agree! Isn't it great? Do you think you can get away and come over soon?"

Van was so excited she didn't have patience to go through the playing part first—the "Hi-it's-me-How-are-things-What-are-you up-to-today" that was supposed to start conversations. She'd rushed to the phone, bursting to share the news with her sister because she thought surely it would lift Cecily's spirits.

It made her own soar because it reassured her the plan, the unrelenting daily regimen she'd set for herself, was working. She was getting well, and with amazing speed.

At first all she'd been able to force herself to do was walk, even outside in the cold, damp spring. She'd pursued that so doggedly she knew now the staff must have thought it some new manifestation of her craziness. Then, as the discipline had driven the fogginess from her brain, she'd tried systematically remembering everything she could. Then she'd gone on to reading, afterward writing down what she'd read so that her mind had been forced into focusing; then she'd learned every fact about her fellow patients, determined to reestablish a grip on reality that she would never let elude her again.

"Cecily?" she repeated, worried a little that the line might have gone dead.

"Yes, Van. That's—that's wonderful."

There was something odd in Cecily's voice. Van frowned.

"I'm sorry I haven't been to see you lately, Van. Things have been . . ."

Maybe Cecily didn't *want* to come see her, Van thought with sudden disappointment at how her news was being received. Maybe she was just another burden to Cecily and wouldn't be any help to her after all, even if she did get out.

Then sharply, almost harshly, Van told herself she was just feeling scared. Just because people didn't respond to her the way she thought they ought to didn't mean it had something to do with *her*. Ben had told her that once, and she had to remember it.

"What's wrong, Cecily? You sound upset."

Van suddenly hated the phone, not being able to see, knowing they were so far apart. She tried to sift through everything she knew was happening to Cecily. She discarded it all back to that day when Cecily had come and wept and wiped her nose on her sleeve.

"Are you still worried you might lose the company?"

There was silence.

"Oh, God, Van! You remembered that. . . ."

Cecily's voice sounded shaky.

"*Are* you, Cecily?"

"Don't worr—"

"*Are* you?"

"No. The board meets tomorrow. Jordan Lyle's married Joao's daughter. He's going to try to take over. But I've—I've made some arrangements. Everything's going to be all right."

She sounded tired. And spiritless. If everything was really all right, why was that? Van frowned again.

"Damn it, Cecily! If I could be there, I could vote with you, couldn't I? But there's no way I can! Three doctors have to meet and agree to let me out of here, and I know they won't—"

"It's okay. Don't upset yourself. Maybe—maybe you'll be

well enough soon so that we can go somewhere together for a little vacation.''

Everything about the other end of the conversation sounded strained, and Van perceived a tension in her sister. She started to press, to try and find out what was troubling her, but Cecily interrupted.

"I've got to go now, Van. Someone's here. Don't worry about me, please.''

It wasn't like Cecily to cut short a phone call. She'd always made time for Van. And there was something . . . the way Cecily had skipped over what the arrangements *were* she'd made. She'd pulled that trick as a child, whenever she'd known Van would veto what she was planning.

Van thought desperately. Something was very wrong with Cecily. That board meeting must be more important than she was admitting. Wasn't there *any* way to get out of this place?

In frustration she stalked back to the dayroom, pacing, ignoring the greetings of a few other women playing cards. She looked at the walls of her expensive prison knowing there were guards, locks, that she could never even make it back to London, let alone to the airport and out of the country.

Then her gaze fell on a magazine left behind by a patient who had left just yesterday for a Swiss hospital. Van picked it up and curled it like a club. She marched to the nurses' station.

"I want to see my husband,'' she demanded firmly. "Tell him if he doesn't come immediately, my sister's going to take me out of here *today!*''

"Here.'' Peter tossed a two-page document down in front of her. He flipped to the second page where Martin's name was scrawled. "Ten percent. The head of the law firm I use drew it up himself. There won't be loop-oles.''

Cecily nodded. "Thank you, Peter. I hope—I'd like to be able to repay the actual cost of it someday. I expect you think that's silly, but I'd feel better about it.''

She gave him a smile she didn't quite feel. Peter *was* doing what she'd asked and she *was* going to be his wife. She owed him the outer gestures of warmth, if nothing else.

He was busy refolding the transfer of shares, fastening it in an envelope. Her words didn't seem to affect him.

"You have a safe, I assume?''

"Yes.'' She rose from her desk.

She wished he wouldn't stand and watch her, but she knew

that was being silly. The churning inside her was over the looming board meeting—and over being short with Van just now.

"Getting this signed took longer than I expected," Peter said without perceptible emotion. "We need to be on our way or we'll miss our plane."

Cecily moved a small carved chest. The safe behind it had been installed for Effie and was at hip level.

"When we get to the airport I'd like to call my sister. I was short with her just a minute ago, before you came in."

Peter handed her the envelope and she dropped it in the small safe, locking the door.

"I really don't think there's time," he said, consulting his watch. "You can do it on the other end—or when we get back. Here, don't forget these."

A white flower in the bouquet he handed her caught in Ben's ruby ring and Cecily swallowed.

It was all right. The part of her that had cared and clung to memories was dead, along with Ben.

She wondered how long a wedding ceremony in Las Vegas was going to take.

"You want *what?*"

Trace MacDonald stood in the dayroom of the Langhurst Clinic looking furious. Van wondered how she could ever have thought the cold perfection of his silvery hair and clotheshorse attire to be attractive.

"I want to change hospitals!" she repeated loudly, pretending agitation.

She *was* very nervous. She was afraid of Trace. In the weeks of walking and pressing herself to remember things, she'd reconstructed completely how he'd caused her to lose Wesley's baby, and flashes of their wedding night as well. She knew he could hurt her. But she had to do this for Cecily.

"My horoscope says I should," she continued. "See—right here—it says so!" She waved Mrs. Wickliff's abandoned horoscope magazine under his nose. "An important day for decisions . . . travel will be rewarded."

Van didn't believe in horoscopes and it wasn't even her own birth sign she was flourishing. She doubted Trace had ever bothered to notice the date of her birthday, though. And people always seemed more concerned about hushing mental patients than about anything else. It was worth a try.

"What the hell does your horoscope have to do with dragging me out here?" Trace snarled.

He'd looked scared when he'd come in—all white and nervous. It was almost like he'd expected Cecily to jump out at him. Then he'd turned angry, said Cecily couldn't get her out, and Van had told him she'd only said that so he'd come, so she could talk to him. Now he was getting nasty.

"It's what's been wrong with me all these years! I haven't lived in harmony with the stars!" Van insisted passionately. Then she changed the subject a little; she'd started to recognize you did that when your mind wasn't right. "I hate it here! The food stinks and my room's too small. Mrs. Wickliff said accommodations are *much* nicer at Belle Porte, only *her* husband couldn't afford it this time. But after all, you're getting *my* money from Effie's shares—"

"You stupid bitch. You're not moving anywhere!" he said in a low voice, stepping toward her

Van fell back a step and felt faintly triumphant. She was not going to let him touch her.

"I'm a lot better, Trace. If you don't let me have my way, I'm going to tell my doctor about our wedding night—and about those pills you gave me. He likes me. He believes me."

She smiled, a smile she hoped was halfway between demented and dangerous.

"Cecily's having a meeting tomorrow, and I could make you miss it," she said in a singsong voice.

He wet his lips nervously.

"I don't *like* it here! I want to go to Belle Porte tomorrow. And I *know* there are openings. Tell them to send me and I won't make any trouble. Someone from here could go with me—or April could fly over."

He'd been weighing it all. She could tell by his eyes. Now he hesitated, looking at her suspiciously. Van's heart fell.

"All right," he said through his teeth as though making calculations.

Van guessed he was thinking about his own flight first thing in the morning—the early one he always took to allow himself a cushion of time before Cecily's meetings. He couldn't afford to miss it.

"Let's see whoever is it I have to see and I'll make arrangements, if it'll shut you up. But just in case you've got some clever plan up your sleeve, I'll pick somebody myself to go along with you."

*   *   *

The door of the hotel where they would spend the night closed behind them. Cecily heard Peter, felt his breath against her hair, but couldn't force herself to turn.

It was done. They were married. She had saved Duvall.

Peter's hands settled on her waist. She tried to relax. He began to kiss her neck demandingly and pulled her against him.

Cecily let her eyes go closed. The days when Peter's touch had stirred her to passion seemed light-years away. She had been someone else then. She hadn't yet seen behind Peter's lost-little-boy look and she hadn't yet known the moods, the remoteness, the burning fire of passion and creative drive and laughter that was Ben.

Her throat ached with unshed tears.

"You're not as responsive as you used to be," said Peter, a coldness creeping into his voice as he released her. "What's wrong?"

She could see him in the great, garish mirror of the bridal suite done in gold and white. Ostentatious. Repelling. Ridiculous for a wedding like theirs. She turned to force a smile.

"I'm tired, Peter. And tense about the meeting tomorrow. I'll feel more like a honeymoon once that's past."

"How flattering."

She let out a breath of vexation. "For heaven's sake, Peter. Don't make it sound so—so—"

"So much like I've bought you lock, stock, and barrel? But I have—I've done exactly that."

He hooked his fingers beneath the collar of her white dress, the deliberate slowness of the gesture almost sinister as his hazel eyes looked into hers.

"Except that I couldn't quite see it on the terms you'd outlined. It went against . . . my basic nature, shall we say? Or maybe it was my basic instincts as an investor. So I made a small change in the agreement with Martin. To guarantee full return on my investment, you might say."

His words were making her want to shiver. In his face there was something cruel, and as she looked at him she knew.

"You put Martin's shares in your own name, didn't you?" Her voice was a whispering fire, about to burst into flame, about to be extinguished. "And tomorrow you're going to vote against me!"

He caught her chin now, hurting her, and Cecily was paralyzed by loathing for her own stupidity.

"You'll be better off without your company," he said calmly. "Maybe when you accept it's gone you'll begin to act like a woman again."

His mouth closed over hers in icy possession, carving out the pleasure he sought there even as she struggled.

"Damn you! You're crazy if you think—"

He jerked her head back, choking off her words.

"You're mine now," he hissed as his kisses ate like acid into her helpless throat and his hand worked swiftly, opening the front of her dress. "I've played games for you I've never played for any other woman. From here on I call the shots. You're going to be my wife and nothing else—well treated if you come to your senses, taught your place if you don't."

He kicked her legs apart and pressed against her, still holding her head back so she could scarcely breathe, let alone resist him.

"Let's call this the first lesson, shall we, my love? I'm going to ride you to my heart's content tonight. I'm going to make up for all the time I've wanted you and couldn't have you—because you were too stubborn to come back to me when I found you—because I had to go to the effort of setting up that charade about Grand Cayman and tipping your husband off anonymously so *he'd* dump *you*—and getting my lip split for it!"

His face loomed grotesquely over her in Cecily's distorted vision. There was only complacency there—no remorse at all. His words sank home.

He had never meant to help Van at all! He'd meant to destroy her marriage! All his life Peter had gotten whatever he wanted. He cared nothing for anyone else.

Half-strangling in her imprisonment, she drew back her hand. Her thumb fumbled with the band that held Ben's ruby and she swung. Her anger and despair for what he had done, not to destroy her last and futile attempt to save Duvall, but to separate Ben and her, drove the blow delivered to his face. He staggered back holding his cheek, the flesh beneath his eye split by the heavy stone.

"Why—you little— You'll pay for that!"

His eyes glittered at her, and Cecily knew there had never been love in them, only possessiveness.

"You never understood how lucky you are I'd even bother with you, have you?" he sneered. "It's going to be fun seeing you put in your place. Seeing you crawl for every little favor you ever want from me!"

Cecily was fastening her dress.

"If I crawl, I should be just about as low as you are, Peter."
She picked up her purse. "If you want somebody to share this
God-awful room with you, I suggest you buy somebody. I'm
going home."

FIFTY-FIVE

V AN BREATHED A SIGH OF RELIEF. SINCE HER IDEA ABOUT HELPING
Cecily, she'd walked that narrow line between being such a
demanding patient the clinic would be glad to lose her and
creating such a commotion she'd be sedated again. She'd been
very careful. And now, when it was noon in London, seven A.M.
in Miami, she was walking toward a passenger gate in Heathrow
Airport.

Some muscleman Trace had hired walked beside her. Big and
burly, he could overpower her easily if she tried to escape, so
Van hoped he wasn't especially smart. Her eyes searched nervously for a familiar face in the passing crowds. What if she
didn't find it?

Then she saw April, her carefully done eyelashes not moving
a dot as she observed their progress. Van sighed in relief. April
removed a shoe and began to hobble toward them.

"Excuse me . . . hey, lady, can you please tell me if this is
the way to shoe repair?" she asked, intersecting their path. "My
heel came loose."

"She doesn't know," the muscleman said curtly and tried to
steer around her.

"I don't know," Van repeated with sweet obedience.

"Ow!" April tottered and caught at the muscleman's sleeve
with fluttering, feminine appeal. "I twisted my foot when the
damn thing broke. Could you just help me back to my suitcase?"

With her head she indicated a small bag near the recess to an
unmarked door. Van began drifting toward it. Now the muscleman
had two reasons to go exactly where April wanted.

Van's stomach was tied in knots. She saw April's free hand
come out of her pocket with something shiny in it. It darted
upward.

Van pounced on the muscleman's other arm as the small
syringe in April's finger drove into his bicep. His struggle for

freedom lifted Van off the ground, making her sure for interminable seconds that they had lost.

Then he slumped between the two of them, unconscious. His back was against the wall

"In there!" April hissed. ⸜

As April looked behind, Van pulled him through the unmarked door. It was some sort of stairwell.

"It worked!" she panted, amazed now that it had.

"Jeezus! I hope I didn't get an air bubble in him or anything!" April said, her grin looking shaky.

They eased him to the floor. Van jerked tickets and passports from his shirt pocket, just as she and April had planned. April stuffed a diamond bracelet and earrings into his pants pocket, part of the bracelet hanging out.

"There. If anyone finds him, that should hold him long enough for us to get away." She pulled Van to her feet. "Come on!" she urged as they fled back through the door.

They began to walk rapidly down a corridor.

"I've lied about six ways and gotten you traveling papers," said April. "From now on you're Kate Ludwigs, a divorcée. Here. Memorize how to sign your name while we get the hell out of here!"

Cecily stood in the office, now hers, where she had first met Effie. She thought of moments she had known there. The quarrels—with Ben, with Effie, among all three of them. The unveiling of the Ringmaster Necklace. The exultant moments of triumph.

She had failed Effie's trust in her. The board was waiting. In a few moments she would lose everything: Duvall; the new, productive mine for which Jenkins had worked so hard and she had gambled so much; a chance to present to the world Effie Duvall's last, inspired collection.

She hugged the sleeves of her black silk dress around her. The blunder she'd committed marrying Peter was nothing compared to the pain she felt at the prospect of seeing Duvall stamped out forever. Duvall was a link not only with Effie, but with Ben. It represented the boldness for which both had stood

Yet a strange new strength held her upright. She knew it was what had fueled Effie's climb to success. It was hate. She would make Peter pay for his faithlessness. She would make all of them pay for the things they had done. And it no longer mattered to her what she did to accomplish that. Anything that Effie had done she could do. Laws and morality no longer held sway over her. What counted was survival—and revenge.

Her telephone rang. She returned to her desk and raised the receiver.

"It's your sister," said Felice.

Images of horror shot through Cecily's head. She hadn't called Van back.

"Put it through," she said.

I'll kill Trace if he's hurt her again, she thought calmly. I'm capable of it. It would be easy. I know that now.

But suddenly Van's voice was bubbling in her ear.

"Cecily? Oh, thank goodness, you haven't started the meeting. Cecily, don't say a *thing!* I'm in Miami."

"What?"

"April's with me. We're at the airport. We've just cleared customs, but we can't make it to the island for another forty minutes at least. Our plane was late.

"Cecily, I'll *be* there! So don't let Trace vote. I—I ran away. I'll explain it all later."

"Van—"

"I've got to go! Just wait for me."

The line went dead. Cecily stood staring at the telephone in her hand, wondering if she had imagined this and if her own mind was breaking under strain. Stunned, she couldn't even think at first what this meant to the voting. Her only thought, like a small joy, a small flame eating through darkness, was that Van was safe.

Then, so humbled it made her bend double and lean against her desk and feel like a child again, she realized what had happened. Van had done this for her—incredibly—against all odds!

Wiping back a tear for this one person who still could elicit her tenderness she moved toward the outer office.

"Delay the meeting, Felice. I don't care how you do it. Tell them I'll be there in an hour. Tell them if they start without me the meeting will be illegal."

She ran, unable to walk, toward the back stairs. As she turned a bend in them a figure loomed out of the shadows.

"Trying to run out on me, little cousin?"

Jordan's tall form and curly hair wavered on her suddenly shattering vision like a shape from her nightmares. It was how she remembered that afternoon at Marblehead—the hair on the back of his hands. They were reaching toward her.

She moved, but not quickly enough. He caught her by the heavy gold chain that held Effie's ruby. He slammed her back against the wall.

"Remember the game we played with Van that day? You spoiled it. So I figure it's only fair for you to finish it. Just a good, hard fuck for you to be thinking about when you watch me take over your company."

Her air was cut off. His words about the present scarcely reached her. She was remembering Van, tied to a tree, screaming and crying. Out of horror and hate she reacted automatically, bringing her knee up hard against his crotch, flinging her arms up to break his hold on her.

"Guard!" she called sharply, knowing she would not get a second chance. She whirled, and with all her weight behind it, drove her elbow against Jordan's stomach. He doubled and lost his footing as the door to the kitchen below swung open. It was only the cook who stood there, but it was enough.

"Get a guard!" snapped Cecily, and heard a shout from the cook and then running feet.

She knew she was safe as she backed away but she was cold and trembling.

"Get this man back upstairs with the others, and see that he doesn't leave," she said to one of Raoul's men who had appeared.

She spoke calmly. She wasn't afraid of Jordan . . . quite. Yet her quivering knees told her had she been a fraction slower, a fraction less quick-witted . . .

He was filthy. A creature who should be caged somewhere.

"You haven't got a chance!" he hissed as the guard yanked him to his feet. "No matter what you try up there, I can destroy you."

His eyes glowed with hate. Cecily turned away. She breathed deeply again and again, blotting out his words.

I'm going to survive! She repeated that single promise all the way through the house and down to the boat dock. Van was free! With her vote they might force the board to a stalemate—depending on Margaux—and the diamonds from Jenkins were on their way. Her heart was leaping, making feeble lurches back toward life. So why this feeling of heaviness?

Because of Peter, she thought, her finger still feeling the weight of the ring he'd put on it yesterday even though it was bare now. Because she despised herself for what she'd done.

But no. Ben was dead. Her move had been logical. It was what Effie herself had done, not once but several times.

Only I'm not like Effie. I can't stop the fact that I still love Ben. That I always will. That I'd feel like a traitor with Peter even if I hadn't learned what he really was, just as I'd feel a traitor with anyone else. That's the difference between me and Effie. I can't stop loving. Even though it was never returned, and even though it hurts.

Peter was powerful, though. He was never going to let her go. The knowledge crushed down on her even though this morning she'd already seen a lawyer, already put in paperwork for an annulment.

Then she saw the boat. It had slipped onto the horizon while she'd stood lost in thought. Already she could make out two patches of blond hair, April's tightly curled and Van's blowing free. The sadness that had crept into her thoughts was pushed aside by joy.

"Why, it's your sister!" said Raoul in surprise.

"Yes!" Cecily laughed. She didn't know what she'd told him when she'd said she was expecting a boat.

The final feet to docking had never seemed to close more slowly. Cecily reached down, impatient. Before the motorboat even seemed to touch, Van flung herself up toward her arms.

They embraced, rocking wordlessly, holding fiercely. Through her own tears, Cecily saw the ones that seemed to lend an odd pride to her sister's eyes.

"Oh, Van . . . April . . . thank you," she managed at last. She smiled at Van. "Do you really want to go in there? If you do, we've got to hurry."

Van nodded decisively. "This is April's lawyer," she said, indicating a man who had clambered out with them. "I'm borrowing him . . . since I don't have Wesley to help me." She bit her lip.

But her head had risen with determination. There was steel in her once clouded eyes.

Cecily, choked with emotion, couldn't speak. She reached for her sister's hand. Their fingers still were locked in mutual support, as they'd often been in childhood, when the two of them walked through the door into the already filled board room.

For a second there was silence, and Cecily saw the alignment of faces: Trace, Chantharangsy, and Jordan seated on one side; Kim and Peter across from them with Margaux a few chairs separate.

Next there was pandemonium.

"We were waiting for *this*?" howled Kim. "Next she'll be exhuming Effie herself to vote!"

At his insinuation, Cecily flushed with protective hate. Before she could answer, Van was moving calmly and unflinchingly toward Trace.

"Get out of my place," she ordered.

He had risen on sight of her, amazement on his face. Now his eyes flicked wildly between Cecily and Jordan.

He hates me for what I did, but it's also made him afraid of me, Cecily thought. It surprised her she was just now tumbling to that simple realization.

"You're incompetent," Trace said hoarsely. "You're supposed to be in a hospital. You've escaped!"

"You murdering s.o.b., you'd better believe I *am* competent!" Van said, taking another step toward him. "And I've got an attorney with me to back me up. You may be smart enough to kill unborn babies, but you're not smart enough this time. Now move!"

Still, for a second, he hovered. Cecily knew he couldn't decide, that he was as fearful of Jordan as he was of her.

Jordan looked livid with rage. He had just lost a counted-on vote for his takeover. Reluctantly Trace moved back, fumbling for a chair near the wall, away from the table, carefully keeping his gaze on all of them.

Van pulled out the chair at Cecily's left and took her place.

"Now then," said Cecily, coming around to the head of the table. "Shall we begin?"

She spared one scathing look for Peter, who, with a butterfly bandage high on one cheek where her ring had hit him, watched her from rock-crystal eyes.

"I'm sure you all know Jordan Lyle has married Ana-Sofia. You may even know that I've married Peter Kemp." She heard Van gasp and glanced at her in apology. "Since he's sure to vote against me, however, feel free to consider him one of yourselves.

"I gather this meeting was called because Joao's mines have been sold? No doubt Jordan would like you to think that's the end—"

"That *is* the end of Duvall," Jordan cut in smugly. "She's lost your source of diamonds; she's sold away your emeralds, it seems. If you let her run things much longer, your interests in Duvall with be worth nothing.

"You know the progress Lyle and Company has made since coming to this area. We've grown. We've established reliable suppliers for our stones because we pay them well. We can live without Duvall's client list, but we'd be interested in acquiring it. And we turn a profit. What about her? What kind of dividends have you had of late?''

There was murmuring from Kim and Chantharangsy. Peter looked grimly satisfied. Margaux propped her forehead against her hand, shading her eyes.

"I'll tell you what kind of dividends you can expect in six months," Cecily interrupted. Margaux's pose made her feel uneasy. She and Van alone, with a five percent margin, could still force a stalemate, but she needed to turn them by capturing more support than her sister's. With nothing to back her up, she made a desperate attempt. "Duvall has its own source of diamonds, a new mine. Jenkins never retired. He's been developing it. The first stones are due any minute, and Duvall—this whole board—owns a one-third interest in the venture."

"Absurd!" said Kim with a wave of the hand. "You expect us to believe such lies?''

"I am offering," Jordan continued calmly, "to buy out Duvall. Open your books to independent appraisal and I'll give you fair market price. Moreover, I'll contract for all the good rubies and sapphires those of you with mines see fit to supply."

Cecily's confidence wavered. She and Van together held a vote of forty-five percent. Her enemies had forty. Margaux's five percent could swing in either direction, keeping them here for hours of if it swung for an even split. And Van, whose day had started five hours earlier than the day did here, and had gone through God knew what to get here, must be nearing exhaustion.

"I'm voting to sell," said Chantharangsy.

"And I," Kim said promptly.

The door opened. Felice, with a look of apology, hurried to Cecily's elbow.

"A courier has come from Mr. Jenkins. He insists on seeing you."

Cecily nodded, though uncertain now whether even this would have effect.

"Send him in."

On edge, and alert to every sound, she heard the whir of a helicopter, directly overhead. That must be how the diamonds had arrived.

"The stones from the new mine are here," she announced, rising as a bookish-looking young man who seemed scarcely more than a schoolboy entered.

"This is diversion! A delaying tactic and nothing more," Jordan protested.

"Wait," said the young man as Cecily reached for the latches on the attaché case he set before her. Reaching into his pocket, he pushed a switch on a tiny box, turning off some sort of electronic alarm that guarded the case, she realized.

At a nod from him, she lifted the lid. Her breath caught at the profusion of clear white stones she saw there. Defiantly she turned the case, flaunting its riches.

"It's bait. There is no new mine," Chantharangsy said and looked toward Jordan.

For the first time Cecily wondered if he'd been allied with Jordan from the day he came here. The meeting was continuing despite these stones that might have spelled victory.

"I call for a vote on the sale of Duvall to Lyle and Company," said Jordan.

Cecily snapped shut the case of diamonds and locked it.

"Wait for me in my office" she said to the courier.

"I vote to sell," said Peter, looking at her with a chilling smugness.

"Also," said Chantharangsy.

"I don't!" Margaux spoke with vehemence. "You're cobras. All of you!"

Van started to speak but was cut off by Kim

"I don't, either." His pale, fat hands were on the table, half raising him as his greedy eyes watched the diamonds leave. "I believe we should have a try at continuing the way things are," he said with a broad, ingratiating smile toward Cecily. "Those who are displeased should sell their shares to those of us who aren't."

They'd won! Cecily was so dazed by the turning of things she could hardly believe it.

"All right!" said Jordan, on his feet as she was.

They faced each other, and Cecily hated him as much as she had that day at Marblehead. Beneath his blond curls his face was bathed with a frightening obsession to win.

"The vote goes her way, but I'm still making an offer. I'll give cash to anyone willing to trade their shares in Duvall for shares in Lyle and Company. Chantharangsy? Kemp? Kim, don't be an idiot trying to suck up to her! Take my stock for hers and you take no risk! I'm going to control this floundering company!"

"I don't think you'll control much of anything for a while," said a voice.

Cecily cried out, catching the table before her for support. Van gasped and turned in her chair.

I must look at Van, see if she's all right, see if this is too much for her, Cecily thought. But she couldn't tear her eyes away.

Ben stood in the doorway, and behind him Wesley. Both were impeccably dressed. The left sleeve of Ben's jacket hung empty below the cuff. *His hand!* It was all of him that had died!

She tried to raise her eyes and couldn't. She could hardly breathe. She could hardly hear above the pounding of her heart, which with disabling beats of gratitude was sweeping her back toward life.

When she did look up it was to meet his waiting gaze. She thought she saw a change there, something undisguised that seemed to be reaching out to her.

"We've got enough proof to put you and MacDonald and your Thai friend here away till you hair falls out," Ben was saying to Jordan. "A confession from the mechanic you bribed to ruin my cassette—that's sabotage and attempted murder. Buying a known abortifacient with a forged prescription. Your sister's murder—"

"Compared with what she's done?" Trace shrieked, pointing a finger at Cecily.

He looked wildly toward the room's other door, but Raoul stood there with his rifle. There were other men with Ben and Wesley, two in the uniform of the sheriff's department. They also had guns.

"If you want a criminal, get her!" Trace cried again. "Ask her about kidnapping! Ask her about—"

"Shut up," said Ben. He swung slightly, looking at Chantharangsy. "No one can pin Thida's death on you yet, but believe me I'm going to work on it the rest of my days," he said grimly.

Cecily wanted to speak but the room was swaying around her. Ben started toward her. She took a trembling step to meet him.

"I want a lawyer," Jordan was demanding, tight-lipped.

"Ben . . ." she whispered, afraid to believe this was really happening, afraid to trust the burning love, the longing and caring in the dark eyes that had never before been open to her.

And then Peter rose, his words filled with chilling authority.

"If you'd clear the way, I'd like to take my wife out of here now. This is all a very great strain on her."

Ben's face lost its color.

Cecily grabbed for the table but was conscious of missing it as she fainted.

FIFTY-SIX

"**S**HE'LL BE ALL RIGHT," WESLEY REASSURED VANESSA. "SHE WAS only out for a minute or two. It's Ben I'm worried about."

Vanessa, in his arms, pulled back indignantly. "Why should you worry about Ben? He stomped off without even waiting to see if she'd be okay! He wouldn't even come back to hear why she'd married Peter—and Cecily was crying!"

Wesley smiled at her, and Van half thought it had something to do with her being angry.

"You're well," he said. "Absolutely, wonderfully well. I've never seen you like this."

His expression grew grave. "You don't know what Ben's gone through since that plane crash, Van. We both thought we were going to die when it was happening. I know that.

"We were upside down, spinning, and Ben had the presence of mind to disconnect the computer. We were already too far down for him to get the engine started again, but he was able to do some things to control the crash a little. He yelled for me to brace and aimed for trees. I don't know what happened next. Noise—such awful noise you can't imagine it—and the wing on Ben's side ripping off. We slammed against something and stopped. I looked over and the window had caved in and—and Ben's hand was gone. Blood was spurting out.

"He was staring at it. He pulled out of his harness and got up. He stood there sort of swaying and swung his arm up over his head. I—I thought he was dying there in front of me.

"But the plane was on fire, you see. There was metal on his side that was already red. He—"

Wesley swallowed. Van held him tightly, feeling him shudder.

"He shoved the stump against the metal and held it there, and then he passed out. I thought he'd gone crazy with pain. But you see, what he'd done was—was seal off the bleeding. Cauterize the wound. I couldn't have done it, Van. I couldn't have done something like that to myself."

Van squeezed his hand. "Then what?"

Despite the modesty of his words she knew he, too, had

418

undergone horrors. She felt more grateful than ever to see and touch and hear him once again.

"I ran back and got two bottles of liquor—Ben says that was foolish, but I don't think he'd have stood the pain without it—and dragged him out. From then till we were rescued, he was pretty much delirious. He said Cecily's name all the time. It was wanting to get to her that kept him alive."

He paused. "I'm not as brave as Ben, but I've learned from him, even then. When I was scared—when we stumbled into that jungle village and they met us with guns—I kept reminding myself that if I made it back, I'd see you again."

Van blinked back tears. "Cecily can get a divorce, can't she? That's what I'm going to do."

Wesley smiled gravely. "There's a difference. I know you love me. Ben doesn't know that about her."

They kissed, and the sweetness of their own fortune made Van all the more distressed at how things were turning out for the other two people in the world for whom she cared. Here Ben and Wesley had gotten in touch with Jenkins, learned about the impending board meeting, rushed here so Ben could save Cecily— and the most important part of it had turned out all wrong.

"What can we *do*?" she asked.

"Nothing, sweetheart."

"Can't we go to Ben and Cecily? Make them see?"

"No. I tried to talk to Ben. He sees Cecily's marriage as proof she felt nothing for him. Let's let her be for a while. Maybe, just now, it's enough she got those diamonds."

Cecily sat at her desk and stared at the transparent stone before her, glittering lumps of carbon, as cold as she felt inside.

She had given orders. Ben was not to leave the island until he came to see her on a matter of business. She knew the hardest battle of all she had ever fought lay ahead of her.

Three angry blows fell on her door. She knew it was he. She had asked Felice to leave. She wanted no interruptions.

With the sense of a destiny she couldn't read flying toward her, she moved toward the door. Her fingers shook as she opened it.

Ben's face was rigidly set. The sweeping crest of his hair, the line of his beard, had never looked more handsome than in this moment when he looked at her with blazing disdain.

"You've got a hell of a nerve demanding that I come here," he said through tight-set lips.

Cecily steeled herself to do battle with him, as they so often had battled.

"I knew it was the only way."

"I suppose I should congratulate you on a good marriage," he said, words bitter with sarcasm. "Effie would have approved."

For once Cecily ignored his barbs. Nothing, no attempt to hurt her, would deter her from her purpose. She closed the door he had left ajar.

"Wesley told me about in the jungle." She searched his face for some sign, even the smallest, that there was hope. "He told me you called my name."

"Bullshit. Wesley's so sick in love he'd like the whole world to be."

"Are you denying it?"

She thought his eyes stirred fractionally.

"Yeah. I'm denying it. So if that's the only business you brought me here for, let me leave."

He tried to turn, but Cecily caught his uninjured arm.

"No, damn it, Ben! For once you're going to listen to me! For once you're not going to run away. You're a damn coward when it comes to the two of us. Do you know that?"

His face lost its color. A strain Cecily hadn't noticed before seemed to be pressed into it.

"Maybe—" Her voice faltered. "Maybe I've been, too. I was so afraid you'd never love me that I didn't fight for you. Well, I'm going to now! I married Peter Kemp because nothing mattered with you gone. It took me about half an hour to see the mistake I'd made. I've never slept with him—not since I met you."

"You want a medal?"

His ridicule hurt, but Cecily plunged ahead. "I married him because I was going to lose Duvall. It was all I had left. And I believed you'd never loved me—you'd never said it, never even hinted it. Why, Ben? It could have made all the difference!"

There was a long pause and his eyes, for several seconds, no longer avoided hers. When he spoke it was dully and rigidly.

"It's too late, Cecily."

"No!"

With both hands she seized the front of his jacket, trying desperately to hold the faint diminishing of distance she imagined she saw in his face. She would not give up now, she would not believe he felt nothing! Ben tried to toss her off, but hampered by the relative uselessness of one arm, lost his balance.

Cecily, fearful of further injury to him, tried to catch him. They fell together, against the desk first, so thunderously that loose diamonds slid and showered down around them, and then to their knees. She heard him swear.

She hadn't fought before and now all that mattered to her was at stake! She could feel herself changing inside, the hardness and hate she'd thought were part of her already evaporating.

Perhaps it was only through pain that she could reach him—the pain that would make him drop the shield he held always before himself.

Capturing his arm she thrust its still-raw stump against her breast. To reach him. To shock him. To make them one. To claim even the least lovely parts of him as hers.

He gasped, in pain or in fury, his face contorting.

"Damn you, Cecily—let me go!"

"No! I'll never let you go! Because you're a part of me, Ben. Because you're in my blood and my heart and my mind in a way no divorce decree—not even death—can ever end. If you never believe me—if you never love me—I can't change that. But you're going to hear me out! You're going to understand!"

Ben struck her hands aside violently, but his eyes were filled with wild confusion. Perhaps it was fear she saw there, Cecily thought.

"Look at me and tell me you've never loved me!" she challenged in a whisper as he loomed above her.

He shook his head. Yet even as he did, his mouth was drawn to hers. She felt the touch, the slow, incredible friction of his lips. She fed, and he took ravenously. But then, as she began to lose herself, Ben jerked sharply back, rejecting even as, for a moment, he had accepted.

Cecily was defeated. It was, as he'd said, too late to reconcile their differences. She couldn't even raise her face to look at him.

"It—doesn't matter," she said, choking over the words. "As long as you're alive and I know that, nothing else matters. You can go."

He was silent for long moments, still not moving.

"You've changed," he said at last, and his voice sounded strange.

From her bowed pose she could see nothing but the outline of his bold, squared chin. His presence overwhelmed her, melting her to nothingness as it had a hundred times before.

"No." She answered low in her throat. "I haven't changed. Maybe you've never seen me before." She raised her head, the pain of knowing she'd lost him forever now blurring her vision. "I don't know why. Because of Effie, I guess." Unable to stop herself, she touched the corner of his mouth.

His shoulder hunched forward, capturing her hand against his face and startling Cecily so that she drew it away.

"I didn't want to see you." His dark eyes swept hers. "What I felt for you was more than any human being should feel for another. It was too risky."

Then his strong, sure hand was tangling in her hair, drawing her toward him. His lips recaptured hers with a fire and intensity such as she had never known.

"Oh, my God, Cecily! I *do* love you!" He gasped the words, his lips rubbing back and forth across her cheeks, her eyes, her temples. "It wouldn't matter if you'd slept with Kemp and a hundred others—I'd still have to love you. I couldn't say it, not even to myself. I was too afraid of losing you. And when I did lose you, I had to face it anyway. You're my life—more than my life. You're my faith, my belief in whatever in this universe brought us together!"

She trembled, afraid to believe. But her heart knew the truth. She raised her arms, holding him to her, circling his neck.

His embrace was somewhat off center. He favored his injured arm. But this was Ben, alive and hers and open to her as he had never been before. Trust, like a sweet elixir, flowed between them.

"If you tell me now that you love me, then God help you," he said, his voice rough with a hint of the rasp that had been in Effie's. "If you do, I'll never let you away from my side again for as long as I live!"

He was holding her chin, none too gently, and Cecily felt all the leaden days inside her turning into gold.

"That's all I've ever wanted," she whispered, longing to wipe the lines of tiredness from his face and prove those words to him for the rest of her life.

"All?" he asked, a last, detectable trace of doubt shading his face now. "Not Duvall, too?"

She took a breath.

"Yes. I want Duvall, too. But I've learned something I don't think Effie ever knew—I learned it when you left, and all over again when I thought you were dead and the pain inside me never stopped.

"I've learned survival isn't the most important thing. It's having someone to survive for—that's what matters."

He studied her gravely, a very long time.

"You're not like her," he said finally.

A wave of fear hit Cecily. She pressed her palms against her eyes and wished she could drive out half of what they had seen. For Ben had been right about so many things, and if there was to be a chance for the two of them now, the way must be completely clear. In the last months—for so long—it seemed she had grown confused about so many things, even who she was and what she was.

"I don't know," she said with a burgeoning sadness. "I've done things—oh, God, Ben! I let Trace Macdonald be castrated! I *paid* someone to do it! Because of what he'd done to Van. And because I had the power . . ."

His hand drew hers away gently. His fingers stroked her closed eyes, traced her mouth, brushed back her hair. Each touch of his fingertips brought expiation for her sins. Their strong, certain movements became a charm against shadows.

"We've both learned things. We both have regrets," his deep voice said. "But that dream about a little girl to wave to on the merry-go-round could still come true for us. If you want."

His lips brushed her forehead. She raised her mouth in answer. His body seemed to capture hers of its own accord. When at last they parted, small sparks of humor were flickering to life in his eyes.

"Not much market for a one-armed test pilot," he said. "Can you use another designer?"

She laughed despite the fragments of regret and self-doubt still lodged inside her.

"You have to audition first," she said. "Like I did for Effie. Take off your clothes."

She pulled him with her down toward the room's thick carpet, thinking of Effie and Bibi and all the days that were to be. He was skillfully unfastening the small buttons of her dress

"I plan on being accepted," he said with a grin.

"You've always been vain."

"I've always been good." He kissed her slowly. "Christ," he said, breaking away to look at her desk as though remembering something. "Aren't you going to lock up those diamonds first? There must be half a million dollars worth."

Cecily followed his gaze and smiled.

"The diamonds will be here tomorrow."

He kissed her, drawing her to him.

"So will I," he whispered. "So will I."

ABOUT THE AUTHOR

Versatile novelist Mary Ruth Myers, author of FRIDAY'S DAUGHTER, AN OFFICER AND A LADY, and INSIGHTS, credits a visit she paid to an international gem dealer in Brazil as her inspiration for COSTLY PLEASURES.

A graduate of the University of Missouri School of Journalism, Ms. Myers wrote for newspapers in Michigan and Ohio before turning to fiction. She lives amid an eclectic mixture of modern furniture and pre-Columbian art with her husband, Henry, who owns a clock shop; their young daughter, Jessica; and two cats. Their house, in the small Ohio village of Yellow Springs, is on the edge of a nature preserve.

Ms. Myers invites readers to write to her care of her publisher.

The
Best Modern Fiction
from
BALLANTINE